FOR THE GLORY

FOR THE GLORY

TOM DeHUFF

PETER E. RANDALL PUBLISHER
Portsmouth, NH

Printed in the United States of America

Design by Debra Kam

Peter E. Randall Publisher
P.O. Box 4726
Portsmouth, NH 03802-4726

Cataloging-in-Publication Data:
DeHuff, Tom, 1946–
        For the glory / Tom DeHuff.
            p. cm.
        ISBN 0–914339–44–3: $19.95
        1. World Cup (Soccer)--Fiction.   I. Title
        PS3554.E424F67   1993
        813'.54--dc20   93–30423
                                CIP

To my wife, Lynn

ACKNOWLEDGMENTS

A great big thanks to:
- My family for your patience, understanding, and sacrifices.
- My Mom and Dad, for all you did.
- Rodolfo Mora (Fofi) for your companionship at the Italian World Cup and many helpful insights into the World Cup tournament.
- Kyle Rote, Jr. for allowing me to use your name as a character in the story and for your permission to use the quotes.
- Members of the Costa Rica National team and Association officials for your friendship and help in Italy.
- Bora Milutinovic for allowing me such close access to the players and for what you've accomplished in World Cup soccer.
- Marcus Byrd for your many suggestions and encouragement.
- Tommy Shields for the loan of your computer when I really needed one.
- Jean Franco and Mickey Elletti for being our host in Italy.
- Becky Cummins for your help and ego-building praise.
- Dr. Tabachnik for permission to use your real name and for your contributions to sports.
- Paul Ott for allowing me to use your name and song.
- Strength Shoes for your permission
- Speed-Chutes for your permssion.
- Chris, Jimmy, and Gene for your help and faith—thanks.
- Darlene Bordwell for your helpful copyediting.
- Peter Randall for all you've done to make this better.

FOR THE GLORY

CHAPTER 1

The first time the water slapped them in their faces Scott and Joel knew the action was fixin' to start. The gentle sounds of the river swelled quickly into the roar of the rapids.

"This is it! Let's see if you've got what it takes. Maybe it will make a man out of you." Scott had to shout to be heard, even though Joel was sitting just in front of him.

In answer to Scott's comment, Joel raised his paddle above his head with both hands for an instant. Quickly, he brought it back down again, however; a large boulder loomed just ahead on the left and the paddle was needed in the water.

"Hard right," came the instruction from the raft guide, just barely audible above the din of crashing water.

The eight-man raft eased beside the rock as the front end rose on the swell. Joel at first was several feet above Scott, then several feet below him as the front of the raft rose and fell with the topography of the turbulent river.

Scott Fontaine and Joel Adams, best friends since kindergarten, along with two other players on their high school soccer team, Rod and Phil, had planned this rafting trip shortly after they had gone canoeing down a very mild river with the youth group from Joel's church. The canoeing trip had been great, the outdoors invigorating. Yet, while the canoe trip had been exciting, rafting was exhilarating and liberating.

After an hour and a half of medium-sized class III and IV rapids the three-raft and four-kayak expedition stopped on a sandbar for a picnic lunch. The sandwiches, fruit, and dessert tasted all the better in the beautiful surroundings.

"I overheard the guide telling one of the others that the two largest rapids are ahead of us," Joel told the others. "He says one is over two hundred yards long! It's called the Boilermaker."

"Yeah? Great! I loved the big rapids back there. It was so loud you couldn't hear anything but the river."

"I know. I got drenched...several times."

"Me too. This sure is a great way to spend a summer day, isn't it?"

"I wouldn't mind doing this a couple more times before school starts."

The second half of the trip proved worthy of its acclaim. The Boilermaker had several class V areas. As they entered the top of the rapids, the boys were nearly intimidated by the view. The kayak in front of the first raft dropped into a trough and disappeared altogether, only to shoot up a moment later.

"Hot dog. Hang on Joel, we're in for it now. This is the big one." Scott was hoping the ride would be as good as it looked, and his enthusiasm showed in his voice, but no one could hear.

The boys gripped their paddles more firmly and dug their feet tightly into the floor stirrups, their only means of hanging on in turbulent action. The raft in front also disappeared from view just as the noise totally engulfed their own craft, the middle of three. Adrenaline pumping, hearts pounding, and veins pulsing, every person in the raft was living the experience to the fullest.

Scott looked back at the guide in the rear of the fifteen-foot raft. He was standing on the last bench with an extra-long paddle, steering the rubber craft through the first course. "Don't know what good he's gonna do in this part," thought Scott. "It looks like we're going the way the river wants us to anyway."

Just then they went down the front side of the trough. The raft seemed to bend in the middle as the front changed direction to start up the far side. At the crest of the far side, the raft started down again.

Joel felt his stomach complain as the bottom dropped. He rose up off his seat and would have pitched forward out of the boat if Scott had not grabbed him from the back.

Forewarned, Scott countered his own upward movement by tensing his crouched body. He had a momentary feeling of weightlessness as they rode over the ridge. From behind him came a yell just as a body landed on the bench between him and Rod, who was seated on his right. The guide had not prepared himself well enough for the moment and was thrown forward, unceremoniously landing in the middle of the boat.

"First time?" Scott shouted at the surprised guide.

"For that, yes. The river, no," came the answer, barely audible in the roar. He grinned at Scott as he scrambled back to the rear again. When Scott looked at Rod, he rolled his eyes back.

The vessel continued to play upon the water, throwing its inhabitants violently about. Going through one particularly rough section, those sitting on the left side were jerked out over the edge of the craft. Water dragged at their upper bodies; only because each had his foot in the floor stirrup did he remain in the raft.

"Move right, move right!" The guide shouted as the raft came through some violent drops and went toward the canyon wall as the river turned left. "Get to the right; everybody to the right—fast!"

Scott remembered the instructions before putting in the river: that the raft could be swamped and flipped over by the upstream waters flowing into the boat. Moving to the downstream side counteracted the downward force of the water. Scott noted Joel was just as quick to move.

"Didn't want to swim through the rest of this," Joel explained as he nodded at what still lay before them.

"Reverse, reverse," came the instructions from the guide.

Joel, Scott, Rod, Phil and the others bent to the task. The distance between the first raft and theirs increased a bit...now it was about thirty yards.

Joel reached back and grabbed Scott's knee and pointed ahead to the first raft. "They're stuck. They're in a hole."

"Reverse. Reverse...hard!"

Once again sinews—muscles made strong by regular workouts—strained to slow the craft.

Inexorably forward they went, closer to those caught in the hole formed by the reverse flow of water seven feet beyond a small three-foot fall. They all knew that the first rafters would be "munched" if they could not exit the hydraulic before the next load of paddlers hit them. The anxious look on the paddlers' faces confirmed they were fully aware of their dangerous predicament.

Still the young athletes and their companions were reverse-stroking to impede their forward progress. Muscles cried out in pain.

At last the first craft exited sideways out of the hole. Scott imagined the oncoming raft stimulated the flow of adrenaline to the arms of those stuck—none too soon.

"Forward. Forward...hard forward."

Scott knew they had to build up speed to overcome the backwash. Again they laid to the task, only this time it was forward.

The boat hesitated as it came over the drop, then moved on.

"Wahoo!" Rod shouted.

"We made it!" Scott squealed, "We made it Joel."

"'Course we did. We weren't about to get caught."

"It was the challenge," Phil added.

The continuing rapids prevented them from watching the third craft, but later the friends learned it, too, had gotten stuck in that same hole.

"That was the best time that I've ever had!" Joel said when they had entered smooth waters.

"I loved it," Scott replied to his best buddy. "How 'bout it, Rod?"

"Fantastic!"

The rafts were drifting toward the take-out point where a bus and a low-boy trailer, hitched behind it, were positioned for the trip back.

Everyone in the group had become even more friendly, having shared a special experience. The talk was constant as many related their feelings to one another. Scott was amazed at the bonding that had occurred as a result of the rush of emotions each had experienced during the tumultuous ordeal.

"You know, you could feel the survival instincts rising within you, back there during those largest and most dangerous rapids. Kind of like you were in another world for a while."

"I know it. You were concentrating so hard, there was no room for any other thoughts. You were experiencing so many new things so quickly. That's what made it so exciting."

"Yeah. That's really living on the edge, isn't it?"

On the drive back to Bethel, the friends discussed the upcoming school year and the soccer season that would start soon. "One thing I really want is to win the state championship for our high school," Joel announced soberly. "Our team should be better than last year, and I felt like we could have done it then. We had one bad game and got put out."

"We'll have to be more consistent, but yeah, it's something I've been dreaming of for a long time." Scott agreed.

"I'd like to play that South Marietta team again and this time beat the crap out of them. They made me mad the way they talked trash during the game. I'd rather beat them than anyone else."

"I doubt they make it to the playoffs this year. Last year almost their whole starting lineup was seniors."

"Extraordinary circumstances call for extraordinary measures of action," Scott thought six months later at the state soccer championships, as he motioned for Geoff to vacate his goalkeeper position and come forward. "Got to make this move now," he told Joel, his co-captain. "Less than five minutes to play and we're still behind 3–2. This is the championship, nothing to lose. We can't lose two years in a row to this same team—not if I can help it."

"OK. Geoff can take my fullback slot and I'll move up with you," said Joel. "And you're right, we can't lose again to these bums, especially since they have so many new guys. They still talk trash."

"The condition of the field has gotten considerably better in the last fifteen minutes. I'm glad the rain stopped at halftime."

"Yeah, the coach was right, this field does drain well, really well."

The Georgia state high school championship was being contested by Bethel and South Marietta. Although a much smaller school, nationally ranked and undefeated Bethel was favored to win, primarily because of All-American forward Scott Fontaine and his best friend, honorable mention All-American defenseman Joel Adams. The game conditions were miserable as a light rain turned into a downpour, soaking the players and spectators and making the field resemble a hundred lakes. Bethel had gained an advantage going ahead two to nothing before the field got so bad, Scott getting one goal and one assist. South Marietta scored before halftime when Joel slipped and fell, opening the defense.

During the second half the puddles began to shrink; since the rain had stopped. The special construction of the subterrain was paying dividends. South Marietta nonetheless continued to fare better in the treacherous footing and scored two more unanswered goals to achieve a three-to-two advantage as the time remaining grew short.

Effective passing had been impossible for the Bethel team, unable to cope with the extremely wet conditions. Things were now beginning to improve, however, because only a few large puddles remained. Traction was approaching semi-normal in some places and control once again swung over to the smaller school.

Once again the opposition talked down to the Bethel players. One player sneered at Scott, "What's the matter, All-American, can't handle a little water?" Others talked trash too. "You guys thought you were so good; you just haven't played a good team before now." "You're wimps."

The taunts grew more numerous and more disparaging as the game clock wound down and the South Marietta players became more sure of themselves.

Just then the ball squirted into the middle of one of the largest puddles. Scott, noting that Rod was open on the left for a well-placed lead pass, darted for the ball. "Got to blast it out of there," he said to himself.

Successfully planting his left foot, he smashed the partially submerged object with his right. Unfortunately, the ball moved only a couple of feet as Scott was sent sprawling face first through the remainder of the puddle and into the mud beyond.

"...That play exemplifies the frustration the Bethel players have had with the field conditions tonight," the radio announcer intoned into the mike. "But Fontaine's back up and apparently unhurt; probably more than a little embarrassed, though."

"Hey, All-American...nice play," the right midfielder said snidely to Scott.

"Thanks," Scott grinned, trying not to show anger.

Bethel again assumed control and moved the ball in nearer to the goal, as the South Marietta team was playing it very close to the vest. Scott was triple-teamed as the opponents knew only too well that his reputation was gained honestly. Time and time again forward thrusts were parried as the prevent defense for the underdogs was doing its thing.

Scott realized the best chance for his team to score was to use himself as a decoy, so he called out "Three-J," a play designed for Scott to run very wide of the goal, drawing the defense with him. Then a midfielder or fullback would run up the middle toward the goal. The play was configured for the ball to be crossed from the off-side from Scott toward the center as Joel (the "J" in "Three-J") became the key man. Rod took the cue and maneuvered the ball to the left side, ten yards from the goal line. Juking his guard so that he could get off a crossing pass, Rod let it fly directly toward the center, where he saw Joel charging toward the goal. Joel came in high and hard. The pass was perfect as Joel met the ball and headed it into the corner of the goal. Tie game!

The listless crowd suddenly came to life. Although only a couple of thousand were left after the heavy rains decimated the numbers, they were vociferous in their cheering.

The regulation time ended soon after the kickoff and the teams huddled together at opposite ends to plot strategy.

During the first overtime period both teams played conservatively and the result was that the score was still tied when play was halted.

During the break between the periods Joel told the team, "Look, there's no way we can chance a shootout with these guys; we have to win it on the field."

The coach interrupted to say, "If we get close to the end—say within the last three minutes—and the score is still tied, I want to take the chance and draw them down close to our end in order to give Scott more of a chance to use his breakaway speed. I think they'll push upfield, trying to get the go-ahead score. I think you guys can stop them. Let's give Scott some working room. If he has enough room, even their whole team can't stop him."

When the first ten minutes of the fifteen-minute period resulted in no score, Bethel drew back into a prevent defense. South Marietta, as predicted, pressed forward. Twice Bethel had to make a great defensive effort to stop a scoring threat. The opposition sensed the team from Bethel was playing for a tie and increased their pressure on goal.

Then the ball played out to the center, slightly to the right, where Scott was. He controlled the ball and started up field toward a duo of South Marietta's fastest defenders. Full speed, he went straight at them. Three steps from the defenders, the All-American stepped beyond the ball with his right foot, picked it up with his left toe onto his right heel behind him, and flicked the ball high up over his head and forward, beyond the surprised duo. Caught unaware, the defenders could only watch helplessly as the ball soared above their heads.

Scott jumped over outstretched legs and burst into the open as he headed the ball further down field.

The crowd anticipated the result: the defense could not cope with the two-time state sprint champion as he dribbled down the field. Scott outdistanced the defense and outmaneuvered the keeper to put the winning goal in the net.

The whole team followed the action down the field and piled on Scott to celebrate the sure victory.

"I love it, I love it," Joel cried out as he hugged Scott. "I can't stand these jerks."

The winners all remarked that it was their opponents' lack of class that made the victory all the more satisfying.

Unknown to the players, or even to each other, three scouts in the stands were making final notes in their briefs. One was from the University of Georgia, one from the United States Soccer Federation, and one from Italy.

———⚽———

Down in Central America another young man, Paolo De Palmer, was conjuring up future glories: glory for Costa Rica and for himself. He was sure one day he would be playing in the World Cup for Costa Rica and that he would be a star.

Paolo's knee hurt. He looked down as he loped along the street toward home. It was hardly bleeding anymore. Some clear, pink liquid was seeping out and down his leg. Paolo smiled to himself; it was worth it! He wished he could have seen himself on instant replay. Eduardo had sent a shot across the front of the goal, a real screamer. Paolo had seen it would be too high to head as he was charging the goal. The perfect time, he had thought, to try that reverse bicycle kick over his head he'd been practicing with his older brother for hours on end. Of course, they practiced on soft ground where landing didn't hurt so much. Paolo didn't think of that when he went up for the shot. The broken rocks strewn on the ground didn't make a nice landing spot. He realized that he would have to angle the shot slightly to get the ball in the goal. So, while in the air, he calculated the necessary twist of his body as he kicked the ball. The problem was he forgot to stop twisting and came down on his right knee instead of his rump or his back like he usually did to protect himself as he landed. The joy of the shot made—he watched it go in the goal as he came down—dimmed the pain. He didn't realize he could hardly walk after he got up. But oh, what a feeling! Everyone was slapping him on the back and telling him what a terrific shot it was. Even the opponents couldn't help but tell him it was a great play. Paolo had been double-teamed most of the afternoon anytime he got near the goal, because the other team knew he was the best scorer for his team.

Best of all, Lucinda was watching. She was not a big soccer fan and didn't know all the rules, but even she told him that the shot was something special. Paolo was on a high anyway, so he had talked to her afterward and asked her if he could walk her home. She had accepted. Lucinda was just about the best-looking girl in town. Paolo didn't know how it happened she was at the game until he asked her on the way home. He still remembered the way it went.

"Why did you come to the game today?"

"I came to see you play."

"Really?" His heart soared!

She went on. "So many people had told me that you were very good, so I asked Jorgé, your teammate, to tell me when your next game was. The nice thing was the game was close to home, only a kilometer or so."

Paolo remembered saying, "I wish it were ten kilometers," as he walked her home. Lucinda blushed and smiled. Paolo thought just then that there couldn't be anyone more beautiful as he gazed into her big brown eyes. She slowed her walk as if reading his mind and Paolo thought Lucinda was considerate also to think of him. Why hadn't he gotten interested before now? he asked himself. He guessed it was because he considered her too good-looking, too popular to be interested in him. Then too, nothing had ever really brought them together, in close contact, before now. They went to the same school, but seldom had classes together.

Paolo remembered thankfully back to that day when a friend of the family had given his older brother and him a brand new soccer ball. Everisto was six and he was four and a half—or so he was reminded later. He recalled the many long days spent playing with that ball. That was all he wanted to do was to kick the ball. Every time Everisto learned a new trick Paolo had to learn it also. He loved tricks, even at an early age. By the time he was seven he was competing favorably with ten- and eleven-year-old boys. When he was twelve he could already outplay many adults.

His thoughts shifted. "I wish I could make that shot in the World Cup. Just imagine. Stadio Olympico in Rome. Eighty thousand people screaming for a goal. Millions more on TV. The high crossing pass comes. Then POW! Paolo De Palmer stuns the soccer world with an acrobatic leap and reverse kick into the goal to beat Germany in the last two minutes of the game. Costa Ricans everywhere are crazy with joy. Paolo, our Paolo, has won the World Cup for our nation. Costa Rica—world champions! That has a nice ring to it. Give me the chance. Just one time. I'd give anything for it."

Then Paolo thought again about Lucinda and their kiss. That was the best part of the day.

Not many miles away two brothers were sitting in the shade of a large mango tree munching on some macadamia nuts. Alex De La Paz and his brother Pepito were also talking about soccer.

"Big B, you really ought to ask about trying out for the national team. Even though you are so young and not yet on a professional team, I think it would be a really good experience for you," Pepito exhorted his older brother.

"Aw, they don't want some kid my age trying out. They only want experienced men. Ones who have played professionally and who have international experience. Heck, I know they would require me to have at least played on the junior national team before seriously considering me for the real national team."

"Well, then try out for the junior national team. You're good enough, I know it."

"Thanks, Little B, I appreciate your support. I'll give it some thought."

"I have dreams occasionally, Big B, that you're playing on a real nice field, with manicured grass and a hundred thousand people watching you play. You are in the World Cup. How could you be in the World Cup in my dreams if you are not going to try out for the team? You've got to get known more than right here in our valley."

"Don't worry. The chances will come for me. I might take your advice though, and give the junior cup team a shot."

"You can make it. I know you can," Pepito encouraged.

Alex's thoughts drifted to a scene in which he was boarding a plane with other Costa Rican players who were on their way to the World Cup. He imagined his mother and father and, of course, Pepito standing nearby waving good-bye to him and the other players. There were lots of well-wishers crowding the gate area bidding them good luck for their departure. He had to admit to himself that playing for his country in the world's largest and most prestigious tournament would truly be something he would relish.

CHAPTER 2

Mrs. Adams called out to her son, "Joel. Joel. Did you invite Mr. Johnson to graduation? Why don't you ask him if he would like to sit with us?"

"Yes, Mom, I called him two weeks ago and again yesterday. He knows it's Friday night. He already knows you're going to pick him up at 6:45 so you can be there early enough to get a good seat. Besides, Scott and I are going over to his house today to help clean up his yard. We promised him we'd help get the place spruced up a bit. I'll remind him once again, but he remembers things pretty well."

"Aw, honey, that's so nice of you two to do that. I didn't realize you had planned to go there. Does he know about you being selected as the outstanding senior?"

"Yes, I told him the day I found out, remember? Almost as soon as I got home I went there to tell him. I picked up Scott and we went together to tell him about all the choices they announced that day and I told him that a thousand-dollar scholarship was part of it. He said he would feel so proud he might burst watching us at graduation. He also mentioned that he wanted to give us a little something for graduation and that we were to come and see him sometime. Maybe that will be today."

"I shouldn't have worried. I might have known you'd have it all taken care of. Mr. Johnson has been so good to you, and you have been good for him. You know he has a little trouble getting around. Some days if it weren't for that cane of his he wouldn't get out the front door. It's just I've been so busy arranging things for both sets of your grandparents and for Uncle Sid and Aunt Mary, and Uncle John and Aunt Janet. They're all coming and I've been busy planning places to stay, transportation, and meals. Did you also remember to invite Susie's family here after graduation? The Fontaines also?"

"Yes, Mom, and they're all coming. It ought to be one great big bash."

"I hope so."

"It'll be fun to see everyone. How long are Grandma and Grandpa and Papaw and Mamaw staying? They'll be here a while, won't they?"

"Yes, Papaw and Mamaw plan to stay a week, but Grandma and Grandpa are going back in three days."

Their senior year was an exceptional one for Scott and Joel. The national acclaim they received for being chosen first team and honorable mention All-American made them local celebrities. Their high school team, having won the Georgia state championship, ended up ranked second in the country by *America Today*, behind a team from Maryland. Scott and Joel both won full scholarships to the University of Georgia, and accepted them on the condition they be allowed to room together. Scott was one of the highest scorers in the country, having scored forty-one goals in twenty-six games and one hundred nine goals during his four-year high school career. Seventeen different colleges offered Scott a scholarship and he was recruited by over one hundred twenty-five schools, most of which held no interest for him. Joel got six scholarship offers and numerous letters of inquiry as well.

Other honors accrued to Scott and Joel. Their senior class voted Scott best athlete, Joel and Susie class couple, and Joel class president. All three won academic recognition on numerous occasions. Joel's most distinctive honor, according to Susie, was being selected the outstanding senior by the faculty and the administration—an honor as well as the thousand dollar scholarship.

Susie and Joel had fallen very much in love and although they weren't engaged, they had privately pledged that they would marry each other soon after graduation from college. Susie had been picked "class favorite" by her peers. As class favorite, she was entitled to lead the entire senior class of four hundred students into the auditorium for graduation and to carry the school flag at the head of the procession. Joel was thrilled at the honors bestowed upon his girl. He thought more of her honors than he did of his own. He was especially pleased that all three of them—Scott, Susie and himself—had been selected as outstanding seniors in "Who's Who Among American High School Students." Susie had also won many awards for being the editor of their yearbook. *The Paragon* had won first place in the state-wide yearbook competition.

In his bedroom Joel reflected on the past couple of years. He was really happy. How much better could things be? He had the girl he loved and with whom he wanted to spend the rest of his life, and who he knew loved him. He enjoyed a very successful high school career and could look forward to a good career in college. A good summer job was lined up that could one day lead to a permanent job right here in his hometown. Susie and Scott were both going to the same college as he. But most of all, he shared a very happy family life and he loved his parents and sisters deeply. He reflected on how much his mom and dad had done for him and supported him, and all those games they had gone to see him play.

His two sisters, Ashley and Amanda, were growing up. Ashley would be in tenth grade next year. She was pretty, perky, very outgoing, and quite popular, he observed. Amanda, too, had a lot of friends; she was the leader of her little group. Joel thought his parents would have their hands full when she got to high school. Amanda was going to be a real knockout; the boys will be after her. She'll have them fighting over her, he chuckled.

Joel and Scott had a relationship that grew considerably closer when they shared a similar experience of becoming a Christian at the same youth conference in the summer before ninth grade. For each it had been a gradual thing, not a sudden, dramatic change; rather, it was a ripening feeling, the accumulation of many years of Sunday school teachings and family beliefs. Each recognized that he had made a commitment, and so their Christian growth became a shared thing that was the subject of many conversations. They often wondered why it took them so long to receive God's gift of everlasting life, when all they had to do was to accept it. There was significant energy between them as they shared this marvelous experience.

When Susie told him over two years ago that she too wanted to become a Christian, Joel's heart practically burst with joy and excitement. He had been witnessing to her off and on without applying pressure. Susie had decided she would accept Christ during a youth conference at her church. She made the decision she would do it, but waited until after she talked to Joel. That night Susie and Joel prayed together in a way they never had before. Their relationship took on new meaning after that night. Joel thanked God he lived in the Bible Belt, where there was so much positive influence. He also enjoyed watching Susie grow as a Christian. She asked him a thousand questions; however, Joel was always very patient with her. They both developed a special fondness for Pastor

Clayton Brooks, Joel's preacher. The Reverend Brooks also set aside a special place in his heart for this young couple and was glad to spend time with them, helping them grow in their faith.

"Has Scott called yet?" Joel questioned his mom.

"No."

"I'm going to run over to his house, pick him up, and go on to Mr. Johnson's. OK?"

"Sure. Please be home at six for supper."

"OK. What's for supper?"

"Fried catfish. That OK with you?"

"Sure, Mom," Joel said as he gave her a kiss good-bye.

The late morning sun shone through the live-oak leaves and the pine boughs, leaving a speckled effect on the front yard at Mr. Johnson's house. The large white antebellum structure lay on the edge of an older section of town. The expansive front yard sloped down toward the street to an ancient sidewalk. In need of repair, with sections askew, the mottled concrete ran interference for the contrast of the green grass and the dark gray of the roadway.

"You know, I think all older homes are painted white. Nothing else looks right," Joel commented to Scott as they drove up in Joel's car.

"They should be anyway, if they aren't. It looks the most natural."

"He sure has a pretty home. I love the screened-in porch that goes all the way around the front and two sides. It's nice to sit in and talk."

Mr. Johnson retained a gardener, who was almost as old as Mr. Johnson himself. He worked three half-days a week. The project that Joel and Scott were to do today was to trim back the azaleas and camellias and an overgrown hedge that had gotten very much out of control. The hedge was one of redtips, as all the kids called them, and it stood seventeen or eighteen feet tall. While the camellias and azaleas could be trimmed with clippers, the hedge required a saw for the biggest branches. These were things the elderly gardener could not do.

Joel had made a list of things to do earlier, so that he knew what tools would be needed. He was thankful for the oversized bamboo leaf rake someone had given his dad. It could do twice the work one of those metal leaf rakes could do. As big as the yard was, with all the pine straw and oak leaves that had to be cleaned up from around the shrubbery and along the edges of the yard, it would go twice as fast with "that big ol' rake."

Mr. Johnson was an older man in Joel's church whom Joel often helped by doing work around the house and running errands. Sometimes, like today, Scott helped. Joel and his family sometimes had Mr. Johnson come to their house for dinner. Mr. Johnson never failed to remember Joel's birthday or either of his sisters' birthdays. Joel and his sisters regarded Mr. Dan, as they called him, as a surrogate grandfather, since both sets of grandparents lived up in Pennsylvania and they only got to see them once a year. Mr. Dan, they all thought, was the consummate southern gentleman. He dressed well, was almost always in a suit, and frequently wore a dress hat when he was outside. It didn't matter if it was hot outside or not, Mr. Dan would wear a hat.

He also owned a 1987 Buick LeSabre that was kept in immaculate condition. When he took the car out, Mr. Dan would not drive fast; he stayed consistently ten miles an hour under the speed limit. As Mr. Dan got up in years he became less and less mobile. He had a problem with his legs in that he had to wear plastic leg supports and special shoes for him to walk at all. He also used a cane. He needed the cane for balance and to help him negotiate steps or steep inclines. When it rained, Mr. Dan eschewed an umbrella, preferring instead his hat and a raincoat. Joel didn't understand why he wouldn't use an umbrella. Mr. Dan's reply on several occasions was that he was used to the hat and raincoat. He never offered more explanation. Joel wondered if Mr. Dan grew up before umbrellas were invented.

Mildred Johnson, Mr. Dan's wife, was in a nursing home, unable to care for herself. Because she had Alzheimer's disease, she required attentive care, much more than what Mr. Dan could give her. The day Mildred first went into the nursing home was a painfully emotional day for Dan Johnson. He knew he had to let go, and yet they had been together now for forty-eight years. It was hard. Except when he was sick, Mr. Dan never failed to visit his wife each day. When he went, he would time his visit to be there at either lunch or dinner so that he could share a meal with her, many days doing both. In these later years he would feed his wife and talk loving words to her, often holding and rubbing her hand. He hoped that at times her mind was clear enough she might just understand some of what he said. He was hopeful that on occasion she still recognized him.

The relationship between Mr. Johnson and Joel was a mutually beneficial arrangement. It gave the older man a youngster to care about and love, and it gave Joel someone to fill the grandfather role in his life. Mr. Johnson and his wife had no children, only nieces and nephews. Mr. Johnson welcomed the love and attention of Joel's whole family, but particularly Joel. Each time Mr. Johnson got together with the Adams's family, he left with a good impression of time well spent and a warm feeling that something good had happened. Joel sometimes did the work at Mr. Johnson's house without receiving any direct pay, but he did on occasion receive some nice gifts, such as the time Mr. Dan used his contacts to buy Joel and his dad tickets to the Super Bowl. Joel had thought that was terrific.

As Joel was sweeping off the walk and Scott was dumping a wheelbarrow load of hedge clippings near the street for pickup, Mr. Johnson came out the front door. "Boys, this sure is nice of you to do this for me. Won't you come in for something to drink and a piece of pie now?"

"Sure," Joel answered, "but first let me finish this walk."

"I must say the whole yard looks really good, maybe better than it's looked in quite a while. You boys have worked really hard."

"Thanks, it's nice to see the place looking good, 'specially those bushes along the house. I'll bet no one has trimmed those in ten years!"

"Yeah, we took two dozen wheelbarrow loads of branches to the street. Look at that pile—it's five feet tall," Scott boasted.

"It is a welcome sight. Now come on in and get something to drink. I have a surprise I want to show you."

After Scott and Joel finished putting the tools away, they went into the house. Mr. Johnson was putting the ice cube trays away and had three place settings with dessert plates and glasses laid out. In the middle of the table were two big pies and a two-liter bottle of Coke. Mr. Johnson shuffled over to a drawer in the counter and pulled out a silver pie server.

"Let's have some pie, boys. Which will it be: apple or blueberry?"

Scott, being the more outgoing of the two, piped up, "I'd like some of both if I may."

"OK. You too, Joel?"

"Yeah, they both look good. Thank you."

"Boys, I truly appreciate the work you've done for me and for the pleasure of having you visit me. It's such a great comfort to me. You know I'm all alone here and even though my nephews and nieces and their kids come visit, when you get to be my age you welcome as much company as will come. Now, I want to show you two a surprise. While I get it, serve yourselves some more pie and get some more Coke."

"Joel, what do you think Mr. Johnson's surprise is?"

"I don't know; he's never mentioned anything to me before, except that he had a graduation gift."

Mr. Johnson slowly came around the corner of the dining room into the kitchen carrying two enormous books, saying, "Clear a place for these, boys." Mr. Johnson set the books down on the kitchen table and carefully settled himself into his chair. When he opened the top book he said, "I've been saving all the news clippings and pictures about the both of you for a long time. I thought you'd like to see what I've got here."

Both Joel and Scott looked up at each other at the same time. "That's really nice of you, Mr. Dan. Gosh, look, Joel, this one's out of the Atlanta paper here. It's the article about our high school team being ranked second nationally by *America Today*. And here's the article itself. Wow!"

"Boy, Mr. Dan, how did you get all of these?"

"Well, I subscribe to *America Today*, *The Atlanta Times*, and our own newspaper. I've just been saving these for a long time; it's been somewhat of a hobby with me. These books that I'm doing will be yours after you finish school. You two will have to figure out how to share these. Scott, I'm sorry these scrapbooks don't go back as far on you as they do on Joel, but I really started this for Joel and then started adding you, too, when you appeared so often together and when I got to know you as you started coming here. So there aren't as many pictures and articles of you."

"That's OK, Mr. Dan, I really appreciate what you've done—this is great!"

"Mr. Dan, this is one of the nicest things you could have done. When Scott and I graduate this year it will end an era, a happy time for us. My mom has kept a few clippings, like when Scott and I made all-state, but not so many and certainly not as organized as yours. This is impressive!"

"I'm glad you two like this. I have enjoyed doing it and anticipated the fun of showing it to you and watching your reaction; I'm not disappointed."

"It's fun to look at articles about yourself. Boy, this is great, isn't it, Joel?"

"You bet! I love this. Thanks again, Mr. Dan."

"I understand both of you boys are going to go to the University of Georgia. Is that right?"

"Yes. Both Joel and I have decided we're going on to college together there. We both like the school and they offered each of us a full scholarship."

"We wanted to go to a school somewhere in the SEC. I liked Georgia, Vanderbilt, or Auburn, but we agreed that Georgia would be the best for each of us. However, we seriously considered the University of Virginia—they've got a real good soccer team—but we wanted to stay closer to home. We've been to Georgia and really like the campus there; they offered Susie a good scholarship also. Everything just kind of fell into place."

"Yeah, it's going to be great to be together throughout college. We're even going to room together."

"That's fantastic, boys."

"Scott, look here—this page has the clippings on our state high school championship. And here's my favorite picture of you sliding through the puddle. Boy, you could train otters with this one."

"Thanks, buddy. Wow, look at this, Joel! This article is out of *The New York Journal*. I've never seen this before."

"Where? Oh, it says 'The state of Georgia has produced three of the finest players in the country, including our pick for the best scholastic player of the year, Scott Fontaine. The future of American soccer looks brighter each year. We don't know of a better player to have come out of our high schools than Mr. Fontaine, a straight "A" student and a speedster with prolific scoring abilities.' Now, how about that?"

"You missed the part about your name being listed as an All American, Joel."

Scott and Joel left Mr. Johnson's house and went to Joel's. There they showed Mr. and Mrs. Adams the scrapbooks that Mr. Johnson had put together. They were very surprised and happy for the boys.

"That sounds like something you two will cherish the rest of your lives. That was very nice of Mr. Johnson to do that. He's a very kind and special person."

"He sure is, Mom. I always feel good when I'm with him. He knows how to make others feel good. He told us his yard hasn't looked that good in quite a while. Look, he gave us each twenty dollars."

"I'll have to drive over past the house to see what you two have done. The money is nice, and I'm proud of you both for spending your day helping Mr. Johnson. You two have something that seldom exists between friends, especially young people. You enjoy each other's company, no matter how much you are together; you like the same things; you never fight or argue; your families are friends; you both have younger sisters; you're both good students and excellent athletes; you're both Christians; and you have generous hearts. I thank God for providing so many blessings. Scott, you are what every mother hopes her son will have for a friend." Mrs. Adams came and put an arm around each of them. "You each have the greatest opportunity to have a rich, rewarding life ahead of you. Trust in God because he is in full control of every aspect of our lives.

"Tell you boys what. I'll treat the both of you to the movies tonight. I know you two were planning to go with dates. We are in love with Joel's Susie. After these two years we practically think of Susie as part of the family now."

"Aw, Mom."

"Mrs. Adams, Susie is probably the most popular girl in the whole high school. She and Joel make the perfect pair; everybody says so. I think she's wonderful and Joel would be a fool to let go of her."

"I have no intention of letting her go."

"What I like about Susie, Joel, is that she has the knack of making everyone feel important and as if she were her best friend. She's really special."

"Thanks, Scott, I know; and I agree with you. I don't know how she does it with so many people, but she possesses a certain touch that makes people feel good. She knows just the right thing to say. She makes everyone else feel important."

Friday began as a beautiful Georgian day. Joel slept until 10:00—much later than usual—because he knew he would be up late tonight, graduation night. The whole family was up already and Grandma and Grandpa had arrived.

"Hi, everybody," Joel greeted as he came downstairs.

"Here comes the prize graduate—almost. How ya doin', son?"

"Fine, Grandpa, good to see you and Grandma." After giving each of them a hug, Joel asked,"How was the trip?"

"Not so bad, it's interstate all the way. We made it here in great shape. How are you feeling, champ?"

"Just fine, couldn't be better, as a matter of fact. It will be great to get all this graduation stuff behind me, though."

"What? The biggest day of your life so far and you're wishing it was already in the past? That seems strange. Why are you trying to avoid tonight?"

"It's going to be OK except that I've got to make a short acceptance speech when they give me the scholarship."

"That won't be so bad. Just thank everybody and act grateful for being chosen. That's all you have to do."

"Yes sir, I know, Grandpa. Still, I don't relish that part of it."

"You'll do fine. Where are you going to college?"

"I'm going to the University of Georgia. They gave me a scholarship."

"Good. I like them. What about your girl?"

"She's also going there. She got a partial scholarship to work on their yearbook staff. She would have gone anyway, though. We wanted to go to the same school. She said she'd go where I went."

"Sounds serious."

"She's just a really great person. Wait till tonight, you'll meet her. Susie and her family are coming here after the graduating ceremonies."

"Good," chimed in Grandma. "I've been wanting to meet this young lady of yours. Your mom has written of her several times. She sounds like something very special."

"She is. She's great. You'll see."

"Mom, I've got to take Susie her graduation present this morning. That OK?"

"Yes. Try not to be too long though. Other guests will be arriving here this afternoon."

"OK."

Joel went to his room and picked up the diamond necklace he bought for Susie. Joel could hardly wait to see her reaction to the present. He bounded down the steps two at a time.

"'Bye, everyone. I won't be too long."

"'Bye."

Joel slipped into the car and drove over to Susie's house, really on a high. Susie opened the front door.

"Gee, you look pretty," Joel offered.

Susie smiled warmly at Joel and said,"Thank you."

Joel grabbed her and gave her a big kiss on the lips as he put his arms around her. "Hi," he said. Then they gave each other a long kiss.

"Hi," She gasped. "Come on in."

"I brought this for you—it's a graduation present. I hope you'll like it."

"I'd like anything you gave me."

"Open it. Open it now. I want you to see it."

Susie opened the present as Joel carefully watched her face.

"Oh, Joel, it's beautiful! It's lovely! Let me put it on. There, how does that look?"

"You look tremendous, and so does the necklace."

"Oh, thanks." Susie said as she kissed him softly. They stayed that way; arms entwined, lips close together, as they enjoyed each other's love.

"Are you looking forward to tonight being over? You've got such an important part to play this evening."

"Aw, it's not such a big deal, but yeah, I'll be glad when it's over. You've got a big part too, don't forget. But I'm not comfortable whenever there's a lot of attention drawn to me. I would much rather be alone with you. Wouldn't that be terrific if we got to spend about two weeks together on a deserted island somewhere? Just you and me."

"Maybe one day we can make that come true, but right now you're dreaming. Joel, my present to you comes tonight, I just know you're going to love it."

"From you any gift will be cherished forever, but it's hard to wait."

"Wait you will, because you have to be a graduate before I'll give it to you."

"OK, I guess I'll have to wait."

"Oh, Joel, I'm going to be so proud of you tonight in front of all those people. Just think, of all the people in our senior class, you got selected outstanding senior. We're all proud of you."

"Yeah, it should be nice for everyone."

"My folks too. You know they regard you now almost as their own son," she beamed. "They think you're terrific."

"So are they. They are both so nice to me. Your sister, Beth, is too. She admires you so much and doesn't seem the least bit jealous of your successes."

"She worships you, you know. Beth brags about you to all her friends. You are both a big brother to her and the man she fantasizes one day will sweep her off her feet. She's got such a crush on you and has had for quite some time."

"I'm spoken for, but she's a great kid and one day she'll make someone a super wife, just like you."

"You're so sweet," Susie said as she stepped close to put her arms around his neck and kiss him. Joel was full of love and kissed her back long and lovingly. He hugged her tightly and wrapped his arms around her. He murmured he loved her as his hands started to roam over the front of her body. But before he got carried away she broke from him and put his hand aside. "No you don't, mister, that's enough. I'll see you tonight at graduation. Don't be late," she cautioned.

"Don't worry," he said with a laugh. "I'll be on time. Scott and I are going together. I'll see you tonight."

With that Joel gave her a quick kiss and said good-bye. He then drove to the store to pick up a few things and went on home. When he got there his other grandparents had arrived and they all spent the afternoon talking.

He liked to listen to stories of the old days…when his parents were kids and the things they did or what they were like. Those stories always amused Joel and his sisters. Sometimes their parents were a little embarrassed by what the grandparents said. It all made for a good time for the whole family.

His sisters, he observed, were now old enough to really enter productively into these family discussions. Ashley, though, was often a little too loud and a little too talkative. But she was smart. Although she studied, everything came easily to her and she understood concepts that taxed even Joel. High A's were the norm for her.

Joel felt a tinge of pride that all the kids in their family got straight A's. Joel had graduated fourth in his class and scored highly in his tests. He had gotten a 32 on his ACT tests, which helped him get a scholarship to Georgia.

"Joel, honey, you ought to get something to eat before you dress and go to graduation. We will have a good bit of food for everyone afterward, but you might get hungry before then. Grab a sandwich or at least a piece of fruit."

"OK, Mom, I'll have a ham and cheese sandwich now and that'll be enough." Joel ate, showered, and then dressed in his best suit. He remembered to put his notes in his suit pocket. His speech wouldn't be long, but he didn't want to forget to thank everyone he should. He looked at his notes: God; family, especially his parents—call them Momma and Daddy—they'll like that; teachers; coaches; administration; all his friends; my best friend Scott; and, not least, Susie.

Joel grabbed the car keys and ran down the stairs. "'Bye everyone, 'Bye Mom—Dad."

"'Bye."

"'Bye, do well; we'll be so proud of you."

"Thanks, see you in about an hour and a half."

Joel jumped in the car and headed for Scott's house. As he drove up he noticed the special balloons and flowers and the big sign Scott's family had put up for him. Scott was the oldest in his family too, so this was a really big event for them. Joel parked the car on the street and went in the front door. Scott's grandparents couldn't come, but he had an aunt and uncle and two boy cousins that had come.

"Hey, how ya'll doing?" Joel said as he went in.

"Joel, Joel, hey, how ya doing? Uncle Todd, Aunt Angie, this is my best buddy, Joel. Joel, meet my aunt and uncle and my two cousins, Reggie and Ricky."

Joel shook hands all around. Scott's cousins were big, he noticed: athletic-looking too. Scott was tall, on the thin side. He guessed Scott was 6'1" and 180. His cousins were 6'2" and 6'1", more or less, but they had to go 220 or 210, worst case. One of them, he knew, was a good football player; the other was a football, soccer and baseball player. They lived in South Carolina; Rock Hill, Scott had said.

"Joel is going to get *the* big award tonight. He was selected the outstanding high school senior in our class. They make a pretty big 'to-do' about that here. He has to do a speech too," Scott declared.

"That's great, Joel."

"Thanks."

"In a couple of minutes we've got to go. Joel, I promised Mom I'd drop these Sunday school papers off at someone's house and pick up some things she's got for Mom."

"OK, sure."

Joel asked Scott's cousin what year they were in college or high school. Reggie told him he was a rising senior—just finished his junior year—in high school. Ricky said he was a freshman at Towson State, almost through his first year there. Joel was trying to think of a way to ask which one was the good football player without offending the other when he said, "Which one of you plays soccer?"

Ricky answered this time. "Both of us play soccer, but I only play intramural and 'rec' soccer now; Reggie still plays for the high school. He's pretty good at it, too. He plays sweeper. I used to play midfielder."

"Oh, I play fullback, stopper mostly, although I've also played sweeper off and on," Joel said.

"Yes, Scott has told us, says you're quite the player."

Scott jumped in. "We wouldn't have done nearly as well this year without Joel. He kept nearly every team from scoring. Joel saved two for-sure goals by himself in the state championship game."

Joel chimed in, "Scott did most all of our scoring. He was a scoring machine! He was so fast and quick no one could stop him. Heck, he was one of the top two or three scholastic players in the country this year. How can ya beat that?"

"I had a lot of help."

"Yeah, Scott."

"Sounds like you both had good years," Reggie said admiringly.

"Scott, hey, it's time to go, you've got to drop off these papers and pick up some things from Mrs. Schwabel, don't forget."

"OK, Mom. About ready, Joel?"

"Sure."

"OK, see ya'll later."

Scott and Joel got into Joel's car and took off to Mrs. Schwabel's house. "How far is it, Scott? You'll have to give me directions."

"They live on State Road 40 about two blocks past Five Points intersection."

"That should be easy to get to."

"Yeah; but I wouldn't want to live there. That four-lane road's too busy.

Too many trucks going to and from the city."

A Michael Jackson song was playing a bit too loud on the radio so Joel reached forward and turned it down. "Are you getting a job this summer, Scott?"

"Yes, I'll be working for David Ingle's landscaping service. That's going to involve a lot of physical work and ought to help build my muscles. At least I hope so. What about you?"

"Yeah, me too. I'll be working for Lambert, Morgan, Reeves, and Byrd, the accounting firm. I'm hoping to get some good experience, as well as the fact they pay pretty well."

"How'd you get that job?"

"Apparently some of the senior partners are real soccer fans and had heard I wanted to be an accountant. So they offered me this job and I said 'Sure'."

"That's pretty neat; that won't hurt you later on when you interview. Maybe they'll even employ you each summer and then hire you after college is over."

"Terrific! What a scene!"

"Then you can get married and settle down right close to home. I can see it now. Big ranch house in the suburbs; two or three kids running around; you and Susie sitting down to supper; you've got it made. Oh, I forgot. Lambert, Morgan, Reeves, Byrd and Adams. That'll make it complete."

"Soothsayer. That all sounds nice, but we'll just have to see."

"We're almost here. There it is—on the left, the white house."

"OK, soon as these cars go by I'll be in there. Boy, the sun sure is bad; I can hardly see. There, it looks clear."

"C'mon in, Joel, while I take these papers in," Scott said as the car was stopping in the drive. Joel and Scott both got out of the car and walked toward the door. Joel noticed two youngsters about seven and eight playing soccer next door. Joel told Scott to go on in; he'd go over with these kids. When he got there he noticed a really cute three-year-old girl out there with them. Joel introduced himself and found out their names were Bobby and Jeffrey. The little girl, he was informed, was Jennifer, Jeffrey's little sister.

Joel started just kicking the ball back and forth with the kids and showing them how to trap the ball and how to kick with both the insides and the outsides of their feet. Joel cautioned them to practice with both feet. "The left and the right foot are both needed in a game," he said. "Force yourselves to practice with both feet. Do drills, practice dribbling with the other foot. Dribble for a while with the outside, then for a while with the inside. Start with the other foot. Do lots of practice, that's how you get to improve. That's it. Good ... Good. Wait, try not to kick with the toe of your foot. See how you have a lot more surface area on the side..."

"Jennifer!" Jeffrey shrieked. "Jennifer!"

Joel whipped his head around. Little Jennifer was crossing the street without regard to traffic.

"Stay here," Joel commanded as he took off as fast as he could after Jennifer.

"Jennifer, stop! Come back," Joel hollered.

Jennifer was paying no attention. She seemed to be oblivious to it all. As Joel ran toward the street he looked to the left, but the sun was so bad he couldn't see anything. He looked to the right and there was an eighteen-wheeler in the left lane passing a car in the right lane.

"She's gonna get mowed down," thought Joel. "Gotta hurry."

Joel sprinted across the sidewalk. The truck and car were bearing down on the right. He realized they didn't see the girl. A car screeched on his left, but far enough away not to pose a threat. Joel could feel his heart thumping. "Got to hurry."

Jennifer was directly in the truck's path, she looked up at the truck coming down on her and froze with terror. Joel was flying.

"Jennifer!"

The trucker laid on his horn. Smoke poured from the wheels as they locked up from hard braking. Joel could see the truck in his peripheral vision. "I can do it! Maybe."

Joel scooped up the girl in his left arm without slowing down and took off ahead, tucking the girl to his side like a football. Joel glanced to his right.

"I'll beat the truck," he thought. "Hope that car is far enough back." Joel's heart jumped as he realized the car was too close—ten feet away and coming too fast. Joel took one more step and dove out as far as possible and threw Jennifer out in front beyond the car just before the car hit him.

The driver of the car screamed when she saw someone appear from in front of the truck directly in front of her. "Oh my God!" she exclaimed as she watched a body fly up over the top of her car. She quickly braked to a stop at the side of the road. As she got out of the car she noticed the truck had come to a stop about twenty-five yards in front, with the trailer partially jack-knifed across the road. She ran back to the point of the accident and noticed that miraculously the traffic had stopped in both directions. She heard screaming from two places. The closest was on her side of the road from a bundle of blue and white lying next to the road. The other was from two kids across the street. Someone had already reached the person in the roadway, so she went to the child next to the road. There was an ugly scrape on the side of her face and she was holding her left arm. She was screaming hysterically. The lady checked the girl for severe injuries and could not see any that were obvious. She thought it best not to move the child until someone more knowledgeable could determine the extent of her injuries. She looked over at the man she had hit and was afraid. "Where did he, they, come from? Why would they be in front of the truck, moving across in front of her? Why me? Why?"

Another man, not a boy, came streaking across the yard and street from the other side of the road. He was dressed in a suit also, like the man she hit.

"Joel, Joel, are you all right? Joel?" His voice was frantic. "What happened?"

"He got hit hard by a car," the second man to get to Joel said.

"How? Why?" Scott knelt down next to Joel and put his ear next to his mouth and looked at Joel's chest. Blood was coming out of Joel's ear. Scott was scared. Joel was breathing and he had a pulse, but his breathing didn't sound right.

The second man answered, "I saw the whole thing. The little girl had gone out into the street. An eighteen-wheeler with a car alongside was bearing down on her. This boy saw her and ran out into traffic, scooped her up and tried to make it across. Just as he was about to be hit he flung the little girl out of the way. The car hit him as he was diving. Hit him hard. He flew up over the roof of the car and landed behind it."

"Why didn't the car see him?"

"Didn't have a chance. He barely made it past the truck. The driver of the car wouldn't have seen him till the last split second, because the truck must've have blocked her view."

Just then a man ran up and said loudly, "I called an ambulance and the police from my car phone. Someone cover the boy up to help keep him from going into shock."

The first man said, "That sun was blinding; it wasn't the driver's fault."

Jennifer's mother had just reached her. Both Jennifer and her mother were screaming. The mother's screams turned to sobbing when she realized her daughter was not critically hurt. She wrapped Jennifer in her arms and hugged her as she continued to sob, "My darling, my darling." Jennifer continued to scream hysterically. Her mother looked over at Joel and the group of people around him with anguish in her face. Jeffrey had told her Jennifer and a boy had been hit by a car, that Jennifer had gone in the street and the boy ran to save her. Jennifer's mother gingerly picked up the girl and made her way over to where Joel was.

"How is he?" she sobbed.

"Not good, not good at all."

"He saved my little girl. Oh, Lord, save this brave boy," she pleaded.

Scott was tending to Joel the best he could. He took off his jacket and covered Joel and someone else provided a light jacket that he put under Joel's head as a pillow. Scott smoothed Joel's hair to try to make it look more normal as he talked soothingly to Joel in an attempt to calm himself and allay his own fears. As a consequence he didn't hear the arrival of the ambulance and the medics. Scott backed up and let the paramedics in. One rechecked his pulse and respiration, the other hooked up an instrument with gauges and wires and dials to Joel's neck and chest. Then he got on the phone to transmit the findings.

"Get a team ready, we're going to need it," Scott heard him say. "Help me get him on a stretcher," the first paramedic said. "What's his name?"

"Joel, Joel Adams," answered Scott.

"Joel, Joel, can you hear me? We are going to take you to the hospital now."

"What hospital?" Scott asked.

"St. Andrews."

Scott searched the crowd for the man who said he called the ambulance. "Man with a telephone. Please call Joel's home." He gave the man the number. "Tell them to meet us at the emergency room, please," Scott added.

Scott got in the ambulance with Joel. Jennifer and Jennifer's mother got in another ambulance. Both ambulances took off, sirens wailing. The paramedic in the back of the ambulance with Joel was talking on a phone almost continuously. Scott was very afraid. The medic was talking fast and excitedly. He said there were massive internal injuries. He asked them to set up an emergency team—arrival time four minutes—and to have blood ready. "Need a head doctor, bone, circulatory, pulmonary, and neuro. Get 'em ready."

Scott said to him, "Is he going to make it?"

"I don't know, he's got severe internal injuries."

They arrived at the hospital and rushed Joel into surgery. Scott filled out the admittance papers and answered questions from the emergency room desk. He then got on the phone and called Joel's house. A lady answered, "Hello."

"Hello. Who's this?" Scott said.

"This is Joel's grandmother. Who is calling, please?"

"This is Scott, Joel's friend. I'm at the emergency room at St. Andrews hospital. I came in the ambulance with Joel. He was hit by a car. It's serious."

"Oh, no. We heard he was going to the hospital, that he was hit by a car, but the man didn't say how bad it was."

"Well, we don't know yet, but he's hurt badly. How long ago did they leave?"

"About ten minutes ago. Everyone left except me, I'm his grandmother."

"OK. That'll put them here in a couple of minutes, maybe quicker if there's not much traffic. Thank you, good-bye."

Scott then called Susie's house. No one answered the phone. He let it ring ten times. "Darn it, they're gone already." Then he tried his own house, but everyone had already left there, too.

Shortly, the emergency room door opened and Joel's whole family came in. His mother and sisters were crying. Scott was introduced to Joel's grandparents.

"How is he?" Mr. Adams asked.

"We don't know. He got hit hard by a car. The paramedic said he had extensive internal injuries."

"Can we talk to a doctor?" Mrs. Adams said, crying.

"How did it happen?" Mr. Adams asked.

Scott explained everything, from his going into the house and Joel going over to play with the two boys, to relating the story told him by the man who saw the accident. He added it appeared the little girl will be all right.

"Oh my poor boy, my poor baby. He must be suffering so much," Mrs. Adams despaired.

"Was he conscious after the accident happened?" Mr. Adams asked. "Could he talk?"

"No, Joel was unconscious when I got to him and he didn't say anything."

"Did the little girl come here?" Mr. Adams requested.

"Yes—with her mother—they came right after us; they are in being examined by a doctor now. I think the little girl, Jennifer is her name, just got a bad scrape and bruises and was scared to death."

"What a night for Joel to get hurt," his grandfather said. "Here he is the guest of honor, so to speak, and he can't even receive the acclaim due him."

"I'll accept it for him if you like, Mrs. Adams, then bring it over here and show him and tell him all about it. I'll tell him there wasn't anything to be nervous about, getting up in front of a thousand people and making a speech." Mrs. Adams smiled weakly at Scott's attempt to be helpful and couldn't help but feel sorrow and love at the same time for her son's life-long friend. She moved over and hugged Scott as they both shed tears. Mr. Adams came over and hugged both of them and said, "It's in the Lord's hands now."

A silence settled on the little group there in the waiting room of the emergency area. Each person was absorbed in his own thoughts and saying prayers. A few moments later a doctor came out through the doors to the trauma area. "Mr. and Mrs. Adams?"

"Yes, that's us," Mr. Adams said, as he took a step forward.

The doctor had a gentle look on his face; he was a kind man with wrinkles around his eyes. "I am sorry, there was nothing we could do to save your son. The injuries were too massive."

"Oh, no!" Mrs. Adams fell sobbing into her husbands arms. "No, no, no, it's just not possible."

Scott sank down onto a chair and put his head in his hands and sobbed. Joel's grandmother broke completely and had to be supported by her husband to keep from falling. Joel's two sisters, Amanda and Ashley, walked to their mother and father and hugged them both while they wailed loudly. The room was full of grief and anguish. The second grandfather came over to Mr. and Mrs. Adams and the girls and just kind of hugged them. All were numb from the tragic turn of events. The grandfather took out his handkerchief and gave it to Mrs. Adams.

"Doctor, did...did he suffer from pain long?" Mr. Adams asked.

The kind doctor answered. "No, Joel wouldn't have felt any pain, he never regained consciousness after the accident. He felt nothing, we are sure of that."

"What caused his..." Mr. Adams tried to ask.

"Joel had both a blow to the head and very severe internal injuries to almost every organ in his body. He died of a fractured skull and massive internal bleeding. We could not stop the bleeding, even though he received a transfusion."

"Thank you, for trying, doctor, we know you did your best."

"We had four doctors working on him from the moment he arrived. There was just no chance."

"Thank you, doctor."

"Would you like to see your son?"

"Yes I would," Mr. Adams answered. "Would you, honey?"

Mrs. Adams, torn with grief, nodded her head.

"May I also, Mr. Adams?" Scott's face was trembling with grief.

"Yes, we can all go. May we, doctor?"

"Yes, of course."

Just then Jennifer and her mother came out through the doors. Jennifer had a big patch bandage over the side of her face and a wrap around her left arm. She was still sobbing a little, kind of catching a sob periodically, as her mother carried her. Her mother looked up at everyone, then at the doctor. The doctor shook his head slightly to indicate the outcome.

Jennifer's mother's face contorted in agony as she faced the parents. "I'm so sorry. Your son did a brave, brave thing, saving my daughter. If it weren't for his brave deed my Jennifer would surely be dead. I don't know what to say. That should be my little girl in there instead of your son. That was a selfless act of courage."

Mr. and Mrs. Adams tried their best to smile.

Mr. Adams reached over and brushed a wisp of hair off Jennifer's forehead. "I'm glad little Jennifer is all right. We can't undo what has happened, but it does help to see your child. That will certainly comfort us in days to come."

The doctor, sensing an awkward moment, said, "This way please," and he took the whole family in.

It was hard for the family; Joel's mother and sisters lost control completely. Scott cried silently. He put his arm around Ashley. He picked up his suit jacket, which had been laid to the side, and put it on, for he was cold. The same thoughts were running through many of their minds. "What will it be like without Joel? Why did it have to happen to him? To us? Why couldn't conditions or timing have been a little different? He's gone on to a better place. Why couldn't he have lived? He can't be dead. This can't be permanent. Maybe he'll wake up and be all right." As they turned to leave another doctor said he would tend to the arrangements to move the body if they had a preference for which funeral home to use.

Mr. Adams said, "It will be Hall's Funeral Home."

"I'll take care of it," The doctor said quietly.

As they turned to leave, Mr. Adams looked at his watch. It was 7:35. "Scott, I can think of nothing Joel would have wanted more than for you to go ahead and go to graduation and, by God, to accept his award. You'll have to deal with why you're accepting and not Joel. I guess you'll have to tell them. But I know Joel would want you to be there. The graduation ceremony started five minutes ago, but you'll be in time for the important events if you leave now."

"Do you think it's the right thing to do?" Scott asked.

"Yes, we do," Mr. and Mrs. Adams chorused. "Take Joel's car."

"I can't. It's back at ... at the accident."

"Then take mine. We'll squeeze into Dad's station wagon. Will you be all right?"

"Yes, I think so. I'm coming over afterward," Scott said.

Scott left and drove to the high school. His mind was racing about Joel, about growing up together, about Joel's family, about the accident, about the graduation, about Susie. "About Susie! What am I going to do? I've got to see her first. She'll go to pieces. I can't just go in and scream, 'Joel's dead.'"

When Scott walked in the back of the auditorium it was dark. There were several people standing at the back because there weren't enough seats. One of his classmates was singing a song. Scott felt dizzy and tried to get his bearings. He borrowed a program from someone standing near him. Best he could tell they were ready for the awards portion of the ceremony. There were four awards. Joel's was last. The first award would be the Music Award. The second and third were for salutatorian and valedictorian. The outstanding senior award and presentation of the scholarship and plaque was last, just before the awarding of the diplomas.

The man near Scott turned and stared at him. Scott had started crying for no apparent reason at all.

"What's wrong? What's wrong?"

"Bad news, very bad news, it's terrible."

"What?"

"My friend—gone."

Scott realized he had better get collected. This was going to be hard. Susie? Where was Susie? He looked out over the sea of mortarboard hats and black gowns and realized he had no chance of locating her in so short a time. He also thought maybe he ought to go around and come onto the stage from the side stage door instead of being so conspicuous walking down the main aisle. Scott left the auditorium and made his way around the building to the side door. "Please don't be locked," he prayed. He tried the latch and was thankful it opened. He went in and up the steps to the stage side.

Susie was looking around. She thought by now she would have located Joel and Scott but so far she hadn't seen them once. Worried, Susie at first thought they were late, then she figured she just couldn't see them without being so obvious about it. The early speeches were boring; most commencement speeches were, she reckoned. Mr. Lee, the principal, seemed to go on and on extolling the virtues of education. He then read off everyone's name who won some kind of honor. This list was long. She heard her own name and Joel's mentioned several times each. Susie did not listen the rest of the time Mr. Lee's voice was droning on. She came out of her daze when everyone started clapping.

"A job well done, seniors," Mr. Lee intoned. "This was perhaps the best class academically, athletically, and achievement-wise we have had here in quite a while."

Susie's mind started to wander again. She thought about how delighted Joel would be with the wall hanging that she had made for him. She had combined macramé, embroidery, and weaving that highlighted most of Joel's academic achievements, National Merit finalist, All-American, yearbook, outstanding senior, and—looking ahead—the University of Georgia. Susie tingled with delight in anticipation of Joel's face when she watched him open it. Tonight at Joel's house—with everyone there, including her parents—would be the perfect time. She estimated she had spent over one hundred hours making that for him. Oh! She couldn't wait till tonight. Where was he? she wondered. "Maybe it's the cap and gowns," she thought. "That would make it much more difficult to pick him out. That's it!" she decided. Then she felt better.

Scott came on the stage side as Mr. Lee was saying, "A job well done, seniors..." Now he had to compose himself and plan how he was going to tell Mr. Lee and everyone else. The very thought of that made Scott lose control for a minute. He bit hard on his lower lip; he knew he had to do better. The Music Award was given. Then the salutatorian. As Mr. Lee called up the valedictorian, Scott broke down again in anguish over all those who were close to Joel: himself, Susie, his family, and when he thought of Mr. Johnson it made him cry again.

"And now, distinguished seniors, parents, guests, and family members; it is my honor to present this year's Kiwanis Club's outstanding high school senior award for Bethel High School, to Joel Xavier Adams." Mr. Lee highlighted a few of Joel's achievements.

"Would Joel Adams please come forward?"

The whole audience started applauding, for they recognized the significance of this award. As Susie was clapping she looked around expectantly but did not see Joel. She became alarmed. "He's still not here. What's wrong?" She grabbed the arm of the guy sitting on her right and squeezed hard when she saw Scott walk out on stage in his suit.

As Scott started out on the stage the clapping got louder, but very quickly people recognized Scott and saw that he was in his suit instead of his cap and gown. The clapping soon dissipated except for a few scattered hands, mostly children.

Scott took a deep breath, then another, before he walked toward Mr. Lee at the microphone. He couldn't look out at the crowd, he just focused on Mr. Lee. Scott drew Mr. Lee back from the microphone and told him Joel had an accident and had died a half-hour ago. Would it be all right for him to tell the people and to accept Joel's award in his place? Mr. Lee was dumbstruck and kind of sagged when Scott told him this. His jaw dropped open as he nodded his head. Scott turned to the audience and stepped up to the microphone. He couldn't focus on any faces through the tears in his eyes. He took another deep breath.

"Th...This is the hardest thing I've ever had to do in my life," Scott thought, then said it out loud. "A very tragic accident happened earlier this evening. Joel Adams was hit by a car while saving a little girl's life." Scott stumbled and sobbed. He had to pause to keep from losing it. He couldn't believe how hard it was to talk, to say words. "H...He died a hero," Scott squeaked, "Less than an hour ago."

Susie screamed along with fifty others. She felt as if someone had punched her in the stomach. Her head was spinning. She grabbed the boy's arm on her right and squeezed as hard as she could. Susie watched Scott break down on stage. "He's g-gone, my love, my life, he's gone," she wailed. Then Susie collapsed, racked with sobs.

Scott halfway collected himself. "Joel lived his life helping and loving others." Scott had to stop again, he couldn't talk. "He also died helping someone." Galvanized by agony and grief, Susie jumped up and through blurred, incomprehensible vision, started forcing her way past students in her row to get to the aisle. "No, no, it can't be; it's not possible," she shouted in her mind.

Susie's father, staggered by the news, was alert to the effect this would have on Susie. When he saw her stand up and move to her left, he moved quicker. As she got to the aisle, he was already running down toward her. Susie turned to run to the back, saw her father and ran crying, "Oh, Daddy." Susie's father felt the weight of the unfair world collapse against him. He cried hard for his daughter as he stroked her hair.

"I'm sorry, Susie honey. I'm so sorry."

When Scott saw Susie jump up, he couldn't talk. All he could do is cry and blow his nose into his already soaked handkerchief. It took two full minutes to compose himself enough to speak, even brokenly. "Joel Adams was my best friend." Scott was forcing the words out through a face screwed-up with pain. The voice didn't sound like his. "He was a friend to most of you. Joel was the best thing that happened...to...to many of us." Scott stopped again and blew his nose. He had to take a deep breath before continuing. As he started to talk, he glanced over to Susie and her father and lost control again. It took a while before he could again speak. His handkerchief was hopelessly soaked. "I...I loved Joel."

Scott and Susie and the principal and much of the audience broke down and cried again.

The whole audience was empathizing with Scott, realizing what a tough thing he had to do; at the same time most were fighting through their own personal feelings.

Scott continued, "Life ended too soon for Joel, but God has a plan for us all. I'm sorry to bring ya'll this terrible news, but with the timing, I knew of no other way." Scott backed away at this point to let the principal speak.

Mr. Lee began, "This is a terrible tragedy. One that we all feel. Joel Adams was an exceptional individual. He was responsible for a lot of good things happening here at this school. I..." Mr. Lee started to go on but broke down and had to wait to regain his composure. "There's something else. I wanted to surprise Joel and his family with this news..." Mr. Lee bit his lower lip hard to keep from losing control. "The school received a letter this week telling us Joel had been selected as one of the top ten outstanding high school seniors in the nation." Mr. Lee reached down and pulled something out of a bag at the bottom of the lectern. "The school has had this letter framed for Joel as a keepsake." Mr. Lee shakily held up the framed letter for all to see. "His family will cherish this forever."

Mr. Lee looked over to Scott and nodded his head for Scott to approach. "I now would like to present..."

Scott whispered to Mr. Lee. The principal then spoke into the mike. "Susie, can...would you come up here please?"

Susie put her hand up in front of her mouth and nose as she looked at Scott and Mr. Lee. She couldn't stop crying, but this request made it worse. She slowly nodded her head up and down. Susie squeezed her Daddy's hand as she slowly walked up to the stage and climbed the steps. As she reached Scott, he turned to her and hugged her while they both cried.

Mr. Lee continued, "On behalf of the School Administration, I now present this year's outstanding student of the year award and scholarship—posthumously—to Mr. Joel Adams, God rest his soul." As Mr. Lee handed the awards to Scott and Susie, someone in the front row stood up, then another person stood. At first slowly, then more quickly, the whole audience stood in silent respect for Joel. Then a single female voice started singing, "Amazing Grace, how sweet the sound." Then another and another voice joined in until the whole auditorium rang with the tune many had known since childhood. Susie and Scott just stood there crying unashamedly, watching and listening to this spontaneous salute to Joel. After the verse was completed the audience returned to their seats.

Scott stepped to the mike. "Joel would have thanked everyone for this award, and he probably would have said there were others more deserving. Because that's the way he was." Something clicked together in Scott's mind as he stood there. He continued. "I have made a decision. I vow to dedicate my career to Joel." Scott stumbled a bit as he made this declaration with fierce determination. Then he stepped back from the mike and let Susie take over.

Through tormented features, with tears streaming down her face, Susie started. "J...Joel would not have talked long, so I won't say much. I...I loved him. We had pledged to be married one day." Susie paused here. "He was a wonderful person." It was all she could muster. Susie tried to say thank you but the words wouldn't come. She just bowed her head and turned to Scott and kind of fell against him as he put his arms around her. There wasn't one dry eye in the audience.

Near the back of the seats a nattily dressed old man stood wearily and shuffled out of the room. Hat in hand, using his cane for support, he limped away, his heart full of sorrow.

CHAPTER 3

The rain shower had passed and the sun shone brightly. The roads were filled with puddles, and mud was everywhere. Alejandro loved the time just after it rained. The air smelled fresh, the birds were chirping and the still-wet flowers seemed even more beautiful. Flowers added so much to the landscape as he walked along the road. So many houses had a variety of tropical flora in their front yard. Alejandro's favorite was the bird of paradise. It seemed so exquisite, yet exhibited strength and beauty. After a rain, with water dripping off the flowers, the pristine scenery seemed vibrantly alive.

Alejandro De La Paz lived on the main road going through town. There was not much traffic, so the road was more of a convenience than a nuisance. He waved to neighbors, sitting on the front porches of their houses. They called out to him to ask how he was.

"Fine," he answered. "Things couldn't be better. How are you?"

"We're doing OK, nice to see you."

As Alejandro reached his house his mother was stepping sideways out the front door sweeping as she went.

"Hi, Mom."

"Oh, hi, Alex. Did you win?"

"Yes, we won 2–0. We really played well."

"Good, I think you boys must be pretty good, you seem to win a lot of games."

"Thanks, Mom. We're not bad. We're good for this area, but that doesn't mean we'll stack up against teams from large towns like Alajuela and Heredia. We won't play any of them until the tournament."

"You'll beat them, too."

"Hope so."

"Honey, Mrs. Martinez next door would like to get some things from the store, but she's not feeling well. Would you be a dear and run an errand for her?"

"Hey, sure, Mom, no problem."

"Thanks, she's a dear friend."

"I'll go now."

His mother had suggested also that he take his younger brother with him, that Pepito wanted to get out somewhere and he could be a help in carrying things home. "Just be careful."

That posed no problem for Alex; he enjoyed being with Pepito and it was good to spend time together doing something useful. Pepito was always a happy boy. Alex and Pepito very seldom had the brotherly friction, name-calling, or fights that often were present between brothers. Alex attributed that to Pepito's good nature and the fact that Pepito idolized him. Perhaps the difference in age also contributed to a harmonious relationship. In fact, the hero worship Pepito exhibited probably would have been more of a rivalry if they had been closer in age.

Pepito asked Alex, "Can I ride my bike along with you?"

Alex said, "Sure, so long as you carry something back with you and you are careful."

Pepito squealed in delight and ran to get a sack that looped over the handlebars and could hold a few things to bring home from the store.

Alex got the list of things Mrs. Martinez wanted and the money with which to buy them. He and Pepito set off at a lively walk and slow ride, waving to neighbors as they passed by. Alex was well liked by everyone. He was polite, cooperative, and becoming something of a small-town celebrity with his soccer playing. His family had lived in this town for years and years. His parents had been childhood sweethearts and had gotten married when they were seventeen years old. Alex was born one year later. A sister followed two and a half years later, and then Pepito, who was six and a half years younger than Alex. Their close-knit family suffered a terrible tragedy when the daughter, Roberta, died from an infection following an emergency appendectomy. This loss drew the family even closer. Pepito, especially, looked up to Alex as more than a big brother; he was also Pepito's hero. His athletic exploits were adulated by the younger brother.

Alex bought the articles Mrs. Martinez requested, having to go to two different stores to make the purchases. Christa, a schoolmate, had asked him about his soccer game at one of the stores. She was a clerk there. Alex knew she kind of liked him. He had no romantic interest in her, though; she just wasn't his type. Alex told Christa very politely that their team had won. No, he didn't score any goals, he played defense and so it would be unusual to have a score. His purpose was to prevent the other team from scoring.

"How many goals did the other team get?" she asked.

"We had a good day and shut them out." Alex was embarrassed to talk about his soccer playing. He liked it when he was present and another person told either a third person or a group about his soccer. In a strange way he liked when someone else told about him, he just didn't want to be the one telling. To him that was bragging. But, yet, he wanted others to know how good he was.

The goods bought in the first store were in Pepito's sack hanging on his bike. Alex told Pepito to be careful because the extra weight would make control a little more tricky. The dry goods were in the second store, where he was talking with Christa.

Pepito had briefly come in that store with Alex and listened while Christa asked Alex about his game. After Alex had answered the younger boy couldn't help but add, "You should have seen Alex today. He stopped two sure goals and kept the other team on their end of the field all day. They couldn't get the ball past him." After saying that he ran outside to ride his bike around with another boy his age who was there also.

"Oh, so you were modest about yourself. Sounds like you had a lot to do with your team winning today."

"One guy can't do it all. The whole team played well."

"It's good that we have a soccer team here that can beat the others. We're such a small town, I like to hear you are beating other, larger towns. Good luck. I hope you keep winning."

"Thanks, I..."

Just then Alex heard a scream and what sounded like an accident. Something gripped his stomach as he hurried outside to look. Out on the street lay Pepito near his bike. Close by was a yellow Land Rover with the door open. Someone was bending over Pepito, looking at the prone figure on the wet, muddy roadway.

"Pepito. Pepito," Alex cried out in anguish.

When he got over to his brother he could see one leg was badly injured; undoubtedly broken. Pepito was unconscious. He looked dead.

Alex was relieved when he saw his brother's chest rise and fall with his breathing.

"I'll call an ambulance," Christa said. She hurried inside to make the call.

"Oh, Pepito, I'm so sorry. I should have been watching you instead of inside talking. I'm responsible for this. Pepito, Pepito, forgive me please." Tears were streaming down Alex's face.

"I'm sorry," the driver said. "He circled back out into the street right in front of me. I couldn't stop on the wet road. I feel sick. Poor little boy. Is he your brother?"

"Yes. Pepito, can you hear me? We're going to get you to the hospital. We've called an ambulance." Turning around, he called to someone standing close by and said, "Please go to my house and tell my mother. Tell her Pepito had an accident on his bike and we are taking him to the local hospital. Use those words, try not to frighten her too much."

The ambulance soon came and they got Pepito on a stretcher and into the converted Isuzu Trooper. The hospital was only two minutes from where the accident happened. Alex rode in the ambulance with his brother. The hospital was really only a medical treatment center to treat minor injuries and sicknesses. The doctor on duty looked Pepito over carefully and told Alex and the ambulance crew that he would have to be taken to a larger facility—probably the hospital in San José—a two-hour ride away. "I'll give him a shot and we'll start an IV on him, but he'll need more than what I can give him here. His leg has been smashed and he has several broken ribs. I'm most concerned about his knee and whether he has any significant head injury. My guess is he has a concussion."

Alex looked back at his little brother and started crying. "C'mon, little guy, you've got to pull through. We're going to take you where they can give you the right kind of help. Be strong, you've got to. I'm gonna be right beside you all the way on this. I won't leave you, I promise."

At that moment his mother came in. The man driving the Land Rover had stayed to pick her up and bring her to this hospital.

"Alex, Pepito. Oh my poor son." She looked at Pepito and saw the anguish on Alex's face and put her arms around him.

"Mom, it's all my fault. I didn't watch him closely enough. He rode out in front of this car."

"Doctor, what's his situation?"

"Mrs. De La Paz, he has a badly broken right leg, particularly the knee, some broken ribs, and a concussion, I believe. We need to get him to San José where they are equipped to deal with injuries like this. We have stabilized his system and will protect his leg and ice it, and as soon as that's complete I'd like to get him going. I'll call ahead and prepare the right people for when he gets there."

"Will he live, doctor?"

"Yes, he should. Unless something I can't see has happened in his head, or something very unusual occurs as a result of surgical procedure, there's no reason to believe his life is in danger."

"Doctor, that's a big relief to us. You just don't know," Mrs. De La Paz tearfully but gratefully replied.

"Mom, let me ride with Pepito in the ambulance. I...I promised him I would stay by his side through this. You come with Dad. OK?"

"All right, son. The driver said he would take me to San José. We'll wait for your father and come in later. I've sent someone to get him from work."

"Five minutes and we'll be ready," the doctor said.

They loaded little Pepito into the ambulance while Alex, after hugging his mom, climbed in and held his brother's hand.

Only when the ambulance had crossed the mountains and entered the outskirts of the capital did the vehicle begin to use flashing lights or the siren. With the way expedited through traffic they were able to reach the children's hospital in downtown San José in just under two hours. They backed up to the emergency door. The moment the vehicle stopped, the doors were flung open. The intensity and swiftness with which the hospital people unloaded and wheeled Pepito away alarmed Alex all over again.

"Has something gone wrong?" he asked the driver.

"No. It is necessary to get him into surgery as soon as possible. They work fast here."

"Thanks, I...was worried."

"I understand. You need to go to Admissions. That's down the hall and to the left."

"OK. Thanks again."

As Alex was answering questions about how the accident happened, he broke down crying in frustration and grief. "Little Pepito was such a joy. A bright light to the whole family. He never got in a bad mood, always had good things to say about everyone." Alex really got scared when he realized he was thinking of Pepito in the past tense. The lady taking the information was patient and empathized with him. After the paperwork was complete Alex went to the waiting room alongside the emergency entrance and waited.

After a few minutes of waiting he went to the phone and called the public phone near his house. He was relieved when Enrique, someone he knew, answered. Because the town where he lived had a population only a few shy of six hundred, Alex knew everyone would already have heard about the accident. Indeed, that was the case. Enrique said so many had stopped by to ask if he had heard anything. "Even got a phone call from Christa," he said.

"Christa?"

"Yes. She said you were with her when the accident happened."

"Yeah. We were talking when I should have been watching Pepito. I'm to blame."

"From the account I heard, I doubt your being there would have made much of a difference. Don't judge yourself so harshly."

"I can't help it. I feel responsible."

"Your mom and dad should be getting there in about forty-five minutes. They left here over an hour ago."

"Good, that's one thing I wanted to find out. Thanks. Did anyone take the things to Mrs. Martinez that we had bought?"

"Yes. Christa found someone to take the groceries and other items to her," Enrique answered. He almost added some of the groceries were ruined and Christa got them replaced, but he thought that information could wait til later. Enrique was very much impressed with how responsible Christa had been through all of this. "She'd make someone a good wife in a few years." Even though he was three years older, she was someone he now wanted to get to know better. "Alex, something else you should know."

"Yes?"

"A prayer candle has been lit in the church here for Pepito."

"Good, I'm glad. He'll need everyone's prayers. Thanks."

Alex dreaded the arrival of his father. How could he face him? What could he say to him? What would his father say to him?

Eventually they showed up. To Alex's relief his father did not seem to blame him. They were more interested in hearing how Pepito was. Did any change take place during the trip into the city?

"No, Pepito stayed unconscious the whole while. His breathing was regular. No change really."

"Alex," his father addressed him. "Son, I know what your feelings are about what happened. While inside us, your mother and I are hurting, our love for you is unchanged. I don't think you would have been able to stop what happened, even if you had been outside."

"I should have been there. I should have cautioned little Pepito to be careful, to watch out for vehicles. I'm the one who was in charge. Mom...Mom told me to be careful. I've let her down, I let you down, and most of all, little Pepito." With that, Alex, still only a boy of fifteen, collapsed sobbing against his parents.

The three of them waited over two hours before any word was heard. Then a doctor came out and told them, "Your son has severe injuries. He has a bad concussion, we had to relieve swelling in his head. He had some internal bleeding caused by broken ribs, but worst of all is his right leg. We are working hard to save it. His knee was destroyed and his leg fractured in three places."

"Is anything life threatening, Doctor?"

"No, I don't think there is any reason to worry on that account."

"Is he still unconscious?"

"Yes, but we've got him anesthetized and it won't be until that wears off that he could wake up. We've still got another two to three hours of surgery to perform on his leg before we are finished, but I wanted to give you an interim report. I've got to get back in there."

"Thank you, Doctor."

The wait seemed interminable. There were long periods of silence, punctuated by short conversations. Alex told them what Enrique had said. They told him of townspeople who had wished Pepito well before they left. Several times Alex quietly sobbed for Pepito.

Finally surgery was over and the same doctor came out. "Mr. and Mrs. De La Paz, your son is doing as well as could be expected. We think we have saved his leg..."

"Saved his leg?" Mr. De La Paz uttered.

Alex put his hand over his face.

"Yes, his right leg has been severely damaged. We've done reparative surgery on his knee and lower leg, but we won't know what the results are for several weeks. I'm afraid he will have to have more surgery to try to reconstruct that knee if he'll ever walk again."

"If he'll ever walk again?" Pepito's mom sagged against her husband.

Alex started crying. He had bought a box of tissues and had gone through part of the box. He gave two to his mom, and got two more out for himself. Then as an afterthought he gave his dad one also when he began tearing up.

"We are hopeful that his leg will be such that he can live a fairly normal life, except he won't be able to play sports."

Alex felt something give inside. "Pepito will never play soccer, he may never walk again; never enjoy all the good things in life. I'm to blame. I should have stopped it."

"Son, son, don't blame yourself." Alex's father could see what was going on in Alex's mind by his body language. "I told you, son, we don't blame you, Pepito won't blame you; you couldn't have prevented it anyway."

"He'll never get the opportunity to do so many things. He could have been a better soccer player than me. He was better at his age than I was. He was stronger and faster than I was. Now that's all lost."

"Alex, you are going to look to the future. Let's do what we can for Pepito to help him the best we can."

"Don't worry, I'll do everything possible to make his life as complete and happy as I can." As Alex said this he knew his life would be reshaped around his younger brother. He owed him that.

Pepito came out of surgery eventually and as he came fully awake his whole family was there. As the anesthetic wore off the pain increased. "It hurts, Mommy. It hurts." They all looked at him with tears in their eyes.

"You've been badly hurt, Pepito. You're in the children's hospital in San José. An ambulance brought you here. Alex rode with you."

Pepito's eyes shifted to Alex. "Did they flash the lights and make the siren go?"

"Yes, they did."

"Wish I could have seen that."

Pepito was in the hospital for nine weeks and had two more operations on his knee. Each time he awoke with a lot of pain. Despite that pain, Pepito did not often complain. Instead, when the pain wasn't too great he was usually cheerful and happy. He became a favorite of the nurses, who appreciated his attitude and optimistic nature. Often he would entertain them with stories about life out "in the sticks" in his small town of Puerto Viejo. He told of times tubing down the Rio Sarapiqui and other adventures. They learned Puerto Viejo often floods during heavy rains because it is at the confluence of three rivers; the town's only gas station goes underwater and only the top of the gas pumps are visible. What he liked to talk most about, however, was his big brother Alex. He was, Pepito said, not only the best player in Puerto Viejo, but also in his opinion the best player in all of Costa Rica. Pepito made Alex something of a celebrity within the walls of the hospital. Whenever Alex visited Pepito, which was frequently, nurses, other patients…and even doctors made it a point to see him and sometimes talk to him. Alex was unaware of his growing popularity. He assumed it was normal that the ever-friendly Pepito received that much attention. There was a friendly competition for Alex's attention by the nurse's aides whenever he visited.

Alex was taller than normal for his age, with deep, penetrating eyes and longish hair. He was muscular, with broad shoulders and a barrel chest. Alex was an outgoing, talkative person and charmed everyone with his smile. Although good-looking, he was not particularly handsome. His nose was a little too big and his ears stuck out. He also had a big mole on his neck below his left ear. It was precisely these imperfections that many of the nurse's aides found so attractive. Combined with his infectious grin and outgoing personality, these traits made him an alluring prospect for all the young female workers.

Two days after Pepito was admitted to the hospital, Alex made his first visit. Pepito was fully conscious. Alex started to tell him that he was to blame for not being there to watch out for him when Pepito interrupted. "Wait a sec, Big B. It was my fault. You told me twice to be careful. I wasn't. There wasn't anything more you could do. I see the guilt on your face and in your eyes. Get off the guilt trip, Big B. I'm not blaming you. You had nothing to do with what happened to me. It was me. I goofed up, goofed up bad. It hurts so much. The doctor told me I may never walk again, but I'm gonna try. I've got to accept what happened and go on; I can't let this ruin my life. I know I'll never play soccer, so I need you to be everything the both of us would have been. You be the best, Big B. You are the best player in Costa Rica. I want you to be the best in the world. Costa Rica will be in the World Cup in two years and then we will be there again in six. In six you be there—for me."

"Pepito, you nut. Worry about yourself, not me," Alex replied shakily. "You have to be strong so you can get better. There's no telling now how much you'll be able to do. With a good attitude and hard work you might come all the way back and be better than I am. I already thought you're a better player than I was at your age. Keep that vision."

"I have the vision, Big B. It's of you captaining the world champion team in the 1994 Cup with me in the stands cheering. I have dreamed about it. I see you winning ball after ball away from the greatest players in the world. You strip Diego Maradona and other world-class players like they were new at the game. You know something funny? Someone else keeps getting in that dream. Do you remember last year when you played that team from Buenos Aires that you played in the second round of the tournament in San José? He's now playing for Saprissa. I think his name is Ronald something."

"Ronald Gonzales?"

"Yes, that's it!"

"Sure. We talked about him once before. He was one of the best players we ever faced. Ha, Little B, you're crazy—you know that?"

"Just don't mess up my dream by feeling sorry for yourself, or for me. Or don't lay a guilt trip on yourself for what you might have been able to do if you were right there. Nothing would have changed. It was my fault, my dumb luck that car was coming when I circled out onto the road. That's it."

"You're something. You know that, kid?"

"Yeah, sure. Look, I'm getting tired, I want to sleep, OK?"

"Yeah, you sleep."

Alex gently rustled Pepito's hair and, with misting eyes, leaned over and kissed him on the cheek. "You sleep." Then he left the room

Stepping out of the room into the corridor, he leaned back against the outside wall of Pepito's room. With his hands behind him and the palms against the wall, he reflected on the conversation they just had. "He's quite a little guy in there. So brave. So mature. Tries to make me feel better instead of complaining about what happened to him." Alex brought a hand up to clear the tears from his eyes.

"You must be Alex."

Alex jerked his head up. "Yes, I am."

In front of him stood a very pretty young nurse's aide. Her name tag on her blouse read Maria Elena. Her eyes showed compassion and intelligence.

"I've been working on this floor and helping your little brother. He's quite a guy."

"Yes, yes, he is quite a guy. Thanks."

"I've been talking to him a good bit. You know, he thinks an awful lot of you." She continued after he nodded his head, "He...he is very worried about what you feel about the accident. He doesn't want you to feel guilty."

"I know. He just told me that. I should have been watching him more closely. I was inside talking to the clerk in the store and I should have been outside."

"Well, what you have to get over, if you can, is the thought that you are to blame. You won't help yourself, and more importantly, you won't help Pepito if you continue to dwell on whose fault it was. He doesn't blame you."

"Why are you lecturing me?" Alex felt annoyed.

"Sorry. You've got a great kid brother in there who hurts a lot and who may be crippled for life. I was just trying not to add your guilt feelings to his already weighty burden—that he has caused you to bear a burden of guilt."

Alex contemplated what she said as he looked at her, standing there so innocent-looking. How did one so young gain so much wisdom? She's right, he thought. What's more, you can see she really cares about Pepito. Everyone is telling you the same thing. Don't feel guilt about what happened. It wasn't your fault. And now, don't complicate Pepito's chances for recovery. Make a decision. It is hard, it is very hard. What have I got to lose? I'll do it. It's the right thing to do. All I have to do is to shake off this feeling and the situation will be better by all accounts. Why is this so hard? One step at a time. Take the first step.

"All right, Miss Maria Elena whatever your name is, I'll do my best to eliminate this complication in the recovery of my brother."

"Gallegos, my last name. You'll see. It's for the best." The young assistant answered him with a sparkling smile revealing her white teeth. Her smile faded as she said, "Your brother will need all the help he can get. His injury is very serious. I'm sorry it happened. Your brother is such a loving person. We all are pulling for him here in the hospital."

"Thanks. Its comforting to know he's well cared for."

In the weeks that followed Alex was a frequent visitor to the hospital. There he found an always cheerful Pepito, who quickly became the most popular patient in the whole hospital. Alex was grateful for the love and attention he saw Pepito was getting. Alex made an effort every time to try to cheer him up, but often it was he who was cheered up. Alex also made many new friends. Every patient in the room with Pepito, as well as most of the nurses and assistants and even a few doctors, became Alex's good friends. With Pepito's upbeat attitude Alex found it easy not to exhibit some of the pangs of guilt that remained with him.

Nearly every time Alex visited, he saw and talked with Maria Elena. He found himself looking forward to seeing her when he came. Those times when he didn't see her left him with a slightly unfulfilled sense, as though she was part of the reason he was supposed to go to the hospital.

One day Pepito told him, "You know, Big B, Maria Elena likes you. You ought to ask her out on a date. She's my number one friend in here. She's so nice to me. I think she's real pretty. It would be different in the hospital here without her. The others are nice too, I'm not trying to say they're not, but she is special."

"Ha. The little matchmaker, huh? We'll see." But secretly Alex was pleased. It had been on his mind as well to ask her out. Alex hated to ask a girl out and get turned down. He was very glad for the information Pepito gave him. It was the security he needed.

After reconstructive surgery was finally completed on his knee, Pepito felt his future cleared somewhat as the doctors said he was capable of being able to lead an almost normal life. He would be able to walk, to work, to drive a car, even to participate mildly in sports; but he would never regain more than about sixty percent of his full mobility and could never hope to be competitive in soccer, like his older brother.

The pronouncement pleased Pepito, who by now had reconciled himself to a worse fate. Likewise, his parents were pleased with the chance their young son would be able to have a normal life. Every nurse who had helped Pepito fight the battles, who knew the long odds he had faced, was also delighted with the prognosis. Only Alex—who, against all advice, had held out hope in a little hidden corner of his world for a complete recovery—was disappointed in the final outcome. Something gripped him in the pit of his stomach as he listened with his family to the doctors relating the condition of the rest of Pepito's life. Finally, it was known how Pepito would be. Alex thought of what Pepito wouldn't have and was sad. Others considered what he would have and were glad. This was something Alex would have to work out or carry with him the rest of his life.

As Pepito convalesced there were more opportunities for Alex and Maria Elena to get to know one another. Not only did they date, but they often took walks in the nearby park, sometimes sitting on the bench just chatting with each other and sometimes holding hands in silence, watching the people go by.

Maria Elena was impressed with the affection and devotion Alex demonstrated toward Pepito. "You must be a very special person to be so devoted to your brother and even more so because of the love and admiration Pepito has for you," she said one evening.

"I think any brother in this situation would do what I am doing. There's...there's a lot of love in our family. We lost a sister years ago and that created close, deepened feelings within our family."

"Oh, I'm sorry. How did it happen?"

"She had an emergency operation on her appendix, which had burst, and she never came out of surgery."

"Oh no. You probably don't have good feelings for hospitals then, do you?"

"I'm never comfortable in one. I could never be a doctor, or do what you do."

"How old was she?"

"It was over three years ago; she was ten, I was twelve. When it happened, Pepito couldn't understand where his sister was or why it happened. He was only five or six. Mom and Dad took it very hard. Since then I have tried hard to please them. Now this."

"I know they are very proud of you, Alex. That's very evident." Maria Elena paused a moment. "Do you realize how popular you and your brother are in this hospital? I'm the envy of all the nurses and nurse's aides. First, because my responsibility includes Pepito, whom everyone likes, and second, because I'm seeing you."

"You ought to get hazardous duty pay instead."

Maria Elena threw back her head and laughed. It perked up Alex when she laughed like that. He thought she was exceptionally beautiful when she laughed. He pulled her close to him and kissed her for the first time. He saw her eyes first widen and then close as their lips made contact. Her hand reached up for the back of his head and it caressed his hair as they kissed.

"You're so beautiful when you laugh. I love it. You look so happy. It really helps me to feel better."

"I am happy when I'm with you. I always have a good time. I care about you. I care about Pepito."

"I'm beginning to care about you too," he blurted out. If it hadn't been for the euphoria of the moment he probably never would have said that, because Alex had a hard time expressing his feelings. He tended to keep them inside of him. In a way he was hard to get to know, to *really* get to know. Alex disliked that about himself. He admired others who could open up to people.

All this flashed through his mind in the instant between the moment he told her he cared for her and when they kissed again. There was a difference, Alex decided later, between a passionate kiss with a pretty girl when you wanted it to lead to something more, and a loving kiss when you really cared for someone. The second was so much better.

The time finally came for Pepito to discharged. The hospital staff threw a big party for him; they all made a big deal of it. Balloons, ribbons, flowers, and gifts covered his bed and room. So many wished Pepito well that he couldn't take it any more and broke down crying. Of the twenty-five or so people crowded into the room, most were embarrassed that they too were shedding tears.

Finally the party ended and the presents and decorations were crammed into the two vehicles that had come to take Pepito home. As they made their way over the mountains Pepito chattered happily. The family was glad to hear his voice and so he entertained them all the way. The mountains were imposing; the sun felt good; the periwinkles, the tree blossoms, and the occasional orchid were again pretty he observed— almost as if Mother Nature had prepared them especially for him.

Pepito was unaware of the welcome home signs and banners that had been erected and would have missed them had his family not pointed them out to him. His eyes opened wide and he squealed in delight. People were good to him in the hospital, but he was glad to be back home again.

Pepito could almost walk by himself but required extra help to negotiate the couple of wooden steps up to the porch in front of his house. They sat him down in a comfortable rocking chair on the porch once he had gone in and looked around the inside of the house. The others were already unloading all the balloons and things and fixing them to the porch and outside of the house—even on the bushes in the front yard. More neighbors and friends came to see Pepito and his family as the news spread rapidly that they were home. Many brought sweets and treats and things to drink. The drinks were especially welcome; it was a hot day, and so many people were there.

Darkness fell and it wasn't until Pepito started getting sleepy that the guests left. As Pepito was put into his own bed for the first time, each one of his family kissed him goodnight and said, "Welcome home."

Later that night Mrs. De La Paz told Alex that the nice nurse's aide—Maria Elena—had asked whether she could come and visit them soon to check on Pepito. "I suspect she would also like to check on other members of this family too while she's here," she smiled. A mother always knows.

At the funeral home thoughts of good times with Joel flooded Scott's mind. Happy days together in school were flashing through his memory. He remembered lots of little things they did with each other and the fun they enjoyed. Scott supposed it was all right to think of happier times at a moment like this. He needed to in order to cope.

Scott was trying to sort out his feelings. Despite his own feeling of personal loss, he was trying to figure out how to help Susie, who was much worse off. Susie was a basket case. She was unable to cope with such a tremendous personal loss; she saw that everything they had planned together was now gone. She felt bitter that all had been taken away from her. What each had felt for the other was an overwhelming emotion that had grown and grown until it had become a comfortable and secure loving relationship.

Scott knew all this from his many conversations with Joel. He had envied his friends, knowing that they had found their mates and one large uncertainty about the future had been settled. Scott had thought at the time Joel told him how their relationship had changed, that he was indeed a lucky man. Scott had confidence enough in himself that one day a girl would fall in love with him and he would love her in return. He prayed that God would deliver just the right girl to him and that he would recognize her when the time came.

Susie now appeared inconsolable. With each passing hour she seemed to grow worse. The shock had sustained her at the graduation, however; and then even later at the home of the Adams. She had shown substantially more grief at home with her family. Today, only twenty hours later, Susie was not in control. She couldn't talk to anyone. She just sat on the couch in the parlor as the many friends filed through the room paying their respects. Susie was crying all the time; she never stopped. Her father had to force her to drink fluids because they were alarmed she might dehydrate. She just stayed on the couch kind of hugging up to Mrs. Adams. As badly as Mr. and Mrs. Adams took the devastating catastrophe, Susie was far worse. The last vestiges of control disappeared whenever she looked at Scott. It seemed the best way he could help Susie was by staying out of the parlor and out of her sight. A couple of times, however, Susie came out to give him a hug, trying to let him not feel ostracized. Scott felt better when that happened knowing that at least her mind was functioning to some extent. As Scott stood there holding Susie, he looked over her shoulder at her father, who was obviously in pain observing his daughter in such an emotional state.

The Reverend Clayton Brooks was steeling himself mentally. He had already spent thirty minutes in solemn prayer asking the good Lord for help in getting through this ceremony. One of his weaknesses, he knew, was not being able to avoid sentiment in a really tragic situation like the one he was faced with today. Three times before he had struggled to make it through a funeral ceremony. Two of those times had been services for children, one a boy of twelve and the other, two children of a family he knew well who had been killed. The other situation occurred when the parents of three children had been killed in an airplane crash. It saddened him to see the oldest, a ten-year-old, trying so hard to act grownup and attempting to take care of his younger siblings. Clayton was doing fine until he looked down at the children and saw the oldest trying to comfort the other two, wiping their tears away with his handkerchief.

Today's service might just be the hardest of all. Clayton had worked closely with Joel for seven years now. He watched Joel grow in the Spirit and mature as a Christian. He watched the sweet relationship develop between Joel and Susie. Watching the change in Susie and the delight Joel had taken in her spiritual growth, Clayton had enjoyed taking an active part in helping the two young people strengthen their beliefs. Knowing what could have been for them, Clayton was not sure of his ability to remain aloof from sentiment during the service.

Clayton took a deep breath and said another short prayer asking God to provide support to the Adams family, Susie, and other close friends, and to grant them understanding that this too was in God's plan. The pastor asked also that Susie and the family be spared the feeling of rage that often accompanies an untimely death; rather, he hoped that they would experience a sense of God's care and concern. He prayed once more for composure for himself.

He then stood up and put on his robe. The time he spent with the family these past two days told him that they would be all right. As Christians they all understood Joel had passed on to a better place and now was with the Lord. Susie was the one that he was most concerned about. She seemed to be by far the most distraught. He had counseled her that in time the pain would lessen, that for now she had to be strong. She must realize that God called Joel home. His reason for Joel's dying was sufficient. Her condition was so bad, however, that he wasn't sure whether she had comprehended.

The family was in the side vestibule, the silence heavy in the room. Everyone looked up at the Reverend Brooks when he entered the room. He showed everyone an encouraging smile. The only ones to smile back were an aunt and her young daughter, he observed. The family's grief was intense.

"Please, let us all gather at the far end of the room for a family prayer—over by Mr. and Mrs. Adams," he began. The pastor then prayed with the grief-stricken clan, asking God for comfort, support, hope, and acceptance during these tragic and trying times. Hope was very important. It allowed the believer to face the grave and death with confidence in the Lord's plan, and enabled the family to cope with the loss and the process of rebuilding to a more normal life again.

Soon it was time for everyone to go into the main sanctuary of the church. Clayton checked with an assistant just outside the door and was told it would still be a few minutes. In a bit, the door reopened and the assistant nodded to the Reverend.

Reverend Brooks had prepared himself for a large crowd, but even he was staggered to see the number of people in the church. The pews were jammed, the balcony was full, with people standing up there in every square foot of space around the pews. People were standing three deep along the sides, and the lobby looked to be packed with those unable to get inside. As he sat in his chair Reverend Brooks thought the church could literally hold no more. Almost as soon as he thought that, people started coming in to stand just inside the doors he had just entered.

Scott sat in the pew next to Susie, whose whole body was trembling. Ashley was next to her, then Amanda, then Mrs. Adams and Mr. Adams. Scott knew without looking that Mr. Dan was in the row behind them, along with the cousins, uncles, aunts, and grandparents.

The overflow crowd made Mr. and Mrs. Adams cry. Susie was already crying, but worsened when she saw all the people. Then her eyes focused on the casket in the center, in front of the podium. "Joel, Joel. My darling Joel. I miss you so much," she thought. Her shoulders shook as she cried. Ashley reached over and took her hand and gave it a loving squeeze.

The organist stopped playing the prelude and the Reverend Brooks stood up and approached the podium. He said a last, quick prayer, asking the Spirit to take over. Pastor Brooks had started to speak with compassion for the family and friends. He reminded them that while Joel had been very happy here in his earthly life, he was now perfectly happy in heaven with Christ Jesus in a place of unbounded glory, beauty, and goodness.

"Yet once in a while there is a giant tree in the meadow that loses its leaves and falls, whose passing cannot be ignored. Joel Xavier Adams was one of these. The people gathered here today are evidence of that. There was something very special about Joel. He was loved and respected by all." Reverend Brooks looked at the front pews as he said this and had to pause to get a hold of himself. When he got ready to start again he looked at Jennifer, the girl Joel saved, and her family, and he realized his voice would betray him. So again he paused. "Mr. and Mrs. Adams, you had a wonderful son. God will help you in the days ahead to get through this most difficult time. My prayers are with you.

"Let us go to the Word to gain more insight. In Romans, chapter eight, we read in verse twenty eight, 'And we know that in all things God works for the good of those who love him, who have been called according to his purpose. For those God fore knew he also predestined to be conformed to the likeness of His Son, that he might be the firstborn among many brothers. And those he predestined, he also called; those he called, he also justified; those he justified, he also glorified.'

"'What, then, shall we say in response to this? If God is for us, who can be against us? He who did not spare His own Son, but gave Him up for us all—how will He not also, along with Him, graciously give us all things?'"

Scott started to cry, thinking about his friend who would not be around anymore. "He's in heaven and is happy, just as Reverend Brooks said," he tried to console himself. Susie squeezed his hand very lightly. When Scott looked over at her he realized how much she was suffering. It hadn't gotten any better.

"'...neither height nor depth, nor anything else in all creation, will be able to separate us from the love of God that is in Christ Jesus our Lord,'" the Reverend continued.

"Joel was the kind of individual who gave of himself for others. People liked him; they enjoyed being around him. He was interested in others and made them feel important. He was a loving person who reached out to many. Have all of us been like that? No, I think God placed Joel here on earth for a purpose; to show us what unselfish behavior is—what love is—and to be an example for us.

"Jesus was the great example; the perfect example. It is after his image that we should mold ourselves. Sometimes, however, we need tangible examples. Joel was one."

Susie audibly cried out and Scott fought against the tears. Reverend Brooks was right. That is exactly what his family and friends thought of Joel. Scott tried unsuccessfully to hold back the tears. He realized it was okay to cry in these circumstances, that no one expected otherwise. His need to cry came and went during the service. His sorrow was not just for himself, but also for the others who would miss Joel. Although a very natural emotion, understandable in this situation, Scott realized it was also a selfish reaction. He would miss Joel terribly; he would no longer have his best friend around; he knew he would feel bad. He felt so sorry for Susie. She not only lost her best friend, she also lost the one she would have spent the rest of her life with. She lost all her hopes and dreams.

There were also the sad thoughts of Joel's promising life cut off. So much future; so many good things ahead for him that now he'll never see. If Joel had not been so highly regarded by others, this might not be so sad. That's what makes this so difficult, he thought.

Clayton himself was struggling; he found it difficult to keep his composure. Several times he had to stop to hold himself together.

Scott heard the Reverend Brooks read from Second Corinthians, chapter one, verses three to eleven. "'...who comforts us in all our troubles, so that we can comfort those in any trouble with the comfort we ourselves have received from God. For just as the sufferings of Christ flow over into our lives, so also...."'"

From these words Scott received comfort. He hoped Susie and the family were cognizant enough to benefit from the words spoken by the preacher.

When the service ended the pallbearers arose as one and moved to the casket, which was draped with flowers. Even thought Scott was one of the pallbearers, he had been seated with the family at their request during the service. The other pallbearers had sat together in a group.

Scott noticed two things for the first time: how many flowers were all around the front of the sanctuary, and that there were three rows of honorary pallbearers who also stood when he stood.

The honorary pallbearers preceded the casket and the men rolling it and formed a gauntlet from the front doors of the church to the street, where the hearse waited. Behind the men in line along the walkway were more than one hundred people who couldn't get in the church, but who had stood outside during the service. Their numbers reinforced the solemnity of the occasion. Already outside, behind the honorary pallbearers on each side, were an additional fifty stands of flowers.

The whole family and their party wept openly as the pallbearers moved to the casket and began rolling it out. Everyone in the sanctuary was standing now. The closest of kin went first behind the casket, followed by other relatives, close friends, and neighbors.

Scott and the others loaded the body into the hearse and climbed in one of the five limousines lined up behind the curtained hearse. A policeman led the procession away from the church and toward the cemetery, five miles away.

Scott agreed with one of the other pallbearers when he made note of the reverence and politeness of the oncoming traffic, most of which pulled off the road and waited while the entire processional passed. This was true even when they got on the four-lane highway. Scott knew from his daddy that this courtesy occurred more in the South than in other parts of the country.

A policeman was stationed at every intersection, hat off and covering his heart. For the first time Scott really knew why they did this. He was glad for it. The respect was deserving.

When the cavalcade of vehicles entered the cemetery Scott could see the location of the grave. "That's nice," he thought. "It's on a hill and it overlooks the high school in the distance."

Scott was surprised to see that there were already close to fifty people here at the gravesite. They must have come here when they couldn't get into the church, he supposed. He started crying again in response to all the love manifested in the numbers of people and flowers present for the funeral.

Shortly after the lead cars came to a halt, the funeral home assistants came and opened the doors to all the limousines. After a few minutes to allow the rest of the cars to arrive, the main party walked to the tent as the pallbearers got out the casket. As Scott and the others carried the casket to the grave, more flowers from among those at the church were put into position. Scott guessed these were selected as being special to the family and were meant to be present at both locations. There were ten or twelve of these.

After helping Mr. Johnson negotiate the hill, Scott again sat with the family, according to their request. Mrs. Adams and Susie seemed to particularly be having a hard time. Again the minister waited for all attenders to gather round. Reverend Brooks opened with prayer and made a brief statement lasting no more than four minutes. Then he closed the service with prayer.

It was over very quickly, mercifully too for the family. The minister and funeral home director came along the front row of chairs, clasping each family member's hand as they said words of consolation.

When the family stood up, each member plucked a flower from one of the stands and placed it on the casket. Scott put his boutonniere on the wooden casket, as did each of the other pallbearers. Scott paused as he tearfully said his last good-bye to his buddy.

People closed in around the family to speak to them and to hug them. Scott moved next to Susie to help support her; she was near to collapsing. Finally, most of the people left. The Adams family and the relatives went to Joel's house and Susie went home with her family. Scott rode back to the church with the other pallbearers in the limo.

Scott slept fitfully that night. So many things were on his mind. He would miss his friend greatly. Never would he forget Joel. Tears streaked his face as he fell asleep.

CHAPTER 4

Three weeks after Pepito's homecoming, arrangements were made for Maria Elena to spend two days with the De La Paz family in Puerto Viejo, accompanied by her mother. It would be a two-and-a-half hour bus trip north from San José. They had to first take a bus from Aguas Zarcas to downtown San José where the bus would pick up more passengers before heading to the Sarapiqui Valley. Puerto Viejo was approximately fifty-five miles north of the Capital City over some very winding mountain roads.

Alex had not lost interest in Maria Elena. To the contrary, he dreamed about her every night. The closer the time for the visit, the more he thought about her. He had not been back to San José to see her since Pepito had come home.

Almost all his free time was spent with his younger brother. He began reading books to him and together they shared these wonderful new adventures. Pepito had gotten nearly a dozen books given to him as presents, and although he could read very well, he preferred it when Alex read to him. Not only could he listen to the story, but he could also watch the facial expressions and body language as his brother elaborated on passages in the books. It became a wonderful time for the two brothers. The bond between them strengthened daily.

Alex still spent considerable time with soccer. The regular season had ended, but Alex still practiced regularly and played in pick-up games and even in informally arranged games with other towns. Heredia's team made good on their promise to come play Alex's team in Puerto Viejo; in fact, the game would be held the day after Maria Elena and her mother came.

Alex was excited that Maria Elena would be there to watch him play. She had never seen him play and only knew of his soccer exploits through what Pepito told her and occasional comments from others in the hospital who had also heard of him. As the day for the big arrival drew nearer Alex got more and more psyched. His whole family noticed his agitated state and couldn't help remarking about it on more than a few occasions. Even Pepito told him, "You look like you think she's coming to see you instead of me."

Alex replied, "It's you she wants to see the most." Silently, however, he was hoping Maria Elena was looking forward to seeing him as much as he was wanting to see her. Ostensibly, Pepito remained the primary reason for the visit. Nevertheless, Alex fooled no one.

Alex asked his father if he could repaint the house before they came; he argued that it had needed doing for a long time anyway. His father glanced quickly at his wife and gave her a knowing look, which was returned in kind. He gave Alex permission to do the painting.

The next day Alex had purchased the white enamel paint and three brushes—two large and one small one. He got Pepito to help him with the lower parts by erecting a crude wooden bench from a long plank and two large blocks of wood—all manu—the hard wood that never seemed to rot. The two of them happily spent the next two days covering the entire exterior—except for the tin roof and the no-glass windows, of course—with a new coat of paint. The floor of the porch was the only portion painted something other than white. The porch got a battleship gray, primarily because that was the only color stocked in porch paint at the store. The paint dried hard within a day and the new-paint smell disappeared a day later. Alex also took it upon himself to cut the grass—a normal chore for him, but this time he did an extra-good job to make it look as smooth as if had been cut by a lawn mower instead of just the regular weed machete—and to trim the bushes in the front and along the side of the house. To Alex it seemed natural that the house be made to look good so a positive first impression was rendered. He didn't realize the underlying implications that were working inside himself.

The morning of the day Maria Elena and her mother were to come by bus, Alex awoke early. He had slept fitfully the night before, having a hard time going to sleep because he was so excited, so anxious to see Maria Elena again. The longer absence from her solidified his feelings for her. Other girls that he ran into in Puerto Viejo who before would have attracted his attention and with whom he would have flirted, no longer were appealing to him. He still smiled and spoke to them and few had realized the change in him, but he definitely had a different feeling for them, a change of which he was very conscious.

Alex got up, dressed, and went out for his usual morning run. He enjoyed the run today more that usual because he could release the tensions that had been building in expectation of the big visit. Alex normally had to force himself to run and it was something he regularly did because he knew the value of conditioning. He regarded it as he did other chores. It was something that had to be done, therefore he did it. Today was different. Today it was relaxing. When he arrived home he felt refreshed. A cold shower washed away the sweat and grime. The showers were always cold; the only hot water was what was heated on the stove. It was not an inconvenience to Alex since he had known of nothing else and therefore didn't miss a hot shower.

Alex had agreed to Pepito's suggestion that they make a sign welcoming Maria Elena and her mother. Alex let Pepito paint the sign and helped him put it up on their front porch banister with one of the ribbons Pepito had saved, making a big bow at the top of the sign. The sign read simply, "Welcome Friends." Alex had argued pleasantly for more words, such as "Friends like you are always welcome at our house," or "Our house is your house" at least, but Pepito wanted to keep it simple.

Alex took most of the money he had saved up and went to town to buy a locket on a gold chain that he'd been eyeing for several weeks. His dad had paid him just enough money that when combined with what he had saved up, he would have enough to buy it. He brought it home and spent long minutes examining the beautiful gift before he finally wrapped it and tucked it under his mattress. He hoped to God Maria Elena's feelings for him had not changed. Would she have thought about me like I have about her? he wondered. He felt sure her coming here was evidence her feelings had not changed. He hoped so.

The bus from Aguas Zarcas arrived ten minutes late—normal for rural Costa Rica—which heightened Alex's restlessness as he waited. He had arrived twenty minutes early with Pepito to wait for the bus's arrival, even though he knew there was no chance the bus would come early. Pepito had insisted on coming with him, even though he had to come almost a kilometer on crutches on an unpaved road. Maria Elena and her mother were the third and fourth persons to get off the bus; the person ahead of them helped get their suitcase off the bus. Pepito's and Alex's faces shone with joy as Maria Elena stepped off the bus. Pepito rushed forward as best he could and accepted a big hug from her as she bent down and kissed him on the cheek. She picked him up off the ground with such enthusiasm he squealed as she hugged him hard. She looked at Alex with a big smile as she hugged Pepito; he too was smiling broadly. As soon as Maria Elena had put Pepito back down on the ground she turned toward Alex. Each stepped forward to close the distance and hugged each other. Alex kissed her ear as he whispered, "It's so good to see you." He kissed her ear again, being careful to turn that side away from Maria Elena's mother. When they unclasped from each other they saw Pepito was already talking rapidly to her mother. They both smiled at the sight and looked at each other. Alex stole a kiss on the lips while her mother's attention was diverted with Pepito.

The four of them, after introducing Alex to the mother, set off hand in hand, four abreast toward their house. Alex had the suitcase in his right hand, and Maria Elena's hand in his left. During the entire walk back to the house Pepito didn't stop talking. He was telling his former nurse how his leg felt, what progress he had made, how good it was to be home, about what had happened the day they got home with the big fiesta, how Alex had been reading to him—she turned and looked into Alex's eyes when Pepito told her that—and how he and Alex had just finished painting the house for them. Alex blushed at that; he had wanted it to seem like this freshly painted house was always how it looked and painting was normal, which this time it wasn't; but since this was the first time Pepito had ever helped paint he had made a big deal of it. Maria Elena sensed this and laughed. Alex squeezed her hand as he watched her laugh. It was good to see her again.

Things went well with the visit. Supper was a happy occasion as the parents of the two boys and the mother of the girl got acquainted. Everyone got along well.

Alex was beside himself wanting to be alone with Maria Elena. Finally the chance came as Alex just simply asked her to go for a walk along the street. Dinner was finished and everyone was already up and moving around.

No sooner did Alex and Maria Elena get out of sight of the house than he turned her to him and mashed his lips against hers. She responded equally and they engaged in a long passionate kiss.

"It's so good to kiss you," Alex choked out. "I've missed you so much."

"Me too," she answered as she kissed him again.

"I haven't thought about anything else almost since I knew you were coming," he told her as he clasped his hands behind her waist and leaned back to look into her moonlit eyes. "You really are beautiful. Your eyes are sparkling." Then he gave her a very tender, loving kiss. When he pulled back he noted her eyes were misty. "What's wrong?"

"Nothing's wrong. Everything is right. I'm crying because I care for you so much and I've missed you a lot."

"Care for me? Is that all? Don't you love me just a little?"

"I love you a lot, Alex. Like you, I've thought of nothing else but coming here to see you since even before Pepito left. I've really missed you."

"Maria Elena De La Paz. Sounds good, doesn't it? If our feelings stay like they are now one day you'll be my wife because I don't want anyone else."

They kissed and discovered their relationship had blossomed into love. Maria Elena urged Alex to hurry back home so her mom wouldn't think something bad. Alex grabbed her hand and started running, pulling her along. They slowed to a walk before they reached the house so they would be able to catch their breath before going in.

Pepito slept with Alex that night, squeezed together in a single bed, while Maria Elena and her mother slept in Pepito's room, where the bed was bigger. Pepito slept blissfully, but Alex lay with his eyes open, thinking back on every word, every action, every event that had transpired since his Maria Elena had stepped off the bus. It was late into the night before he finally dropped off to sleep.

The next morning Maria Elena said she wanted to see the pineapple farm where Alex and Pepito's father worked. She had never seen pineapple grow and would love to see it. Mr. De La Paz agreed, since it was only a ten- to fifteen-minute walk from the house. When they all got there Maria Elena and her mom were so impressed: waist-high plants, deep green in color, were everywhere.

"It's beautiful," Maria Elena exclaimed. "Look how those rows wind along the contour of the land." The plants were in double rows, with about thirty centimeters between the double rows and twenty centimeters between plants within the same row. The plants were in a raised bed a little less than a half a meter wide. She could see this more easily as Mr. De La Paz took them to a newly planted area. He further explained more than fifty thousand could be planted on a space equal to a hectare, including the tractor roads. The plants took from thirteen to fifteen months to grow a mature fruit, and only one fruit grows on a plant. He took them to an area where there was mature fruit and found one along the tractor road that was already yellow in color.

"Perfect," he announced. "This matured a little earlier because it's on the edge; sometimes they do that." Mr. De La Paz snapped the fruit off the plant by grabbing the pineapple and forcing it sideways and down, bending the stalk just below the fruit. He showed them where the mother plant was already producing new plants just beneath the fruit. "These new plants are called 'sons' or 'slips' or 'seeds.' Plant these and you get a new plant." They had broken off with the fruit so he detached all three and gave each lady one. He pulled out his machete and grasped the pineapple by the crown. He then proceeded to whack off the external shell to expose the yellow fruit inside. "This fruit is for export," he explained. "The variety is Yellow Cayenne-lisse and tastes different from the white Montelirio you are used to." He then cut off the very bottom and next cut a thick slice through only to the core, making three cuts to complete the circle. Then he sliced down to free a large chunk of fruit and offered it to Maria Elena's mother. Next he offered one to his wife and the third to Maria Elena. The rapt expressions and 'mmmmmm' noises told him what he already knew. There is nothing quite so good as a ripe pineapple freshly picked. After a moment's pause he cut another thick slice making three more pieces out of it, giving one to Pepito, and one to Alex, keeping one for himself.

"I've never tasted anything so good," Maria Elena said. "This is delicious."

"It is good. It's so sweet," her mom said.

It was no special treat for Alex and Pepito. They had access to this fresh pineapple all the time. While they both loved the taste, it was not new or impressive to them. They just didn't realize that most of the world did not enjoy that privilege. They picked three more ripe fruit and two not quite fully mature—ones that would last several days after the mother and daughter returned to their home in Aguas Zarcas—before heading back toward their home. On the way Mr. De La Paz took them past an area where the plants were flowering to show the visitors how pretty that stage of growth was.

"The flower is shaped like a very small pineapple with reddish-purple blossoms all over it. Each place a blossom appears will later be one 'eye' of the pineapple." He pointed out the diamond-shaped eye on the mature fruit that constitutes the skin or shell of the fruit. "By the way, the sweetest part of any pineapple is toward the bottom. The closer to the crown you get, the less sweet the fruit."

"Those are beautiful flowers, aren't they?"

"I think so. Here, take one of these home also." Mr. De La Paz answered as he cut the flower off.

"Do you ever work here?" Maria Elena asked Alex.

"Yes, I have, but so far only when they really need help, like if they have a lot to pack."

Mr. De La Paz enjoyed showing them what he did for his work. As a foreman at the farm he enjoyed a higher standard of living than did many of the other Ticos in the valley. He explained the owner of the farm was a gringo from Mississippi who came to Costa Rica eight or ten times a year. "It seems like it is a good business, although I'm not privy to the profit numbers. They have been expanding, so it must be good. We now export three or four truckloads per week to Europe and the United States."

"Dad, I have to get back. My game starts in a few hours," Alex pointed out.

"OK, son, we've seen most everything anyhow."

"Señor De La Paz, thank you for showing us the pineapple farm. This has been a great experience for Maria Elena and me," her mother said.

"It's been my pleasure. I'm glad you were interested."

The game was at two o'clock that Sunday afternoon. Alex had eaten as soon as he got home and left for the game trusting the others to follow soon after, to get there before the game started. The field lay parallel to the road and slightly below it so that one could sit on the wall that formed the edge of the sidewalk and look down the three meters to the playing field. There were far more people than usual to watch the game this Sunday. Normally fifty to seventy-five people come to watch. This day, however, because of the calibre of the opponent, almost two hundred people were sitting and standing watching the game.

Heredia had gained a reputation throughout Costa Rica for their always strong junior teams. Puerto Viejo had lost to them this year 2–1 in the semifinals of the National Junior Championship. They went on to win the championship with a 3–0 victory over Limon. The game against Puerto Viejo was so well played on both sides, that the teams agreed to meet again after the season was over. Today was that game.

Maria Elena sat next to Pepito and sometimes held him during the game. She was entranced by what she saw. She knew the game, of course, and was amazed at how well the teams worked together. Maria Elena had seen several pro games—enough to know how the game should be played. The score was 0–0 at half-time. During pauses in the defense Alex had looked up at his new love. Each time he felt renewed inspiration. So far it had been a good game for him personally. He had marked well their high scorer, a guy named Paolo De Palmer, the same one who had scored two against them in the semi-finals. He was good, observed Alex, perhaps the best he'd ever faced. He had a natural instinct for the ball and some very shifty moves that were extremely tough to defense. Twice during the first half Paolo had told him "Nice play" when he had intercepted a pass. Alex had the feeling for the first time in his life he was facing a superior player his own age.

The second half was as intense as the first. Heredia controlled most of the play, but couldn't get the ball in the goal. If Puerto Viejo had a particular strength, it was defense. Besides Alex they had two excellent fullbacks and a very good goalie. Today they needed all that to stave off a vaunted offense. The game ended with no score. Because this was an exhibition game, no overtime and no shootout was played. With a tie everyone gained some measure of respect for themselves and from the audience. The players congratulated each other and many commented on the fine quality of players on each other's team. Paolo said to Alex that he hoped they would see more of each other. "Maybe next year for the Junior World Cup team. I will recommend you to the coach. What's your last name?" he asked.

"De La Paz, Alex De La Paz. Thanks, that's what I'd like to do, but it's hard to get noticed out here."

"I think that can be overcome. Maybe your two fullbacks, too. They should be given an opportunity anyway. Will you write down your name and their names so I can remember them?"

Alex did that and they shook hands. The Heredia team members then got in their three vehicles and drove off.

Pepito was all smiles. All during the game he had pointed out to Maria Elena what was happening, even though most times she already knew. She smiled frequently when Pepito said good things about Alex. His pride in his older brother was very evident. Pepito felt great. Never one to dwell on his own misfortunes, he completely forgot everything else during the game except the action on the field.

Maria Elena commented to the others that perhaps the game for Pepito was the single best therapy he could receive. "Look how animated and excited he is. During his long hospital stay it was the soccer and Alex that he talked most about, and that's saying something, because as you know he talks constantly. Did you know, Mr. and Mrs. De La Paz, it was often Pepito who cheered me and other aides and nurses when we were down? Your son here was always a ray of sunshine for us all. Despite the great pain he suffered he nearly was always a happy, positive patient. I wish all my patients would be like Pepito. It's helping people like Pepito and seeing him get better that motivates me to want to be a nurse."

Mrs. De La Paz answered, "Maria Elena, it's very sweet of you to say those things of our son. We think both our boys are special and we are proud of both of them." Mrs. De La Paz reached around Pepito and gave him a one-arm hug as she smiled down at the crippled youngster. "But I have the distinct feeling you are something extraordinary yourself. I know both my sons think the world of you."

Alex came toward them at this point. He looked at Maria Elena almost the whole walk over toward them except for occasional glances at each of the others and more often at Pepito. She sure looks good, he thought. Hope she liked the game and hope she liked watching me. Man, hope she thinks I played good. That was one of my best games. If she wasn't impressed by that, she'll never be. "Hi," he said out loud.

"Hi. Nice game," they chorused.

"Way to go, Big B. You shut 'em down. Zilcho—*nada*. Their ace couldn't get past you. Way to go." Pepito then gave Alex a high five in the tradition of the Americanos, except he was sitting.

Alex ruffled his hair. "Did you like that?"

"Yessiree. You bet. Fantastic."

Alex looked at Maria Elena and everyone there could tell what the look in his eyes meant. Maria Elena blushed because it was so obvious. "Great game," she murmured. This time she kissed him on the lips, even with all the parents right there.

On the walk back home they had time to talk over the whole game, mostly at Pepito's insistence. Pepito kept asking Alex how he felt when this happened or that happened. How did he know a certain play was going to occur? How did he communicate to his fullbacks? The younger boy was full of questions.

Later in the trip home, Mr. De La Paz remarked to Alex that the other team's center striker—number five—was particularly adept and clever with the ball. Alex told him that was Paolo De Palmer, probably the best junior player in Costa Rica and a member of our Junior World Cup Team, even though he was only fifteen years old.

"Dad," Pepito interjected, "that's the guy all the newspapers say will be Costa Rica's first international star. They say he has as much talent as Diego Maradona did at this age. He's incredible! But did you notice who it was that shut him down? Alex did!"

Alex laughed at Pepito but did add, "He's very good; easily the best I've ever played against. He told me after the game he would get several of us tryouts on the Junior World Cup Team. He was impressed with our defense."

The rest of the visit by Maria Elena and her mother went very well. Alex and Maria Elena had an emotional parting. They knew being away from each other would be hard, they wanted each other so much. Alex promised he would go to visit her soon.

His mom told him she was a wonderful girl and she was happy they liked each other. Her mother, she said, was also a very nice person.

"She means a lot to me, Mom, and to Pepito, too," he added needlessly.

The sun broke from behind the cloud cover and promised a jewel of a day for the citizens of Bethel, Georgia. From the hilltop and driving toward the field complex Gene could not help but marvel at what had transpired their last seven years. It had all started with Bill Lewis, the engineer who had moved into their town eight years ago. Bill was a real dynamo. A man who never stopped, Bill would work tirelessly all day if necessary. He was full of energy and enthusiasm and had talked a group of people into helping to start a youth soccer program like the one he had been a part of in St. Louis. He had raved about how their program was such a good thing for the kids in that area—boys and girls—and how interest in their program had mushroomed in the last several years, eclipsing all other sports in the level of participation. Bill had predicted the same thing here in Bethel. The thing, he said, was to get a core group of interested parents, convince them of the virtues of the game and how it promoted healthy physical fitness; that everyone got a lot of action, not just the best players; that practices could be made to be fun; and that the sport would help develop good body coordination in each youth. "The best thing," Bill had said, "was that because the parents wouldn't be 'experts,' you didn't have the pressure on their children or the negativism that sometimes showed up in little league baseball."

So Bill had come to Gene, recreation director for the town, no more than two weeks after he first moved to Bethel. He had it all laid out. The plan for the first five years was all set down on paper, from the necessary initial meetings to the visits to the local grade schools to a physical layout that provided for three fields. No new construction would be required; what was already available would suffice. Bill himself was a licensed referee and volunteered to do all of the officiating that first year if at least two others would commit to become referees. He had trained all the new coaches and taught them ten or twelve practice drills to use, as well as the rules. That first year they had started with several small parents' meetings, and Bill had gone before all three of the civic clubs to explain what soccer was all about.

Eight teams in three age groups were formed. That first year seventy-eight individuals participated, the youngest of which were five years old. Sixteen kids from the neighboring community had joined the sixty-two from Bethel. Bill wasn't satisfied. He organized coaching clinics and got new coaches certified. He also got several more referees qualified.

The second year the program grew larger, and the third year, larger still. That fourth year saw the building of the first phase of the new soccer complex, which included five fields and a refreshment building. By the sixth year they had doubled the number of fields and lighted three of them. Today the registered players numbered four hundred thirty-five, ranging in age from four to seventeen years.

Gene could see the demonstrable improvement in the players since that first year. They now had boys and girls on state-select teams, and one of Bethel's teams had won the state championship. That team included Scott and Joel.

Just as Bill had predicted, soccer was now the number one sport in town—in fact, in the state. With the burgeoning grass-roots growth, quantum leaps in ability were occurring and Gene could quite easily imagine the United States eventually competing successfully in international play.

Bill had gotten transferred during the sixth year of their soccer program. Gene knew how satisfied Bill felt about having worked so hard to achieve a first-class program here. He could look back on the development with no regrets about not having done as much as could be done by one individual. Fortunately the program had expanded to the point it was no longer a one-man show. They had an official soccer organization with officers and many helpful volunteers.

Gene's eyes and mind focused on the sunlit scene before him. Below him on the expanded soccer complex stood eleven fields, eight of which were now lighted. Soon there would be people everywhere.

The two tournaments they ran last year provided fourteen thousand dollars to the city coffers. The board had reviewed one plan already to build a small, three-thousand-seat grandstand to replace bleachers on one of the fields. No other recreational sport made money or brought the number of fans that soccer did.

Gene liked to come up here to the top of the hill. It gave him a perspective on the whole scene and allowed him to contemplate the past.

This was a sport where everyone played who wanted to play. No one was refused. He wondered why it took so long for the country to "discover" soccer. It was our loss, he reasoned, that we were tied so closely to more sophisticated sports like football. There was room for all the sports. Today soccer was not a big spectator sport in the United States, but Gene figured when these kids grow up soccer could blossom into a sport to rival baseball, basketball, and football. He hoped that one day soccer in the United States would be played at the level played in Europe. He smiled. By the time some of these youngsters got to college, the faith he had in the good ole US of A told him some of these kids would be able to play competitively anywhere in the world.

They had just announced that the 1994 World Cup tournament had been awarded to the United States. Perhaps with the impetus provided by the showcase he knew the World Cup to be, the soccer federation's efforts to promote the sport would finally bear fruit. The groundswell of support and enthusiasm he was seeing right here would, perhaps, gel into tangible evidence all over the country.

Bill had been right on the money when he described what would happen, Gene mused. He had experienced exactly this same thing near St. Louis, where he came from. Of course it took a lot of work, much of it Bill's, but it had been well worth it. Gene still corresponded occasionally with Bill. He was quite a guy.

Today, Gene's own daughter, Allison, was playing a game to decide the league championship. He was pleased at how the coach had developed the girls into a well-coordinated unit. They had transformed from individuals who kicked and passed into a cohesive team that worked the ball up the field and created scoring opportunities by using each other's abilities to enhance their own. The other team had better talent, he judged, but they did not work as well together. No matter what the outcome of today's game, he knew his daughter had enjoyed a good time this year and had learned a lot about the game.

CHAPTER 5

The schoolhouse windows were open, and a fresh spring breeze was coming in on Paolo De Palmer, who was day-dreaming and looking out the window. The day after tomorrow would be his sixteenth birthday, and he had discovered his mother was throwing a surprise boy-girl party for him. He was wondering whom she had invited. He knew she would include classmates and members of his soccer team. He was hoping his mother invited the right girls to the party. The problem was his mom's idea of the right girls were not the same as his. Paolo liked girls who were pretty, vivacious, outgoing, and who liked to party. His mother, he knew, would prefer the quiet, shy, and socially inept ones. He was sure this party was going to be a drag, and, in fact, cause him some embarrassment among his friends. How could she spoil his birthday like this!

Paolo thought he might start dropping a few names of girls he wanted at the party. Three came to mind immediately. Maria; now there was a girl whose body never quit! What a girl. Rosita, her dark eyes were so inviting; and Lucinda, who was the prettiest girl in the whole school; those are noble thoughts, he told himself. His thinking focused on Lucinda. Ever since that day when she came to watch the soccer game she had been very friendly, often stopping to talk between classes. It's too bad all the girls have to wear those school uniforms, he mused. Paolo fantasized what the days at school might be like if the girls could wear what they wanted instead of those blue jumper uniforms. All the schools required students to wear uniforms, so Paolo couldn't feel too bad about it. Lucinda would sure be better to look at in a nice tight sweater over a pair of tight pants, he thought. She sure has a great figure. Paolo again started dreaming about her.

Lucinda had inviting lips, the kind that often showed her white teeth, the two front ones, even when she wasn't smiling. Her upper lip kind of curled up in the middle. Paolo would often watch her just to see if she would close her lips all the way. He thought her upper lip remained open just a bit when her mouth was normal. Her mouth was attractive, however. Her lips just identified her face as something unique. Lucinda was special, anyway. All the boys thought she was pretty. But Paolo couldn't stop thinking about her lips. He wanted to kiss her. The more he thought about her, the more intense his desire was to kiss her. Not only would he finagle an invitation to his party for her, but he'd figure out a way to get her alone and kiss her, too. He continued to scheme as he sat at his desk in the classroom at school, feeling the breeze on his face.

Scott Fontaine had finished his sophomore year at Georgia when the Italian World Cup was held. He tried to talk his parents into sending him to Italy to watch it, but their answer was expected. "Scott, there is just no way we can afford that. If you can find a way to pay for it without drawing out of savings, you may go if you have someone responsible to go with." Scott figured the cost without hotels or game tickets at a minimum of twenty-five hundred dollars. He tried lots of different ways, including asking his home soccer association and newspapers—figuring he could write articles about the matches for them—but couldn't find any interest.

Many of the games were carried on cable TV, and Scott taped every one of them. Then he would watch these over and over again. Scott, like thousands of young U. S. soccer players, was studying the moves of the best players in the world. When Scott came to an especially good move on tape, he would run it back and forth time after time while he tried the same move. Some of these he practiced hundreds of times in his living room before even going outside to practice them "on the fly" or while dribbling the ball. Scott was really impressed with the players' ability to turn the ball in a different direction and to fake their moves without touching the ball as they challenged a defender. By the end of the summer of 1990, Scott felt he had jumped two or three levels in his ability to control the ball and to play soccer.

How many other Americans were thirsting for this kind of soccer? he wondered. How many others are doing just like me—learning by practicing what they've watched?

The answer, yet to be manifested at high schools, youth soccer, and colleges around the country, was, literally, thousands. American soccer took a quantum leap forward thanks to the televising of the '90 World Cup and the magic of videotape. Scott felt so strong about what he learned that he sent Ted Turner at TNT a thank-you letter "For contributing more to United States soccer than any other individual in America. I just want you to know for at least one person how much your televising the Italian World Cup meant." He described what had taken place with him and how much he practiced and some of the moves he learned.

Scott was surprised when one week later he received a letter in the mail from Ted Turner himself. Scott showed his letter to his mom and dad. They suggested he get it framed, and at school he hung it proudly in his room above his desk, alongside a motivational sign he made for himself that said simply, "1994—World Cup Champion, United States of America."

When Scott returned to college that fall he found almost all of his teammates also had taped World Cup games and used them to practice new moves. The coach was tremendously impressed with the elevation of skills demonstrated not only by his existing team, but also of the incoming freshmen. All echoed the same thing. They had spent hours and hours practicing the things they saw on TV.

After the first fall practice he told his girlfriend the difference in the players was unbelievable.

"I know other schools are experiencing the same thing, but we're gonna be dyn-o-mite. God bless Ted Turner for putting it on TV. Look out rest of the world, here we come."

So excited was Paolo about the party tonight that he couldn't eat much of the early supper his mother had prepared. He had been told they would be eating an early meal so his mom could do something special tonight. Paolo had acted nonchalantly, as if he were not interested; but he was. He knew he had successfully implanted the three girls' names without overplaying it and revealing his purpose. At least his Mom didn't let on. Paolo wondered why it was that the more he thought about Lucinda the more important she became to him. So much so that he wanted to spend all his time with her. She had become an all-consuming thought for him. He looked for her at school at every chance, just to glimpse a sight of her. He kept her image in his mind at other times. His heart would beat faster when he saw her, and he would plan what he would say to her. Paolo also remembered that quick kiss she had laid on him when he walked her home after that game a while back. He hoped to get more, much more from her before long. He knew he had worked himself into a new mind-set that viewed Lucinda as a more mature girl. Still he was amazed that without much change in his interaction with her or her interaction with him that he discovered that he liked her; that he wanted to be with her constantly. Was this what love was like? the sixteen-year-old youth wondered. Whatever it was, it sure felt great.

His mother announced, as he was finishing his meal, that he might want to clean up a bit and put on a nice shirt because she expected some company could possibly come over tonight. "You know, some of the family perhaps," she smiled.

Paolo smiled pleasantly and answered that he would. He not only changed, he also took a shower and put on some cologne. There was a blue-patterned, blousy shirt that he thought looked sexy on him. Now was the time to wear that.

The trick, Paolo thought, was to arrange for him to walk Lucinda home afterward. Somehow he had to get alone with her. Hoo-boy, what a disappointment it would be if she didn't come tonight. He had worked himself into a state of mind that centered on Lucinda solely. Maria and Rosita had largely been forgotten. Paolo struggled to reopen his level of receptiveness for them. They were fun, gorgeous, and available. He forced himself to include them and not shut them out so he could have a good time tonight—and maybe later. Then he realized he also needed to include the guys—his pals—who would also be there. None of them better make a play for Lucinda, though. He would be polite to the other girls, but he sure wasn't going to worry about them. They would have a good time among themselves or with the other guys.

How were these people going to come to the party and have it be a surprise? Paolo hadn't figured that out yet. He also wondered how many people would be here tonight. Probably at least twenty, if not thirty. That's quite a few.

When he finished dressing he went back out to the living room. "How's that look?" he asked.

"Nice," said his Mom and Filipe, his younger brother, together. "Paolo, would you go get some things from the store for me, please? We need three bottles of Coke and one diet Coke and some Doritos with some bean dip. Would you please go get those and hurry back here so we have them for any company?"

"Sure, Mom, glad to do it," Paolo said, as things clicked into place. "Need some money, though."

"Here you go. Don't be too long."

"I won't. Be right back in ten minutes. 'Bye."

As soon as Paolo left, his mother, father, and brother swung into action. Mrs. De Palmer looked up at the clock and announced, "OK, time to call Juan and tell everyone to come, Paolo'll be back shortly." In short order they had the house decorated as best they could. At least a festive atmosphere had been created with the balloons and crepe paper. Dancing was planned in the courtyard, which had a brick floor. Mrs. De Palmer was thankful it was not raining. Dancing was a big part of the activities she had planned. Paolo, her boy, was a young man tonight. Sixteen years old—no longer a boy. She was aware that Paolo's interests now very much included girls. She hoped she had invited the people Paolo wanted for tonight. There were supposed to be twenty-four people if everyone came. She had worried that several boys she knew should be included weren't going to come or else there would be too many boys at the party. Paolo, however, had unsuspectingly provided her with three more girls' names just in the last several days that made it all work out. She was sure Paolo didn't know a thing about it.

As the young people arrived, Mrs. De Palmer met them all at the door and told them to come in. Mr. De Palmer watched them enter and for a while wished he were twenty years younger. The girls all looked good, some exceptional. The young boys also shone. A real good-looking group, thought Mr. De Palmer; there's no substitute for youth, he mused wistfully. Mrs. De Palmer made them go around the room and introduce themselves. Mr. De Palmer noted three girls in particular. Rita was stunning; she could win a beauty contest; Lucinda was very attractive—a kind of girl-next-door look. The one he thought was the best-looking girl, though, was Maria. She had a smile that captivated him. Together with those dark eyes that flashed exciting messages, her smile made Maria stand out. As the people introduced themselves, Mrs. De Palmer also noted those same three girls. There began a tingle of doubt about how successful she had been in keeping the party a secret. These three weren't here because they had become friends with him at school. She knew they were here because Paolo wanted them here; she knew how Paolo was about pretty girls, and these three certainly were pretty.

Filipe thought so, too. He was in heaven! The girls certainly looked good. They all wore dresses or nice outfits, and boy, did they look nice. The girls his age just couldn't compare. They were little girls compared to these young ladies. Man, Paolo is going to have a good time, he thought.

Mrs. De Palmer gave them instructions to shout "surprise" when Paolo walked through the door. Barely did they get ready in time. Less than one minute later Paolo came in the door.

"Surprise!" they all shouted.

Paolo looked properly surprised—and pleased—as he saw all those people in the room. He looked around at all his friends, his eyes catching each person as he registered who all had come. A tingle went up his spine as he saw Lucinda. She was beautiful! He couldn't help but notice some of the others also. Rita and Maria sure looked good. Surprisingly, so did the rest of the girls. Amazing what real clothes could do for you, he thought.

Mrs. De Palmer got out some drinks and snacks for the kids to enjoy. She had planned an activity—a guessing game—that would force everyone to mingle and start them all talking and getting into a party mood. In about a half an hour they could turn down the lights and dancing could begin. She noticed how many girls had given Paolo a birthday kiss and realized they must think him quite good-looking. As she compared him to the other boys, she realized he really was handsome. She also noticed he had turned on the charm and was the center of attention. She felt pride for how popular he appeared to be. Both the boys and girls seemed to want to be around him.

When she got a chance to talk to Paolo she mentioned that dancing would occupy most of the night and that he had to dance with every single girl that had come, every single one.

Filipe was the one to turn off the first light. Soon most everyone was dancing. Paolo was skillfully working his way through all the girls, saving Rita and Maria and Lucinda for last. Only two others to go, he thought. When a slow song was played, however, he grabbed Lucinda's hand and started dancing. The feeling of her so close was almost overwhelming.

"You look absolutely gorgeous tonight," he told her.

Lucinda drew her head back a little and looked into his eyes. "You look good, too. Happy birthday." He squeezed her close to him and marveled at how happy he was. He could feel every part of her body against him. He wished he could spend the whole night dancing with her like this. She was really special, so much more mature than all the other girls her age. Paolo hoped she was experiencing some of the same feelings that he was. Was she thinking about him as often as he was thinking about her? Did she look for him between classes, like he did for her? Did she find her thoughts wandering toward him and unable to concentrate on anything else? Paolo was dying to ask, he but knew that would not be cool.

"I've been thinking about you," he whispered in her ear.

"Oh?"

"Yes, not only did I want you to come to this party, but I also want to spend some time with you; maybe we could go to the movies together sometime."

"Ooo. I'd enjoy that."

"Lucinda, can I walk you home tonight after the party?"

"Yes, that would be nice. I'd like you to."

Paolo's feet never touched the ground the rest of that evening. Paolo danced with the rest of the girls but wasn't aware of anything else that was going on except that he noticed how good Maria smelled and that Rita was a good dancer. Paolo did fast-dance with Lucinda one more time and marveled at what a smooth dancer she was, too. Graceful, he thought. Provocative. He loved the way she moved her hips. She could really dance!

One time when Paolo was getting something to drink he looked across the room and saw Lucinda watching him. He flashed a broad grin and saw her smile back. Why hadn't I noticed before what soft, creamy skin she had? he wondered. Something strange, something new is happening to me. This is not like anything I've ever experienced before. All of a sudden it bothers me to see her talking to other boys, or dancing with them. My whole being is becoming centered around Lucinda. I can't stop thinking about her. I'm looking for her at every chance. I can't enjoy other girl's company like I used to. Maria is so pretty, but now just doesn't compare to Lucinda. What's happening?

"Lucinda," whispered Rita, as she sidled up close beside her. "Have you noticed how Paolo looks at you? I think he has a crush on you?"

"I hope so. I've kind of got certain feelings for him. Look how good he looks in that shirt."

"Honey, Paolo looks good to me in anything he wears, or nothing." They both looked at each other and giggled. "I'll bet his body is rock hard, as much soccer as he plays," Rita added. "You do know he's generally considered the best young soccer player in Heredia, don't you?"

"Yes, I've heard he's good. I've even seen him play. How interesting it was!"

"How interesting! Lucinda, you're too much," laughed Rita. "I think you're caught on him all right. Well, good luck."

"He's asked to walk me home tonight after the party."

"Really! What'd you say?"

"I said 'OK,' of course."

"Romantic. Wow. Oh, tell me about it afterward. I want to hear all about it."

"We'll see." Lucinda again looked over at Paolo to see a small crowd of boys around him. Paolo was talking and the other guys were laughing and seeming to hang on his every word. She knew it wasn't just because it was his birthday party. Paolo was one of the most popular boys in school. All the kids respected him, especially the other boys who played sports. She reflected on what Rita had said about how good he was in soccer. That must be one reason why the other boys liked him so much and why they so often gathered around him, listening when he spoke.

Paolo glanced over at Lucinda and saw that she was watching him. That gave him a really good feeling. He was looking forward to taking her home. He knew where she lived. Appropriately, there were two back roads they would have to walk along to reach her house; two very dark back roads. Paolo imagined taking Lucinda in his arms as they walked along those very quiet, very private roads. He wondered if she would be receptive to his advances.

The party started to draw to a close. Shortly after the first person left, everyone else started to leave. Before long only Lucinda was there.

"Mom, I'm going to walk Lucinda to her house, OK?"

"Oh, I didn't realize there was only Lucinda left here."

"She lives a little more than three kilometers from here, so I guess I'll be gone more'n an hour; we won't hurry."

Mrs. De Palmer cast a doubting glance at her obviously enamored son and bid them on their way. Mr. De Palmer raised one eyebrow, having taken in the situation immediately. "I wouldn't hurry, either," he whispered to his wife.

Lucinda picked up her purse. "Thank you so much for inviting me to your party. I had a lovely time, it was a great party."

The two teenagers walked out the door and walked less than thirty meters before Paolo reached over and took her hand in his. "Lucinda, I haven't been able to stop thinking about you these last few days. I've been so anxious for the party to happen so that I could see you here tonight. You look very pretty."

"Thank you, Paolo, you look good yourself."

"Yeah?"

"Yeah."

Paolo stopped walking and turned to face Lucinda as she also turned toward him. Awkwardly at first, Paolo put his arms around her and kissed her fully upon the lips. Lucinda put her arms around him and returned the kiss.

"I can't explain the feeling I have, but I don't think I have ever felt this good in my whole life. You are terrific, he murmured."

"So are you."

They again began walking hand in hand in the direction of her house. As they strolled along, Paolo asked a lot of questions to find out more about her. "Do you have any brothers and sisters? How old are they? What kind of work does your father do? What do you think of school?" They talked easily and enjoyed getting to know one another. She asked him about his soccer. She asked him what his dreams were. He told her very quickly that he wanted to help win the World Cup for Costa Rica.

"Are you good, *really* good."

"Yes, I am."

Lucinda knew he wasn't just bragging. His tone of voice had turned serious and she had heard enough about Paolo from others to know this wasn't just idle boasting. Certainly the time she saw him he looked exceptional. Although she knew he wanted to impress her, something about the intent look in his face and the hardness of his body told her this was something extremely important to him.

"I'll have to come and watch you again sometime."

"I'd like that, I really would."

They were walking along the first back road where there were no lights close by. "Look at the stars, aren't they beautiful?"

"I love to gaze at the stars. Look, there goes a shooting star. Did you see it?"

"Yes, I saw it," he forced out. "I think tonight is incredibly romantic, and you are incredibly beautiful."

Again they kissed, more passionately this time. Paolo was definitely savoring the delights of his first love. They stopped several more times on the way home to kiss. He hated for this night to end. Before finally saying goodnight to her, though, he made a date for the movies with her.

Paolo alternately jumped into the air kicking his heels and shouting his joy, as he walked back home. At this moment he could conquer the world. Tonight's experience, he knew, had set a new direction in his life. Nevermore would he be the same. What a fox that Lucinda was!

———⚽———

"Aw, Mom, I don't want to go. I really don't. I want to stay here and do things with some of the guys."

"No, Scott. You are going with us, that's final. You're already at college, this may be our last year together as a family, and your father and I want you to go."

"But I had things I wanted to do with my friends here."

"You can do them after we get back. We are only going to be gone one week."

"Mom, please."

"No, Scott, that's final. We leave Saturday morning and you are going with us."

And so with great reluctance Scott joined his parents and his two younger sisters on a vacation to Destin, Florida. His parents had reserved a condo on the beach. Scott had heard how nice it was in Destin and Fort Walton, but he had hoped to go to Atlanta to see the Braves play, and then go to the amusement park with some friends.

The smell of the salt-sea air awakened memories of years ago when the family used to go to the coast on vacation. They had not been there since he had started high school and now college. Five years it had been. Scott's sisters were anxious to get there and go out on the beach in their new swimming suits. They just knew there would be lots of boys their ages there to admire them.

"Hey, you two need to help us unload the van before you go out there and wow those boys," Scott teased.

"Scott, you stop it," Dawn retorted.

"Yeah, it's as if you want us to think you are not going to look at any girls or anything," Karen chided.

"Everyone will help us get settled in before you beach it," Mr. Fontaine said. "There will be plenty of time for everyone. Besides, we'll be here a whole week."

"Daddy, you're not going to go to the beach to watch girls, are you? You're married to mommy."

"I don't know what's going on in that fuzzy little head of yours, Dawn, but a fellow never loses his appreciation for a beautiful girl; no matter how old he is."

Mrs. Fontaine spoke up. "There's our condo. Edgewater Beach. See the big building that looks like some giant stairs to the sky. That's our building; I recognize it from the brochure."

"Wow, look at that. I like it," Karen said, awed.

"We've got number 506. The lady said we could take an elevator here, close to the office where we check in, or one down closer to our unit."

"Let's take this one. It's a glass elevator and we can see the ocean as we go up."

"OK."

Check-in was easy and they entered the unit in no time at all.

"Look at this, kids. So much room. This is lovely."

"Two bedrooms...*and* two bathrooms, Mom. Big bedrooms, too," the girls added.

"I like the view from the balcony; you can see the ocean and all those swimming pools," Scott proclaimed from the outside on the balcony.

The others all rushed out on the balcony to share the vista. The condo turned out to be a pleasant surprise. They were not expecting anything so spacious and nice. It had a large kitchen, a dining area, a living room with two queen-size sofabeds, and two large bedrooms. The kitchen area included a washer and dryer, ample storage, and a microwave. The kitchen was done in an off-white Formica trimmed in light natural wood. The living room and dining area had a very tasteful, expensive-looking light beige wall covering. The paintings and other adornments added to the pleasant impression. They all knew this was going to be a good week.

"Mommy, Mommy, do Karen and I get the other bedroom with the twin beds? We need our privacy."

"Privacy? Well, Scott do you mind sleeping out here in the living room? The sofas fold out into beds."

"I guess I really don't mind. I might just sleep on the couch as it is. This seems pretty comfortable."

"There you go, girls. Thank your big brother for giving up so easily."

The two girls ran over to Scott and each hugged him and gave him a kiss on the cheek.

The rest of the day turned out well as they enjoyed themselves on the beach and at the pool. The girls were already making friends; neither was bashful. Scott joined in a game of beach volleyball. There were quite a few high school and college aged kids there, to Scott's surprise. The game was pretty intense with fierce kills and a lot of diving after balls. Scott showed his athletic prowess, displaying his quickness and agility. When he joined the game, his side had lost the first game. Then they came back to win two close games. One girl and one boy on his team held their own, but the others were more of a liability.

The other players were naturally attracted to him because he proved to be the best athlete among the young people. He agreed to meet some of them the next morning to play some sand football. Scott was the type who liked any sporting activity; he loved the challenge to compete. The vigorous activity was just what Scott needed to quench his natural competitive desires.

"Looks like it's going to work out all right after all," he thought to himself. "At least there's something worthwhile to do."

The next morning the girls had gotten up and eaten before Scott woke up. Already they were down on the beach. Dawn had wanted to build a real sand castle; Karen wanted to construct a sand sculpture of the Edgewater building. They decided to do both, asking their Daddy to take a picture of them when they got done.

Scott went out to the pool a bit earlier than "the game" was supposed to start and lay in the lounge chair, absorbing the rays. He was kind of half-sleeping, half-awake when he noticed two girls across the pool. One was blonde and the other was a brunette. Both were pretty. He kept one eye on them, watching from a distance. Before long they both got up and dived in the pool. He could tell they also had nice figures. The brunette obviously had been a competitive swimmer; she broke a sizable wake swimming across the pool.

At the appointed time for the football game Scott got up and went to the beach. Most of the players from yesterday were there, as well as a few new people. Many of those already there said "Hi" to Scott and called him by name.

They played for more than an hour, enjoying the fresh air, the exercise, and the competition. Scott was glad to go into the ocean to cool off when the playing stopped. It was past the normal lunch time, so Scott decided to head up to the condo unit to eat something.

When the elevator door opened, Scott was momentarily surprised to see the brunette swimmer from earlier already in the elevator.

"Hi," Scott uttered as he entered the elevator.

"Hi!" she replied.

"Didn't I see you yesterday at the beach in an orange bikini, and again today at the pool?"

"You might have. I wore one. Where were you?"

"Mostly playing beach games—Frisbee, football and volleyball."

"Oh, you're Scott, aren't you?"

"Yes, how'd you know my name?"

"My brother told me about you. He was quite impressed with your athletic ability. He...he said your speed was awesome."

"Ha, your brother said that? What's his name?"

"Andy."

"What's your name?" Scott's heart was pounding.

"Diana. Diana Paolin." Scott's new friend reached out to shake his hand.

"Nice to meet you, Diana Paolin. I'm Scott Fontaine. Tell Andy he's a pretty fair athlete himself."

The rest of the trip up was spent in silence, each pondering thoughts about the other. As the door opened for Scott to get out, he turned to Diana.

"Would you like to meet me at the pool later today? Say around three?"

"Sure, that'd be nice. Lower pool?"

"OK."

As he stepped out he looked back and saw her smile at him and wave a cute little good-bye with her right hand.

"WOW!" Scott jumped in the air after the doors whispered shut. "Things are looking up."

The next couple of hours seemed to drag. Scott stayed in the condo after lunch playing Questure and Pictionary with his sisters and parents. He couldn't help checking frequently to make sure there were no storm clouds brewing that might prevent his rendezvous.

After lunch he put on his new bathing suit, even though it was still damp from his early morning swim. He had a dry suit but figured the newer one being wet wouldn't matter; it looked better on him than the old one.

By two-thirty he was out at the pool catching rays on a chaise lounge. His sisters joined him, wanting to swim again since someone was there to watch them.

Scott tried not to look for Diana too often. He did not want to appear overly anxious. He jumped in with the girls one time to swim a little, mostly because he thought the time would pass faster.

When he saw her walking down the steps from the middle pool, he was relieved to see another girl her age with her, as well as Andy. Scott knew he wasn't the greatest conversationalist and the others, together with his sisters, would make things easier.

Diana wore a cover over her swimsuit that did little to hide the curves he remembered from earlier. She was bright and perky and handled the introductions well. Scott admired the ease with which some people like Diana managed introductions. Scott was as apt to forget someone's name.

Often, too, he didn't introduce people in the correct order. This time, however, things went well, despite the pressure he felt.

Andy was obviously going to be an asset to the development of any relationship with Diana. He was about a sophomore in high school and easily impressed.

"Scott, Scott Fontaine. I'm going to remember that name. I don't know what you do or if you play any sports, but if I see you on TV, someday, I'll know who it is," Andy gushed out.

"Why, thank you, Andy. Don't be so sure you'll see me, though."

"He's a soccer player, goes to Georgia, and is an eligible bachelor," Karen chimed in, eyeing the two pretty girls.

"Karen, hey, watch it," Scott said, but inwardly was delighted. He knew Karen was proud of him and it looked like she would be helpful.

"He's real good; he was the number-one ranked high school player in the country as a senior," Dawn added.

Scott could see perhaps Karen had ulterior motives, the way she was eyeing Andy. Scott didn't think of that connection before, but was amused at the similarity of their thoughts.

"I knew it. I knew it. You had to be somebody with that kind of speed and agility. I was right." Gina, the blonde with Diana, was not subtle in her admiration of this information about Diana's new friend. Scott was glad that his sister was so outspoken.

"Soccer games don't get on TV much—at least not college level soccer. So you probably won't see me on TV. Here, I've been saving these two lounge chairs with the help of my sisters. There's another one over there. I'll get it."

"I'll get it, Scott. Let me," Andy responded.

"Andy used to play soccer until he broke his leg last year. He hasn't been interested again. Maybe you would kick some with him, that might rekindle his interest," Diana told Scott when Andy went to retrieve the chair.

"Be glad to. I like Andy. He and I were on the same volleyball team yesterday." Silently he thought, "And I like him even more now that I know who his sister is." Out loud he added, "Ready to go in the water?"

"Sure."

Scott had found out Diana was here with her parents, Andy, and Gina for the week, just like his family. Since today was Monday, that left at least four more days to do things with the Paolins. Scott had very much wanted to do something tonight with Diana, but he thought he better not push it too fast. He knew he shouldn't come on too quick. It was important to maintain the element of challenge in the relationship. Most people, when chased, will run away.

Incredibly, the perfect situation developed.

Karen mentioned loudly to all that she wanted to go on the water slide tomorrow, and maybe the go-karts.

Andy picked up the idea with enthusiasm and said, "Why don't we all go together?"

Scott watched Diana carefully as he signaled with body language that it was fine with him if it was with the girls. Both girls responded favorably, and so the next get-together was arranged for tomorrow morning at nine. Scott's impression of what Karen schemed created a new image of his sister. He realized she knew what she was doing. He just wasn't sure whether it was all conceived on her own behalf toward Andy or if some of it was to also help him with Diana. In any case the result was achieved in the best way possible.

Scott asked Diana which condo they were in so that if any plans changed he could call. He gave her his own unit number when she asked him. A small thing, but he thought it important that she asked.

Back in their condo unit Scott thanked his sisters. "The afternoon went great, just great. Thank you girls for helping me. It's nice to have you feeding the girls so many nice things about me. I'll treat you to some ice cream the first chance we get."

"Oh boy. OK. It's a deal."

"Thanks, Scott."

His parents were still out shopping, but it didn't take long for them to hear all about the day when they returned.

"One thing about Dawn, she doesn't keep secrets," Scott told them as he hugged her to his side. "Your daughters are growing up, though. They were quite the young ladies out there."

"I'm glad you had a good time, dear. It's nice you're making friends your own age."

"Diana and her friend go to college together in Florida. They're juniors there, or will be in September," Dawn continued to be helpful.

"I have to say things are going better than I expected. I'm glad you forced me to come. Would it be all right if I asked Diana to dinner sometime?"

"Do you mean here, or on a date?"

"Well, either, Mom. Both."

"My goodness, are we smitten?"

"When you only have a week I guess you try to cram in more than you might otherwise," he laughed.

During activities at the water slide and racing go-karts, Scott thought perhaps he should switch the target of his attention. Gina seemed to be a whole lot friendlier than Diana. In fact, the situation of relationships was a curious montage of feelings that were rapidly changing. Scott couldn't figure out what to do—to ask one or both to dinner, or to include Andy or what. Then it came to him, the best solution would be to have both families go out together for dinner. So that's what he proposed.

Surprisingly, everyone liked the idea. Scott was taken back by the response Diana showed. Normally she was more quiet than Gina. Scott got further confused in trying to sort out his feelings. He also didn't understand what was going on in the minds of the girls. He guessed things would sort themselves out.

Both sets of parents accepted, and plans were made to go to Scampi's that same night.

"Scott, Scott, would you look at this and see if it looks OK?" Karen asked.

Amused, Scott helped her pick out just the right clothes. Karen was obviously more interested in boys than he was girls at that age.

Diana's parents were very pleasant, very friendly and helped to make the evening go well. Diana switched back on to Scott right from the outset. She was warm and friendly and talked a whole lot more than on previous occasions. The first feelings Scott had for Diana returned even stronger. The confusion and uncertainty about which girl he should pursue disappeared with the developments that unfolded. At one point Scott was skeptical that Diana was putting on a show for her family—that tonight's behavior was not genuine.

Diana explained much after supper as they walked together toward the cars. "You undoubtedly don't know how to take me. I want to explain. When Gina and I went swimming with you and your sisters yesterday, she developed a crush on you. So I backed off a little—not from any lack of interest on my part, but really to give her sort of an equal chance. Boy, this sounds stupid, doesn't it?"

"No, it's helping me understand you."

"Well, she really liked you and just because I met you first shouldn't take away an opportunity for her to develop a relationship—a serious romance possibly. That was further complicated because my brother showed an obvious affection for you. So what I tried to do was to provide her with access to you without extracting myself from the picture. I afraid all we've done—all I've done—is confuse you. So Gina and I talked today and I reaffirmed my interest while she was willing to step aside, having tested the waters, so to speak. I could see the confusion and consternation in your face. Gina could, too. I sensed all along that you felt something for me, but maybe you would feel something for Gina, too. But with so short a time together here this week, Gina and I decided that either I would spend time with you or neither of us would...that is, if you want to."

"I don't know quite how I'm supposed to feel. You were the one I was interested in, not Gina. Yet Gina sort of stepped in. I thought you lost interest and I was trying to figure out whether to just be friendly to the two of you and forget about developing any kind of relationship with you, or to ask you what was going on. Then abruptly tonight you were the same girl I first saw and then talked to that afternoon at the pool. I...I almost feel like a commodity that was bought and sold."

"Scott, I'm sorry. I have feelings for you. Good feelings." Diana stopped walking and turned to Scott. "This is how I feel about you." Then she kissed him. "Hold me, Scott Fontaine."

Scott felt the juices flowing. He was quite blown away by the last five minutes. A strange feeling came over him that he was protecting the girl in his arms; from what he didn't know. Did she even need protecting? What primeval instinct generated the desire to hold this girl close, to protect her from all things bad? Scott was perplexed at the new sensation sweeping over him. He squeezed her tightly.

"I wish this moment would last forever," he whispered to her. "This seems so right."

"For me, too."

"Diana, we have three full days left here and then we have to leave Saturday. I'd like to spend as much time with you as possible to get to know you and to see more of you."

"I'd like nothing better. My thoughts are the same. It was better you suggested it than me, though. It's funny how much you want to push things when you know you only have a short time together."

"Exactly. I doubt everything would move this fast or that we would have had this type of conversation if we both lived in the same town."

"No way. Let's see where the next three days take us."

Scott took her hand gently and walked toward the cars where everyone was patiently waiting, themselves engrossed in conversations.

Both sets of parents sensed something different about the young couple, as though it were branded on their foreheads.

Mrs. Fontaine glanced over to her husband who caught her eye as she silently said, "Oh-Oh."

The next several days whirled by for Scott. He couldn't remember being so happy. He and Diana spent nearly all their time together. They went swimming in the ocean, happily splashing in the waves and building sand castles and covering each other up with sand. They played volleyball with other young people and miniature golf with the rest of the two families. On Thursday they went to Big Kahuna's, a water park with great slides, several miniature golf courses, dune buggy and go-cart tracks, and other activities. Everyone had a great time there.

They discovered paddle ball on the beach was a favorite activity. Scott could tell both Diana and Andy were good tennis players by their abilities on the sand with the wood paddles. It was a game they all enjoyed. Scott's and Karen's tennis background stood them in good stead against the tournament-tough Paolins. They even rented one of those ocean-sized water tricycles that you pedal to propel the large, over-sized tires. In everything they shared their joy. The fragile bond formed that night at the restaurant gripped tighter.

Twice Scott ate at the Paolins' place, once for lunch with his two sisters and once for supper, and twice Diana ate at the Fontaines'. Andy and Gina came with her for lunch. Every moment together was a delight for them both. Karen and Dawn came to think of Diana as their friend, too— a big sister sort who was very nice to them. Both girls talked all the time about how much they liked Diana.

It helped that at Big Kahuna's Gina met another guy that she liked. It seemed to take some pressure off—to remove the last vestiges of awkwardness that remained.

At night Scott and Diana enjoyed walking along the beach hand in hand or arms around each other as they talked. These night walks provided the opportunity to really get to know each other, to say who they were and to reveal their dreams. The daytime activities built up a strong comfort zone and time to enjoy one another. But it was the nights and the moonlit walks on the beach that made them begin to fall in love.

Each understood exactly what was happening between them. Each wondered if this was just a summer romance or if it would transcend the time they would be separated from each other. They talked about it. Both said they hoped with all their heart that their feelings would not change.

CHAPTER 6

The newly-elected President of the United States Soccer Federation, Alan Priestaps, had just recently returned from a meeting with Joao Havelange, president of the international ruling body of soccer, known as FIFA. It was Priestap's first official meeting with the international officials since becoming the president of the USSF. It was critical to begin making immediate plans to organize the World Cup. The tournament was to be held in just over three and one-half years. To that extent he organized World Cup—USA as an organization for which the sole task was to plan and execute all the aspects of the World Cup tournament. He, himself, would undertake the overall supervision of the multidimensional job of preparing for such a huge event. It was evident outside assistance would be needed in several areas: making the draws, security, referees, and logistics. He needed people who were familiar with how a World Cup is run and all the various rules and requirements FIFA placed on the host country.

Mr. Priestaps sent a memo to each of his assistants requesting a meeting with them in two days' time:

"Gentlemen, I have had my secretary type my notes I took while meeting with Mr. Havelange and his assistants. You'll notice that many of my notes deal with decisions that will be made by FIFA and not by us. For instance, venue locations and stadiums are not within our decision-making power, although we will be allowed some input and recommendations.

"I have taken the liberty of roughing out an organizational chart for you to look at. This is only a thought-starter. I want your full input and suggestions. I know you'll be able to make substantial improvements in what I hurriedly put together. Then, too, we need to talk names. Who should have what specific responsibilities?

"Please come prepared to discuss our assembling a top-flight organization to successfully accomplish this enormous task. I want to deal with main functions defined, potential names for those responsibilities, then to define second-level functions."

When the time for the meeting arrived, Priestaps asked his secretary to come to the meeting to take notes. The meeting started off with vigorous discussion.

"Alan, I would like to suggest the addition of a public relations group." Henry opened up the discussion; he was not one to hold back if he had something to say. "There will be an immense effort required, not only dealing with the public, but also in getting information and regulations out to cities interested in hosting teams as well as more information dealing with the venue cities. Maybe even traffic control, signs, maps, schedules, etcetera."

"I think directional signs and the like should be under logistics," Brad added.

"Thank you both for your input. Let's first take the six main functions I've listed and see if it would be better to have them arranged differently or to have more or fewer directors. OK, we show security; television and sponsor activity; logistics; tournament draws; competition committee; and tickets, venue, and stadium selection."

Harry broke in again. "If I may, I'd like to show the details under logistics to show how mammoth that task is. That's why I'd like to break PR out of it and make it a separate function. Under logistics I've got these main areas: travel; refreshments; utilities; FIFA liaison; hostesses; hotel accommodations; practice fields; liaison efforts with teams; translators; World Cup logo; legal; World Cup licensing; airlines; and public relations, which includes maps, signs, the media, schedules, as well as regular PR functions."

"Who would you have responsible for things such as ballboys, and bands, and advertising, and tour hosts, and referees, and limousines for dignitaries."

"FIFA chooses the referees."

"I'd put advertising under TV and sponsors, and I'd sure as hell get some good people for logistics."

"OK, OK, that's good discussion. What are the advantages of having that as a separate group instead of under one good individual who is under logistics?" Priestaps asked.

And so the discussion went. The entire group eventually decided that it was best to leave public relations under the director of logistics so as to have as much continuity and direct communication as possible.

The meeting lasted all day. In fact, they ordered out for lunch and for supper. By the time the meeting broke up at nine-twenty, though, they had a good feeling for how their organization would function and quite a list of names to consider for the various positions. One surprising outcome was the feeling that so many expert consultants would be needed: some just to help a specific group get organized and some that would be needed for the duration, until the tournament was over.

In March, 1991, Alan Priestaps introduced Kori Gaborakov to the media. "His proven track record in the last two World Cups is unparalleled for having taken teams and advanced them beyond what most people expected. He is exactly what the United States needs for World Cup '94, and his association indicates the level of commitment the United States is willing to make to achieve competitiveness internationally. We are delighted to have obtained the services of one so talented as this great coach from Yugoslavia.

"I am now delighted to present the world-renowned soccer trainer, Mr. Kori Gaborakov, the new United States National Team coach."

"Thank you, Mr. Priestaps. If you pardon me, I speak through interpreter, so I don't say something bad."

At this point a young man stepped forward and stood beside Kori, and at the microphone Kori spoke softly to him and paused while the interpreter translated to the crowd of reporters.

"I am happy, very happy, to be selected as the trainer for this great country of yours. You are partaking of history in that in three years you will host—for the first time—the World Cup of football. We must prepare your team to be competitive. We must get more international experience and utilize all the great resources this country can bring to bear. I am convinced we can be competitive and win at the World Cup level. We must believe in ourselves. I thank Mr. Priestaps, the other officials in the U.S. Soccer Federation, and all of you for giving me this opportunity. I have no style of play I impose on the team; rather, I try to tailor the style of play to the makeup of the team. What works best for the group of players on a particular team is what I go with. Italy plays differently from Germany. Scotland is not like Holland, nor do Argentina and Brazil play alike, nor Uruguay and Columbia. Every team has its own unique style of play. So will it be with the United States."

"How good is Kori's English?" asked one reporter.

"Coach Gaborakov—Kori', as he likes to be called—speaks seven languages. English is not one of his strengths. We have made arrangements to immediately start tutoring Kori in English," Priestaps replied.

"When will he take over the reins of the team?"

"He'll observe the team for a month or two. Interim coach, John Kowashak will manage the team in South Korea next month when we play the Korean and Olympic teams and on a trip to the Middle East that currently is being negotiated. After that we expect Kori will take over."

"How many prospects did you consider?"

"We looked at over thirty different prospects, and narrowed the field down to two. Kori and a former Dutch coach," Priestaps said.

"Do you anticipate that Kori will be better able to tap the ethnic talent here in the States?"

"Yes, definitely," Priestaps replied. "The ethnic pool of talent, because so many of them don't go to college, has been largely overlooked. We expect and encourage more of that talent to be made available to be looked at. We need some players who spend ten to twelve hours a day, all day long, playing soccer. The only place in the United States that occurs is in our ethnic communities, people whose fathers and mothers came from Yugoslavia, Hungary, Brazil, Mexico, Argentina, Chile, and other places where soccer is everything."

"Kori, you had great success before in the World Cup, but I'm not sure you ever faced such a great task before. Will you comment?"

"For me this is a big challenge," Gaborakov replied through his interpreter. "My dream is to be one more time in the World Cup and to win it. I'll be most happy to win this championship. Yugoslavians have a saying: 'The third time is victory.' If I wasn't sure we could have reasonable success, I wouldn't have taken the job."

"What made you choose Kori over everyone else." This question was directed back at Priestaps.

"First, his proven success in exactly the same circumstances as we have here to turn a modest team into a winner. Second, he is both an accomplished international player with experience and a great tactician and motivator of players. Third, we like his style. Kori gets involved with the players in practice and has fun doing it. His enjoyment and love of the game are contagious."

"Does the U.S.A.'s noted lack of interest in the game of soccer bother you and can you change that?" a reporter asked Kori.

"I am hopeful that success will generate interest. As the team begins winning more and more—even before World Cup action—interest will start to build. As the time for the World Cup approaches here, as in Mexico and Italy, the newspapers and TV will be filled with stories about the championship and the upcoming competition."

Priestaps added, "The war in the Gulf has built up the level of patriotism substantially, and the hope is that this feeling for our country will translate into support for our country's team. You all have noticed so many more people wearing red, white, and blue ribbons, clothing and such, and look at flag sales. There are twice as many flags flying now than there were before the war. We are convinced the country will support a good product in soccer as in every other sport."

"What do you, Kori, feel America needs to improve on the most. Offense, defense, or something else?"

"The United States players need more international experience in order to effectively compete. However, I'd say defense is always the cornerstone on which to build a team. Defense does not mean the goalkeeper and the fullbacks only. Defense involves the whole team, each player doing his part."

"We need to draw this to a close and let the coach go to work," Priestaps interjected. "Thank you—all of you—for this strong show of support. We are excited to have this talent associate himself with America's World Cup effort. We look forward with anticipation for good things to happen."

Gaborakov put in one last word. "I'd like to thank publicly the USSF officials who have chosen me with such an important task. I hope I will be worthy of that trust and the enormous responsibility that carries with it. Thank you."

Reaction from every direction was positive in supporting the United States Soccer Federation's decision to hire Kori Gaborakov as the trainer, as most of the soccer world calls its coaches; it was a move well thought of and supported by many throughout the world. Those in the know were aware Kori could also have gone back to Costa Rica as their national team trainer. Costa Rica had made him a very lucrative offer to return through the 1994 World Cup and by doing so forced the United States to up the ante in order to get Kori. The willingness to do so showed the world soccer community that America was committed to improving its soccer program and serious about the 1994 World Cup—a positive indicator all around.

For Scott the summer passed slowly. The feelings for Diana raged within him and the hurt he felt not being able to be with her grew as the weeks passed. The phone bills skyrocketed and Scott needed a substantial part of his summer job income to pay for his calls to Diana. The frequency held steady at about three calls a week. The problem was that many of the calls were quite lengthy.

Arrangements were made for Scott to visit Diana shortly before the end of the summer. He got so excited about going to see her that he proved almost useless around the house. Karen and Dawn teased him and felt envious at the same time.

Happily for the two young people, the intensity of this relationship only grew as time passed. Neither suffered any doubts about the other. As they talked more and more on the phone, their knowledge of one another expanded rapidly.

Scott started packing five days before his departure date. During the next several days he changed his mind on what shirts and other clothing he would take with him. He found it more and more difficult to sit still. He had to be doing something. He started playing tennis every evening just to help the time pass faster. He was surprised that his skills returned so quickly. It had been years since he had played serious tennis. The tournaments he had played in as a kid now seemed so long ago. Diana had mentioned how much she liked to play and that Andy was pretty good. Scott guessed that's probably what prompted him to get out and play. He also wanted to look good when he played with Andy and her. She had told him to bring his racquet, that they would probably play when he was down there. She said her father played quite a bit and was still ranked in the seniors for the state of Florida.

Scott was to stay at their house. Mrs. Paolin said they had room and that it wouldn't be a problem. The four days he was to be there, he knew, would pass quickly. He would try to have as much time with Diana as possible, but he knew her family would have to be included in much that went on. That was part of getting to know her. Scott believed that often the mother would give a strong clue as to what the daughter would be like later on. Scott was anxious too to see what the family life was like. Hopefully, everything would be normal and happy

Waiting for Scott's arrival, Diana stood at the exit to the concourse at the airport. She, too, was very anxious that all would work out well. She was sure it would. This visit would be the test for both of them to see if the relationship was real or not. Scott was so nice and yet not stuck on himself like so many others. He was the first real gentleman she had dated. The best part was she knew he liked her for herself and not for her family—or worse, her money. She hoped the size of her family's estate wouldn't blow him away. She decided that she had better prepare him prior to their reaching the compound.

There she is! Scott's heart soared when he saw her standing in front of her father. She's cut her hair little shorter, but boy, does she look good!

Diana broke into a big smile when she saw Scott. He looked as good as ever to her. As he came close she allowed herself to be swept up into his arms for a big hug. They squeezed each other tightly before kissing a very warm hello.

As Scott released Diana, he looked to Mr. Paolin and warmly shook hands.

"Nice to see you, sir."

"Did you have a good trip?"

"Yes sir, no problems at all. The hardest part was waiting to get off the plane to see Diana ... and you, sir."

He quickly looked back to Mr. Paolin from Diana's face as he sought to include him. His face got a little red, even though he knew they both understood.

"Is this all your luggage?"

"No sir, I have a suitcase I checked. This is the only carry-on."

As they started toward the baggage area Scott put his left arm around Diana's waist.

"I believe it's hotter in Atlanta than it is here."

"We get a cooling breeze off the gulf. Helps to keep it from getting so hot."

As they got close to the baggage area Scott forced enough distance between them and her father to whisper, "You look so good. I've dreamed of this time all summer. You're beautiful." Then he kissed her quickly and smiled his best smile.

"Me, too. I had a hard time these past few days, waiting for today. I'm so glad you're here. Scott, there's something I have to prepare you for before we get home."

"What's that?"

"It's our house: where we live."

"Why do you have to warn me?"

"Well, it's so large. I don't want you to be surprised and angry with me for not telling you."

"I couldn't get angry with you about anything."

"Still, I'd rather you know ahead of time."

Despite the attempt to prepare Scott, he was not ready for what "home" was. A mansion would be more like it. He guessed there were twenty acres fenced in around the main house and other buildings. Expensively fenced in, he silently noted. He loved the huge live oaks all around. He saw a barn, or rather a stable, for horses, a swimming pool with a large pool house, a clay tennis court, and servants' quarters in a separate building.

"Nice place you've got here. This is beautiful, it's incredible."

"Thank you. We enjoy it here."

"Holy cow. You grew up here?" he whispered to her.

"Yes, I warned you."

"Does everyone in the Fort Myers area live like this?"

"Sure, silly. You should see the others."

Scott smiled at her humor. That was one of her many endearing features.

Andy came running out and bounded down the steps from the porch.

"Hi, Scott. Scott's here, Mom," he called. He came running over to them.

Scott shook Andy's hand and could feel the friendly greeting in his grasp. This was going to be a great visit.

"I'll get his suitcase, Dad. Oh boy, did you bring your tennis racquet?" Andy asked when he saw the carry-on bag that was big enough to hold a racquet.

"Yep. Understand I can get a few lessons from you."

"I'll try, but if I can't give you a lesson, Dad can."

"Does he still beat you?"

"Most of the time he does. He can put the ball anywhere he wants."

"I might be able to show Scott how to hold the racquet. I have the feeling he doesn't need any lessons," Mr. Paolin chuckled.

"Soon as lunch is over, let's play. We can play doubles and then singles later."

"Whoa, let's let Scott put his stuff away."

"OK, c'mon, Scott. You and I are sleeping in the pool house," Andy bellowed.

So, Scott and Diana and Andy went first to the pool house to put his things away. The boys were to sleep on the second floor. There were two bedrooms up there, one large and one small, connected by a bathroom. The large one was for Scott; Andy took the smaller one.

"It's nice of you to sleep out here with me and keep me company, Andy. I appreciate that."

"Heck, I wanted to. It'll be fun. I used to sleep out here all the time in the summer."

"Pretty nice accommodations, I'd say. This is nice, very nice."

"I hoped it would be OK. My parents thought this was the best way."

"This is fine."

"And look, this overlooks the tennis court. You can open the door and go out on the balcony. Makes a great place to watch the action on the court," Andy pointed out.

The three went into the main house to greet Mrs. Paolin, but not before Scott stole a kiss from Diana just as Andy passed out of view.

"I'm so happy to be here with you. This is great."

Scott noted that Mrs. Paolin had a cook and a servant to help with lunch.

Must be a tough way to go through life, he thought. So this is how the other half lives.

Strangely, Scott did not feel intimidated by the situation. He was glad he had met Diana in other circumstances, though, where none of this could obscure his true feelings. This way he had no confusion, no mixed signals.

The tennis was fun. Mrs. Paolin watched while the others played. Scott was glad he had practiced before coming here. Andy was quite good, better than he expected. Mr. Paolin was deceptively good. Andy was right. He could put the ball anywhere he wanted, and surprisingly, he could still cover court fairly well, too. Scott learned Mr. Paolin turned forty-six later this year, so this was his second year in the forty-five senior division. Diana was no slouch either. Scott found himself admiring not only her tennis game, but also the way she moved and her competitive spirit. She fit right in with the rest of the athletic family.

Having come here and seen the estate with the tennis court, Scott could now understand why such a tennis-playing family did not play tennis on their vacation to Destin. They had it here any time they wanted. This was one question he didn't have to ask.

Andy continued to be enchanted with Scott. He didn't expect such a good game of tennis out of his sister's boyfriend. For sure now Andy wanted his friends to meet Scott. If things worked out well and Scott agreed, he would have Scott scrimmage with his own soccer team. He was confident that Scott was indeed the soccer player he believed him to be. Anyone who started for the University of Georgia would be impressive if that's all he was. Karen and Dawn had convinced him, however, that he was more, much more than just the average college soccer player. Andy could tell his speed was exceptional. Andy guessed, after seeing him play tennis, that he was probably a standout in every sport he played.

"Scott, do your sisters play tennis also?"

"Yes, Karen is playing on our high school team as a freshman and Dawn has started playing tournaments this year."

"I knew it. Your whole family is athletic, isn't it?"

"Yeah, I guess you'd say that. From what I've seen no one in your family is too shabby at anything, either."

"Scott, I've got a big favor to ask of you. Our high school soccer team is having a scrimmage day after tomorrow. Will you scrimmage with us? I really want to see you play—and so do all the rest of our team."

"Well...I don't know what Diana has planned." Scott turned to his partner.

"Yes, that's fine if you want to. I'd like to watch you, too. I've never seen you play."

"OK. I'd like that, but I didn't bring any soccer shoes. I almost did, then decided against it."

"That's OK, we'll get you some," replied Andy. "Hot dog. I can't wait."

After tennis the three younger ones went swimming. Scott and Diana relaxed in the warm water. They engaged in a lot of friendly play, splashing, diving off the shoulders, and touching each other. Scott felt wonderful just being with his girl. Several times they kissed underwater. The afternoon passed quickly as the two shared companionship they each had longed for.

Supper, to Scott's relief, was an informal affair. Despite the presence of the servant, who served each dish, dress was casual and so was the atmosphere. Scott felt like he belonged rather than being an outsider, or worse, an intruder. It was a feeling of immense satisfaction and warmth to be accepted so easily. He sensed no tension, rather a feeling of being liked and accepted from every member of her family. As if this was supposed to happen, he thought. He glanced over at Diana and saw her flash him a big grin. He reached over and laid his hand on her bare leg. The look in her eyes confirmed that everything was all right.

After supper Diana asked Scott, "Would you like to walk with me around the grounds?"

"I'd love that."

Diana took his hand as they went out the door.

Behind them Mrs. Paolin looked at her husband until he met her eyes.

Words were not needed as Mrs. Paolin nodded slightly.

Once at some distance from the house, the pace of their walk slowed. Scott broke the long silence.

"You know I felt like one of the family in there. That's a great feeling. I was apprehensive about how it would be, about how I would be received."

"Mom and Dad definitely approve of you, if that's what you mean."

"Yes, that's it exactly."

"So do I."

For the first time they really kissed. It had been so long. The ardor with which they engaged told them more than words.

"I'm so glad to be here, to be with you, and to have everything be just as it is. Nothing could be more perfect. The feelings I've experienced and the reception by your family couldn't be better. It's everything I hoped for."

"I've missed you so much. I wish you could stay here the rest of the summer. I, too, feel everything is just right."

As they kissed again, Scott couldn't help himself, "I love you, Diana, I love you."

Her eyes sparkled in the moonlight as she answered him with a full embrace. She reached behind his head and twined her fingers in his sun-bleached hair as she pulled him even closer. When they drew their heads back Scott could see tears in her eyes. She couldn't talk. So he hugged her again. Finally the wave of emotion subsided enough for her to force out, "I love you, too," and break into tears.

Scott had never seen anyone like this before, but he surmised the emotions of the moment were too much for Diana to handle.

"I'm sorry," Diana apologized, wiping away her tears with her finger. "I don't mean to fall apart on you. I'm just so happy."

"I love it. Don't be sorry. I like seeing the depth of your emotion. It tells me what I want to know."

The young lovers talked of so many things that night. It seemed they never ran out of things to say, or of thoughts they wanted to share. It was a dynamic period, yet one of peace and contentment for each. They laughed at each other's funny comments and agreed on what was important in the world. Scott was glad Diana didn't have any weird notions, that she was conservative in her views, and endorsed all the normal things in life, without being a crusader for any particular cause. That, he knew, would be a turnoff to him; something that might make his new-found love dissolve if she pursued such a course.

When they got back to the house Diana's parents had already gone to bed and Andy was out in the pool house watching TV.

"Your parents have gone to bed. That shows me they trust you. That's good."

"Yes. They always have. I have wonderful parents."

"I agree. I really like them. Andy, too. He's a riot."

"He's a mess. He was almost as excited about this visit as I was. Oh, I almost forgot to tell you that I've asked a few friends over for a small party tomorrow night. Hope that's all right with you."

"Of course. I'd like to meet them."

"Gina will be here and others, too."

"Others, too?" Scott mimicked and laughed.

After they kissed goodnight, Scott went to the pool house. He was sure he had never been happier. Ever since Joel died a shadow had been cast over his life. This was the first time the sun fully burned away the fog— that the darkness of the forest had been penetrated. Scott was happy.

"How'd it go?" Andy invited.

"Couldn't be better. She's a beautiful person. Ya'll are a wonderful family. By the way, Karen and Dawn said to say 'hi'."

"That's nice. 'Hi' back to them. They are super."

Andy and Scott stayed up another hour and a half talking. Andy was quite intelligent and had his feet firmly on the ground. Very much so, thought Scott, for a sophomore in high school.

The party the next night was a mixed bag for Scott. While he knew Diana wanted him to meet her friends and he knew it was necessary, he would have rather been alone with her. In spite of that he had a good time and met two girls who were in Diana's sorority at the University of Florida.

"So this is the famous Scott Fontaine, who swept Diana off her feet. Nice to meet you," Mimi responded when they were introduced. "I've heard so many interesting things about you from both Diana and Gina."

"Well, now that we've met, I'll be able to know who you are when you pick up the phone. I'll probably call once or twice when she's at school."

"Hi, I've heard so much about you, I feel like I know you already," Darleen, the other sorority sister, said.

Both comments made Scott feel good and reinforced in him the knowledge that Diana truly cared for him.

He overheard Darleen tell Mimi, "He's gorgeous. No wonder she's got the hots for him."

That made him chuckle, although he tried to hide the fact that he heard it because Diana, who was next to him, had to have heard it also.

When all the guests had left Diana asked, "Did you have a good time? Or was it a bore?"

"No, I enjoyed it. I liked them all. I liked Gina a lot. It seemed different now that the roles were clearly cast. And Mimi, I liked her too. I even liked Darleen, the one who said you had the hots for me."

"Scott, you're a rat. You heard."

"Of course. And I loved every minute of it."

"I'll bet you did."

They sat on the living room couch and watched TV in between times of making out. Finally, at one o'clock they kissed goodnight and parted.

The next day at the soccer scrimmage Andy introduced Scott to the coach and purposely stayed away from any praise of Scott, knowing now that it was unnecessary, that it was better not to oversell a product, and that Scott would prefer it that way.

Scott's new shoes felt good. He told them he preferred to borrow some, but Diana's family would have none of that. So they had gone shopping and the Poalins had bought Scott a brand new pair of Nikes. They rationalized that since he was doing this for Andy, they should spring for the shoes.

Diana watched Scott perform on the field. She was impressed with his cool handling of the ball and his smooth, easy gait at three-quarters speed. He looked so graceful. She could tell he really was in his element.

Scott took it easy on these high schoolers, not wanting to show them up too bad. There was clearly a difference in their level of play from his own. Not that they were bad. They were actually quite good. Still, the gap was there. Only two or three times did he put on a burst of speed. Mostly he tried to set up some of the others to score. He didn't want to hurt their pride. Still, Scott was conscious of Andy's wanting him to look good, so a few times he exhibited some fancy ballwork.

One of the fullbacks started riding Andy, telling him that his friend was OK, but no superstar; that he had played against plenty just as good. Andy didn't have any love for this guy anyway so he explained the situation to Scott and asked him for another favor.

Three minutes later Doubting Thomas was on his back and Scott had scored almost over the top of him. Andy came over and high-fived Scott as he said simply, "Thanks."

"Glad to do it," he replied with a smile.

At the end of the scrimmage Andy challenged all the players on the team to race against Scott. "I'll bet anyone of you he can beat you in a fifty-yard dash with him spotting all of you ten yards."

Scott had fun during the scrimmage and albeit reluctantly, he agreed. "But I'll run sixty to their fifty."

If the guys on the team weren't impressed with Scott beforehand, they certainly were after the race; Scott beat the closest racer by three yards.

"My goodness. I wish one of you had that kind of speed," the coach told Andy. "That's incredible."

"Yep. Told you he was quick. Fastest white boy I've ever seen."

Diana felt proud watching Scott race. She too knew he had spectacular speed. She was pleased also to hear Andy retell the story of Scott's accommodating him with that fullback he didn't like. She was warmed by the loyalty and friendship that had developed between Scott and her brother.

Later that afternoon they took Scott to the home of Thomas Edison. Scott was so impressed with that huge banyon tree that he decided the banyon tree was now his favorite type, replacing the live oak. He loved the way the large limbs were supported by 'trailers' that grew into structural supports as they touched the ground.

"Those huge limbs need that. No way the trunk could support those alone." He pointed out to Diana. "I'm impressed."

"I love to come here. It does something for me every time I come."

He put his arms around her. "I hope it makes you randy," he teased.

She pushed away laughing. "You wish."

That night they took another walk, Scott having requested it earlier during their tour of Edison's home. The strong bond of love grew larger. Scott knew, he really knew this was the person he would one day marry.

When the time came to part, it was hard for everyone—the parents more for empathy with their daughter, but they too had grown fond of Scott. Andy gave Scott a picture of himself, "To give to the girls," he said. "Maybe they'll fall in love with my picture."

Scott laughed. He would miss Andy also. Their daily singles match had gotten closer and closer. Scott told him it was a good time to leave anyway, or soon he would start losing. Andy laughed it off, but he wasn't so sure Scott wasn't right. The soccer superstar seemed to improve every day on the court.

When Scott got home the girls made him retell some of the stories—especially those with Andy—four or five times.

"He really said that?" Karen exclaimed when Scott handed her Andy's picture.

"Yep. Word for word, as I remember."

"Gosh. Can I go with you next time?"

"Me, too." Dawn chipped in.

"Oh, I don't know. We'll see."

"Their place sounds fabulous."

"When will you get your pictures back?" Karen asked. "I can't wait to see them."

"Probably in two days."

Scott could tell without their saying anything that his parents understood fully Scott's relationship by his exuberance and by what was left unsaid.

The day for tryouts for the United States national team, held at the headquarters of the United States Soccer Federation at Colorado Springs, was balmy and overcast. Invited to these tryouts were sixteen players from the regional teams and the junior Olympic development program. Upon special request from certain influential soccer people, three others were also invited. One of these special invitees was a sweeper specialist, a young black man from New Jersey by the name of Robert Hastings. It had been explained that because of his recent conversion to soccer from basketball, he was not so well known and not a part of the system that pushed the best players toward the top. The right person had been convinced to give the kid a chance, so he was flown out to Colorado for the two-day tryout.

Kori was opposed to the idea of these extra people because it would take away from the attention he wanted to give the others. Political considerations were such that he had to humor whomever it was that had foisted these three upon the two-day event.

At the beginning of the tryouts, measurements for certain physical abilities are taken: the forty-yard dash, the hundred-yard dash, the standing high jump, the running high jump, the mile run, and a shuttle run, in which each individual is required to run back and forth six times between lines ten yards apart. These times and measurements are regularly taken by the assistants and those assigned to help them. On the day of Robert's initial tryout, his recorded results for the two high jumps and the shuttle run were so spectacular that all the coaches were called together to observe. Robert's standing high jump measured forty-four and three-quarters inches, three and one-half inches higher than anyone had ever measured in the ten years this test had been done.

Kori was sitting in his office finalizing plans for the rest of the two-day period when one of the helpers came running in out of breath. "Coach,

Coach, you've just got to come and watch this one guy. You won't believe it. He can jump over my head. The other coaches sent me in here to tell you to come."

When Kori got there they had Robert redo his high-jump feat for the benefit of the head coach. This time he jumped forty-four and seven-eighths inches. When the kid from New Jersey did the running high jump he touched a spot over the marked digits. When they extended the markings and placed two coaches on chairs to observe the jump, they had him do that jump again. The registered mark was forty-nine and three-eighths inches. Never before in his whole career had Kori seen the likes of these marks. He truly was taken aback. When the coaches told him that Robert's first attempt had resulted in a mark of fifty and one quarter, he was even more impressed. The other players were incredulous. No one, but no one, had ever seen that kind of performance before. All the other players had gathered around to watch. Robert kind of laughed off all the attention. He was used to it. Every time a tryout for some kind of select team was held they always did some measurements. The high jump and the fifty- or forty-yard dash was always among them. Robert smiled inwardly; they had not yet timed him for the running events. He would show them something special there, too! Each time a measured result was announced the other players clapped and shouted encouragement. Coach Kori couldn't help but notice the effect this was having on all the other players. It was a feeling of having something special in their arsenal.

Robert's time in the forty-yard dash was 4.32, second only to team member Scott Fontaine's previous time of 4.26. That was exceptional time for a sweeper. In the shuttle run Robert had the best time of all. He seemed to be able to stop, turn around, and be at full speed in his second step. Scott was the only player faster off the line; however, he lacked Robert's turning ability. Several times during the tryouts the coaches had Scott and Robert race each other. Kori noted the positive effect this had on the players. The players sensed that no team they would face would have two players as fast as these, or one player who could jump like Robert. That jumping ability was valuable for a sweeper, the last line of defense, who often had to get up in the air to prevent a header into the goal by the other player. Heading the ball out of danger was an event that occurred many times in every game, and so the ability to get higher than anyone else was a tremendous asset. Often that could mean the difference between winning and losing a game.

CHAPTER 7

Scott's senior year was a demanding one from a lot of perspectives. For one, his studies required significant amounts of time. He was determined to graduate in the top ten percent of his class. At the end of his junior year he was ranked thirty-nine out of two hundred forty-five, so he had to improve his standing to achieve his self-imposed goal. Second, providing for time on the phone with Diana was hard. His relationship with her grew deeper as their love matured. He still called her regularly, but not every day, and lengthy conversations were minimized.

Once soccer season was over, Scott's time became a little freer. He was able to travel more often down to see her. He stayed at the Pi Kappa Alpha frat house, having gotten to know some of the brothers who dated girls at Diana's sorority house. He found he liked the brothers there nearly as well as those at his own frat house. It became well established between them that they would get married and they even talked of what kind of engagement ring Diana wanted. After a long, loving phone conversation, in which quite a few "I love you's" were exchanged, it was the right time, Scott decided, to officially pop the question. This decision was made after an extensive time of separation. Scott wanted to make it something really special, so he called Chris Peterson, his best friend and president of the University of Florida Pike fraternity. Chris was engaged to a sorority sister of Diana's.

Scott was pleased that Chris sounded enthusiastic about his plan. Chris told him, "Hell, Scott, a lot of the guys here know you so well it's just as if you are one of the brothers here. I don't see any problem. Sounds like fun. I know we can muster up at least a dozen guys."

"Great. Thanks, Chris. This is really special to me."

Scott decided on the ring and purchased it, having to finance twenty-five percent of the cost. He then made a phone call to his parents and told them he was going to Gainesville for a big weekend there. The other arrangements he knew he could make once he got there on Friday.

Scott was impressed that Chris had gotten twenty-one brothers to participate. They seemed to even be enthusiastic about the idea.

The time was set for Saturday, six-fifteen, right when Diana's sorority would be eating supper. Since it was February it would already be dark, enhancing the effect of the candles that were involved with the plan.

Chris told Scott he had gotten word to his financée at the sorority that something would be happening and for her to alert the others. What he didn't tell Scott was that something extra had been cooked up between Chris and his girl.

Scott showered, changed, and picked up Diana. Scott was so full of love for his future mate that he almost blew it by proposing that night. They went to their favorite restaurant and enjoyed prime rib under candlelight. It was romantic and certainly set the scene for following night.

"Tomorrow I'll come pick you up at seven, after you eat. I need to do some studying and I have a paper to write, so I need to study during the day. Or we can study together most of the day."

"Sure. As long as I'm with you I'm happy," Diana replied.

They studied together, mostly at the library, touching hands, sometimes talking. Scott found it difficult to concentrate and get his work done.

They ate lunch together at the sorority house, invited guests being commonplace on Saturday. Sandy, Chris's financée, winked at him when they said hello to each other. Scott smiled knowingly.

Later that afternoon when they were walking back to the sorority house, Scott asked Diana to wear her black skirt with her white sweater tonight.

"It's one of my favorites," he explained.

At six o'clock the brothers all gathered at the Pike house. Chris passed out small sheets of music and a candle to each brother. Fortunately he had purchased a couple of extras because he had forgotten to count himself and Scott when figuring the amount required.

They went through the songs once, including the portion Scott would sing solo, and rehearsed exactly what they would do. At six-ten they left the house and made the short walk to the sorority.

Chris went to the door to tell Sandy they were ready while everyone else went to the balcony overlooking the group. Fortunately the wind wasn't blowing and all the candles were easily lit.

In another minute Sandy came out of the double doors onto the balcony leading Diana and a bunch of sisters. As the fraternity started to sing, Diana didn't realize right away that all of this was for her. Only when she saw Scott out in front of the group did she realize. At that point she started crying. Scott's solo part was toward the end of the first song, and he handled it well.

When the second song began, Scott left the group, went inside, and around to the balcony. There he joined Diana as the ensemble continued. She was still crying as he kissed her.

At the moment the second song finished, Scott took his arm away from around her and reached into his pocket. He dropped to one knee, opened the box, and in a husky voice asked, "Diana Paolin, I love you so much. Will you marry me and become my wife for the rest of our lives?"

Several girls ooohed in delight as they watched Diana, one of their most popular sisters.

"Scott Fontaine, my love, I would like nothing better. Yes. Yes. Yes."

Scott got up and kissed his fiancée in front of everyone as he put the ring on her finger.

"Hip, hip, hooray! Hip, hip, hooray! Hip, hip, hooray!" shouted the brothers.

Then as Chris and Sandy had arranged, the sisters organized a response and sang their sorority anthem back to the brothers on the ground. Both Scott and Diana were surprised, not knowing of the plans.

The sorority sisters closed in on them afterward offering congratulations, many kissing both Diana and Scott.

Mimi offered, "Well, I don't know how any of us are going to top this. What a wonderfully romantic setting to get engaged! I love it. Was this your idea, Scott?"

"Yes, I wanted this moment to be something really special. Diana deserved at least this much."

"I've never seen it before," Gina asked, "How did you get the idea?"

"One of my friends at Georgia told me about one of his friends who was a part of one and he said that it really came across well."

"Well, so did this, Scott. You two make the perfect couple and I wish you all the best," Mimi gushed.

"Me too. I hope you two are really happy, and that you have lots of beautiful children." Gina said.

"Thank you, Thank you," Diana and Scott responded.

By that time the fraternity brothers had made it up to the balcony and an impromptu social happened. Many congratulated the happy couple and said how much they enjoyed this proposal and glad they were to be asked to participate.

Sandy and Chris came to them and Sandy scolded Chris. "You didn't tell me Scott was going to ask Diana to marry him."

"I know. I wanted it to be a surprise. But I thought it was neat that you got the sorority to sing back to us. Thanks."

"You were in on this?" Diana questioned Sandy.

"Yes, Chris told me they would be serenading you and us and could I make sure we would be ready. Then we decided to provide a response to the fraternity. But I didn't know you were going to pop the big question to her," Sandy answered, turning to Scott.

"Chris did exactly what I requested, except he added a little extra with you singing back to them."

"I loved it, Honey. That was the nicest thing that's ever happened to me. I loved all of it." Diana kissed Scott to cement her feeling of total contentment.

"Come on. I want to call my family and tell them. Andy has asked me three times if you've asked me yet."

"He has? OK. Then I'd like to call my family also."

"I think everyone's going to be excited, especially when we tell them how you did it."

"Dear Mr. Gaborakov:

"Not so many people know about our product yet; our advertising budget is small. As a former soccer player and having tried these shoes myself, I know the difference they can make. Three results occur: People who wear these jump higher when they change to normal footwear, leg conditioning improves, and speed improves. As you know, these attributes provide an advantage in soccer.

"In addition to the enclosed testimonials, I have personally witnessed more than twenty individuals, athletes and non-athletes alike, who used our product and reported results no less than an inch increase in jumping ability and some achieved more than a two-inch increase. I swear this is true.

"Enclosed you will find a brochure that more fully explains how to use the Strength Shoe in training and what it can do for your players. Also enclosed, obviously, is one pair of size ten shoes for you to try to really see that our claims are true.

"You may reach me at the address above for correspondence or to place an order. I can also handle any telephone orders.

"Best regards,

"Philip Emery, Assistant Marketing Director"

Kori examined the enclosed brochure and was amused at the apparent shape of the shoes. They had a very high platform under the ball of the foot. Otherwise, they mostly resembled a tennis shoe with very little heel. The shape was obviously designed to force the calf muscle to work all the time by not allowing the heel to rest on the ground. There were no special exercises one needed to do in order to reap benefits from the shoe. It made sense to Kori that the shoe could indeed provide extra muscle for jumping.

Just then there was a knock at the door and Scott Fontaine poked his head in. "Coach, can I talk to you for a minute?"

"Sure, come on in."

"My kid sister graduates from high school in two weeks and I want to be there."

"What date exactly?"

"The sixth of June. What I'd like to do is to fly home, be there for graduation, then fly to Miami to catch up with the team the day before our game with Russia, uh, the new Russia."

"What size shoes do you wear?"

"What?"

"What size shoes do you wear?"

"Size ten. Why? What's that got to do with anything?"

"Well, I need a guinea pig to try out some new style of shoes. So I'll let you go if you'll wear these special shoes just like they say to do. Oh, and we'll cover the airfare too."

"OK, deal. Where's the shoes?"

"Right here. I haven't opened them yet. Let's look."

When they got the shoes out of the box, Kori broke into a big grin. They looked funny. "Try them on."

"These? Aw, come on, coach. You're not serious?"

"What's your sister's name?" Kori replied impishly. "Try them on."

After Scott tried them on and stood up, he told Kori, "I feel like I'm leaning forward."

"Jump a few times."

"They feel different."

"They are supposed to make you jump higher when you change back to regular shoes."

"Yeah? You mean I don't have to play in these?"

"Not during a regular game, anyway."

The next day at practice Scott took a whole lot of abuse. Eddie and Ricky, teammates already, were particularly hard on him.

"What are those?" Robert inquired of Scott, pointing at his feet.

"Medicine."

"Medicine?"

"Yeah, they help cure white man's disease."

Robert laughed good naturedly, so Scott used the same line on Jebedoah with the same good results.

Kori had Lester, one of the statisticians, remeasure Scott jumping with regular soccer shoes and then with the Strength Shoes in order to establish a "before" benchmark. He jumped higher with the regular shoes. Twenty-six inches and twenty-four and five eighths inches were what was recorded and reported to the coach.

Two weeks later, just before Scott left for home, he was remeasured. "Twenty-six and one-half," Lester called out. "According to my records that's the best you've ever done."

"Let's try it with these shoes on," Scott rejoined enthusiastically as he changed back into the Strength Shoes.

"Twenty-six inches flat."

The two of them went to Kori. "Coach, you oughta order these for everyone. They work, they really work. I've gained one-half inch in my vertical leap and my legs feel springier."

"Springier? What's that?"

"My legs have more spring."

"Let me see his chart."

Lester handed him the clipboard with a grin and a slight nod of the head.

"Order one pair of shoes for every player and one for me. I want them here when we get back from Miami."

The day the shoes were passed out in the locker room was one of joking and light-hearted jesting. Word had spread quickly on the improvement Scott had obtained, so the acceptance level of the players was just slightly above tolerable.

In nine weeks' time the shoes were regarded as everyone's best friends. To a man they all felt better and all had shown improved results. The least any of them improved on their jump was three-quarters of an inch. Several had gained one and one-quarter inches. Times in the forty-yard dash showed less positive results. Three did not improve at all, but the rest demonstrated marginal improvements. Scott's time improved by one hundredth of a second.

After six months, continued advancement was observed in jumping, speed, and endurance. Robert had gained one inch on his vertical leap and Scott's forty-yard dash time was down to four and twenty-two hundredths of a second.

The coach ordered a second pair for everyone. He also cautioned them not to tell anyone about the Strength Shoes so that other teams did not find out. "Let's keep this Yankee ingenuity to ourselves, huh?" He purposely did not answer the letters of inquiry sent by Philip Emery.

Jimmy Greenawalt was excited about being chosen as one of the TV announcers for the World Cup games. He had played soccer as a youngster and loved it. In fact, that may be why he was picked, he surmised. The network was committed to provide quality broadcasting for the tournament. They picked up Kyle Rote, Jr., to work with him. Kyle would be doing the commentary, but Jimmy felt really good about being selected to do the color commentary on the announcing team.

Jimmy had just returned from the library, where he had picked up some books about soccer. Although he knew the rules, Jimmy wanted to have as much background as he could about the game and about the World Cup. He wanted to know everything there was to know about the history of the sport, the great players, the past World Cup tournaments, the great games, the upsets, and the personalities who influenced soccer history. Jimmy would know it well enough to insert factual information during the telecasts.

Helping him in his research was Sam, a good friend who often provided Jimmy with ideas to use in his commentary. They often would talk about big telecasts and bat ideas around. Sam enjoyed his part—it made him feel important, as if he impacted millions by what was said on the air—even if nobody except them knew it. Sam, for his part, was rewarded with choice seats to many of the sporting events.

Jimmy was thorough in his preparation for these big events. If Jimmy did his job properly, the viewer could be as informed as an insider. He especially wanted to enhance the viewer's perspective of what was happening on the field.

So it was that Jimmy and Sam were reading books about soccer, looking for interesting information. As something noteworthy was discovered, Jimmy or Sam would make copious notes and file them on four-by-six-inch cards for future reference.

Jimmy was looking through a book called *The Early Days of Soccer* by J.R. Fitch and Andrew Grise when he spotted something extremely interesting about the game's history.

"Hey, Sam, listen to this. 'The English used to play football on Shrove Tuesday. Large numbers of men played on each side. Often it was one town against another. This began in the third century in Britain. Anyone and everyone could participate. It was a virtual free for all. Hundreds were often on a side. There were no rules, almost any tactics were acceptable. A score was made when one side forced the ball through the opponent's goal. Violence was an integral part of the game. For that reason sometimes the game was outlawed. Various rulers tried with limited success to ban the sport. People were at times jailed for playing in a game such as this. At the end of the eighteenth century rules were introduced to make the game a little more civilized. The prevailing opinion was to make the sport one in which gentlemen could participate. Hence the rules today are riddled with references to gentlemanly behavior.' What do you think of that?"

"Extraordinary!" exclaimed Sam. "I think we can pick up on this to help the viewer understand why there is such violence at certain games, particularly in England. The English think violence is part of the game. My God, they grew up with it."

"I think I can get some mileage out of that."

"Agreed. A significant portion of your viewers will have heard of the violence over in England. There have been several tragedies over there but our public doesn't understand why it happens."

"Yes, you're right. Remind me to look up accounts of several of those incidents..."

So Jimmy and Sam spent the whole afternoon pouring over material from the books and periodicals. Jimmy had fifty ideas running through his head at once. He knew he was getting some good material. He and Sam would do this twice a week for about a month, until Jimmy felt he had enough material to work with.

Jimmy realized with a start that he ought to make sure he knew what the rules of the World Cup were. Maybe, he thought, there were differences between what he knew from his playing days and what was used for international play and specifically for the World Cup. Substitution rules were definitely different. Only two substitutes were allowed for international play. Recreation play allowed unlimited numbers of subs. Also in World Cup play he knew the subs have to come from a pre-named pool of five from the seven that are potentially available. There must be other differences, he reasoned. I'll write to FIFA and get a book of rules. Then I can make a list of the differences. After all, many of the viewers will be familiar with the rules of rec soccer.

Other ideas came to mind of ways to additionally prepare himself. He went through the records of all the previous World Cups and also sent for information on the various stadiums around the world that had been used in World Cup play.

Jimmy enjoyed the research part in preparing for this type of event. It was part of being a good color commentator. It was fun as well as challenging to learn about something new. He enthusiastically threw himself into gathering information. Two things prompted his keen desire for details: one was the letters he received after telecasts from viewers who enjoyed his work; the other was not wanting to give out incorrect information over the air. It was one thing, he hoped, that set him apart from some of the others. It was a commitment to excellence. No half-hearted attempts to prepare himself would do.

"Godfrey, Godfrey, there's someone I want you to talk to!"

"Not now, Andrew, I've got too many things to do, I don't have time. We've got the tour of homes coming in two weeks and there's way too much to do."

"I won't take no for an answer. This could have a tremendous impact on our town; much, much bigger than the tour of homes."

Godfrey was sorry he answered the phone. He hated to be interrupted, particularly when he was so busy and would be up very late that night working on plans for the tour. Yet he valued Andrew's help and wise counsel. Andrew had contributed so much to the town with his enthusiasm and energy and hard work in the chamber and other civic organizations. He knew when Andrew got enthusiastic it would be something worth listening to. He also knew he could not refuse Andrew, not after all that he had done for Godfrey, both campaigning and for helping his work as mayor of

Ashton, New Jersey.

"OK, OK, Andrew, you know I'll do it. Who is he?"

"Someone I ran into on the plane into Newark. He's an official with the United States Soccer Federation and he's in the area to talk to the city officials about hosting some World Cup games. I got him to come here and talk to us, he's here now. I'll bring him over."

Soon after, Andrew walked in with a dark-haired man in his forties and dressed in a blue blazer over gray slacks; very much what Godfrey might imagine a soccer federation official would look like—whatever that was. He was introduced as Thomas Cothern.

Andrew hurriedly explained, "One aspect of the World Cup that would involve a small community like ours was an opportunity to host a World Cup team. Each World Cup team will be scouting a location to stay and to practice and prepare for the games and generally they prefer a small-town setting to a major city. One that would not be too far away from the game site, yet tranquil enough so that the players would have peace and quiet. It would be a great opportunity to enrich the local culture with a foreign team and to claim a bit of the global spotlight that follows the World Cup. Think what it would do for our tourism," Andrew said. "The town's name could get in front of much of the United States and even the rest of the world. Over twenty-five billion people watch the World Cup each time—every four years."

"Whoa, whoa!"

Godfrey stopped Andrew because he could not keep up. He turned toward the hazel-eyed Mr. Cothern,

"Walk me through some details, please—such as, when is the World Cup? How many people are involved with a team? What would it cost us? And how could we expect to benefit?"

Mr. Cothern smiled pleasantly and patiently explained: "The World Cup will be held in the United States for the first time ever in the summer of 1994. The organization I work for, the United States Soccer Federation, is finalizing locations to play the World Cup matches. We are pretty sure we will have one group play here at the Meadowlands. The World Cup is composed of six groups of four teams, twenty-four in all. Each group plays its matches in a different locality. For instance, in Italy last year each group played its round-robin matches in a pair of cities— kind of spreading the World Cup opportunity around, giving each city a chance at the big tourism dollars that flow in.

"So each of the four teams that might play here in New Jersey would be hunting a home, a place to locate their headquarters. The teams might also spend some of their time near the location of the games—eating and even staying the night before and the night after. But they also want a relatively secluded area away from all the hubbub and noise.

"The tournament would begin in June and end in July. The teams might be here five weeks or only two and a half if they lose in the first phase, which reduces the teams from twenty-four to sixteen. The official contingents include about thirty people; eighteen players, three coaches, and perhaps another six to ten people. Then there are the officials from their own soccer organizations and also some VIPs—even the president of the country perhaps and all the families. Then, too, would come many fans and countrymen following the team, as well as media.

"The town that hosts a team would be expected to provide housing, food, communications, practice facilities, medical care, logistics, additional transportation beyond the buses and cars FIFA provides, and not the least is the financial fee paid to the team for the privilege of hosting it."

"A hosting fee, you say? How much?" Godfrey asked. "And what is FIFA?"

"FIFA is the international soccer federation—the governing body of soccer throughout the world. There are more than one hundred seventy-five member countries in FIFA. The fees—well, that depends on the team. In Italy some weaker, lesser known teams got maybe $50,000. The best teams commanded over one-half million dollars, The Brazils, the Italys, the Germanys would cost over one-half million dollars. The Rumanias, Koreas, and Costa Ricas, for example, would be on the lower end of the scale. They also garner less of the world media attention.

"How would we gain from this?" asked Godfrey.

"There's no larger sporting event in all the world. The World Cup, except for, perhaps, the Olympics, is followed by more people everywhere else in the world. More media attention is given to the World Cup than to the Olympics because it is one event with all participants and teams playing the same sport. The Olympics, however, are many different events. The media in World Cup analyze everything: the team, the players, the coaches, the diets, habits, where they stay, how they practice. The in-depth analysis by the media is much more extensive than what you might expect. Coverage is extended to newspapers and TV broadcasts throughout the world.

"It also involves expensive, community-wide commitment. You will provide all those services I mentioned and more without charge to the team and their officials, and to the FIFA officials. Volunteers and other help will be required and will require much time. The townspeople must be willing to accept and support this. Traffic will increase. Reporters will examine everything; interview many, many people. Inconvenience will be the norm. The team expects—and the USSF will demand—gracious and generous hospitality."

"What time frame will we have with which to plan and decide and get ready for all this?"

"In December 1993, the World Cup draw will be made and at that time it will be decided and announced which teams will play, and where.

"Almost certainly New Jersey will be chosen as one of the sites for the matches. You will then know what teams you would have playing here and could decide whom you would like to host, if any. The four teams will be placed so that each group gets one team from the best six, one team from the second group of six, one from the third group of six, and one team from the last or least-regarded teams. Part of my job later will be to help the teams find appropriate headquarter sites. You will be competing with offers from other towns for the right to host a team. Hopefully each team will have three or four interested locations wanting to provide that for them. Next year we can provide literature and helpful information for how and what to do. There are also some consultants who can be hired to help you do this. The locations for the World Cup matches will be finalized, we hope, a year and a half before the draw is made. Much will be required of the cities and the stadiums also to conform to security standards as well as capacity and FIFA regulations. All of this will be available in printed format in a timely fashion. You are really getting a preview ahead of time because the host location effort won't begin for another six months or so. Then we will go out and make presentations to communities working to develop the correct way to apply for positions as host communities."

"Whew! That's a lot to digest for one who's not so much into soccer as to be familiar with how a tournament is run."

Mr. Cothern smiled. "Much of this is fairly common knowledge in Europe and in Latin America, but is almost unknown here. We have a lot of educating to do."

"What do you think? What do you think?" Andrew asked Godfrey.

"I think its a great chance to promote Ashton. Imagine the press and TV from all over the world descending on our town. Wouldn't that be fantastic?" Cothern prompted.

"I need more time to think about this," Godfrey reflected.

Cothern looked at his watch and begged forgiveness for being on a tight schedule. "I really need to be going. I've got three meetings today and have got to move on. We'd like you to consider the opportunity if you have that interest."

Godfrey took Cothern's card and shook his hand as he thanked him for taking the time to come and talk with them.

"We will certainly consider this and consult with the appropriate leaders here in our little community. It's a big decision because it will require an extensive financial as well as personal commitment. Let's see what the flavor of opinion is here."

"All right, thanks and good luck," Mr. Cothern called back as he then walked out with Andrew to be taken to the city for his first meeting.

As Godfrey continued to work on his mayoral duties, his thoughts went frequently back to this meeting with the USSF official. Godfrey had been around enough to imagine how much work, how much preparation would be involved for the town and its people. Yet soccer had become really big here in the last six or seven years, with over nine hundred kids participating in their recreation program. Maybe, just maybe, the support would be there. He did some quick computing to figure how many people would be coming to their town and how much each could be expected to spend every day. Then using a multiplier of three and one-half he was startled to see that over $4 million would be generated in sales for their town if he included the ripple effect. "That's a figure that will grab people's attention," he concluded out loud.

Scott awoke early in the morning—too early. Once he was awake he knew it was hopeless to try to go back to sleep. His thoughts were on the big day's schedule. Thankfully the wedding was set early in the afternoon, at one-thirty. Once they were married it wouldn't be so bad. The time waiting for the wedding would be hard, though. Scott got up and showered, but didn't shave. He wanted to wait until he got dressed to shave so no signs of a beard would show in the wedding pictures. Then he went downstairs to the restaurant area for some breakfast. Chase Anderson and Marty Wilcox were still asleep in the other bed. They were the only two players who were coming to the wedding, but they were two that Scott had become fond of. Wanting a tie-in to the National team, Scott had asked them to be ushers.

When he returned from breakfast the other two still had not awakened, so he went for a walk. The air was pleasantly cool, for the day had not yet turned hot. The breeze was blowing in off the Gulf and the branches of the trees stirred pleasantly. Scott enjoyed the solitude of his walk and the time to have his own thoughts without so much distraction. The past two days had been fairly hectic getting ready. He had not had much time to himself. Today, the most important day of his life, he welcomed the chance to meditate. Eventually he recalled days spent with Joel. He remembered that day with Mr. Johnson when he and Joel had seen the scrapbook for the first time. He reviewed that fateful day of graduation that had changed him so much. Once again he knew that the Lord was in control of all things. He said a silent prayer of thanks for all the good things that had happened to him, particularly for bringing Diana into his life and for preparing this very special woman to be his wife.

Happy thoughts of good times with Joel came to mind also. He smiled when he remembered the time they had double-dated together. He drifted back to that time. Scott chuckled and shook his head as he recalled vividly the circumstances.

Joel had always been more active, more comfortable with girls than he. As a matter of fact Scott had never been on a date before his junior year. Joel had told him that was a crime, that dating girls was fun, socially acceptable, built character, and presented a challenge—much like sports. "You can't be well rounded socially, Scott, if you can't get along with girls. I can't believe you've never had a date!"

"Well, it's not exactly something I advertise, you know. It's my time. I've always been so wrapped up in sports."

"So have I, but that doesn't mean I have to miss out on some of the best things in life."

So Joel had persuaded him to ask Pamela Eichly out. Scott knew she liked him; at least, she was very friendly and spoke to him all the time at school.

They decided to double date and go to a movie. Before that first call to ask her, Joel had given him some dating tips.

"First of all, act confident; don't give away that this is your first date. Be interested in her—they like to talk. When you first see her, compliment her on something—how she looks, for instance. During the movie comment a few times on the movie; at least talk a little about something. Hold her hand and put your arm around her, she expects that. Buy her popcorn and a drink. And most important of all, when you take her home and walk her to her door, kiss her good-bye. It's all pretty easy."

So Scott worked up the nerve to call Pamela. He remembered exactly word for word what was said. "Pamela, is this Pamela?"

"Yes, who is this?"

"This is Scott Fontaine."

"Hi, Scott, how are you?"

"Fine. I was wondering whether or not you would go to a movie tomorrow night with me?"

"Yes, sure."

"You will? Great. See you tomorrow."

Scott had turned to Joel to give him the thumbs up sign and the good news only to see Joel sitting there with his hands covering his face. "What? What's the matter?"

"Not bad. Not bad. What time are you going to pick her up? You didn't give her much information."

Just then the phone rang. Scott picked it up. "Hello, this is Scott."

"Hi Scott, this is Pamela. I need to know what movie we are going to see and what time you're going to pick me up."

"I'll pick you up at eight o'clock. We're going to see *Ghostbusters* and we will be double dating with Joel and Susie."

"OK, that will be fine. I'm looking forward to it."

Scott remembered that while he was getting ready and then while waiting for Joel to pick him up that he had to pee several times from being so nervous. He laughed, too, at how many times he checked his billfold to be sure he had enough money.

Joel had not been dating Susie much before that, maybe only two or three times. Since the weather was so warm Joel had the convertible top down on the LeBaron. After they got to Pamela's house, Scott recalled the gate to the picket fence he walked through to get up to her porch. When the door opened Scott could still picture the scene. She looked beautiful! He stood there just looking at her in amazement. Finally his silver tongue checked into gear and he said, "Gosh."

Actually, as he observed her reaction, it couldn't have been a better compliment. She must have known the impact on him made all her efforts worthwhile. He did remember then to say, "You look terrific."

They got the tickets and went inside and bought the popcorn; as Scott turned to leave and enter the theater, Pamela asked him sweetly, "Aren't you going to get your change?"

"Oh yeah, I forgot. Thanks."

They found some good seats. Joel went in first, then Susie, then Pamela, and lastly Scott. They had worked that out ahead of time too. Scott had still not held Pamela's hand or put his arm around her. "Oh well, plenty of time," Scott remembered thinking. After he finished the popcorn and the drink he hung onto the cups so that he had something to do with his hands. She had not yet finished with hers. After a while he looked over at Joel and Susie—only to see them smooching.

Scott laughed as he recalled thinking, "She's going to think I'm a real Klutz—didn't give her the time of the date, gawked at her, didn't get the change, and here I sit not holding hands or anything. I've got to—want to—hold her hand. She looks so nice."

He then looked at her profile. Pamela turned and smiled at him. Now's the time, he thought. Here I go. Here I go. I'm just going to reach out and hold her hand. I'm just going to grab her hand. It's right there on her sweater on her lap. Scott looked over at Joel again; he had his arm around his date. Scott's hands began to perspire. He wiped them on his pantlegs from his thigh down toward his knees to dry them off. On three. Ready. One, two, three, four, five....

Idiot. Ready. One, two three. Scott reached over and grabbed Pamela's hand and pulled it up to the armrest. Pamela turned once again to him and smiled as she disentangled her sweater from their clasped hands.

Scott and Pamela stayed that way until the movie ended. Scott at least felt like the pressure was off. Afterward Scott again took her hand, the other hand, to walk out of the theater.

On the drive home Scott again recalled how Susie sat right next to Joel in the front seat, while he and Pamela were spaced a bit apart from each other in the back. At her house they got out and Scott walked Pamela up to her door.

Scott recalled once again the feeling he had as he stood there talking to her. He was telling her about his soccer. He wanted to be kissing her, but instead stood there making small talk. She just stood there patiently. In his mind he was saying Kiss her, dummy, kiss her. At one short pause Scott leaned forward and kissed her on the lips. "Goodnight," he muttered.

She smiled and said, "Goodnight."

Scott felt terrific! The adrenaline was flowing. The next few moments were crystal clear in his mind. He jumped off the porch, skipping the three stairs, and ran down the walk. His left foot kind of slid on some mud but he kept his balance and ran forward feeling great. The picket fence was only a little over three feet high. Adrenaline flowing, feeling super, Scott decided to jump the fence. He noted afterward that he almost always takes off on his left foot. This time his right foot happened to be the one at the right place to jump the fence. He guessed he wasn't used to picking up his right foot and that's why he didn't quite clear the fence. The feeling that he had looking up at the other two laughing at him was embarrassing. He really didn't care, though. The mission was accomplished.

"Way to go, lover boy."

Once they had dropped off Susie, Scott and Joel laughed about the whole evening as Scott related what had happened throughout the date.

Scott's reflection on the times of growing up with Joel was refreshing to him. He wiped the wetness out of his eyes and looked down at his watch. He had been walking half an hour. He turned and headed back to the hotel.

When he got to his room, Chase was on the phone with Andy. He was making arrangements to play tennis in about an hour. Scott nodded his assent when Chase glanced up at him. Andy was to bring four racquets and some balls. Chase and Marty hurried up and got dressed while Scott changed into some tennis clothes. Scott forgot that he had his racquet, but knew that an extra racquet wouldn't hurt. It would be good to play to take his mind off this afternoon and make the time pass more quickly.

Andy loved being with the guys. Getting to know Chase and Marty had been a real treat for him. Marty kept him in stitches at the rehearsal and the dinner afterward. Andy thought Marty was the next best thing to sliced bread, Scott figured. He viewed Andy as one who enjoys life and certainly one who likes to be with older guys, especially good athletes. When Andy found out Chase had played tournament tennis he had told him that he would call in the morning to set up a game.

Marty knew he was outclassed on the court as soon as he saw the others start hitting. He was teamed up with Andy, who maybe was the best, but he realized who the weak link was going to be. The four had a good time together; the points were competitive even if the final result wasn't. Andy told Scott that was his wedding present from him. Marty more than made up for his lack of tennis skills by supplying much of the good-natured commentary that ran throughout the match. All agreed it had been fun and a good way to spend the morning. At eleven-thirty they quit in order to get ready on time.

Marty and Chase left for the church before Scott, having to be there one hour before the wedding to perform their ushering duties. Scott had let them finish in the bathroom first. He was going to ride with his parents, who were staying in this same hotel. Scott called his parent's room to confirm the exact time for departure.

"Well, how's it feel to be almost married?"

"Feels pretty good. Have the girls already left?"

"Yes, Gina came by about ten minutes ago and picked them up. They were so excited. They tried to call your room about an hour ago but no one answered."

"We went to play tennis. Andy came and picked us up."

"Oh. Too bad Karen and Dawn didn't know that. They would have gone, too."

"I should have thought of that myself. I'm sorry."

"Well, don't worry about it. The girls are going to get to play with Andy tomorrow at their house. They can't wait."

"I'll bet this whole thing has really been a blast for them."

"They said last night how much fun they were having. They feel right grown up."

"That's good. Is Mom there? I'd like to say something to her."

"Sure, just a moment."

"Hi, Scott, how are you doing this morning?"

"Fine, just fine. It's hard to not want the time to hurry."

"The wedding will happen soon enough now. It's only one hour away. Daddy said to tell you we're leaving in ten minutes. Will you be ready?"

"Yes, I just have to put my cummerbund and jacket on. I'll come to your room when I'm ready."

People were filing into the church when the Fontaines got there. Scott's mom and dad went to the back of the church while Scott went in the side door near the Sunday school rooms. Mr. Fontaine joined him in a few minutes, having deposited his wife with the other women.

"Diana looks absolutely magnificent."

"Does she? I can't wait to see her in her wedding gown."

"All the bridesmaids are here, and so are all the ushers."

"No one got lost, huh?"

"No."

"Did you remember the ring?"

"Not sure. Let me see."

"Aw, Dad."

When the right time came for them to go out into the sanctuary, Scott felt relieved. It was finally here! They went and joined the minister and turned to face the back. Scott could see the bridesmaids lined up at the door. Dawn was in front with Karen just behind her. Both of them had been looking for Scott and gave him their biggest smiles. Scott could tell they were excited. The wedding coordinator was standing alongside of Dawn.

"Here she comes!" Scott watched Dawn walk alone up the aisle. Then came Karen. Karen was a doll. One by one the bridesmaids came up the aisle. Scott looked at his mother to see how she was handling this. So far she was not crying, but he figured that would happen soon enough. Scott knew where his emotional side came from.

Then he saw Diana and her father. The wedding coordinator was straightening out her gown. Then the music started that Scott so long had wanted to hear. Diana was beautiful. She looked positively radiant. The white dress was truly the right one for her. Boy, does she look good! he thought.

At last he heard the minister pronounce the words "...man and wife. You may kiss the bride."

Scott raised the veil and kissed Diana for all he was worth. Then they turned to face the audience as the minister said, "I now present Mr. and Mrs. Scott Fontaine."

The reception was at the house. If the grounds looked good before, they now were wonderful. Several tents had been set up for people to get out of the sun. Flowers were everywhere. The caterers had five different stations set up, forming a circle about sixty yards in diameter, each with five cloth-covered tables holding different kinds of food. There were crab claws and shrimp and oysters and scallops at one table, cheese and crackers and small sandwiches at another, fresh fruit cocktail at another, an array of hors d'ôeuvres, including chicken and water chestnuts wrapped with bacon occupying the last two. At both ends of each station also was a young lady serving punch. Then there were three bars set up, two at opposite sides of the circle and one very close to the pool house. Two bartenders dressed in tuxedos manned each one. Wandering among the guests was a quintet of violinists, softly playing a variety of popular and light classical music.

The wedding party was the last group to arrive. A procession of nine vehicles brought the group from the photo session at the church. When Marty and Chase saw the expanse of the layout, they came over to where Scott and Diana had just emerged from their limousine.

"Boy, you hit the big time," Marty declared. "Diana, is this your family's summer cottage or did ya'll live here, too?"

Diana laughed good-naturedly. "This is where I grew up. Of course, we didn't have the tents back then."

"Why do you guys think I married her?"

"Some sure have it made."

The photographer stayed busy taking pictures all afternoon. Arrangements had been made for an aide with a tape recorder to be with the photographer when he took pictures, taking down on tape people's names and hometowns so that duplicate pictures could be sent to them later.

Scott and Diana enjoyed the reception. It was a good time to visit with relatives they had not seen in a long time and to meet each other's extended family. The moments spent with friends from high school and college were great, too. Diana later told Scott that six hundred and twenty people had been invited and that they expected almost five hundred to come. Scott could see that Chase, especially, but also Marty, were enjoying themselves. Chase was in his element. Not only was he flirting with the bridesmaids but also most of the other young, attractive ladies that were present. There were a lot of them too, Scott noted.

Karen and Dawn were having the best day of their lives. They had never participated in a wedding before or seen anything quite like this reception. Since both were outgoing and enjoyed a good party, this occasion maxed out their abilities. Sometimes Dawn would come running over to Scott to tell Diana and him about some wonderful new experience she had just had. Then, too, the girls were having a good time with Joel's two sisters. Scott was glad that his sisters were enjoying the festivities.

Scott made it a special point to introduce Mr. and Mrs. Adams and Ashley and Amanda to the Paolins and others. He noted that his mom and dad were careful also to include them as often as they could. Scott knew it must be a bittersweet day for them. He was glad they had accepted the invitation and had come to the wedding, but felt sorry for the feelings they must have, and that Susie couldn't make it.

At four-fifty Scott and Diana left the reception to change in order to leave on time for the airport. They were flying to the Virgin Islands for their honeymoon. All the guests gathered around the limousine to see them off. The young couple tried to remember all the faces they saw as they drove off. Everyone was happy.

CHAPTER 8

One thing the coach really liked about coaching for the United States was the ready availability of superior resources. More so than with any other job he had, Kori felt the U.S. was capable of providing special equipment and other items to make training more valuable and to better analyze game technique and strategy. From the availability of those things developed a support group that had come to be called the "techno team." Chief in their responsibilities was to develop computer programming and the computer hardware tied to the filming of the games that would enable the coaching staff to thoroughly analyze play. Statistics of their own players as well as those from other teams could be entered into the computer and analyzed fully.

The coach planned with the techno group to evolve the statistical analysis to even a greater degree of precision. He would know how many times the other team brought the ball up the right side and how many times up the left, and then how many times straight up the center. Did the other team tend to try for fast breaks? He would know exactly how many in each of the games they played. When a player received a ball and was closely defended, which way would he make his move to get around the defender behind him? The computer would have that as well. He knew the computer would prove more helpful against the European teams than the teams from Latin America because the Latin teams were more extemporaneous. There was no telling who would be in their World Cup group this next time.

Coach Kori had shared with Scott and the other players just exactly what the techno group was doing in order that they would have confidence in the final output that would guide their preparations for each opposing team. These practice tours were not only for the players to practice against other nations; the techno team was working very closely with the coach to develop the statistics gathering to make them more meaningful.

In the 1990 World Cup the United States was grouped with three European teams. In ninety-four it could be any assortment of teams. They would have to be prepared to play whomever was in their group. One thing for sure, there would be at least one very good team somewhere in their group. FIFA seeded all the teams. Each team was ranked as the best six teams, the second best six teams, the third best six teams, or as the lowest rated six teams. These were then drawn with one team from each category playing in a group of four teams. In 1990 the group with the U.S. in it was considered the weakest group *because* the U.S. was in it. Coach Kori acknowledged to his players that would be the case this time. As host, the U.S. would be seeded as a "best" team. Although articles were appearing in international soccer publications extolling the improvement in the North American contingent, on the merit of the team's play, they did not deserve a top seed. Several scribes were now predicting the U.S. might just make it into the second phase of the World Cup tournament. Still, it was the prevailing opinion that the host team—for the first time ever—would not be a serious contender for the title.

Coach Kori and the U.S. Soccer Federation were hoping that by employing the very latest in technological advances, the odds could be shortened a bit. They planned a scouting program that was second to none. As much as could be known about the players and the teams would be tracked, analyzed, and studied prior to the start of the tournament. Every game played in the World Cup would be filmed and analyzed. The computer would identify weaknesses and strengths of each of the teams, further modifying the information as more and more games were analyzed. The computer could even project the effect of substituting one player for another against a particular team. Every vulnerable area against a potential opponent could be emphasized in practice in an effort to shore up that weakness. The U.S. Olympic committee became very much involved in this techno research early and, when the soccer people saw that, it became a joint effort between the Soccer Federation and the Olympic Committee.

This techno analysis had developed from a takeoff of programs used by several teams in the NFL and the major leagues for baseball. Some of the best soccer coaches in the country had been called in to help set up the structure of the program to analyze play. Three new programming whiz kids were hired to implement every new concept that made it past the approval committee, consisting usually of the coach, one assistant, and one consultant. Not only did they adapt the programming to soccer, but they further refined it.

Many of the other international teams knew the U.S. was doing an inordinate amount of scouting. Their representatives were everywhere. League play in Italy, Germany, England, Brazil, and Argentina all saw two man camera crews attending the games. International contests often had multiple cameras from the U.S. filming the contests, the various leagues having rebuffed their attempts to obtain films of those contests.

"Where are you going this time, Scott?"

"We are going to Mexico, Honey. We play three games. The first is in Juarez against their National Team. The second will be in Guadalajara against a second division all-star team. Then the third will be in Mexico City against their National Team again. I'm looking forward to the trip. It will be my first time in Mexico."

"Scott you know I worry about you when you travel. It isn't bad enough you are away and have to fly, but you also go to some of the most out-of-the-way places. Do you know what hotels you will stay at in Guadalajara and Juarez?"

We'll stay at the Hacienda Hotel in Juarez and the hmmm, let's see. Aha, here it is. At the Palacio Real Hotel in Guadalajara. I'm sure it's going to be very nice."

"I guess I shouldn't worry, but I do. I suppose it is necessary for the team, and you *are* getting to see lots of new places.

"It is necessary, even essential, for the team to get as much international experience as possible. Mexico always has a strong World Cup team. They will no doubt be a strong test for our team. It may be also that they will be the team to represent the Concacaf in the World Cup in addition to the U.S."

"The what?"

"The Concacaf. That's the North American, Central American, and Caribbean region in the World Cup qualifying. Two teams can qualify from that region, one of which must be the U.S. this time because we are the host country. The World Cup tournament is the best twenty-four teams that qualify for the event. There may be as many as a hundred and fifty nations that attempt to qualify. At the Italian World Cup the U.S. qualified second to Costa Rica."

"That sounds impressive. Well, have a good time, Sweetie. Good luck and have a safe trip. I love you." Scott's wife hugged him and kissed him goodbye.

There was excitement in the air as all the team gathered at the Marriott Hotel in El Paso the night before they were to cross into Mexico. Although they had gotten consistently beaten in Europe on an eight day tour, no team had beaten them badly, and they had beaten Hamburg two to one in their best game. By the end of the tour they were playing the teams almost even. That contrasted with the first couple of games, in which they had been blown away: three–nothing and four–one. Despite being forewarned by Kori, they had been illprepared for the quick transition game employed by the Europeans. In the last two games the players had learned to adapt and to defend that kind of game. That was the whole purpose in the team going to Europe.

Then in the Marlboro Cup back home the team lost to Mexico, then beat Canada. The game with Mexico could have gone either way, but the U. S. had dominated Canada, outshooting them twelve to two. There had begun a growing feeling of confidence that they could play with the big boys. The new coach from Yugoslavia had already made a difference. After each of the games they played, the team reviewed the films together, looking at the mistakes that had been made and copiously discussing even the minutest detail of the strategies employed by the opposition. He also taught them some complicated transitional maneuvers. A zillion practice sessions succeeded in moving the field further up—that is, keeping most of the activity closer to the opponents goal. The coach had also analyzed the team members and pinpointed their strengths. Plays were designed to utilize those strengths. He had been very impressed with Scott's speed.. Now they had several new ways to utilize that speed.

In the Marlboro Cup tournament the new coach's techniques had made a difference. Twice Canada displayed a pattern that the U.S. fullbacks recognized and had practiced against. They stopped one or two goals because of the coaching techniques.

So it was with very high spirits that the team had met in El Paso. Most of them had a week off prior to this trip. The midfielders and several of the players on the fringe of making the roster and three or four new faces had practiced this past week. All of the ones who had a week off stayed active, however. The desire to exceed and to please their new coach, if not the need to stay on the team, was sufficient motivation. Some of the new players were pressing hard for positions. They all would be at peak conditioning, for soccer was a game of endurance. Each one had enough experience to realize the value of being in tip-top shape.

The Europeans had shown them what that could do. At the end of several of those games, it became obvious that they were in better shape than the Americans. The players had all received weighted jackets upon their return to the United States and were told to wear them as they trained. Each one weighed approximately forty pounds, although those of the larger players had slightly more weight than the smaller players. Too, each player got a set of ankle weights. Scott could feel the difference as he ran his six-miles-a-day workout, especially when he ran the sprints before and after his run. The first three days he had to take off the weight jacket to run stadium steps. He was so exhausted that he feared he would fall down the steps if he left it on. But by the fourth day he was able to carefully negotiate the stadium steps with the jacket on. By the end of ten days it was almost as if he no longer had the extra weight. He had gotten used to it. It was funny, Scott noted, all the players upon getting back together had acknowledged the same result: extreme soreness the first couple of days, but at the end of the week a kind of getting used to the extra burden. Almost all had admitted the extra weight gave them a feeling, true or not, that they were now in better shape than before. Each had related their own efforts to cope with the additional burden. Some had given the jacket a nickname. One had called it the elephant, another the baby grand, but a couple used the term "monkey." It seemed better to say "they had the monkey on their back." They all were glad to play some games instead of having to run with the monkey.

As the players arrived one by one from their various rooms they congregated in the hotel lobby, waiting for the predetermined departure time. Scott felt a renewed sense of direction among the team. That they had all suffered the same experience at the same time—although separately—seemed to do something to draw them together. If they had not all sensed the same gain in physical fitness, the experience might have provided them all with a common hatred for the dreaded monkey. Scott had the feeling they would be given more opportunities in the future to share that most pleasant of experiences.

Scott saw Chase approaching and gave him a warm hello smile.

"Morning Scott."

"Morning."

"I don't know about you, but I'm psyched up to kick butt down there in Mexico."

"I feel the same way. Somehow I think most of the team feels this way."

"Coach has a way to do that ya know?"

"He understands people very well."

Across the lobby Eddie and Ricky were cutting up. "Those two always seem to be in a good mood and ready for anything."

"Yeah, know what you mean."

"Everyone seems relaxed. No one is uptight. That's good."

The team left the hotel and went down Airway Road to have breakfast at a place called The Village Inn. The coach required everyone to eat breakfast and over time had learned it was almost impossible to make everyone eat if the meal was taken at the hotel. Invariably someone would skip the meal to get a little extra sleep. So the schedule now included time to stop and eat breakfast.

The Mexican Soccer Association had assigned a tour host for the American contingent named Sergio Villarreal, who was seated at Scott's table. It was his job to help facilitate their travel arrangements, getting them through customs and assisting with hotel and other transportation arrangements. The players took to him right away. He was very personable and liked a good time. He was telling some of them of the good night spots in Juarez and Mexico City. He was going to have a good time and anyone else who wanted to was welcome to join him. He said this was his first try at this sort of thing so he didn't know what was supposed to be done or not supposed to be done. So he wouldn't let a little matter of rules stand in his way to help them enjoy themselves. So long as they could do things within what rules Coach Kori set for them Sergio wouldn't be the one to slow them down.

The entourage took up eight or nine four man booths with several taking a two man booth. When Scott saw double blueberry pancakes on the menu he knew what he was going to order. He loved blueberries. Some of the other guys had known Scott long enough that they could predict that's what he would get. Scott happened to sit in a booth that included their tour guide Sergio, Robert Hastings, and Terry O'Shay.

In the adjacent booth Scott could hear nothing but laughter. Together there were Eddie Jackson, Ricky Breeland, Jebedoah Wright, and Marty Wilcox. Anytime you put Eddie and Ricky together, that's what you're going to get, Scott said to himself. Adding Marty is just like pouring gasoline on a fire. Jebedoah wasn't doing much talking; he was always laughing. He was kind of quiet. Jebedoah was the second black on the team. "It was funny though," Scott thought, "that Robert and he weren't really friends. Derrick White was the third black on the squad and perhaps was a little closer to Robert than he was to Jebedoah."

"Hey, hey, I got another one," Ricky said. "These three drunks were staggering home after a long session in their favorite bar. They got lost and happened upon some railroad tracks. As they were following the tracks one said, 'Thish sure is a long shet of stairs.' 'That's not sho bad,' slurred the second. 'The worst thing ish the hand rail is sho low.' 'Well we won't have to worry much longer,' added the third. 'Here comes the elevator.'"

Jebedoah spoke up. "I've got a good one. This guy was hunting in Africa with his gun-bearer. It was getting dark and they had been hunting all day without success. From somewhere close by they could hear the repeated roar of a large lion. They could tell he was getting closer. All of a sudden the gun-bearer sat down and changed his boots to put on sneakers. The hunter exclaimed, 'What are you doing? You can't hope to outrun that lion, even with those on.' 'I don't have to outrun the lion,' he answered. 'I just have to outrun you.'"

"Hell, no wonder you like that one," Eddie shot back, laughing.

Later that day, as the players stepped off the bus and walked inside the Hotel Hacienda in Juarez, there were a lot of favorable reactions. Scott and Chase were two of the first ones into the lobby, followed closely by Eddie and Ricky.

"Awwrright," came the remark from Eddie, as he looked around.

Scott was mentally agreeing with him. Behind the lobby of the hotel was a figure-eight pool that looked inviting for later that evening. He turned to say something to Eddie and stopped when he saw Eddie staring at the girl behind the check-in counter. She was absolutely beautiful. Not just pretty, but actually stunning. Scott reckoned she'd draw quite a crowd. Her name tag showed Lucia. She looked to be nineteen or twenty years old, was about five feet two inches tall, had dark hair and dark eyes and a creamy smooth complexion. Scott all of a sudden realized what Eddie was so eloquently remarking about. It wasn't the interior of the hotel.

Eddie headed over to her. Good ole Eddie, count on him to put a move on any and every pretty girl he sees. By now most of the guys were in the lobby and were also looking around. Sergio too was headed for the counter along with the coaches. The bellboys were bringing in the luggage.

Scott heard Eddie say to the girl "Do you speak English?"

"Yes, of course. May I help you?"

"Yes, you just might could help me. I don't speak Spanish. Don't I look like someone you recognize?"

"No. No, should I recognize you?"

"Yeah. I was Paul Hogan's double in the movie *Crocodile Dundee*. I do all of his stunts. Did you see the movie *Crocodile Dundee*? Don't I look like him?"

From behind them and to the left someone said something that Scott couldn't understand. But the girl and Sergio burst out laughing. Lucia flashed her eyes up at Eddie and covered her mouth with her hand while she continued to laugh until she got under control.

Eddie asked, "C'mon, what's so funny? Tell me what he said," nodding toward the bellboy.

Scott looked over toward the bellboy who had spoken and who was now smiling broadly and showing some brown teeth. He was obviously enjoying his own remark.

"C'mon, tell me what he said, what's so funny?" Eddie repeated to the beauty behind the counter.

"He said," she answered, "you look more like the crocodile than Dundee to him."

Hearing that, the entire group laughed loudly. Scott had tears in his eyes. It was the perfect squelch.

Thus a new name for Eddie was born: Crock-a-dee-a. It was a mixture of Spanish and English, but it stuck.

"Hey Eddie, your reputation has preceded you here," someone called out.

Another called out "Eddie you've been upstaged by a bellboy."

Eddie shot back. "Look at her, she loves it. Hey baby what are you doing after work tonight? Let's go have a drink."

"Thanks, but I've already got plans."

Sergio watched Eddie carefully, looking for any signs of animosity. Instead of getting mad or withdrawing and sulking however, Eddie just seemed buoyed up all the more. He was laughing too. Sergio couldn't help but marvel at the mood and comraderie that prevailed among the players. He could see the team was going to have a good time on this trip, and so was he. Sergio knew he would be asked questions by the trainer of the Mexican National team. He had been primed beforehand. Who were the leaders? What was their mood? Did they argue? Were there any fights? Were they tense and uptight? Had they discussed any strategy? Sergio knew his answers would not be what the trainer for the Mexican team wanted to hear. He hoped he was not asked in front of the team.

Scott leaned over toward Marty and spoke softly. "Marty, have you read the book *Wind in the Willows*?"

"No. Why?"

"The main character in that book is Mr. Toad. It's a children's book and is an allegory—all the characters are animals. Mr. Toad has a personality that can't be deflated. No matter what bad things happen to him Mr. Toad bounds back from adversity and setbacks just as cocky and sure of himself as before."

"Eddie?"

"Yeah. Look at him. You'd never think the bellboy just put him down. He's still trying to flirt with her."

"She is gorgeous. I don't blame Eddie for trying. I don't think I've seen ten women in my lifetime as pretty as she is."

Eddie was, in Scott's opinion, the visual epitome of the southern rebel. With his beard he was exactly the image Scott thought of when he envisioned a rebel in the War between the States climbing over the embankments, going into battle. Except for soccer, Scott didn't know anything Eddie took seriously, unless you counted chasing after women. Scott didn't like the language Eddie or Ricky used but he knew he wasn't going to change that. Ricky was a redneck cowboy who participated in rodeos in off times. Bronco riding was his specialty, Scott recalled.

The whole team got registered and settled in their rooms. Lunch would be at one o'clock, and they were all to meet in the lobby at five minutes to one. The coach had them all set their watches because time in Juarez differed by one hour from time in El Paso. The guys were allowed to pick their own roommates. They slept two to a room. The newest players were having to select a roommate right there in the lobby. Most of the older roommates knew with whom they would be staying, although some changing around did occur on each trip; the players sometimes just wanted to get to know someone else a little better. However, Eddie and Ricky always stayed together on every trip.

The game that day was scheduled for five in the afternoon. Everyone had already been given the timetable. They would leave the hotel at three-fifteen. The stadium was about one half hour from the hotel, even in traffic. "Dress for the game in your hotel rooms," the coach had announced during lunch. "Wear white tops and blue shorts...blue socks also." The coach knew from experience that some of the locker rooms were not the best in the world—sometimes even lousy, compared to what they were used to in the U.S. Some had no lockers, they just had hooks. Of course it was not wise to leave any valuables in the locker room. One of the team manager's jobs was to keep the "lock box" with him at all times. Everyone put their wallets, watches, and other valuables in there. It was a team rule, in fact, that all valuables were kept in there when not on one's person. They could not be left in the room or on the bus or anywhere else. That way things didn't disappear. Another little travelling rule the coach liked was to assign everyone a number. Kori was number one, the two assistants two and three, Scott was number four and everyone else had a number, with the managers having the last two. When boarding a bus or a plane the coach had everyone "sound off" and call out their number. You didn't mess around during that little procedure. One time someone did and the coach suspended him for the next game. By sounding off the coach always knew who was missing. He liked it better than having someone count heads.

The game that day was not a physical game as such. The Mexicans used superior ball handling to forge a two to nothing lead. Then the U.S. scored a goal on a shot by Scott that Chase deflected into the goal. The second U.S. goal was a gift. On a corner kick by the U.S. contingent, a Mexican player got jostled and headed the ball into his own goal. He had screamed at the referee afterward, claiming foul and that he had been pushed, but the goal stood. Mexico's star right wing, Francisco Orpinal, had been shut out of the offense by an aggressive picket defense that kept a man in front and a man behind him at all times. Francisco had been far and away their leading scorer, with nearly thirty-five percent of their national team's goals. With eight minutes left in the game Francisco broke across the middle, picking Eddie against one of his own teammates. Twenty feet in front of the goal he stopped as a midfielder fed him the ball. The only defender on him was the fullback just behind him. Francisco took the pass, chipped the ball up into the air—head-high—and performed his patented bicycle kick, taking the shot toward the goal, but facing away from the net. Robert, the substitute sweeper for the U.S., recognized the situation, however, and raced across behind Francisco just as he was kicking the ball. Right when contact with the ball was made, Robert leaped. The ball caught him flush in the chest and bounded away; Eddie cleared it out of harm's way.

The sizeable crowd roared in excitement for the two outstanding plays—one by their star forward and one by the gringo substitute. The Mexican coach was amazed. He had never seen that shot blocked before. The U.S. defender must have leaped one meter or more into the air to get up high enough to block that with his chest. It was certainly one of the most outstanding defensive plays he had ever witnessed. He turned to his assistant and said something about designing a way to keep the sweeper away the next time that opportunity came up.

The game ended tied two apiece. The U.S. team and its coach were elated. This Mexican team was considered to be as good as any of the teams in Latin America except for Brazil, Argentina, and possibly Uruguay. Scott knew this team was the one to beat to qualify for the one open spot in the Concacaf region. Only Costa Rica was considered to be a serious threat to this team to challenge for the qualifying spot. True, Mexico had actually outplayed the Northern team and they had outshot the U.S. twelve to eight, but corner kicks were about even and time of possession was nearly the same.

Coach Kori was pernickety about what charts were kept. Missed passes, fouls—whether called or not—good plays, bad plays, all of these were what the coach kept up with during each game. One assistant coach kept a plus and minus chart, the plus for each good play and a minus for each bad play or mistake. It often served as the basis for deciding starter role status for a player. The computer kept all the records so that the coach could weigh each statistic as he liked. It also allowed him to evaluate trends and to practice to head off problem areas. The techno team continued to refine the analysis of play.

Peculiar to itself was the goalkeeper position. The keeper coach kept his own set of charts and data separate from the rest of the charts. Goalies are much like kickers in football. They have their own training regimen, they practice apart from the other players at times, sometimes they are treated differently, and often they are loners. Cornell, the starting goalkeeper for the United States tended to be more a part of the team than most goalies.

The game today told the coaches the value of the scouting report and computer analysis. Robert Hastings admitted afterward that he recognized the situation from the tendency chart on Francisco. He said, "I just took a chance that he might try that. He's a bit of a hot dog and the situation seemed right for him to take it." Other players echoed the feeling that they were helped by knowing more of the opposition than what they were used to. A tie today was considered a good performance because Mexico not only had a good team, but they also played well in the contest. The level of play had been brought up to that of the Mexicans. The next game in a few days would be even more telling. The local team would definitely be more motivated to win in their capital city. If they were taking the Northern bunch lightly, that would be rectified the second go-round. Kori gave instructions that the stats on today's game be entered into the computer as soon as possible and run through the analysis programs. He knew the output would be ready early in the morning.

For dinner that night both teams were treated by the Mexican Soccer Federation to a meal at a restaurant that specialized in seafood. Several of the players ordered lobster after having it explained that it was the specialty of the house. Marty was one of those, but he knew he would have ordered it anyway, that being one of his favorite meals. He sat at a table that included Sergio, Scott, Chase, Fong, and a couple of Mexican players. Fong had already gained a reputation for prodigious consumption of food after games, so the guys were in a light mood as they kidded him about how he was going to satisfy himself tonight.

"I don't know about you Fong, but I'm really hungry," Marty Wilcox baited Matt. "I think I'll just eat the shell and all when my lobster comes."

Fong tended to giggle when teased. He seldom answered such challenges, nor was he offended easily.

Chase was sucked right in. "You can't do that. No one eats the shell. I'll wear my skivvies backwards for a week if you eat the whole shell."

"You're on."

Something about the way he said it made Chase question those stories he suddenly remembered about Marty eating strange things.

Only one or two of the guys even have a chance to know I always eat the shell when I have lobster, Marty said to himself.

Sure enough, when the food was served Chase made sure Marty got the biggest lobster.

Even though they knew it was going to happen, the other players at the table couldn't help but cause a scene when Marty started eating. The sounds of the shell cracking made them all laugh. Soon players from other tables started coming over to see what the commotion was all about. Then people from other parts of the restaurant came to see if it was really true—that someone was eating the shell of the lobster.

When the waiter came around to check if they wanted more bread or water, his eyes grew wide with surprise. He started to laugh. The six players at the table got a kick out of his reaction. In a moment the waiter disappeared but soon returned with the chef and three others. There was no question that Marty had become the center of attention.

The nickname "Lobster" stuck on Marty from that moment on. Scott knew he was in the company of one of the great characters he had ever met in his life. He couldn't wait to tell Diana about him.

Intuitively, Coach Gaborakov felt uncomfortable with the sweeper position. He had initially opted for experience in that area that formed the heart of the defense. Reluctantly he released the most experienced member of the squad, having made the decision to add Robert. He wasn't sure whether Robert would even get to play in the tournament games, but he just couldn't pass up someone like that. Too, the chemistry with Robert on the team might prove to be better. Gregg, the sweeper Kori let go, seemed to hold some resentment that the coach didn't keep more players from the national team three years ago.

Kori consulted with his assistants later that night and told them of his feelings about starting Robert every game for a while to see how he developed. "Robert's lack of experience is his only drawback. He has good instincts, he just doesn't recognize situations quickly enough to prevent them from happening—at least at this level of play. The advantage the techno team gave the U.S. squad might just make up for some of that. This was evidenced today with Robert's block of the bicycle kick shot. Now was the right time to give him that chance. One or two spectacular plays like the one Robert made today would keep the adrenalin flowing in the other players. God only knows that we're going to need a lot of that when we play in the tournament. I feel at least we need to see if he can develop the way he has the potential to do."

Robert Hastings was an interesting addition to the team, having grown up near Trenton, New Jersey, and being an outstanding basketball player. In fact, he was sixteen years old before he ever played any soccer. The coach of his high school team invited him to come play when two of their star players got hurt. He made the basketball coach mad by playing two sports at once, but he decided "if Bo could do it, so could he." It at least offered Robert the opportunity to learn the game. He was put on defense because he did not have the usual ball-handling skills of the others. That high school coach realized right away he had something special. Robert progressed so rapidly in his junior year that he made second string allstar for the eight teams that formed their high school league. He developed into an aggressive, attacking defenseman who intimidated many of the opposing players with his size and athletic prowess. His superior speed and jumping ability astounded all who observed his play.

Scott was really impressed with Robert's athletic ability. He knew Robert was really the better athlete, and there weren't many that he would put in that category. I'll bet Kori thinks he can teach him enough between now and the tournament to allow him to contribute, Scott guessed.

Not surprisingly, Robert was to have several strategy sessions with the coach as Kori worked to hone the rough potential. The talent was clearly there, only experience was lacking.

Robert took the news of his starting very positively. He told the coach, "Thanks, I welcome the chance to get more game experience and to prove myself worthy. I am sure that I will make some mistakes, but I hope I will continue to improve at a very rapid pace. I appreciate the opportunity. Ever since I watched the World Cup play in Italy, this is something I wanted to do. I want to play for my country."

Scott talked to Robert when they were back at the hotel. "Robert, I understand you are going to get more playing time. That's good. You will get no better opportunity to learn than from Coach Gaborakov and in playing international contests. From what I know of your background you've come a long way in a short time."

"Thanks Scott, one big worry I've had was whether a newcomer like me would be resented or not."

"You won't be resented if you can help the team."

"Well I know that if one new person is added to the team, that means someone leaves the team. That person may be very popular and good friends with many."

"You can't worry about that. We all understand that each of us is only on the team until someone better comes along to displace us. Heck, when Coach Gaborakov took over the Costa Rican team he made at least a half a dozen changes less than eight months before the start of the Cup."

"Thanks. This is something I've really wanted to do. I'm an intensely patriotic person and want nothing better than to play for my country. I get tears in my eyes when I watch the Olympics, knowing how proud they feel to have won a medal for their country. When the National Anthem plays I'm a basket case. I can envision the feelings, the emotions of those standing on the platform accepting their gold medal. I'm a real turkey at times like that. I even cry when I watch all kinds of movies. It doesn't even have to be particularly sad and I cry. I've never seen another man as emotional as I am."

"I might just give you a good race. Anyway, welcome aboard. I think you will prove to be a real asset to our team."

The rest of the tour through Mexico went very well; the team showed consistent improvement. Coach Gaborakov told the players he was very pleased.

Alex had just turned eighteen and was enjoying the celebration with the other guys. The Costa Rica Junior World Cup Team was in Brussels playing some elimination rounds that would advance them to the final phase of the Junior World Cup to be played in Sweden. They had beaten Israel, Romania, and Paraguay. If they beat France, they would advance to the quarterfinals. The coach had just concluded a team meeting in which the message he had delivered to the players was one of satisfaction of how the team had played. He reminded them to maintain their level of intensity and to concentrate on the transition game. Against France the key would be to score first. Although a good team, France had on occasion gotten rattled when they fell behind.

Alex left the meeting and went with Ramon, Jorgé, Paolo, and Manuel out to a nightclub. Tonight they had a one A.M. curfew since there was no game the next day. Tomorrow night they knew curfew would be at eleven P.M. and their time would be limited.

The group made their way down to the Grand Place area of the city, only two and one-half blocks downhill from the central railway station. Ramon was in his glory at the Grand Place. An aspiring architect, he was fascinated with the buildings arranged to form a square in the interior. From the giant cathedral with the many stone figures carved on the front to the gilded facade on the ancient commercial buildings at right angles to the massive church, it was breathtaking. Ramon often begged off some side excursions to local lace shops or chocolate shops to stand in the middle of the stone square, gazing at the beautiful buildings around him. The areas that lured Paolo and Manuel were the side streets with the many restaurants and open-air cafes. That's because that's where the girls were. Alex and especially Jorgé were encouraged to come with them because they spoke English—Jorgé more so than Alex—and in Brussels English was more generally used than Spanish. Jorgé had even picked up a smattering of French words, which he tried on nearly every native he talked to. He knew from learning English the more you use a language the easier it is to learn.

Paolo's intent, as always, was to try to pick up some girls. Alex couldn't believe the success he had—even handicapped by language. Girls just gravitated to him. He had obvious good looks and he had charm, but there exuded a sex appeal that women couldn't resist.

Alex had mixed feelings staying with Paolo. Paolo was a favorite of everyone on the team because of his stellar play and his magnetic personality. Everyone had a good time when Paolo was around. Yet he knew if he stuck with Paolo and the right situation presented itself, he would have sex with a pretty girl. Not a whore, though—he wouldn't do that. He had already made that decision, although he felt guilty because he loved Maria Elena so much. He was sure they would get married, maybe even within the year. He knew he should be true to her, but the attraction of the wild, free lifestyle was too tempting to ignore for now. Too, if he didn't try it now there would be an increased likelihood of his being tempted after he was married, and for him being married meant being faithful.

There was something inherently attractive about being on the Junior World Cup team from Costa Rica when you are in Western Europe. Being a soccer player helped, and being from Costa Rica provided just the right exotic touch. It wasn't long before they had joined up with enough accommodating young girls to match their numbers. So what started out as Paolo and Manuel alone the first foray into the city streets several nights ago, now numbered five and would grow to include almost the whole team as more learned of the results achieved. By the end of the tournament they were also meeting some of the same girls who apparently also enjoyed their nights out.

Costa Rica won their next game easily. In a surprisingly weak display of soccer, France wasn't up to the level of game that Costa Rica displayed. The Costa Rican coach had expected a much tougher game than the two-zero shutout. France had begun to make a name for itself in the junior age competition.

The home team of Belgium was next. Again the team had a day's rest between the games. The game against France did not wear them down. However, Belgium had a particularly tough game against Spain from which they had to recoup. The coach worked his guys hard in the off day between games. Satisfied they were still physically fit, he told them he believed they could wear down Belgium in the second half.

Paolo made two spectacular plays during the game with Belgium and scored on both of them to lead Costa Rica into the finals three-two. On one play he dribbled past four defenders who all had a legitimate shot at tackling the ball, then out-maneuvered the goalkeeper to score. Even the partisan fans witnessing that run by Paolo knew they had seen something special. It was not unlike the run Diego Maradona had made in the 1986 World Cup, when he dribbled past five separate defenders to amaze the crowd and the world viewing audience. That one play alone made Maradona, even if he had not had all the other spectacular plays in his career. The television highlights proclaimed Paolo's play on a level of the men's World Cup, not just the younger group. Some commentators wondered aloud whether Costa Rica didn't have a young Maradona they were foisting on the soccer world for the first time. What's more, the kid still had another year left in the junior age group.

Costa Rica's thrilling campaign came crashing to a close when Spain, the favorites, upheld their number-one world ranking for junior teams and prevailed over the Central Americans three to one. Alex, who had also drawn accolades all through the tournament, was frustrated by the attacking Spaniard offense. It was the first game in which Costa Rica had given up more than one goal. Alex felt he had let his team down. He just couldn't cope with the number of offensive players Spain threw at them at once. Twice goals were scored when the defense had become confused and disorganized. Those goals Alex blamed on himself. As defensive captain he was responsible to keep organization and communication among the group. It just seemed like no one had a great game—no one, that is, except "Cujo," the goalkeeper. Cujo made at least seven great saves.

Cujo had picked up his nickname from the American movie of the same name because he changed personalities so dramatically when he stepped onto the field, and became like the mad dog Cujo himself. He was decidedly unfriendly to the opponents and took advantage of his large size to frequently knock into them when opportunities presented themselves. He never seemed to get seriously hurt, although his teammates often noted the ugly black bruises that marked his body the next day.

That night after the banquet in the team's honor at their hotel the guys again went out on the town. Once again their friends were waiting for them. Alex spotted the same girl he had been with two nights earlier and made his way to her. He was surprised and pleased to hear most of the girls had seen not just today's game, but some of them had seen two or three of Costa Rica's games.

There was no curfew tonight—it would have been ignored anyway—so the players and their dates partied all night. Although Alex thoroughly enjoyed himself, he realized it wasn't the same. He missed Maria Elena. That thought grew stronger now that the team would be heading back home. He had managed to keep bouts of homesickness to a minimum, but now thoughts of her overwhelmed him. It started after he had danced with his date a second time that night and when she questioned him what was wrong, he poured it all out to her that he missed his girl back home. She was the one who would be his wife. The girl listened for a while and tried to bring him out of his sad, selfish feelings, but when she realized she couldn't, she got angry and went home. That left Alex alone, and a renewed sadness swept over him. Slowly he confirmed what he knew he had already decided some time ago. When he got home he would set a date and marry Maria Elena.

Right away the coach and players could see the merits of the idea. The extra wind resistance from the parachutes forced the running muscles to work harder and the runner to strain more in the right places. The runner naturally wanted to lengthen his strides as a result of the wind drag. The runner also was forced to take the correct angle of lean as he ran in order to pull the parachutes.

There were some snickers as the chute idea was unveiled before the team. The testimonials from professional football teams were enough that Kori arranged for the developer of the parachute training method, Dr. Ben Tabachnik, the former head of speed research for all sports and an Olympic coach for the U.S.S.R. When his credentials were read to the players, their attitude became one of intense interest. They learned that more than six professional teams engage Dr. Tabachnik as a consultant.

"The Speed Chutes," Dr. Tabachnik explained, "do not interfere with the proper running techniques or mechanic; rather, they enhance those techniques and mechanics. The chutes can be used running curves, changing directions, and even running backward. There are three sizes of chutes—small, medium, and large—creating six possible combinations of Speed Chutes. These allow an athlete to improve his speed without ever hitting a speed plateau, if you follow the program. In addition, the chutes can be released during a sprint.

"We experienced very favorable results in the Soviet Union using these parachutes as a training technique. Times in the one hundred meters were reduced by two-tenths of a second to four-tenths of a second for most of our runners. Inches can be added to your vertical jump because of the leg strength that is developed.

"By starting off with a couple of medium chutes, then changing to one small and one medium chute, then to two small, then one medium, and then down to one small chute of three and one half square feet, you'll never hit a plateau or get frustrated with not changing or improving. Finally you'll do what we call a release, in which the chutes are released during a full-speed sprint. You'll feel as though a rocket kicked off behind you."

Several demonstrations were done in front of the whole group. Then Dr. Tabachnik worked with a number of the players, helping them to obtain the proper running form. Scott was one of those and he could easily see where the chutes would help to develop the leg strength to further improve his speed and quickness. Dr. Tabachnik recommended a six-month regimen with the chutes, and then to lay off and do other conditioning for about four months, then to repeat the whole process again, timing the sixth month to end just before the start of the tournament. He assured them they would all be faster, quicker, and in better shape than if they had not used the chutes.

At the end of the first six months Scott's time had improved to a dazzling four and eighteen-hundredths seconds in the forty-yard dash. Robert turned in a sparkling four and twenty-four hundredths. Chase had lowered his time to four and thirty-two hundredths, and now four more were under the four and four tenths mark. Kori was positively salivating at the thought of such a team. Never before had he coached or played on a team with the speed this one had. Undoubtedly, his team would be the fastest in the field of twenty-four, and quite possibly, the best conditioned.

Alan Priestaps introduced David Starr to his organizing committee. "Mr. Starr is one of the foremost experts in the world in security matters for this kind of event. He is from Manchester, England and has been involved in both of the past two World Cups, each of which was carried off without incident. He will be working as a consultant with the FBI, U.S. Customs, and all the state and local governments. One of his primary duties will be to provide special training to those responsible at each site for the security of the players, the soccer officials, and the fans. He has already inspected each and every site in order to make specific plans for each one and to make particular plans at each site for the special needs there. As I understand it, he has mapped out security plans for every level of involvement. I now present Mr. David Starr."

"Thank you Mr. President", Starr began. Gentlemen—and lady, I'll try not to trivialize your already vast experience in dealing with major events such as your Super Bowl and various national tournaments that are themselves a huge endeavor. Rather, let me deal with what will be unique to an event such as this. First, we have an international event of mammoth proportions. You must control entry into the United States. Crazies exist in nearly every country in the world, and many of them or their organizations would like nothing better than to cause embarrassment or worse for your country. They may be motivated by political objectives or personal ones. They will know that taking a player or a coach into captivity would generate enormous and immediate pressure for capitulation to their demands. We must be proactive and prevent such an episode. The first place to do that is at border control. Consequently, border control efforts must be stepped up very shortly. A well-laid plan may place someone in position weeks or even months ahead of time.

"Next, each hotel that headquarters a team must have exquisite protection for the players, coaches, and other related personnel. Each and every exit must be controlled at all times. Each team will also need to practice at some local field. Arrangements must include those facilities. Travel for the teams will also be a concern. The teams will travel locally in FIFA-provided buses to and from the stadiums, practice fields, restaurants, and so on. From city to city they will travel in chartered planes. I've outlined each separate area of concern for all of you to look at and consider the best plan to provide safe passage and conditions.

"Third, stadium security; access to the stadiums must be tightly controlled. Every person entering the stadium must be searched, *every one*. You must have control over the personnel in the stadium security forces. In Italy we had a situation where someone tried to replace a security guard without anyone knowing of it. So use guard forces where everyone is known to each other and an outside agent would immediately be revealed. Every stadium has, or will have, crowd control impediments separating the crowd from the fields of play as well as from other sections of the crowd. These are mandated by FIFA. You've all heard of the unfortunate events that have occurred in England and other places during soccer matches. Believe me, the fervor felt by soccer fans for their team is unmatched by anything else I've seen anywhere. Prevention is the best effort toward crowd control."

David Starr digressed from his purpose of telling the group how important and how thorough security needed to be to illustrate the depth of passion felt by soccer fans from throughout the world. "Back in 1969 El Salvador was playing Honduras for the last open spot for the 1970 Mexico World Cup. The game was badly called and the fans grew exceptionally rowdy. Midway through the second half, fighting broke out in the stands. The police never fully controlled the crowd after that. El Salvador lost three to nothing, and their fans spilled over into the section of the grandstand occupied by fans from Honduras. The situation was really ugly; forty people were killed that day. El Salvador's fans couldn't get out of the city because angry Hondurans effectively blockaded the ways out. The government of El Salvador heard what was going on and, believe it or not, launched a full-scale war on Honduras. Tanks, Planes, infantry, the works. Hundreds, even thousands, died those first few days. Only when the OAS stepped in did cooler heads prevail. These countries take their soccer seriously.

"You've all heard about the hooligans from England. I am somewhat of an expert in that regard. Number one it's not just the hooligans from England that might be a problem. We have identified twenty-eight individuals who are problems in England and have made plans to contain them in the country as much as possible. These are the hard-core problem people that seem to actually be trying to cause dangerous situations at the soccer matches. Every customs agent at every border in Europe and the United States, as well as Mexico and Canada, will have a list of names of these individuals. In addition, we have a similar list of individuals from Ireland, Brussels, Holland, and other locations. These will also be distributed.

"Terrorist activity is probably our gravest concern. Some of these organizations have a suicidal desire to achieve certain objectives. At times there is extensive planning put into a scheme to disrupt events. We will have well-placed sources throughout the world keeping a watch out for any news about activity in that regard. There is no reason to suspect serious trouble at all. Nevertheless, we have to be prepared for anything. For each match there will be a specially trained SWAT team on hand in case something should happen; their primary objective is to prevent any occurrence. Naturally, as the level of play escalates into the later rounds, these SWAT teams will grow in size.

"I suggest you read the brochure I've prepared and then let's get back together so that I can answer questions any of you might have. At that time we can also discuss some specifics," he concluded.

CHAPTER 9

Alan Priestaps was reaching his limits. He was under heavy fire from both ends. First there was the pressure to develop a competitive team and to give as many players as possible the necessary international experience. At the same time, trying to field two national teams was having a debilitating effect from several directions. The cost of sending two teams abroad was stupendous. It wasn't just the players. One had to add the coaches, the managers, the statisticians, the film crew, and a couple of techno boys. He sensed, too, that the ability to compete was somewhat sapped by having to spread the talent out in two teams. The two-team concept worked great when visiting teams were brought to the United States and they could play them both, each coached by Coach Gaborakov. When they traveled that was impossible. No, the two teams had to become one. When the tour to Italy was complete, so was the existence of two teams. After more than one year for both teams, each had the opportunity to go to at least three different countries already, and Italy would make the fourth. This was the first time that both teams traveled at once and to the same country. He wondered how that would work out.

The other factor that weighed heavily in making the decision to consolidate the two teams into one was that planning for two teams was too time consuming. Planning sessions were kicked up a notch in the preparation for the World Cup. That had to take precedence. There were so many things to be dealt with. The governing people at FIFA had disallowed their appeal to waive the seventy-five-yard wide rule for the fields at the various venues. The rules for World Cup differ somewhat than those for international play. The field size can be as small as seventy yards wide and as large as eighty for international play. The World Cup, however, specifies the fields must be exactly seventy-five yards wide. That means several of the possible venue sites have to make significant renovations to the physical facilities in order to accommodate this rule. Mr. Priestaps just finished notifying those sites affected. Happily, not one of the proposed venues backed out. It simply meant that monies would have to be allocated to provide the necessary area.

Mr. Priestaps told his staff that this trip to Italy by both teams would be the last time that two teams traveled. Kori did not disagree. He thanked the staff for allowing the two teams as long as they did. He responded that the timing was actually pretty good to draw the players he wanted together into one. In fact, he had transitioned the team mostly into a number-one team and a number-two team, even though he often switched players to get a look at certain combinations. The second team had a lot of new players, who were constantly being tried. He still had the opportunity with one team to evaluate new individuals.

Kori told the staff to watch the progress of the teams in Italy. He felt that certain things were beginning to mesh. Even though they had lost down in Brazil 2–0, he could see signs of progress. "It is time we make our move to the front," he declared.

The plane landed in Rome right at the scheduled time. The players were met at the other side of the customs office by Giovanni, one of the Italian Soccer Federation representatives, who took them to the hotel straightaway.

The coach told them to get some rest before they started practicing at 5:00 P.M., or 17:00 hours. "You will start using military time while in Europe because all schedules are on the twenty-four-hour clock," he explained.

Scott and "Pu" roomed together. Pu was a young guy just graduated from Clemson. He had earned the nickname "Pu"—pronounced "Pooh," as in Winnie the Pooh—while pledging his fraternity. One of the tasks of a pledge was to learn the Greek alphabet. Pu's pledge brother thought it a good joke to teach him an extra letter at the end of the alphabet. As Pu tells it, the brothers roared with laughter when he recited the alphabet in front of them all during Hell Week. It also spoke something of Pu's naiveté as people were all the time pulling his leg or playing a practical joke on him. He was regarded as an easy mark, not really worth a serious challenge to a committed prankster.

Both guys fell fast asleep and were awakened, only by a phone call the assistant coach had arranged. Thankfully, the coach did not have a long or a very hard practice. It was timed to get the guys up and to work out the stiffness from their bodies after the long trip and change of hours. Both Pu and Scott were famished when it finally came time for supper. Food had been available for those who wanted something when they first got to the hotel, but most had skipped that and gone to bed. Supper made up for it, though; they were served a six-course meal, plus dessert. Coach Gaborakov got up afterward and thanked their host for a wonderful meal and then told the team there would be two practices tomorrow—both long. The team loudly booed that announcement. The coach changed that to cheers when he said the second practice consisted of a visit to the Coliseum and Vatican City.

The practice that next morning was hard. The coach told them they had all had too much rest and were getting out of shape. "This morning," he said, "we will correct that."

Scott couldn't remember many practices quite as demanding as that one. They practiced three hours and never stopped the whole while. As practice closed the coach told them he was doing them a favor, hoping now they would sleep well tonight.

That afternoon they went to the Vatican. Scott knew the Vatican was a walled city within Rome controlled by the Catholic Church and largely exempt from Italian rule. They even have their own post office and bank, he read. He liked the uniforms of the Swiss Guard. The outfits reminded him of movies he had seen of the 16th century in Europe. The Conquistadors, that's who wore outfits like these, he remembered.

As they walked through the Vatican Museum Scott commented to Pu how interesting the exhibits were and that their value was so much it was impossible to estimate. The wall hangings were impressive, as were the frescoes on the walls and ceilings. When Scott saw Pu hanging on every word, he thought he would see how far he could take it with him. Scott told Pu there was more gold here at the Vatican than there was in the whole rest of the world. When Pu bit on that, he also told him in one of the exhibits downstairs they had Vincent Van Gogh's right ear—the one that had been cut off. Pu acted a little strange with that remark. Scott could tell Pu wanted to believe it—that was his nature—but it sounded a little far-fetched, even to him. Apparently the other guys have been working him over on his gullibility, Scott decided.

After walking through an indeterminable number of rooms they reached the Sistine Chapel. Scott was unprepared for the wonderful way everything worked together. Although there were many different scenes, not always related to one another, the majesty of the art was overwhelming. Scott sat down on one of the benches along the side and just marveled at the artwork. At first he thought the columns and figurines were part of the ceiling structure, then he realized those were painted into the ceiling like everything else. "Talk about realistic," he said out loud to himself. Scott knew he had never been so impressed with anything as much as he had this. He thought about Michelangelo lying on his back, painting the ceiling. How could he keep the proper perspective on all of this—everything the right size and facing the correct, no, the best, way—while lying on his back? Scott drifted in his thoughts, trying to imagine himself as Michelangelo. What a great man! If he had done nothing else but this, he would be great. But he'd done so much more. The statue of David, for instance. Think of the realism of the muscles and ligaments and tendons! Just outstanding. The beautiful scene depicting the Last Judgment was particularly moving.

Scott wasn't the only one overwhelmed by the Sistine Chapel. They all were. The whole team spent twenty minutes just in that one place, gazing at the stupendous result in front of their eyes. Scott told Pu the Sistine Chapel was the very room in which the Cardinals meet to elect the new Pope. By now, however, Pu was so skeptical of all information he wouldn't even acknowledge hearing Scott's words.

Next they took a bus to St. Peter's Basilica. St. Peter's was the main entrance to Vatican City. It was the place from which the Pope greeted the people. "Huge, huge, look at this," Pu said. "Look at those statues all around us."

"Magnificent," agreed Scott, "You certainly don't see this kind of thing back home, do you?"

"Not where I come from, you don't."

The Basilica itself was equally impressive. Pu overheard someone else say that this church was the largest Christian church in the world. "That I can believe," he muttered.

Scott had the feeling he was stepping on hallowed ground. He tried to picture a mass being held in here as he looked around, but somehow the right picture just wouldn't develop for him. Michelangelo's Pieta was here. Again, the man could really make things come to life, Scott thought. What a wonderful talent he had. And there were so many who had talent during the Renaissance time period. Where was the talent now? Surely the know-how wasn't lost, he asked himself. Even Eddie, who displayed no interest in culture, was awed by the splendors just witnessed, Scott observed.

The Coliseum was nice but it was a little bit of a letdown because it looked so much like the pictures Scott had seen of it. Two things detracted from it. One was that the city—the streets and other buildings—had infringed on the ambiance of the structure. Second, they had just come from some of the most impressive works of mankind in the Vatican: Things to which photographs just don't do justice. Had they seen the Coliseum first, it might have been more impressive.

That night they were invited to a different restaurant and again were served a scrumptious meal. Scott knew they'd all be fat as pigs by the time they left if they kept up this eating. The coach told them tomorrow evening would be their first game—against the second-division team, Ancona.

"Don't let that second-division label fool you," he warned. "Second division here is first division in most of the rest of the world. They are going to be tough. You've got to be tougher. It's been a tiring day for me, so let's all go get some sleep."

That last comment drew a lot of feedback. "If it was tough for him, what about us?" was Pu's comment. Scott smiled at the psychology of the coach.

The next day they played horribly, losing 2–0. Scott wasn't sure whether they were all still tired or whether the other team was that much better. They seemed to be everywhere. The U.S. offense couldn't connect with passes, and the opponent's offense stormed the U.S. defense. Scott didn't play in that game, and several other starters were also held out. Scott wondered whether the coach was setting up both our players as well as the other Italian teams they were to play. He wondered, Why would he tire us so much the day before, then not start half of the regulars? The score could have been four or five–nothing, the advantage was that great to the Italians. Well, the coach got our attention about how good these teams would be.

They took a bus the next day, straight down the coast to Pescara, where they were to play their second game. Again, it was a division-two team. The coach told them what kind of strategy they used and who the main players were.

Once again Scott did not play, although this time the coach came to him ahead of time and told him he wanted to give some of the others a chance, and also not to reveal Scott's speed until the big games with Bari and Napoli. The coach said that especially Napoli would be the big test. He told Scott to watch and observe so he learned from these first two games.

This second game went much better. Scott and Marty sat out the whole game. Eddie and Pu were substituted into the action just after halftime. The United States team ended the game tied at one. All the players felt better than they had during the first game, but the coach reminded them these were second-division teams and there was a significant difference between the level of play of first- and second-division clubs. The U.S. team began to get more acclimated toward the Italian style of play, with the quick transition and power offense. The coach had told them before they left the United States what it would be like, yet until the players experienced it, they really didn't comprehend; worse, they couldn't react to it until it was too late. That was how Pescara scored the goal. The United States had really outplayed the other team and should have won, Scott felt. We had ten or eleven good scoring opportunities that we didn't convert, he told himself. The coach told Scott, the other forwards, and the midfielders, "Watch for opportunities to run straight up the middle without the ball and look for a pass. Maybe the other clubs won't have the same weakness, but they'll have to show us," he said.

The next day was a bus trip to Bari with a practice later that day. On the way down to Bari the players couldn't believe how pretty a drive it was. On their left was the Adriatic Sea and the coast. "The highway itself is one long 287 kilometer garden," someone said. Indeed, the center had a flowering shrub of beautiful white and pink and lavender and red flowers. The grass was trimmed and the plantings of trees and other landscaping placed near bridges and tunnels were lovely. "It was one of the nicest roads I ever traveled," he told his mother and Diana later. "Maybe things looked much better because we played better," he mused.

The coach worked on strategies that afternoon—both offensive and defensive. Afterward he told them they had a real chance to beat this club. He said that the first game was just a learning experience,—and they were tired and played tired. "Tomorrow we'll find a lot out about ourselves."

The locker room after that next game had to be one of the neatest experiences in which Scott had ever partaken. There was so much whooping and hollering he couldn't believe it. The old coach was a wily one! He had set the Bari team up for a fall and they took it. Coach Kori said they had played a good many subs in the game and not to get carried away with a little ole 2-0 victory, but his eyes were sparkling when he said it, and you could see the smile a mile away.

Both scores had been on runs straight up the middle, and in both of them Scott had figured, with an assist on the first one and the second on a shot he took that the goalie couldn't handle cleanly and that Chase Anderson followed up and put in. Everyone was jubilant!

The coach told them, "This is going to make Napoli take us seriously, so expect a much tougher game day after tomorrow when we play them. Meanwhile, enjoy it. Hip, hip, hooray! Hip, hip, hooray! Hip, hip, hooray!" The whole team joined in to shout with their foxy coach.

The next morning the team left for Naples, or Napoli in Italian. The coaches had a huddle and decided to give the team the day off. They could go to the beach if they wanted. Of course, they all opted to go to the beach. They were grossly disappointed, though, that the girls at the beach kept their tops on. Later they were told it was mostly in northern Italy and in only a very few places in the south that tops came off. They all marveled once again at how pretty were the Italian girls.

Scott couldn't remember when he had seen so many pretty girls. Some of the guys got the coach to say they could invite the girls for supper if they could get any of them to understand them and they paid for their meals. Now challenged, some of the guys would stop at nothing to get some girls to eat with them. Amazingly, getting the girls wasn't so tough after all. Some of the guys got two or three to say they'd come and then got those girls to bring more.

As it turned out, ten girls showed up at the restaurant. The girls who had helped make the arrangements, by common consent, were paired with the guys who got them to come. All the extra girls were apportioned among the tables such that there were at least two girls at each table. The guys were all in a festive mood, Scott noticed, including himself. Surprising what the addition of good-looking girls does to the atmosphere, he reflected. And these girls were good-looking! Five were blonde and five had dark hair. Scott had been surprised to see so many blondes, especially girls, in Italy. His image was that of dark-haired girls with what he thought of as the Italian nose. While there were plenty of those, they were not in the majority. Scott estimated thirty to thirty-five percent of all girls he saw had blonde hair. And the Italian nose was in a decided minority of girls. Of the ten girls, Scott categorized three of them as beautiful, four were very good-looking—two just good-looking, and only attractive one. The three beautiful ones were as fine looking as any he had ever seen. One particularly was stunning. She was one of the ones the guys had talked to. Her name was Raphaela and she was at the table next to Scott's.

The two girls at Scott's table were in the very good-looking category and their names were Brigitta and Stephania.

Scott was amazed at how much could be communicated when neither person knew the other's language. Most of the guys had learned some basic phrases and, adding universal words such as football, one could actually communicate some thoughts. When guys or girls really got stuck, they asked the interpreter to help. He had become a very popular person.

Toward the end of the long meal the coach stood up and told the guys they would have to say *ciao* to all the pretty girls because they were all going to the hotel and to bed, as tomorrow was an important game.

Chase Anderson—the guy who asked the stunning brunette, Raphaela, to come—asked the coach, "Could we have tickets for these girls at the stadium—to come as our guests?"

The coach looked down at the interpreter/guide with a questioning expression.

"I think we can arrange that. Let's see, ten tickets at the stadium," he answered.

"Twenty! Hell, get at least ten more to come with these. I'll take two," Eddie, who was one of the guys sitting at some distance from any girl, shouted.

The interpreter/guide laughed and said, "OK, we'll make it twenty-one. One for me, too."

The result was a loud cheer from all the guys. One or two of them, Chase included, stole a kiss from the girls.

The interpreter stood up and explained to the girls, "The coach is sending the team straight to their hotel tonight, so there will be no more time for socializing. However, the team has requested that all of you attend the game tomorrow night—as their guests—at 7 o'clock at the San Paolo stadium. They have made arrangements for free tickets to be left for you—at Gate two, I believe. In addition, they have requested you each bring a friend so that a total of twenty tickets will be available for you and your friends."

One of the girls shouted, "Bravo," and all the others joined in with another. Smiles were all around; this development left everyone happy. Chase took that opportunity to get in another kiss, Scott noticed. Can't blame him for trying to establish territorial rights to that girl, he thought. She sure has a pretty smile. It's her eyes though that make her so enchanting.

Cornell, the goalie, told one of the girls that after the game perhaps there would be time to go dancing. In fact, the words he used to get the idea across was, "First football, second dance, understand?"

Andriata was her name. She smiled her understanding and indicated back, "I say others OK." Cornell nodded his head vigorously in reply and said, "*Si, capito.*"

There were a lot of *ciao*'s said and kisses on the cheeks as the team left the restaurant and boarded the bus. Scott's attention was directed toward Chase and Raphaela and noticed Chase gave her a good one on the lips. For an instant Scott wished he could move that fast with girls. Even though he had no need to or really any desire to now that he was married, it is every guy's wish to be popular and well liked by girls, and to be able to have success with girls. Not necessarily ending up with sex every time, but to be able to advance beyond first base whenever you wanted to—that would be great. Chase had that quality, and Scott wished he did, too. It also caused a pang of homesickness in Scott. He missed Diana at that moment. For the first time this trip, it really hit him.

They were under instructions not to go to the beach and not to swim the next day. They had a skull session at 14:00 hours but the rest of the day was free. A few went shopping; some played cards and others read books. Several had an inordinate capacity to sleep. Scott did not require a lot of sleep and, in fact, couldn't sleep late as a rule. He marveled at those who could sleep twelve and fourteen hours at a time. If Scott got six hours a night he could function well the next day. Even two nights in a row at four hours wasn't a problem. The third night, though, he needed six or eight hours to feel good the next day. However, he always tried to get eight hours the night before a game. Frequently, he woke after only six, but if he woke earlier he usually did not need more.

The stadium in Napoli, San Paulo, did not have the free-flowing design of the one in Bari, but Scott had seen few stadiums that could compare to Bari. As the team unloaded from the bus Scott wondered where all the people park. As far as he could see there was no organized parking of any kind. Curious, he asked the interpreter, Giovanni, about it.

"Look all along the streets. There's room for one car on each side, maybe with two wheels up on the sidewalk sometimes, but every street gets parked on just like these right over here." Giovanni pointed to some, parked inches from a guardrail on the right. "Every street will be filled up for blocks around and further when it's a big game."

Scott started to shake his head.

"This is Italy, not Boston, Massachusetts," Giovanni laughed as he told him the obvious. "Haven't you noticed some differences in handling a car here in Italy? Number one, you park anywhere you don't stop traffic. Number two, if you can squeeze through an opening—go for it. There's one cardinal rule of the road here. Never look directly at the car, or its driver, when you're trying to squeeze ahead of the other vehicle. If you do, you've lost. Once the other driver knows you've seen him there, he also knows you will stop before letting the cars hit each other."

"I guess I've been looking around at the sights and haven't watched the driving so much. Maybe it takes some getting used to."

"Yeah, you Americanos are too polite when you drive; it takes the fun out of it. It's much more of an adventure here."

"I'll watch a little better next time we ride."

"Scott, Scott, let's go. Coach wants us, someone hollered."

"Got to run, thanks."

"*Ciao.*"

"Go for it." Kori told his listeners, "I want to beat these guys so bad I can taste it. This is the cream of the crop. You don't get any better than this team." The coach talked to them about the first fifteen minutes of the game. "If we can hold them out at the beginning it will be a toss-up game. We can't let them score in the early minutes of the game. Play good, smart defense."

Right from the opening whistle Napoli was trying to take it to them. It seemed like they were everywhere. The young U.S. team couldn't even get the ball much past midfield, without Napoli getting it back. They converged quickly on the one with the ball.

Scott told his teammates to pass it quickly. "Don't hold onto the ball," he shouted. "One touch or two, then pass it off."

The good part was Napoli didn't score at all in the first half. Neither did the United States, though. In the second half Napoli came out like a *blitzkrieg*, putting a lot of pressure on the U.S. defense. Scott found himself going back to defend frequently. If we can just mount an attack of our own, we might just be able to break this juggernaut of theirs, Scott convinced himself. He traded places with the right midfielder, hoping to introduce some confusion. Sure enough, the defenders against the right side of the United States were not expecting to have their area flooded on a push out. They were a split second late in recognizing the situation, and therefore the United States mounted a dangerous right-flank attack. No score occurred, but the pressure let off just a bit. The complexity of the game shifted as once again the two teams played evenly. But it was the United States that now was making it dangerous for the other team.

The crowd of about twenty to twenty-five thousand started getting into it more, realizing they were seeing a pretty good game. The United States would get cheered and applauded just as loudly as Napoli. Each good play for either side was appreciated with applause by the knowledgeable crowd. They were here to see good soccer, even though many came not expecting it. As a matter of fact, at times it seemed like the crowd was more for the United States. It was as though the fans knew who the winner would be, who it could only be, but wanted the teams to make a good show of it while they could. Each renewed threat by the United States was approved by the soccer crowd. Each deft series of passes received their approval. The fledging U.S. team noticed this and took substance from the support.

The game ended in a scoreless draw. One of the assistant coaches, whose job it was to chart the game's activities, found that in the second half the United States had possession twenty and one-half minutes, Napoli twenty-two minutes—almost even. In addition, the United States had four corner kicks to Napoli's two in the latter period. Crosses into the middle were five to four in favor of the United States after halftime. "When you analyze it," Kori said, "we may have outplayed them in the second half."

The crowd gave the United States and the game a standing ovation at the end. Most thought they had gotten more than expected. They appreciated the two attacking styles. It made a good game to watch.

Giovanni told them afterward how surprised several of the Napoli players were that the United States didn't fold under the pressure, that they didn't make defensive mistakes, and that their individual skills were much improved from what they faced in 1990.

Scott asked Giovanni if the Napoli players had given it their all. Giovanni responded with, "After you guys beat Bari, they were determined to show you soccer Italian style. No, they didn't let up. For a game that had no meaning, they played damned hard. I could see that."

Giovanni's statement made the whole team feel good. Scott made it a point to go speak to each of the defenders and midfielders to tell them what a heck of a job they did defensively.

Pu told Scott, "For a while it seemed they were coming from everywhere. I don't know what you did up front there, but when you guys pushed out and took it to them it made all the difference in the world to us. They had to worry about their own defense. I don't think we could have held them off the entire game without a score if something hadn't changed like it did."

"I don't know how the defense managed as long as you did. They just never had the right chance. They never got open across the middle. You had 'em marked each time. Nice goin', anyway. Good game. *Great* game, Pu."

That conversation reflected the sentiments of everyone. The defense did an outstanding job covering and shutting Napoli down, but when the offense took it to Napoli it took a lot of pressure off the defense. Everyone was more or less happy with a 0–0 tie. They had played well against a superior team. They had even shown enterprise with a few dangerous runs of their own, creating a game that was not lop-sided and was very entertaining.

Giovanni told the team, "The people watching got their money's worth. That was a good soccer game. I think now America has the respect of at least a portion of our nation. Word will spread of what you have done. I guess, too, it depends on how your other team is doing in the North."

The fact was the other team beat the first second-division club they played 1–0; then they tied Torino 1–1; then they lost to Milan 2–1. Milan had a strong club also, but the American team played them a strong game and came away with their respect.

After the game in Napoli the players cut short their locker room celebration. The guys sent Lucas, the manager, upstairs to see if there were any girls waiting there for them. Lucas begged Giovanni to accompany him so he could communicate to them, so the two of them went.

They recognized Raphaela right away. She was standing with a whole bunch of girls at the players' exit. Lucas's first thought was, I wonder what the Italian players are going to think when they come out and see these girls waiting for us. Lucas couldn't help noticing once again that girls in Italy either didn't wear bras or else what they wore didn't matter anyway. He was glad he brought Giovanni, though. Lucas and Giovanni kissed Raphaela on the cheeks and the other girls they remembered from last night. All the girls were dressed very nicely, and really looked super. All sorts of thoughts about how the guys would react went through Lucas' head. He decided he would tell the guys not many were up here and they were just going to say *ciao* and leave. Lucas could imagine the looks on their faces when great expectations were dashed and disappointment replaced it. Lucas heard Giovanni tell them the players would be out in about ten minutes and that they had sent them up to make sure the girls were there and to tell them it wouldn't be long. At least that's what Giovanni told him he said on the way back down. Lucas made Giovanni a co-conspirator to his plan to miss-inform the team.

When they got back to the locker room Lucas said, "There's good news and bad news."

"Uh oh. What's the bad news?"

"The girls are up there all right—at least some of them—but they won't be going anywhere with us."

"Why not?" several called out.

"Liar," Chase said, as he threw a shoe at Lucas. "Tell us the truth."

Lucas ducked the shoe and broke into a broad grin. "There's a ton of nice-looking girls up there just waiting for the right guys to come along and take them out tonight. I say, let's go celebrate!"

Eddie Jackson, the tall, raw-boned rebel from the South, shouted, "Awwrright, let's go get 'em and party." Everyone, it seemed, started to hurry a little more.

Coach Kori told the team he was real proud of the way they played and that they bent but did not break defensively; that they played a heady game, a smart game. "Sometimes you've just got to weather the storm. That's what you guys did tonight. A very important lesson learned here. You can win some ball games you might not otherwise if you remember tonight. Good job on offense, too. We stuck it in their eye. They knew they were in a battle. Now tonight you boys have a good time. Remember you represent the United States of America, so conduct yourselves accordingly."

Eddie Jackson answered for them all, "We'll show them us red-blooded Americans are no fags."

The team all laughed at the way Eddie expressed himself in such a straightforward way. They were all in a good mood and ready for a good time.

When the team exited the stadium they were pleased to see how good the girls looked, and to see them there waiting for them. Those like Chase who already had matches, went right to their girls. Some of the others like Eddie—after an initial "Awwrright" upon first sighting—went straight to one they never met before and laid a claim. The remaining guys and girls sort of grouped together in bunches of three and three, or four and four, putting off for a while who was going to be with whom.

"The girls," Giovanni announced happily, "have selected a place near here for a quick bite to eat, then on to a discotheque called The Enchanted. I know it. It's really quite a good one."

The place they stopped to eat just served sandwiches, pasta, and pizza. In less than an hour's time they were out of there and headed for the disco.

The disco was actually on the lower floor; a lounge occupied the main floor. When they descended the steps the throbbing of the music grew more intense. Below was one very large room with a bar on each wall.

The dance floor was in the center, down two steps from the surrounding area. The dance floor flashed lights as the floor itself would randomly light up blocks of two-feet square. The steps around the dance floor were black but had little lights that also flashed off and on that looked like the lights some airplanes had on their aisles, pointing the way out. The dance floor was full, but not crowded. In the spacious end areas around the dance floor were tables with chairs. At one end there appeared to be enough places for all of them to sit.

Eddie and his girl, a beautiful blonde who was wearing a black top with white skin-tight stretch pants, and Marty and his date immediately went out on the dance floor. The others all sat down first. Chase told someone to order the right drinks for him and Raphaela, then he too went to dance. As soon as all the drinks were ordered, all but the group of four and four were dancing. They sat boy, girl, boy, girl but were still trying to figure out who was with whom. Scott was in this group. He kind of held back because he thought the others should have first pick. He would have a good time no matter what and wasn't interested in anything more. They sat and talked somewhat awkwardly during that first dance. Then as one record spun into another—they were playing American hits as well as Italian songs—two of the guys and girls got up. So Scott took the one girl next to him and signaled for the last guy to get up and go dance and soon everyone was on the now-crowded dance floor. Scott found it easier to communicate while dancing than he did when sitting and talking. A smile here and there did a lot.

After five or six dances everyone made their way back to the tables where the drinks were waiting. In short order Lucas stood up, held out his drink, and said, "I propose a toast. To all the *bellisima regazze* in Italy. May they live forever."

That was accompanied by a chorus of "Hear, hear!" and cheers, and salutes as all took a drink. Giovanni interpreted for the girls, but most of them got the meaning because they heard *bellisima regazze*—beautiful girls.

Then Chase stood up and proposed a toast. "To an evening that we'll all remember forever."

This was again accompanied by "Hear, hear!" Scott could hear Eddie hollering "Yeah, man." And, of course, "Awwrright." As some finished their drink they headed back out to the dance floor. Before long they were all out there. The dancing was a little wilder this time. The girl with Marty was really moving sensuously, shaking her hips and just plain look- ing good in her miniskirt. Marty was a good dancer, too, and together

they made a great couple. Marty was very young. He had not long graduated from high school and had played two years of college ball at Penn
State. He was a somewhat unconventional, fun guy who Scott had taken a
liking to. He hadn't gotten to know him as well as he'd like, but everyone
was saying he was different, a completely uninhibited person. A little
crazy even. Someone said he had seen him eat a glass after drinking a
beer. Scott already knew how he liked his lobster.

When a *lambada* song came on, Marty and his girl immediately started
dancing a very respectable *lambada*. Pelvis together, one leg pressed
between the partner's two legs, they swayed and twirled around in a very
sexy dance. Two or three other couples, not players, were also dancing
the *lambada*, but Marty clearly was the best. He was having a good time.
Scott got the impression he liked being the center of attention. Maybe
that's why he did all those crazy things. When the dance was over, all of
those standing around—including the whole team except six or seven
who had their try at the *lambada*—applauded the dance and Marty and
his partner. Marty had given it his all, dipping his partner backward so
that her hair touched the floor and making pronounced hip movements,
sometimes with the girl not holding on to Marty but with just him holding her as she lay back.

Another regular dance followed that one when everyone danced again.
One or two players had changed partners. Scott couldn't tell if it was just
for one dance or that they figured out they'd be better off switching. An
interesting point to follow up, he thought. He noticed Ricky, the right
fullback, was one who had switched. The next dance after that was quite
a lively tune. Scott liked the Italian music. It had a good beat and was
easy to dance to. The dancing was really wild to this record. Arms were
flying around, dancers jumping, turning, and twisting higher and faster
than before.

A circle formed around one Italian couple who had been dancing wild-
ly. The on-lookers started clapping rhythmically as the action got more
intense. As soon as the first couple tired, a second entered the center and
started really going at it. Most of the Americans by this time had joined
the ever increasing circle. Shortly, the second couple retired to the fringes
of the circle.

All of a sudden Marty dropped down into a crouch, folded his arms
across his chest, shouted "*Olé,*" and started dancing the Russian sailor
dance. A widening circle of clapping dancers grew around him as the rest
of the people stopped dancing and started watching. Scott laughed. He
had seen the Russian saber or sailor dance on TV before (he wasn't sure

what it was called) and knew that it was extremely hard to do. He had half tried it himself without any success. Marty must either be a talented guy or he's worked on this a long time, he figured.

Marty was having a good time. He was really enjoying putting on a show. Back and forth he would go, shouting "*Olé!*" every time he turned around. After about five times up and back he stood up and kind of backed into the circle. Everyone cheered loudly and clapped for his performance. His dancing partner then jumped into the middle and did this crazy, sexy dance Scott had never seen before. She can really dance, Scott thought. Her dancing was accompanied by a calls of "Bravo" from the crowd. Soon, she backed up and retreated into the circle. After the shortest of pauses Eddie jumped in the middle and went down on the floor. He was squirming around on the floor doing the Alligator. The Alligator Dance looks more like a turtle swimming than an alligator. Scott didn't know how it got its name. In no time at all Eddie flipped over on his back and stuck his hands and legs up waving them all around. "That's the Turtle," Scott said to his partner. "He's on his back trying to flip over. Turtle," he indicated, nodding his head in Eddie's direction. Scott realized the girl couldn't understand him, but it was a chance to talk to her anyway.

Two more people danced in the middle of the crowd with the people watching and clapping rhythmically all the while. When the dance ended they all returned to their tables. Scott watched Marty field the questions the other guys were asking him. Scott decided once and for all that Marty loved being the center of attention.

The next day the guys all judged the night before to be one huge success. First the tie with Napoli, then the meal and disco with the girls, and judging from how tired the guys were the next day, Scott observed the night didn't end there for many of them.

The team was taking the train from Napoli back up to Genoa, where a bus would pick them up to take them to their hotel. Scott had heard so much about the European trains he was glad they would have a chance to ride one. The train ride proved to be a mistake.

Ricky came through and asked Scott if he wanted to join Eddie and him as they walked all through the train. Scott declined and told them to have fun. Fresh from their adventure the night before, they were primed to expand on that experience. In the next-to-last car they saw two girls as the sole occupants of an eight-passenger compartment, so they went in and sat down to "talk" with them. The girls giggled; about all Eddie and Ricky were able to get across was that they were football players from America and their names were Eddie and Ricky. The girls' names were

Elisa and Adriana. Then after much laughter and frustration both guys fell asleep there. After they woke up, they again started trying to communicate.

Ricky asked, "Where go?"

They understood his rudimentary Italian and answered, "Bologna."

Then they asked the guys in the same way, "Where go?"

When they answered "Genoa," the girls looked at each other before talking excitedly to Eddie and Ricky.

"*Grande problema.* No, No!" Ricky and Eddie knew by the way they were gesturing something was wrong but they didn't know what. The girls continued to press home that there was a problem, but weren't getting the exact message across to the guys.

Finally one of the girls got up and pulled Eddie up to go out in the corridor. Ricky got up to follow figuring they'd be better off together and he'd find out too. They went through that car and into the next. When they got to the end of that one there was only the locomotive in front.

"We've been had," Ricky turned to Eddie. "Somehow we are now on a different train than the one earlier because we walked through at least five cars before we got to these girls."

Through a complex explanation by using their hands, Ricky finally understood what must have happened. At some point the train separated, the front going to Genoa, the rear going to Bologna.

"What do we do now?" Ricky asked after Eddie finally understood.

"Damned if I know," was Eddie's answer.

Ricky turned to Adriana, following him. "*Necesito* Genoa, *necesito* Genoa."

She took his hand and they walked until they found the train conductor. The girls explained to him what had happened and that they were Americanos.

He started talking excitedly and loudly to the girls, gesturing with each statement. Eddie and Ricky could well imagine what kind of dumbass names by which they might be referred now. The conductor seemed to have little sympathy for them. Once again Adriana asked what they could do to get to Genoa. Once more the man gestured and spoke loudly and very rapidly.

Once he finished, Adriana turned to Eddie and said, "*Prima* Bologna, *segundo* Genoa."

Both guys understood what that meant.

"When? When?" asked Eddie, who was trying to think of the Italian word for when.

"*Si* " said Ricky. "*Quando?*"

"*Domani, domani.*"

"Uh oh! That sounds like tomorrow to me," Ricky confided in Eddie.

"Crap, what the hell are we supposed to do now? I don't have any real money with me. What's your situation?"

"Mine's not any better. I left my wallet and money with my bag. God damn. Hope those guys get our luggage. If not, I've lost money—two hundred fifty dollars—and my credit cards and driver's license and everything. Crap. Crap, crap, crap. What'll we do now?"

"I dunno. Ask these girls for some help," Eddie said hopefully.

"OK. *Ragazze per favore. Necesito va a Genoa, domani. Para treno.* You, *tu*, help Eddie and *mio?*" Ricky had to use pidgin Italian with some English because he couldn't speak the language. In fact, he wasn't so sure it was Italian as he was prone to mix some recently acquired Spanish with the few Italian words he had just learned on this trip.

"*Si, si,*" the girl answered. She then held her hand for them to wait there while she went somewhere else. In a minute or two she came back with another person, an older Italian woman.

"Can I help you? She says you are in some trouble but she can't understand what you are saying, so she asked me to talk to you."

"Hot dog, she speaks English, Eddie."

"I know, dolt. I got ears."

Ricky then explained to the lady, "We are American soccer players traveling with our team to Genoa when we walked to the back part of the train and fell asleep. The train separated, I guess, and now, if I understand these girls, we are headed to Bologna. We need to get to Genoa, tonight. Can we get there?"

The lady rapidly interpreted what Ricky said to the girls. One of the girls spoke very fast back to her.

The lady then turned to them and spoke. "You can only get to Genoa by going all the way to Bologna today, staying the night, and catching the morning train from Bologna to Genoa. That's what the conductor told them."

"Crap. You mean we can't get to Genoa tonight?" Eddie burst out.

"No, at least that's what the conductor said. They usually know what they are talking about."

"We have no money and no place to stay and no way to catch up to our team in Genoa," Ricky told her. "What can we do?"

"Do you know where they are staying in Genoa? What hotel?"

"No, do you, Eddie?"

"Hell, no."

"Any ideas, lady? We're fresh out," Ricky pleaded.

"Have you any contacts in Genoa, any at all?"

"None that I know of. You, Eddie?"

Eddie shook his head. "I would have had with a little time and any chance at all with some girls."

Ricky ignored Eddie. "The only thing I know is we are supposed to play the second-division soccer team in Genoa day after tomorrow."

"The only thing I can think of," the lady answered, "is to call some official of the Genoa soccer club after you get to Bologna and inform them of your plight. You guys are in a fix."

"Yeah, looks like we really did it this time. Coach'll be awfully pissed at us," Eddie told Ricky and the others. He looked at the two Italian girls, who were really quite nice looking, as an idea formed in his head.

"Would you ask these girls if they can get us a place to stay tonight that won't cost anything?" He spoke to the lady but was looking at the girls, smiling.

She launched into a long discussion with them, apparently suggesting several things. The conversation alternated between her and the one girl, Elisa, and then between both girls. Elisa glanced over frequently at Ricky during the conversations.

When they finished, the lady turned to them. "They say you can stay with them. They are next-door neighbors. They live in Bologna, not too far from the station. They feel they can arrange something for you."

"*Grazie, mille Grazie,*" Ricky said, smiling and looking at the girls.

"Awwrright," Eddie said loudly. "*Grazie*, ladies, *grazie.*"

So Eddie and Ricky returned with the girls to the compartment. The conversation was more lively this time as there was now a bond among them all. They were also getting more used to communicating with each other.

The train was scheduled to arrive in Bologna at 9:20 P.M. or 21:20 European time, and they arrived within one or two minutes of that time. The guys carried the girls' luggage off the train and walked toward the station. As they were walking through the station they heard their names paged twice. "Eddie Jackson, Ricky Breeland, come to central office please," in English. They got the girls' attention and managed to get them to understand the page.

When they got to the office there was a message. "Wait here for a phone call at 21:40. —Giovanni."

"They know we're here," Eddie shouted as he slapped Ricky on the back. He then grabbed Adriana's hands and skipped around in a circle, with her trying to keep up and understand what was going on.

"*Me amicos,*" Ricky said to Elisa, showing her the paper.

When the phone call came, they were waiting.

Ricky took it. "Hello, hello, Giovanni? Boy, are we glad to hear from you. Yeah, you figured it. What time? OK, we'll be on it. Things are fine here." Ricky said as he put his arm around Elisa's waist. "OK. Tell the coach we're sorry it happened. Nah, no way. We weren't shook. Had plan B in place. Just weren't sure how to pay for the train back. OK, see you tomorrow. *Ciao.*"

"It's all set. They will have tickets waiting here for us on tomorrow morning's train to Genoa. It leaves at 8:05 in the morning," Ricky told Eddie. "*Molto bene, molto bene,*" Ricky said to the girls.

"*Signore. Bigletta a Genoa—due, per favore.*" He leaned over the counter to get the agent's attention. When the agent gave him the tickets, he thanked him and turned to Eddie.

"We're all set now. I have the tickets. What shall we do now?"

"Let's party. Party time," Eddie danced another little jig with Adriana. "This may turn out to be a lot better than what the other guys have. We're starting a string. Two nights in a row."

"Wait a minute, I have to go to the bathroom. There's one over there. Wait for me. *Momento.*" Ricky held up his forefinger in a gesture communicating they should wait, and then showed a very small gap in between his thumb and forefinger to show how short the wait would be. He then turned and walked toward the bathroom.

Eddie talked in English to the girls, trying not to appear a total idiot while Ricky went to the bathroom. The ploy seemed to work as the two girls strained unsuccessfully to understand anything at all from what Eddie was talking about, but were entertained nonetheless.

Shortly Ricky came hurrying over to the others. "Eddie, Eddie, you gotta go to the bathroom here. Even if you don't have to, you have to. You won't believe it."

"What? Why?"

"I won't tell you. You have to see for yourself. It's right over there." Ricky had a mischievous grin on his face as he pointed the way.

Eddie went in the door indicated for men and to Ricky's delight came right back out and looked at the sign. He glanced at Ricky with a wolfish grin and went right back in.

When he finally reappeared, Eddie came back over to the group and declared, "That's damn sure something you'll never see in the States."

"You got that right."

"I stayed until I figured out why all those women were in there. They're cleaning the ladies' head and have shut it down. Hell, they were coming in there like it was nothing special, no big deal. Hell, it must be normal for them."

"I was standing there pissing and they walked right by me. I was paying more attention to who was walking behind me than what I was doing myself."

"Me, too. The strangest thing, though, was that there were no toilets to take a crap, just holes in the floor with sort of ceramic foot pads. Did you see that? How is someone supposed to take a shit?"

"Yeah, I saw that. No, thank you. I don't know. Hey, how in the hell are women supposed to go? They must piss all over themselves. I could never squat to do it."

"Me neither. I have trouble when there is someone in the next stall. This is unreal. They had a lady in there cleaning, too. Did you see that?"

"Nothing to it. Another day at the office for her."

Both guys laughed over this episode and knew they would have a great story to tell the others.

"*Viva Italia!*" Ricky shouted as they started off together for the evening.

Neither Ricky nor Eddie played in the game against Genoa, which the Americans won 2–1. Eddie told the story to the other guys several times. Ricky shook his head sometimes, laughing at how Eddie embellished the tale.

After they beat the Genoa team, everyone's spirits were very high. Business was concluded now in Italy. They had an extra day that was allowed for sightseeing, so the players, after huddling together and arguing about what to do, ended up voting to go to Monte Carlo and Nice. But the decision was made only after a long struggle by those who wanted to go back to Naples. That idea of going to Naples was finally rejected as impractical; it was such a long way. To some, like Chase, it would have been worth it.

They presented this argument to Giovanni and the coaches. Train schedules were consulted and after much huddling it was decided they could go to Nice if they left the next morning and returned very late that next night or on the all-night train back to Rome. The team voted for the all-night train, which got them to Rome in time to still do some things the next day. In fact, it arrived at 8:20 the next morning.

Two attractions were drawing them west: the beaches of Nice, where they were sure to see girls sunbathing topless, and the sights of Monte

Carlo and Monaco, with the chance to gamble.

All the players put on their bathing suits under their warmups or shorts the next morning before getting on the train. Those who had forgotten bathing suits just put their shorts on. They were not going to miss the beach scene.

The beaches themselves were a disappointment. There was little or no sand, just small stones. They got there at about 10:15 and had until 21:30 in Nice.

"Watch the sunburn!" Giovanni warned.

The scenery at the beach was everything they expected it to be. The guys, as a group, started walking along the beach near the water. Scott estimated more or less fifty percent of the girls were topless. Most of them were just lying on their back face up. Some were on their stomach, propped up on their elbows or lying flat. As the team walked along they caused quite a commotion because they were whooping and hollering and talking loudly, praising this one or that one or jeering fat, older ones who, in their opinion, shouldn't have taken off their tops at all. Scott and Pu were walking together mostly just looking, or making quiet comments to themselves. Eddie's and Ricky's comments were the loudest and spiciest. Eddie's language was almost always somewhat vulgar, but he had a down-home way of saying things Southern-style that just made you laugh at him. He could get away with saying things that others couldn't. Eddie and Ricky would frequently make suggestions to the girls they passed, but very few sunbathers spoke English. Several girls said something back to them. A few times, when they spoke English, the commentary flew fast and furious. Some times it turned a bit nasty. Some of the girls didn't like their comments. Sheer numbers and boldness overwhelmed the girls, so the guys backed off of nothing. Apparently the code there was to treat the topless situation as if it were nothing special, Scott observed to Pu.

"When you think about it," Pu answered, "why shouldn't they be able to take their tops off and have it be a very normal situation? It's only in the States, because they are always covered, that we think this is really something. Everyone, every girl, has 'em. It's not really anything special."

"Yeah, I guess you're right. Still, I like to look."

"Oh, me too, me too," Pu responded. Right then Pu groaned because he saw an exceptionally nice set of boobs on one girl. He turned to Scott to draw his attention to them when he saw Scott's gaze riveted on the same girl.

"She's beautiful," half-whispered Scott.

"Now, I could stand here all day and look at that. I tell you."

The other guys caught up to them at this point and interrupted Scott's thoughts.

"Look at that! Geez, look at that!" Ricky gushed.

"Awwrright!" Eddie drawled out his favorite expression.

The guys liked this girl so much, it became consensus she was number one of all they had seen on the beach so far. They were obvious in their admiration. It was hard for twenty staring guys to be subtle, anyway, but none made any pretense of it here.

The girl was embarrassed at all the attention. It wasn't long before she put her beach coverup on to the accompaniment of a chorus of boos.

As the guys moved along, their favorite thing was to watch "the ceremony," as they called it. "The ceremony" happened upon the arrival of newcomers to the beach. When new girls came to the beach, and seventy-five percent of everyone on the beach were girls, they'd settle on a spot. First thing they always did after they layed down what they were carrying was to lay out their towel. Then the girls would sit on the towel. From that point it varied somewhat. Some put lotion on their arms and legs and shoulders. Some fiddled in their beach bags getting sunglasses and books out, or putting shoes or sandals in. Then they'd either stand up and pull off shorts or pants or they would pull them off sitting on the towel. Next would come off whatever coverup they were wearing up top. About ten percent of the girls had no swimsuit top. Of the majority who did wear a top, there was usually some intervening procedure of searching in their bag or rearranging the towel—something to delay the next step. What made it interesting was that suspense element. Will she, or won't she? Only half took their tops off and so every time the guys waited, holding their breath, to see if the girl would pull off her top before laying down. This ceremony was more fun than looking at those already disrobed. A few of the more enterprising girls would come to the beach in street clothes, wrap a beach towel around themselves, and proceed to undress completely underneath the towel, then to put their bikini bottom on before removing the towel. The first time they saw this the guys just stared, not really believing what they were seeing.

After a while, Scott and Pu walked up into town to see what it was like. Eddie and Ricky said they were going to stay right there on the beach. The city of Nice had many pretty flower beds, well cared-for. A couple of blocks from the beach they came to a large moon-shaped sculpture at one end of a sort of town square that was one block wide and four blocks long. Beautiful flowers, manicured lawns, sidewalks, and fountains made a very pretty, relaxing atmosphere.

"Boy, this is nice here, no wonder you hear so much about the French Riviera," Pu remarked.

"Yeah, I like it too. One day I'd like to bring Diana back here and spend a real vacation at this place. I'm getting to see and do so many things that I'd like to share with her."

"Sure sounds like you love her."

"Yep. That's why I don't mess around like many of the other guys. I won't do that to her. When I married Diana I made some commitments to her that I won't break. We're very much in love."

"Hope one day I find a wife I feel that way about. I envy you, Scott."

"Diana is special, very special. She is who I want to spend the rest of my life with. I love her very much. And just now I miss her. Let's go."

When they got to Monte Carlo, some of the guys went straight to the casinos, while some went to Monaco to see the palace. Scott found Monaco a little eerie. So this is why Grace Kelly left the United States, he thought. Nice place, nice lifestyle. The view of the harbor was tremendous, with all the yachts and cruise ships docked. What dominated the landscape, though, were all the houses and buildings on the surrounding hillsides, mostly white, overlooking the harbor. That's beautiful, what a picture, Scott thought as he stared at the scene in front of him.

"Bet you'd have to have lots of money to afford to live here," Scott stated to Pu, who was also looking at the scene.

"Lot of millionaires here, I betcha," Pu answered.

"Have to be, to live here."

Later that night Scott and Pu played blackjack at the casino. Scott won four hundred francs, and Pu lost sixty. The money won allowed Scott to pay for the Monte Carlo sweater he had purchased for Diana in the shops up in Monaco. Now he wished he had bought some more things for her. They'd have no more chance here; they were to leave late that night.

Because Eddie and Ricky had already experienced some misinformation on the train, they were all required to be at the train station forty-five minutes early. The scheduled departure was 0:05, or five minutes after midnight, so they were to be there by 23:20. Miraculously, everyone showed up before 23:30, although several appeared a little inebriated. The stories of what each had experienced were related to one another while they waited for the train. After the first several spectacular hours on the beach together they had broken up and gone their separate ways. Some went into town, some gambled early, many remained on the beach, while a couple slept in the hotel room they had gotten so they had a place to shower and change.

The trip back to Rome was long but uneventful. Eddie and Ricky were frequently asked to join someone for a look-see through the train, but they usually smiled while declining the invitation.

Scott didn't sleep well during the all-night trip. He wished he could sleep sitting up—others seemed to be able to—but he dozed fitfully.

The next morning it was light when Scott opened his eyes. He realized he must have slept almost two hours, his best rest of the whole night. The others in his compartment were still asleep, so Scott got up and walked out into the passageway. Hay fields with large round bales greeted his view. Interspersed between the hay fields were sunflowers. Scott had not realized before coming to Europe how much land was used for agriculture. He had always had this notion that people would be everywhere. Funny, though, the people seemed to live in the same towns, the same houses, for ages. Very little new housing was evident. Not at all like the United States. Towns here were the same size today, it appeared, as they were fifty or one hundred years ago. The buildings, made of stone or brick, looked that old, anyway. Evidently the population of Italy, and maybe Europe, had not increased all that much over the years. Scott wondered what the Old World countries would look like now if they had grown like the United States had in the last two hundred years.

Before long, one of the coaches came by and told Scott to wake the others in his compartment, that they would be in the station terminal in twelve to fifteen minutes. He then went on and Scott could see him poke his head into the next two compartments, presumably waking up the players.

After waking up Pu and Cornell, Scott went back out to the passageway and reflected on the trip. He had enjoyed so many things. The team's performance was the overriding factor in making everything else more fun. After the first game the team had played very well. Scott wondered whether this team could now beat the other U.S. team. He didn't believe they would have done any better and probably not as well. This team had really built camaraderie with this trip. More so than with the trip to Brazil. More things happened here. In fact, the Brazil trip was kind of dull compared to this European experience. He liked Rome and the ancient culture better than Rio, also. Maybe it was the team's performance that colored his feelings, too, but there was a definite camaraderie evident with this team that wasn't there in Brazil. This team has character. We have fun together, and that helps everyone's attitude. Plus, on this trip Kori was the coach. Scott wondered if he was coaching each of the two teams in order to get as good a look at as many of the players as he could in real situations. Kori was a fun guy and added a lot to the team morale.

Scott was still deep in thought when people started crowding the passageway as the train was slowing, coming into Termini Station in Rome. He grabbed his bag, thankful that they'd been able to leave much of their luggage at their headquarters in Rome, so he only had one bag to carry. When they got off the train, they had a long walk to get to the terminal, because they were in the ninth car from the end. Giovanni asked them to wait together until all of the players and coaches were ready, to be sure no one got lost in the train station. When everyone was assembled they started off. The players' mood was melancholy, however, because they sensed this was the end of their trip in Italy. The adventure was over. Consequently, there was not a lot of conversation among the players.

As they approached the exit turnstiles, Scott could see there was a bottleneck getting through. As he glanced to the right there was also a steady stream of travelers coming to that point at the same time, further clogging the bottleneck.

"Great. Gotta wait to even get out of this station," he said to no one in particular.

As the team and Scott reached the point where progress was delayed, the people packed tightly behind them. Italians are always in a hurry, just like their driving, he thought.

He could feel the crowd pressure from behind and resented such close quarters. Just as Scott stepped through the turnstile he heard someone say, "Gone."

"Hey, my wallet's gone! God damn, my wallet's gone."

Immediately Scott felt his back pocket and was horrified to realize he'd had his pocket picked too.

"Mine, too. Somebody picked my pocket!" Scott called out as he turned to his right to try to spot the pickpocket. As he turned, someone in a grayish-white T-shirt pushed through past him into the crowd ahead.

"Hey, there he is!" Scott cried. "Get him!"

But the pickpocket, about seventeen or eighteen years old, tall and skinny, was disappearing into the many people emerging from the turnstiles.

Scott partially turned to the player next to him without looking to see who it was and said, "Watch my bag."

With that he took off, pushing through the crowd as though his very life depended on his getting through. He heard someone else close by say, "We gotta catch him." It sounded like Ricky but Scott couldn't take time to turn and look, he had to keep his eyes on the figure in front. Ahead he saw the pickpocket look back at them. When he saw them coming hard after him, he redoubled his efforts to escape. His hands were shoving and pulling people out of the way as he entered the fringe area of the crowd. Now he could weave and dart through the people. The space between the pickpocket and Scott widened noticeably, and as Scott got to the fringe area, the pickpocket cleared the crowd and started running full speed through the terminal.

Scott, with Ricky close behind, accelerated as they made their way through the less crowded area. Ricky hollered, "Stop that man, he's a thief," as he pointed ahead to the pickpocket.

No one made any move to stop the fleeing thief, but happily, people who looked up at them moved enough out of the way so that Scott and Ricky made good progress through the edge of the crowd.

Seeing the effect, Pu, who was trailing Ricky, yelled "Thief, Thief!" As the last few people cleared out of the way, Scott focused on the figure sprinting ahead. This was no ordinary race. The man in front was stimulated by the sight of three bigger men, obviously in their prime, chasing him. Scott, filled with adrenaline from the fury rising in him for being victimized, was a driven man.

The pickpocket had often fled from the scene before when he'd been found out. Most pickpockets drop the goods and pretend their innocence, counting on escaping as the victim bent over to retrieve his valuables. But this one had relied frequently on his superior speed to get away in the past, when he had been found out. He had supreme confidence in his ability to outrun anyone who might pursue him. After all, he was a champion sprinter in high school who had found a way to use his abilities to make a living. Once again he would outrace his pursuers. He smiled as he pictured the frustration on the faces of his adversaries as he left them behind.

Scott was amazed at how far away the foe in front of him had already gotten. The distance looked to be thirty-five yards or so. Nonetheless, Scott bent to the task and, feet flying, took off at full speed in hot pursuit. The man in front, Scott noticed, had sneakers on. He must have planned for the chance he'd have to run, he thought. He's pretty fast. He's no slouch.

Fortunately, Scott also had sneakers on, as well as his warm-up suit. As Scott sprinted after the man, he started closing the gap ahead of him and opening one on Ricky behind him.

The teenager burst through the doors at the end of the station and ran out into the drop-off area in front of the parking lot.

Scott poured it on. He did not want to lose his target outside the building. He too burst through the doors, flinging them wide as he followed the culprit outside. He still had him in view as he passed into the bright sunlight. Scott wondered what the guy would do, once outside, to elude any pursuer. He didn't realize the pickpocket seldom had anyone stay with him this far and had never had someone catch up.

The pickpocket never had to look back. He knew by the sound of the doors bursting open that he was in trouble. He wondered who the hell he had picked on. Was this a track team? Was this their champion sprinter? He should have studied them more closely before deciding to steal their wallets. When he heard the doors slam open he made two decisions: First, he threw the wallets away—off to the right. The cardinal rule is never get caught with the goods. Second, he began to plan some evasive tactics. He looked ahead to see how he could evade a pursuer. His spine tingled as he thought of potentially unpleasant consequences. Being on some kind of a team, his adversary was probably in great condition, so he couldn't hope to outdistance him.

Scott pointed to the area where the wallets were thrown as he glanced back at Ricky and Pu. "Get them!" he shouted.

Ricky stopped to gather up the wallets. He too had seen him throw the stolen articles to the side. "Help Scott," Ricky called to Pu. "I'll get these."

"OK," Pu puffed, as he continued after Scott.

Ahead of the pickpocket was a two-and-a-half foot fence with a three-foot gap to allow passenger flow out of the parking lot. The way was clear, so he dashed through the opening and ran into the parking area. One hundred yards ahead was the road, crowded with cars. The same road ran around the parking lot to the left, only thirty yards away. He made the necessary decision and broke to his left toward the closest way out.

Unfortunately for Scott, a mother and toddler were arriving at the opening of the fence at the same time he was. He didn't slow down one bit; rather, he hurdled the fence just next to the toddler. Thanks, Mark, he said to himself. Mark was a high school buddy who taught Scott how to jump high hurdles at track practice. Even though Scott never ran them in competition, he had learned the basics of sticking the forward leg out front and picking the trailing leg up with the knee to the side.

In a flash Scott was over the fence. Just as he touched down he saw his objective, only seven yards ahead, take a sharp turn to the left. As Scott matched the direction of the desperado in front, he slipped on some loose gravel and went down hard on his left hip. His left hand went down to break his fall and was the first element of recovery as he pushed back up with lightning quickness. The fall allowed Pu to catch up with him but it also widened the gap on the fugitive to fifteen yards.

"Let's get that bastard," Pu wheezed. They had already run close to one hundred fifty yards at full speed and so conversation was short and strained.

Off they went again, eager to capture the thief and bring him back to the police. Scott was angry he fell and let the target, who was almost within grasp, get ahead again.

At the sound of someone falling the pickpocket turned and glanced back at the two men pursuing him. Good, he had opened up the space again, providing him some new options for escape. He looked ahead at the traffic flowing through the street. As he watched the vehicles flow past, an idea came to him. He looked back at what was coming and saw a dark blue pickup in the nearest lane of traffic. Perfect—if I can just reach there in time, he thought. Just as the teenager reached the street the truck passed the same point. Up he jumped into the bed of the truck and landed on all fours. As he recovered from his landing he saw the truck was gradually pulling away from his pursuers. For the first time, he got a good look at who was chasing him. He saw a runner with blazing speed chasing the truck and almost staying even. He wondered how quickly he would give up. Surely he realizes he can't keep up with the truck. It won't be long, nor can he keep up that speed very long. I'm tired; he's got to be, too, he thought. Behind the lead runner was another one with good speed. He's faster than I am too! The pickpocket was reevaluating his strategy. Maybe running away has to be a selective course for action. *Madre de Dios.* Why did I pick on these guys?

Even further back was a third person in the same warmups and same tennis shoes. Never again someone with tennis shoes, he vowed. Coming out of the station were a group of the same players, he observed. Glad I caught a ride.

In fact the truck was spreading the distance between the pursuers and the pursued. The young thief felt a surge of relief and couldn't help blowing a kiss to his nemesis. You bastard. You wore me out and I threw my profit away—I should've kept it. Then he kind of leaned back and gave Scott and the others a good-bye wave.

Pu shouted, "He's gotten away!" at Scott, who was sprinting ahead of him.

"Nope, red light," Scott answered.

"What?" Pu gasped.

"Red light," Scott repeated. "Look." He then pointed to the traffic light around the corner, well ahead of the truck. The first three cars in the near lane had already stopped, but the slowing traffic had not yet affected the truck.

Scott knew the thief did not realize that his escape was being jeopardized. The problem was to stay close enough so that when the truck slowed down he would still be within striking distance. He was angry that someone would take something from him, and the pickpocket's arrogance in the truck further inflamed Scott's feelings. Gotta get him, Scott declared to himself.

The thief couldn't believe Scott was still chasing him. He thought he would wave to him one more time; make him mad, really mad. He restyled his wave by using fewer fingers. "Here, this is for you," he mouthed.

Just then the pickup shuddered as the driver put the brakes on hard. The pickpocket jerked his head around quickly to see what the problem was. His face grew ashen when he saw the line of traffic stopped ahead of him. He scrambled to his feet and moved to the right. As he placed his hand on the side of the bed he vaulted over the side, back down on to the street. He didn't gauge the effect of the forward movement of the truck just right, and instead of hitting the ground running, he stumbled forward, straining to retain his balance. Swearing, he strained mightily to bring himself upright so as to be able to sprint again. Eventually he regained his form and speed.

When Scott saw his target leap out of the truck his anticipation of immediately catching him was crushed. I'm not going to let that bastard get away, he thought. So Scott hardened his resolve and was immediately rewarded with the sight of the stumbling figure ahead. Adrenaline surged anew as the yardage between them was eaten up with each step.

"Move, move," Scott shouted silently.

The thief reached full speed along the street just as he heard the footsteps behind him. But it was too late.

Scott launched himself into the air from two yards away about the same time his nemesis topped off. He knew he had him. "Now," he cried out loud as he leaped for his objective. The flying tackle was perfect. The youth went down hard under Scott's weight slamming into him. Down they went on the pavement.

Scott scrambled higher on the body underneath him as he straddled the form with his knees. The pickpocket was twisting and turning, trying to get Scott off him and get away.

"No you don't, you prick. I've got you now," Scott hissed to him as he pressured his neck back down to the ground with his forearm.

Pu came to a stop alongside them and, breathing heavily, said,"Way to go, way to go." He grabbed the pickpocket's right arm, which was reaching back to grab Scott's hair. He roughly pulled it back away from his teammate.

"Whoa, this jerk still has some fight left in him," Pu said as he gave the guy's arm a little twist.

Eddie came running up at this point. "Let me at that son of a bitch. I'll teach him to try and steal from us." Then he reached down and whomped him on the back of the head with his full hand opened. "Get him up so's I can do some real damage."

"No," Scott commanded. "Let the authorities take care of him."

Scott and Pu hauled the pickpocket up to his feet and held him tight.

Eddie got right up in his face and said, "You've seen the last of the outside of a jail, asshole."

The thief retaliated by kicking Eddie in the shins.

In a flash, Eddie hit him with a right across the cheek. "Try it again, moron."

The youth slashed out with his feet again at Eddie. Instantly Pu, the third biggest player on the team, grabbed him around the throat with his arm, pulling him away from Eddie while twisting so his own body was between Eddie and the thief.

"Enough horseplay. Let's get him back to the station." Then Pu took control of their prisoner. "Let's not mess him up too much, boys, or the police might not take too kindly to our good Samaritan efforts here."

The pickpocket was speaking rapidly in venomous tones to Pu as he was jerked off his feet and spun around by the much bigger soccer player.

Scott grabbed one arm again and told Eddie to follow behind. As soon as they started toward the station, Ricky, Marty, and four others came up to them.

"Nice going, glad you got this asshole. Someone needs to teach him a lesson," Ricky declared as he walked up to him and grabbed his shirt and twisted it under his chin. "Boy, you picked on the wrong ones this time. I even got the goods you threw away, see."

Scott stuck his leg across in front of the teenager to prevent him from kicking Ricky, but the youth, now grossly outnumbered, reconciled his fate and did not try anything. Instead, he stared with intense hatred right into Eddie's eyes as he looked up into the taller man's face.

"Let's get him to the cops," Pu told everyone. He gently moved Eddie aside with his free hand and started off with the prisoner, Scott on the other side.

Several of the guys slapped Scott on the back and told him, "Way to go," and "nice going," and other compliments for running him down. All of them realized the pickpocket was a pretty fast runner. "Too bad this guy took a wrong turn somewhere; he'd have made a pretty good striker on someone's team," Marty remarked.

Several of the players turned to look at Marty, half thinking the same thing, half thinking Marty was crazy, which they already knew.

When they got back to the station the coaches and the rest of the team were waiting with Giovanni and three policemen.

The pickpocket immediately started jabbering to the cops, nodding in the direction of first Eddie, then Scott.

Giovanni told them, "He's telling the cops you guys called him a lousy Italian swine and pushed him in the crowd and when he pushed back you chased him and beat him up when you caught him, that two of you held him while the third punched and kicked him."

Scott and Pu and Eddie declared at once, "He's lying." Eddie then used more colorful language in describing what happened between the pickpocket and himself.

Scott told Giovanni to show the wallets Ricky still clutched to the policemen and make them believe their side of the story.

Giovanni replied, "Oh, I don't think that'll be any problem. They know who he is already. They know he's a pickpocket. They told me he is known as Smoke because when he runs that's all he leaves someone to catch. No one has ever caught him before. Even the police. He's gotten away every time. They said he's extremely fast."

Eddie, who was listening, piped up, "He didn't know what he was up against. There's no one faster in the whole world than Scott. Scott could catch anyone. Pu here is awfully fast, too. He'd 'a caught the mother, too."

"No, I wouldn't have. The bugger was about as fast as I was. Without Scott he'd have gotten away for sure. I'm not surprised no one has caught him. He needs this, though. I think back there when we were close together, he was trying to tell me just how thankful he was that finally he got captured." Pu broke out into a real big grin with that statement.

Scott and the rest of the posse all had many opportunities to explain their little adventure to the other guys and also to people back home. Scott enjoyed the raw form Eddie used to tell the story, although it seemed to get better and better each time he told it.

CHAPTER 10

Scott cried from the strong emotions brought on by the headlines in the sports pages: "U.S. Women Capture First World Cup." The story continued: "November 30: Guangzhou, China—A scrappy defense and the golden touch of striker Michelle Akers-Stahl powered the USA women over Norway to capture the first ever FIFA world championship for women. Norway forced the USA out of its normal attacking style of play and gave the Americans all they wanted before succumbing 2–1 to a gritty squad of focused and determined combatants." The article went on to describe more details about the game and the strategies employed by both teams.

Apparently the United States did not dominate this contest as they had so many of the others leading to the title game, Scott concluded. He knew, however, that the American contingent lost twice before to this Norwegian team earlier this same year. Must have been a real battle, he continued thinking. He read on to see that Akers-Stahl, the striker, had scored both goals for the United States. That news made him emotional, realizing he held the very same position for the men's team.

What really got Scott going, however, was the information that so many of the women had sacrificed so much to participate in this World Cup. Several had to quit promising jobs, many postponed a family, Mia Hamm left college. The personal sacrifices were enormous. When he read how midfielder Shannon Higgins played the whole game with a broken foot, Scott had to get up and get a couple of tissues to blow his nose and wipe the tears off his face.

She was quoted as saying, "Fight and desire got us through." The article used her situation as that which best illustrated the grit of the players on the team.

Scott had been following the progress of the tournament in the papers as the games unfolded. He was excited to see the paper every day, wanting to know how they did. He got so psyched up after reading about their eventual victory that he sent the team a long and involved congratulatory letter expressing his personal appreciation for their accomplishments. He told them how proud he was of their victories and that they had come through so much to achieve their ultimate goal.

Scott had gotten to know several of the players through occasional meetings with them. Twice the USSF had initiated some activity that brought the two teams in contact with one another. The determination of all the women, and particularly of five or six of them, had truly impressed him, enough so that he realized maybe they were more dedicated to their goal than he was to his. It forced him to conduct some introspection, which resulted in a fierce determination to strive to accomplish his one goal that he had focused on: to win the World Cup!

"You don't know the first thing about being a coach," Paolo shouted. "You treat us like children instead of grownups! Rules, rules, rules. No freedom for us. I feel like a prisoner when I am with this team. Ridiculous! Maybe I just go back to Spain to play with my team. I don't need this hassle!"

"Calm down, Paolo, calm down. You are not being treated like children, but there are a few rules that you are required to observe. One of those is a curfew during the tournaments and the night before any game. It is too important to the rest of the team for each player to be well rested, to worry about how you feel about the curfew rule. You will observe curfew or you won't play on the team. Look, Paolo, we need you and your abilities, but only if you have the correct attitude. I don't want you disrupting the rest of the team. You must make a decision whether you really want to be a part of this Costa Rica national team or not. I want you if you can decide to be a part of the team. If you want to be an individual, then go back to Spain and don't play World Cup. Think about it!"

Paolo De Palmer went off and sulked a little, though he knew the coach was dead right, and that he, Paolo, wanted badly to be a part of the national team and all that comes with it. He dreamed of being the center of attention of the press and all those adoring fans—especially the pretty *muchachas*. He dreamed of scoring the winning goal in a World Cup match and receiving adulation from all the fans. It had happened that way in junior soccer, but how much more magnified the reaction would be in a World Cup match!

The coach walked down the field toward the defense. He shook his head. That Paolo. He's got so much talent, but he is so immature. He's got a lot of growing up to do. All he thinks about are the ladies. From what the other guys tell me, he is quite successful, too. I imagine the girls respond to his good looks and charm. He's popular with the other guys, too. They like him, they like to be with him. He's got an attractive personality. Paolo could have such a positive effect on the team if he would channel his energy toward the goals and objectives of the team.

Paolo is the key, thought the coach. If I can get his mindset directionally correct and he performs with the same level of intensity as he now wastes on distractions, the team might just gel around Paolo as the nucleus. He's got a world of talent. The very best thing is his uncanny ability to be in the right place at the right time. It's as if he knows ahead of time what's going to happen. As if he has viewed films of the action ahead of time. Nowhere have I seen a player anywhere with instincts like Paolo.

The coach had only six months to develop a team from among a bunch of individuals. The first elimination round for the '94 World Cup would be here before the national team is ready, he lamented. It would be tougher this time. Last World Cup, Mexico was disqualified for using an overaged player in the Junior World Cup competition. With Mexico out, it was a wide-open opportunity. Costa Rica had finished first with eleven points and the USA second with ten points, barely squeezing out Trinidad-Tobago with a 1–0 victory in Trinidad in the last qualifying game.

The coach was glad the USA received an automatic berth as host, for their national team had been showing some muscle as of late. They have more team speed and seem to play better as a team. The USA, he recollected, had upset Peru, Bolivia, Uruguay, and almost Argentina to finish second in the America's Cup this year. They could have won the game against Argentina, too. The USA team may be very representative. The coach allowed himself a smile. The whole Concacaf region will be well represented. The Mexican team always does well. And now his Costa Rican team could, with a few improvements, supply a few surprises of their own.

Coach Lopez, since coming last year, had instituted several changes of his own. When he arrived he spent three weeks reviewing films of the team's past performances. The team, he figured, could be improved with a new offense and a new defensive scheme. The midfield was pretty strong, a good sign. The center midfielder, an Indian, would fit in nicely with the plans for the transitional game. There were a few holes to fill, but by and large the team worked well together. The coach smiled as he thought of some of his training techniques that would yield positive results. This was a team he could work with. What was really promising was that the younger team (the under nineteen-year-olds) had done so well in the past several years. He saw several really good players among that group. There was also the majority of the team left over from last year's World Cup in Italy. Ronald Gonzales looked every bit as if he would become a great team leader. The coach hoped so. He was also as fine a person as one could meet. Yes, Ronald was needed to add stability and maturity to the team.

Coach Lopez pulled himself back into the present. He looked off at Paolo and wistfully hoped things went the right way. Paolo could be the key. He had the talent that could develop him into one of the stars of soccer. Diego Maradona of Argentina had the same knack for timing and passing and scoring as what he saw in Paolo. Coach Lopez had seen Maradona as a youngster before star status arrived. It was the same with young Paolo. He had the same sense of greatness around him as what he saw in Maradona. If only, if only, the coach dreamed on.

One of the reasons Coach Lopez took this job as coach of the Costa Rican national team was the sense of commitment he felt from the National Soccer Committee. He smiled as he remembered how they had approached him. Yes, they had done their homework and had known all the right buttons to push. They knew what would appeal to him. What had surprised him was the financial commitment behind the World Cup effort. They had garnered industrial sector support and healthy contributions from wealthy individuals, placed a tax on gasoline, gotten all the professional teams to kick in, and had gotten a generous amount from the public through a "support the national team" campaign.

Forty-five years ago, he mused, Costa Rica could play with any team in the world. They had a strong team with excellent players at every position. Then a transition occurred. The best players had come from the middle class, people who were well educated and who, perhaps, held professional jobs such as teachers and engineers. That slowly evolved into a situation where the poorest people became the best players—to escape the financial conditions they had grown up with. The game of soccer changed in Costa Rica. Soccer became the way out for many. While Costa Rica today has very little poverty as such, many played with financial gain in mind. When that transition occurred, something was lost, not to be regained—even with the subsequent development of their professional leagues.

Now it was his job to restore the days of yesteryear. The fans wanted it. There were great soccer fans in Costa Rica. They had even "adopted" Brazil as their country to root for in World Cup and other international play because Costa Rica was generally put out early in the competitive rounds. It was a phenomenon that seemed peculiar to outsiders but one that was perfectly natural to these Ticos who thought nothing was unusual or strange about their allegiance to Brazilian soccer.

The coach had to develop a strong defense, which he considered his top priority. He had some good players, but some, like Roger Flores, were getting a little long in the tooth. The coach would have to carefully select his complement of players. He also would have to be on the lookout for additional help. Every once in a while he saw someone who could help but who might not be used properly in their current situation. Often it was the defensive scheme and how the player fit in that determined how well he played. Coach Lopez would keep an eye out for that certain player as he watched the professional games. He also kept trying new players in exhibition matches that the national team played with other international teams.

Paolo continued to impress him. It was uncanny, his ability with the ball. The ball seemed a part of his body. Whether Paolo was deftly moving the ball with his feet, or heading it, or making a body trap, the ball always was where he had full control. He had seen no one else who could take a pass at full speed from any angle and immediately have complete control of the ball. It was an extension of him. He would work on some offensive schemes that could get the ball to Paolo in opportune situations, he decided.

It had always been a strong desire of Maria Elena to get married at the church in Zarcera. Ever since she was a little girl and had fallen in love with the beautiful landscaping, it had been a dream of hers. That church was not the one that she regularly attended; rather, it was her grandparents' church, and the one in which her parents had been married. Too, she and Alex had invited and expected a much bigger crowd than the little church in Aguas Zarcas could handle.

Maria Elena had spent the night in Zarcera with her grandparents many times, but never had her emotions been flooded with remembrances of days gone by as they were tonight. The church rehearsal had gone well and everyone enjoyed a meal afterward here in her grandparents' house, just a scant two hours ago. Now she lay in bed, too excited to sleep. Tomorrow she was to be married to Alex. She would become Mrs. De La Paz in just over twelve hours! People would be coming from all over. Alex had so many friends from soccer she was sure there would be an abundance of eligible young men for all her friends to pick from. Her thoughts drifted back to how she and Alex first met. She had seen Alex when they first brought Pepito in. She was immediately attracted to him, not just by his good looks, but also by the demonstrated love and concern he showed for his younger brother. Pepito, dear precious Pepito. He was one of a kind. Even though he never recovered full use of his leg enough to allow him to run, he never let that affect his positive, always upbeat, outlook on life. Pepito had taught her something about life. That young man let nothing get the best of him. Maria Elena sincerely believed no matter what Pepito faced in the years ahead, he would be able to successfully cope with it. She loved him with all her heart, just as fully as she loved Alex, although, of course, in a different way. She wondered though, if Pepito were older, would she have loved him differently?

Twelve hours. A long time to wait. Maria Elena went through the ceremony as they had practiced it and tried to imagine what the real thing would be like with people in the church and a wedding dress and bridesmaids and music. It was glorious every way she pictured it. She pictured Alex, so nice in his suit. She hoped he was as excited as she was. They had talked so much about their future together. Actually, other than their moving in together as man and wife, nothing much would change for now. She would continue nursing in San José while Alex continued to play soccer for Saprissa. Maria Elena remembered well the day Saprissa signed Alex to a contract. Alex bounced into the hospital and danced with her in a circle. She didn't think she'd ever seen him so happy. He didn't stop talking. His future was settled. He would earn a handsome salary, more than enough for them to live on.

The day dawned bright and sunny. Maria Elena could tell her mom was a nervous wreck. Usually she was calm. Not today. Today her only daughter was getting married and she was beside herself with so many things to do and, more importantly, that she was losing her daughter and giving her up to be married to a boy. Fortunately, Maria Elena's aunt was taking care of most of the preparations.

The church was nearly full. Most of Alex's teammates from the junior national team were there, as well as those from his Puerto Viejo team. In fact, it seemed like half the town of Puerto Viejo was there. On Maria Elena's side were many of the nurses and some of the doctors she worked with at the children's hospital. Old friends of the family who still lived in Zarcera also attended.

The ceremony was short for a Catholic wedding. Afterward there was a fiesta held outside the church on the main entrance to the church, the one that went underneath the arches made of shrubbery. The fiesta also spilled over into the sidewalks along the main street of town. Those who had never attended any kind of service here at this church were amazed at the beautiful topiary displayed at this county church nestled deep in the mountains. In one place was sculpted a whole bullfight arena, including the bull ring, the spectators, and the matador fighting the bull. Other beautiful shapes of animals presented themselves to all who wandered throughout the topiary.

For their honeymoon the young couple went to Puntarenas on the west coast and stayed in a cabin on the beach that one of Maria Elena's relatives owned and lent to them for their time together.

Both Alex and Maria Elena thoroughly enjoyed their first days together. The feeling that continued to grow within them further ripened the love they felt for each other. Neither had expected such a strong bond to have developed so quickly. They came to depend on each other for so many things, including support when things weren't going quite as planned.

In the years ahead Alex would welcome that support.

Antonio Montini was chastising himself for not having thought of it first. His boss in New York called this morning to suggest they consider this World Cup of soccer and to explore the various money-making opportunities. Antonio was born and raised in the United States and didn't know the first thing about soccer, at least the rules. He did know it was the most popular sport in the world, far and away more popular everywhere else than either football or basketball. He knew his boss was right. If there is that much interest throughout the world, then there have to be opportunities to exploit. So Antonio called a meeting of his group leaders for this afternoon in his office in a building that overlooked two of the gambling casinos in Atlantic City.

"Gentlemen, Number One suggested we look at ways to make money during this soccer tournament this summer, the World Cup. This is a really big deal throughout the world. We just need to figure out how to capitalize on an event this big. Now, this is an idea session, and I want to hear what you guys think about it."

"Well, one obvious way to make money is to make book on the games using our network. We'd have to get the word out that we are doing it so our customers know about it," commented one.

"Good. Whose line will we use?"

"Cleopatra's Palace; all the big casinos will take off of their line. We'll just tie right in to theirs, like we do for the basketball."

"OK, what else?"

"Along that line, we can offer types of bets that legit places won't offer. They'll do win-lose of course, and they'll do over-under probably. I'll try to find out what else they'll be offering, and maybe we can come up with others."

"Good. Nick, you run with those, OK?"

"Right, Boss, you got it."

"Open up a little, let's be innovative."

"How's about us fixin' a few?"

"Well, how would we do that? They all speak different languages, and most of the players are already well paid. It's hard for one guy on a team to make enough difference."

"It's always possible to find someone willing to throw one, Boss. Maybe one guy is pissed off at his coach or sumptin' else. And certainly we can find someone who speaks the right language, once we've decided who's the target. I know Italian's no problem."

That brought a chuckle from the others in the room.

"If we choose to try that I want to be involved at each and every step. Something like that can backfire, you know. What else can we do?"

"How 'bout the ladies? Unless I miss my guess, most of the people traveling to the United States will be men, not couples or families. The men are the most avid devotees of the sport."

"That's an easy one to do. Carlo, you find out all the cities where these games are going to be played. Then you start lining up taxi drivers, bus drivers, hotel workers, and our other usual contacts. Joe, you start working on getting the girls."

"I'll use as many locals as possible, but we may have to move some of them around to meet the demand."

"OK, keep me informed."

"What about the hotels? Can we muscle a percentage from the room bookings?"

"Nah. As I understand it, the rooms have been booked already, several months ago. They started soon after they started selling tickets."

"Is there any opportunity to get some protection money?"

"What about kidnapping or extortion? Is there any potential for that?" Vinnie asked.

"Let's be careful with those. I imagine security will be at peak levels for an event such as this."

"There are always openings for a well laid-out plan, Boss."

"Let me think on these for a while. Unless anybody else has any really big ideas, let's start running with these. I'll call Number One and let him know what we talked about. He'll have to approve everything. We'll meet again on Friday at, say, ten in the morning. Any problems with that?"

Coach Gaborakov looked out the doorway and shook his head. The rain was coming down harder than ever. He decided perhaps today would be the day to try something a little different. In order to help build team unity today, the players would go through some planned interpersonal exercises to develop more camaraderie among the players. The purpose was to develop a more cohesive unit. He turned away from the doorway and headed to his office, where he had a file full of notes and ideas about how to do this.

Some of the activities had been given to him by a friend of his who worked for General Motors, which had used them in training the salaried workforce prior to opening a new plant. The activities were designed to help the people to get to know each other better, to be able to relate to one another. The theory, his friend had explained, was the more you knew about your fellow worker, the more you knew where he was coming from, maybe what motivated him, and how he might react to certain situations. The plant startup had gone exceptionally well. The level of commitment among the hourly and salaried workforce was exceptional. The plant became a showcase for GM and a leader in management techniques, having delegated authority and responsibility down to the level of the operator to a greater degree than anywhere else at GM.

It had been a number of years since the coach's friend had experienced this, but he told the coach recently of the lesson learned from the up-front effort and training investment and how it paid off for the largest corporation in the world.

Two of the things Kori wanted to accomplish were to get each player to reveal something of himself that had influenced him and his life and to have the players have an enjoyable time doing it.

He had expected everyone to show up; they had been told to come to practice rain or shine. Even the coaches and managers could participate. The players would benefit from knowing more about them, too.

The file was exactly where it was supposed to be, and the coach spent the next two hours detailing and preparing the exercises for today's practice. By the time he had finished putting his plan together, the players had all arrived. They were all in the locker room or the weight-training area. Some liked to work out before practice; some liked to do their assigned workout after practice.

The physical fitness trainer had done a splendid job developing the players. As a group, in seven months of workouts designed by the "doctor," as he was called, the team had achieved some startling advancements. Overall team speed had improved substantially. Every player had increased his forty-yard dash speed by at least three-hundredths of a second. All could now jump higher. The minimum increase was three-tenths of an inch, but half the team had advanced more than one-half inch, and three players had scored an astounding one-inch improvement. Their body-fat content had decreased six percent. Their times in the mile run had diminished an average of nine and one-half seconds. The doctor had been recommended by the United States Soccer Federation and arrangements had been made for him to spend two months with the team full-time in the summer and consult part-time during the rest of the year. It had been an agreeable arrangement and allowed him to continue his full-time job at USC in the same capacity. Practice was due to start in twenty minutes. The coach called all the assistant coaches into his office and explained what he wanted to do. He didn't expect enthusiastic support for his plan and he didn't get it. But all were willing to go along with his idea and to participate.

The coach waited until everyone was assembled before he entered the room. One little thing that implied authority, he felt, was the control that was gained by being the last one to a meeting.

"The weather is terrible outside, gentlemen, and I've decided today would be well spent getting to know each other a little better. Just relax and enjoy these little exercises we're about to do. I want to start this off by having everyone take one minute to tell the others a little about himself. Include if you're married or not, how many kids you have, where you grew up, and at least one item of information about yourself that you've not told anyone else here. I'll start it off.

"I'm married and have two children, ages eleven and eight. My wife's name is Maria and the kids are Daniel and Matthew. We live in an apartment on the East Side near the swim club, courtesy of the United States Soccer Federation. I was born and raised in Yugoslavia. My father probably had the greatest influence on me of anyone. He played soccer for Yugoslavia in one of the earlier World Cups. He also was an exceptional coach and only an untimely death kept him from coaching the Yugoslavian national team, in my opinion. When he died I was very affected and it was more than one year before my life again became somewhat normal.

"I was a member of the 1978 national team until three months before the start of the tournament, when I tore my knee up and ended my playing days. As soon as I was rehabilitated I turned to coaching. It's been a lifetime ambition of mine to coach a World Cup champion, although I never figured it would be for the United States."

Applause broke out after he said that.

Each of the assistant coaches and players took his turn and told the roomfull of listeners things about themselves. Some told funny stories, some mentioned pet peeves and little things that revealed another side the other players might not know about. Some were serious all the way through, and some had everyone in stitches laughing at the things that had happened to them. Marty Wilcox was one whose tale made the others laugh so hard tears streamed down more than one face. He told how he had won bets doing goofy things and how some of them had backfired, like the time he tried to eat a beer bottle and the unfortunate after-effects. His proudest achievement had been going a full six days in the hospital after knee surgery, eating every meal—and even surviving an enema—without a bowel movement.

The way he told it had them all holding their sides: how the nurses would try to force him to do it and ways he convinced them he had already. He had a way of telling stories so that people just naturally laughed. When he finished—more than two and one-half minutes later—someone called out that Marty missed his true calling. He should have been a comedian.

Other guys told of major events in their lives: things like falling in love, a divorce, losing their virginity, being dirt poor growing up, winning some championship, and other personal bits of information. When Scott's turn came—he was next to last—he told about his conversion to Christ, how that had changed his life, his falling in love with Diana, how he got engaged, and getting married. Then, very emotionally, he told his team-mates about his inseparable pal, Joel, and the events that transpired the night of his graduation, when something inside him died along with his best friend and how, in front of his classmates, he had dedicated his career to Joel. He interrupted his talk frequently to avoid breaking down as his eyes flooded with tears and his voice caught. Scott ended his time by rolling up his right sleeve to show them the black arm band he always wore in practice and in games. "Many of you have asked about this and I wouldn't talk about it. Now you know."

It was another thirty seconds or so before the last person, a coach, could start his short speech. He kept it somber out of respect for Scott, but he also revealed that he had an autistic sister at home and how hard that had been for his parents.

The coach was very satisfied at how the first part had gone. It had been quite interesting and began a kind of bonding among the team members. He was glad Scott's turn had been near the end. His poignant tale had been just the right way to end the round of revelations, but would have destroyed the jubilant mood that had mostly prevailed once Marty got started.

"OK, now everyone should take a three-by-five index card and pencil as we pass them out. No pens, use the pencil only, please. Write on the card at least two and no more than three items about you that are kind of special: interesting facts about yourself. These will be read to the entire group and then we will all try to guess who it is that these bits of informa-tion are describing. Everyone got it? Any questions?"

"Yeah, I got one," Eddie Jackson called out. "Can I put anything I want to on this?"

"Sure. It's wide open, except it has to be about you or describe you."

The coach wrote up his own card, then waited about five minutes for the others to finish. He called for the cards to be turned in. Most of the guys got up and brought them over to the coach. Several had not finished, however, so the coach told them, "Two more minutes, then turn in what you have."

After everyone turned the cards in and they were shuffled, the first card read, "(1) I was engaged four times before I finally got married. (2) Chinese food used to nauseate me, now it's my favorite. (3) My favorite movies are Westerns." The coach read the first fact and everyone looked around, kind of snickering, wondering who it might be. Several guesses were proffered. Eddie, Chris, and Jebadoah were all mentioned, but each denied it. Then the coach read the second statement and more guessing occurred. When the coach read the last item, several guessed correctly that it was Stewart, the goalie coach. That drew a good cheer from most of the guys.

The next card read by the coach said, "(1) I once ate supper with the richest man in America. (2) I was elected outstanding high school senior from a class of four hundred. (3) In third grade I was excused from music class because I sang so bad." The guys had fun guessing and wanted explanation on the dinner. Sam, a substitute, explained his father was a manager of one of Wal-Mart's distribution centers and their family was invited to eat dinner with Sam Walton when he came to town once. The third card was one that drew much laughter. It read, "(1) I almost beat Roger Kingdom in the high hurdles in a close finish. (2) I hated soccer when I was ten years old. (3) I was elected homecoming queen as a senior in high school." It turned out to be Terry O'Shay, which surprised everyone because Terry was perhaps the slowest runner on the team. They all demanded to hear how he almost beat Roger Kingdom in the hurdles. Terry explained that his school met Roger's school in track his senior year and, of course, they all had heard how great this Kingdom guy was and only a junior at that time. Terry said when the gun went off they all got a good start but Roger was moving well out in front. At the second hurdle Roger was four steps ahead of everyone else. On the third hurdle Kingdom caught his foot and went down. Terry said he could tell it was a bad fall because Roger fell face down and slid on his chest and chin. "As I approached the finish line this guy, Kingdom, blew past to finish two to three yards in front of me." The whole room broke into laughter at his description of how he "almost beat Roger Kingdom."

Other interesting facts surfaced. One person's secret desire was to visit the Taj Mahal in India. Another had lived in seven different countries. Another was elected mayor of his town. Still another player had twice saved a person's life. One of the players revealed he had played on a Little League World Series finalist team. Eddie declared he was descended from Robert E. Lee. There were revelations of a sadder nature also. The equipment manager had two friends commit suicide when he was sixteen years old. Another disclosed his uncle had been murdered.

Once again the coach was very satisfied at how things had gone. The players were opening up to each other and sharing a bit of themselves. One of the coaches, who had not really been in favor of doing this when

Kori described it to them prior to practice, even came up to him and said this was a great idea and was working out fine.

After a fifteen-minute break to allow everyone a chance to get up and stretch, go to the bathroom, and get a drink, the coach moved into some team-building exercises. One of these forced each member to rely on all the others to put together solutions for a problem. To make this more effective, the large group was broken into four separate teams. The coaches and managers formed one team, and the players grouped into the other three. Each group's objective could only be reached if they worked together, because each participant was given his own set of instructions and his own set of data with which to work. A lack of cooperation would yield the wrong result.

Three of the four groups came out with the best result. The fourth group missed it, but had come close. After that session the coach explained the theory of the exercise and related it to how this team as a whole, to be successful, had to work together, had to rely on one another, and had to have utter confidence in each other to be successful. "People are going to make mistakes, we all do. But you guys have to know each other well enough that a mistake does not destroy your confidence in that person to get the job done or in the team's ability to win. Two mistakes, however, may mean the coaches have lost confidence and you'll be taken out." That brought a round of nervous laughter from the players.

The next activity stressed communication. Here the coach had tailored the exercise to be more in line with how a soccer team must communicate while on the field. This was followed by a talk from the coach about a past World Cup championship team that attributed their success to their ability to work together on the field and to know what was going on and translate that into anticipation offensively and defensively. Anticipation. That was the coach's key word at every practice and in every speech. The team who anticipates wins. Good communication—both verbal and physical—could enhance anticipation immeasurably.

The next undertaking for the day's program was an activity that built team unity as well as bonding. It would force reliance among the players to achieve the objective of the exercise. It was also designed to let all the participants enjoy themselves while doing it. It too went very well and left the coach with a very satisfied feeling.

The last agenda item was to have each player put his name on the top of a three-by-five index card and write on it what their goal was in this World Cup. After they had finished the coach asked each of them what would they be satisfied with achieving in the tournament. Everyone could then turn in their cards and go home or go to their workout, if they had not already done so.

As the coaches were going through the cards they separated them into three categories. The first was those that gave some abstract or some personal objective not related to winning. The second pile was for those cards that listed World Cup champion or win the World Cup. The third pile was for those that were satisfied with a lesser result. These included "Win a game," "Advance to the second phase," "Reach the quarter finals," and so on. The coach was disappointed there were so many of these, yet, at the same time, he knew the players were being realistic. Five of the players had listed the championship as their goal. Of those, two had said they could be satisfied with reaching the quarter-finals; one indicated the semi-finals would be enough. Only Robert and Scott indicated winning the whole thing was what they would settle for.

It was strange, Coach Gaborakov reflected. Scott was one of three players he was considering to be the captain of the team. The events of the day and the reactions of the players to Scott had pretty much decided in his mind Scott was the man. Now looking at the card in front of him, he was certain. The team had a captain.

It would take emotion to reach the level necessary to compete against the better teams, and it was clear Scott was a very emotional person. The coach was sure one more piece of the puzzle had just fallen into place.

CHAPTER 11

Scott gazed out of the window down at the harshly cut features of the land and the many small, white houses with aqua-colored roofs. The flight attendant announced preparations for landing over the P.A. system, informing the passengers that arrival in Guatemala City would be in ten minutes. "Escarpments" was the one word that kept coming to mind as he looked below. Cliffs and river valleys and table-top mesas were prominent everywhere. Ominously, houses and other buildings were placed right on the edge of the flat, elevated areas, with sharp dropoffs only a few feet away. Scott wondered if collapses ever occurred as the terrain eroded away.

The plane bounced twice, then settled down on the runway. The strong deceleration of the aircraft forced everyone to lean forward. The result was that many strained to look out to see why the pilot was in such a hurry to stop. As usual, it was a crossing roadway between runways that allowed the Boeing 727 to avoid a longer taxi run back to the terminal. Scott could see the expected objective just ahead as the plane neared the crossway.

Guatemala City was an intermediate stop between Houston and San José, Costa Rica. Having had a college fraternity brother from Costa Rica at Georgia made Scott more anxious than the rest of the players to go there. His name was Hernando Obando, and was one of the most fun guys in the house. Hernando was a great party person and never said no if asked to join in some activity or adventure. Also, for some reason, the girls were always attracted to him; he was always the gallant gentleman. In fact, Hernando was a great showman, too. He played varsity tennis and was always hamming it up for the crowd. Scott smiled as he remembered more than once Hernando coming over to the grandstand between points and ostentatiously blowing a kiss to "a pretty *señorita*" sitting in the stands. If his girlfriend was there he always embarrassed her by asking loudly for "a kees, just a leetle kees" in front of the audience. Scott hoped he would be able to see Hernando while he was in Costa Rica. He had written him a letter to tell his friend they were coming.

Outside, next to them, was a Lacsa plane from Costa Rica. The sight of that made Scott anxious to get to San José and see the country he heard so much about from Hernando. He remembered his frat brother telling of the mountainous terrain, the volcanoes, the waterfalls, and the beaches. Scott could picture Hernando holding spellbound a group of brothers while he described the wonders of his land. "Come and visit me sometime and I will introduce you to the most beautiful country on earth. You will be enchanted by our natural wonders and, of course, by the beauty of our women. Come and I will take you to El Pueblo, a city of shops, restaurants, and nightlife. Come with me to my favorite disco, Coco Loco, where the Latin music is lively and the *muchachas* look divine."

Well, Hernando, Scott thought, you will finally get your chance to show us what you have been talking about. We'll see if you were bragging. Scott had told some of the other team members what he recalled from those times Hernando spouted off about this nation of wonders. He tried to think back to what his Latin friend had said about soccer in Costa Rica. Naturally, soccer in the United States was second rate compared to that in his country. He had talked of their professional leagues and compared soccer up north to that of a mediocre second-division team. Scott knew not to believe all of what Hernando said, but nonetheless was eager to find out how the United States national team compared. Kori obviously was a lot of help in describing what he remembered about Costa Rican soccer from his time coaching there, and in particular providing information from the very successful Italian World Cup, as well as updates of recent results. Apparently Costa Rica was very good, accounting itself well in the Gold Cup tournaments, the Marlboro Cup, and particularly of late, in tournaments in South America. This tour would be a telling opportunity to judge this team's capability.

The two-team concept had been abandoned by the USSF and now they were down to one. They had played several matches against traveling professional teams from Egypt, Finland, Tunisia, and Chile national teams. So far this combined U.S. unit was undefeated and gaining a lot of recognition. Kori would acknowledge to them only that they were meeting his expectations; by the same token, both Kori and the USSF were out beating the drums, getting publicity and to some minor degree raising the level of public support and awareness for this national team. Even Pele came out with a public statement that American soccer was very much improved with Kori Gaborakov as the coach. Kind of a good feeling to know I am a part of this team, Scott thought. Scott was just starting to get to know some of the players who had played on the other team and who were now a part of the national team.

Nick Jankowski was one new man added to the squad. Nick had probably played more soccer than anyone else. He grew up in an ethnic community outside Pittsburgh and played neighborhood soccer as a very young boy. His grandfather was from Yugoslavia and had played semi-pro ball before coming to the States. Nick's dad had played soccer in the United States also, but never had a chance to play pro, because there were no leagues then. Nick not only played in youth leagues growing up, but also played the rough adult league. Kori could tap into the natural ethnic talent better than anyone did before him. Nick possessed just that kind of talent. He was quite a versatile player also. Nick could play any of the defensive positions except goalkeeper, and he could play left or right midfield. Of the new guys added to the team, Nick was the smartest. His knowledge of world affairs and everyday matters was formidable. No one could beat him in Trivial Pursuit. It was funny, Scott reckoned, how you could usually tell when someone was smarter than yourself. Nick was the only one on the team, however, whom Scott put in that category, although Chase Anderson was nearly Scott's peer. The other thing about Nick was he seemed to accomplish whatever he set out to do. He didn't give up until his goal was reached. Scott liked that about Nick. It was Nick that Scott chose to sit next to on this plane trip down to Costa Rica.

Matt Fong was another new player on the combined roster. Even though he had gone with them to Mexico, he really had played on the other team. His was an interesting story. Seven months ago he acquired citizenship in the United States. Previously he had been on China's national team. His parents had lived for years in California, then went to China as missionaries. He seemed to be a happy-go-lucky kind of person. Scott saw him to be someone who enjoyed what was going on around him. Already he had integrated well with the team; everyone seemed to like him. From what Scott had heard, Fong, as everyone called him, was a pretty good forward who could also play midfield on the outside. It was said he could lay in almost perfect corner kicks every time, from either corner.

It wasn't long before the plane was over Nicaragua. Below was Lake Nicaragua. Scott could see the volcanoes jutting above the lake, so he pointed them out to Nick.

"Kind of an interesting view, isn't it?"

"Yeah, my first volcano. You never forget your first volcano. Sort of like your first date."

"Know what you mean."

"You know," Nick added, "Lake Nicaragua is the only lake in the world with freshwater sharks,"

"Really? Nah, you're pulling my leg."

"No. Really. That's true. Sharks adapted to the fresh water. The theory is once it was a part of the ocean, but got separated. As fresh water fed the new lake, it gradually turned from saline to fresh. The sharks evolved, too."

"Looks interesting."

"They say Nicaragua is a beautiful country; can't say, though, that I've got any real desire to go see it. Not at this time."

"I dunno. I wouldn't mind."

It wasn't long before they crossed over the border into Costa Rica. Scott looked down at the rugged mountainous terrain.

"Looks wild and untouched."

As Nick leaned over to look he replied, "Costa Rica is one of the few conservationist countries actively working to preserve tropical forests. They have several huge national parks that are preserved as rainforests."

Scott thought he should lay a fact or two on Nick as well. "Did you know more than two-thirds of the population of Costa Rica lives in the Central Valley? Mostly in and around San José, the capital."

"That's interesting. Doesn't leave many people for everywhere else, does it?"

"Nope. For a country the size of West Virginia, thirty percent of two and one-half to three million people have a lot of room to spread out. I understand coffee, beef, and bananas are their chief exports, and that citrus, cut flowers, and pineapples are coming on."

"You know what I always thought would be neat, to walk out your back door and pick an orange off the tree for breakfast. I'd like that."

"Me, too. That would be nice. I like fruit of all kinds. My friend Hernando told me they grow every tropical fruit here in Costa Rica. A fruit lover's paradise is what he called it."

"Do you think you'll see your friend?"

"I hope so. I wrote him to tell him when we were coming, and that we were staying at the Cariari Hotel."

"Did you hear back from him?"

"No, but he didn't really have time. I only wrote him eight or nine days ago."

"Well I hope you run into him."

"Thanks. Me, too."

Scott could see lots of mountains as he looked down. He thought he glimpsed another volcano also, but the clouds partially blocked his view.

After they landed and exited through the jetway into the main terminal, they walked to the *aduana*, the customs and immigration area, and then downstairs to get in line at the check stations, where everyone's name was entered into the computer. Scott noted the beautiful wood ceiling and walls.

Happily, they were able to bypass the normal customs inspection of luggage as some person met them and arranged to bypass the incoming inspection everyone else went through. Everyone carried his own duffel bag and suitcase up the stairs and out to the waiting area just outside the building.

There the American contingent was met by Ricardo Servilla Aymá, the soccer association president, as well as several hosts and hostesses. As each player emerged, Ricardo shook his hand. Scott was favorably impressed upon first meeting him.

"Scott, Scott, over here!"

It was Hernando! He had come to the airport to greet him.

"Hernando!"

"How ya' doing, buddy?'

"Good, real good. Well, someone finally came here to check on you."

"Great, that's what I've been wanting. It's about time someone came down here to God's country."

"I've told some of the guys on the team all the good things you say about your country. Hope at least half of them are true."

"Half! Hell, it's all true and more. You're gonna love it here. I know you will. How much free time are you going to have?"

"Some. Not exactly sure how much yet. We'll get our schedule finalized tonight at a team meeting. I think Kori already has most of the details worked out, with Lucas doing most of the work. Lucas is our manager, but he's an all-right guy."

Scott saw Nick approaching. "Nick, Nick. This is Hernando, the fraternity brother I was telling you about. Hernando, meet Nick Jankowski."

"Hello, Nick, nice to meet you."

"*Mucho gusto, señor, equalamente.*"

"Oh. You speak Spanish, huh?"

"No, not really. Just a few words."

"*Bienvenidos a Costa Rica.*"

"*Gracias.*"

"Your whole team is staying at the Hotel Cariari, right?"

"Yes, five days."

"You certainly picked a good time. The Miss Costa Rica contest is going to be there Wednesday night. You're going to see some beauties. My girlfriend is one of them."

"Yeah? That's great. We'll have to make sure that's programmed into our schedule."

"I'll see to that," Nick offered enthusiastically.

Word of the beauty contest spread rapidly. Before long Scott heard a loud "Awwrright" from twenty paces away. He smiled. He knew who that was without looking. Eddie certainly had a one track-mind.

The players boarded a bus to be taken to the hotel. Armida was their tour guide and told them several interesting facts. "This road," she indicated as they pulled away from the airport, "is a part of the Pan American Highway. Costa Rica was discovered in 1502 by Christopher Columbus, ten years after he landed in the United States. He named Costa Rica for its rich coastal area on the Caribbean side. Our country was settled by Europeans, just like yours. Our population is about two and one half million with most of those living in this Central Valley. As you see, we are surrounded by mountains. Notice the beautiful, tropical flora. Costa Rica is especially known for its beautiful bougainvillea that you see in ten different colors along the roadways."

"Look at those orange blossoms on those treetops," Marty called out to everyone close by. "I've never seen anything quite like that."

"They're all over the tops of those trees. Look, lots of them," Pu added.

"They certainly are lovely. I wonder what the name of those trees are," Scott thought out loud.

"I'd like to know, too," Nick replied.

"Costa Rica has sixty-seven different climate zones," the guide continued, "from the very dry Guanacaste area in the Northwest to the Monte Verde National Park, a tropical rainforest. Our country offers a great diversity for agricultural endeavors as well as choosing the temperature

and climate in which you want to live. We basically have year-round tem-
peratures that vary from 50 degrees Fahrenheit to 90 degrees Fahrenheit,
depending on the elevation. Many people from the United States and
elsewhere come to retire here in Costa Rica.

"Your hotel is called the Cariari, which is the same name Costa Rica
used to have before Christopher Columbus renamed it."

"Tell us about the beauty contest," a voice with a drawl hollered. "Are
you in it? You're pretty enough."

Armida laughed and relaxed a little more. "OK. Our annual Miss Costa
Rica contest will be held at your hotel Wednesday night, I think at eight
o'clock. This is the finals and includes girls from every province, plus a few
specially sponsored ones. There are fifteen competing in all. I'm sure you
will enjoy it, and no, I'm not in it, but thank you."

The bus stopped at a traffic light. The tour guide told them, "We're
nearly there. I know you will enjoy your stay and hope you will return
again one day."

The team gave her a round of applause, and she smiled brightly.

The bus pulled off on a frontage road and passed another hotel before
pulling into the Hotel Cariari.

The players were immediately impressed. The hotel looked different
from U.S. hotels. They liked the Latino atmosphere. The lobby was a
large circular room that was open to the outside. You could feel the
breeze.

"Look at the wood, Nick."

"Yeah, Scott. The grain and color is just gorgeous. I wonder if it's
mahogany. They grow a lot of that in Central America."

"I don't know my woods very well, but this looks more like teak to me."

"Could be. We're meeting at one-thirty, right?"

"Yep, half past one. That's thirty-five minutes from now."

Scott was assigned to room with Robert Hastings, the first time the two
had stayed together. The rooms were pleasantly large, with two queen-
sized beds in each room. Scott and his roommate stored their gear in the
room and joined several others to wander around the grounds.

The six players were impressed with the signed pictures on the wall of
the walkway to the casino and restaurant. Presidents, actors, singers,
sports stars, and even astronauts graced the wood-paneled wall.

"Look, Carter, Reagan, Bush, Shultz, and a bunch of others have been
here."

"Look, Bjorn Borg and Jimmy Connors were here," said Chase
Anderson, the tennis player.

"They hold a tournament every year in Costa Rica, called the Coffee Cup, that attracts players of that caliber," Scott offered. He had heard that from Hernando, who also had played in it a couple of times.

"I didn't know Costa Rica had an astronaut. Here's a picture of Franklin Chang."

"He went up in the last flight before the Challenger disaster, as I understand it."

"Bet he's glad he went on the one he did," someone else remarked.

They progressed down the slight incline toward the restaurant. As the young men looked in they saw a well-coordinated indoor restaurant with an outdoorsy look. Tropical flowers and plants were everywhere.

"Dining here is like eating in the middle of a jungle, almost," Pu stated. "It's neat. I like it."

"You half expect to see monkeys swinging down and swooping up your food," Eddie added.

They all agreed they'd like to eat here, if the opportunity arose.

They practiced that afternoon in the National Stadium, which wasn't so big. Scott figured it held twenty, maybe twenty-five thousand at most. Hernando came to watch them practice and later told Scott that there were two other stadiums in the country larger than that one.

As usual, Kori was participating in the practices and taking his turn—it was his turn whenever he wanted it to be—at taking passes on the fly and shooting at the goal. Kori was always enthusiastic and constantly demonstrated his zeal and love for the game. That spirit of enthusiasm was infectious to the rest of the team, as Kori meant it to be. He continually told them they must first love the game. You practice better and you play more creatively when you love the game. Scott knew that was true. Certain skills, certain techniques had come more easily and without pain because he had enjoyed practice so much.

Scott reflected on the successes the team had had since Kori became the trainer. He guessed it really started with the 1991 Gold Cup in California when the United States contingent did so well beating all the other teams in Concacaf to emerge unbeaten and untied. That team was largely composed of players from the 1990 World Cup team, but already Kori had a great positive influence in just a few months. Then came their success in the Pan-American games in Cuba, when they upset a favored Mexico team for the Gold Medal.

Now the makeup of the team had evolved to more younger players, although several key positions were still filled by the experienced "old guard." In fact, the team, as it was now, had six players from the 1990 Cup team and twelve new ones. It was not yet clear who Kori was going to start. He used one lineup one time and a different one the next time.

Scott asked the coach if his friend, Hernando, could join them for supper this first night and he said OK. Kori was pretty good about including friends and relatives if the teammates requested that sort of thing. Scott didn't know if that would hold true for the World Cup itself, but he had been told Kori kept a relaxed atmosphere in Italy when he had coached the Costa Rica team.

That first night they ate at a restaurant called Rias Bajas in El Pueblo. "So, finally I get to see El Pueblo," Scott told Nick as they rode to the restaurant. "Hernando's told me so much about it, I feel like I've already been there. Coach did say we can stay after the meal and go disco, didn't he?"

"Yes, don't you remember Eddie?"

"Oh yeah. How could I forget. He's quite a character. Totally uninhibited. He'll do anything; Ricky too. And Marty, he's really nuts. It's hard to know whether all those stories about him are true."

"Well, you've known him longer than I, but from what I've seen he's capable of anything."

"That's for sure. I like him. You need to see him eat lobster. I like Eddie, too. He's a little crude but he pulls it off with his likeable personality and how he says things."

They arrived at El Pueblo and had a very satisfactory meal of *paella*, which was a Spanish dish of seafood and rice. Hernando was in his glory, entertaining much of the team. He amplified his accent as he described the wonders of Costa Rica to his listeners just as he did at the fraternity. Eddie and Ricky were positively drooling over his description of the women of Costa Rica.

"Don't take my word for it though, come and see for yourselves after supper. We will go to the Coco Loco disco, my favorite place. There you will behold beauty as God intended for us to see."

Scott knew Eddie and Ricky would have braved tanks, at that point, to go to the disco.

The beat of the music welcomed them into a new environment. Eddie was already dancing his way through the doorway. Hernando had arranged an exemption for all the team of the normal cover charge of one thousand *colones*. As their eyes grew used to the darkness, it became evident why Hernando bragged so much about this place and the Costa Rican women. Good-looking, unattached women were everywhere. *Really* good-looking, Scott thought.

"Awwrright!" Eddie was announcing his satisfaction.

There were at least thirty unattached girls there, and nearly every one of them was attractive, if not beautiful. Scott made his way over to Hernando, who was beaming from ear to ear.

"I can't believe this is the way it is every time. What'd you do, stack the deck?"

"Oh, *señor*, you hurt my feelings. Why do you say such a thing?"

"Because I know you, Hernando."

"In Costa Rica, beautiful ladies are everywhere. This is no exception. It is always good here. I am sorry, I did invite my girlfriend to come and she brought a couple of friends," Hernando added, as if to be perfectly truthful. "Come, let me introduce you to her."

"Rosibel, allow me to present my best friend from the United States, Mr. Scott Fontaine. Scott, this is Rosibel Vargas, one of the most beautiful and nicest ladies in Costa Rica."

"*Mucho gusto*. Hernando has positively bragged about you. I feel like I already know you, Scott."

"Thank you. *Mucho gusto*. Hernando has been known to exaggerate at times. I must say, though, this place is everything he said it was, and so are you. So many pretty girls here."

"Thank you. These are my friends Pierina and Marta. Their English is not so good." Rosibel then turned to explain to her friends who Scott was. As she did so Scott could feel the heat crank up a notch as both girls turned on their best smiles.

Not long after Scott sat down at their table he looked out on the dance floor. Already Eddie, Ricky, Marty, and Cornell were dancing. He saw several more guys, Terry, Pu, Robert, and Chase, go ask girls to dance. Scott told himself he shouldn't have been surprised that all the girls accepted, but he was. This is too good to be true, he thought.

Nick came over shortly and asked if he could join them. Hernando and Scott stood up as Hernando introduced the girls, Scott already having presented Nick to them. Nick sat down between Scott and Hernando and immediately ordered drinks, for himself as well as those who wanted a fresh one. "My first impressions of Costa Rica are excellent, Hernando. I get a special feeling about your country and the people here."

"Thank you, that's good. I love my country. I wish more people knew how good it is here. We have the second oldest democracy in the Western

Hemisphere and a way of life that we all enjoy."

"I can see that."

Scott was looking at Rosibel, wondering if she was the most beautiful girl he had ever seen or if Pierina was. He was reminded of that Norman Rockwell painting of the boy approaching two very pretty girls sitting on chairs, trying to decide which one he was going to ask to dance. The two Costa Ricans were both stunning. As he looked around the room a realization set in.

"Nick, you know there are only two places I've ever seen so many nice-looking girls."

"Where's that?"

"In Italy—all over the place—and in the better sororities at Georgia and the University of Florida."

Hernando and Rosibel got up to dance and left the other four to fend for themselves.

As usual Scott held back to give the other guy his choice. Nick picked Marta, and so Scott also joined the dancers with Pierina. As he fast-danced with the young Tica he couldn't help but admire her beautiful face. These people, he thought, are just like us in so many ways. They want many of the same things we do. Also, their philosophy of life is just like ours in the States. It must be that democracy spawns the same things. I'll bet if it were a dictatorship, things would be different. It's Maslov's hierarchy of needs at work here.

The music shifted to something not conducive for dancing and all six found themselves retreating to their table at the same time. Shortly after they sat down Hernando called out, "Fofi, Fofi, come here."

Scott and Nick looked up to see a mustachioed Tico in a coat and tie come with a drink in his hand toward their table. Hernando stood up. "Fofi, I'd like to present an old schoolmate and fraternity brother of mine from Georgia, Scott Fontaine. And this is Nick, Nick..."

"Jankowski. *Mucho gusto.*"

"How do you do. Rodolfo Mora," Fofi said as he shook their hands.

"Although I may regret it, may I introduce you to these young ladies also," Hernando continued. "This is Rosibel, my girlfriend, and Marta, and Pierina, friends of Rosibel's."

"*Mucho gusto. El gusto es mio.*"

"Fofi likes the nightlife and knows simply everyone, it seems. He is an attorney and a director of the soccer team you will play Thursday—Saprissa. He also went to Italy in 1990 to watch the World Cup games for six weeks. At one time Fofi played goalkeeper for Saprissa when they won the national championship."

"Well, quite an introduction. Please pull up a chair," Scott invited.

Fofi had dark wavy hair and penetrating eyes that shined full of life and enthusiasm. You could tell Fofi lived life to the fullest. Gregarious and handsome, the type that probably had girls falling all over themselves; the Latin lover type. Fofi stood about five-ten, maybe five-eleven and had a solid build. Scott guessed he was about thirty-two years old. Looking at the three Ticas and how they looked at Fofi, Scott knew his assessment of him was accurate.

"How is it that you went to Italy to follow the World Cup? That's something I wanted to do also. How was it?" Scott asked.

"A client of mine, a gringo from Mississippi, asked me to go with him. He got the tickets and we went. Italy was beautiful. The soccer was terrific, the soccer stadiums were magnificent, the culture was impressive, and the women gorgeous. We had a really great time."

"Your English is excellent. Where did you learn to speak it so well?"

"I went to college at L.S.U. in Baton Rouge."

The conversation expanded once again to include all of those around the table. Fofi was engaging and certainly livened up the table. Scott admired how both Fofi and Hernando always appeared to be happy and full of fun. The girls, too, he noticed. Costa Rica certainly is an impressive place.

At twelve-fifteen all the team members had to leave the disco. The bus was to depart for the hotel at that time and the coach had imposed a twelve-thirty curfew for all to be back to the hotel.

On the way there the young men voiced their approval of how the evening had gone. Some had ventured out to some of the other discos and piano bars at El Pueblo. Scott learned there were five discos and six piano bars there. All of the players reported favorable impressions.

"Hernando would have enjoyed hearing this," Scott commented to Nick.

"And why not? So far I'm impressed. Those three girls at our table were as good as they come anywhere. They were pretty, friendly, and they all enjoyed themselves. The meal was great, the El Pueblo area was nice, and I especially like the hotel."

"Oh, I agree. There's another quality I noticed, too. Did you see how much Hernando enjoyed life? He was like that the whole while I knew him. I thought that might just have been his personality. Now I'm not so sure. Everyone here is like that. They must have a high quality of life."

"I think that's perceptive of you. I've been thinking much the same thing. They do indeed seem happy."

Most of the players vowed to return to El Pueblo before they had to go back to the States.

"I damn sure am going back there. There were 'nuff pretty ladies there you could take your pick. I near 'bout had three of them wanting to come home with me to the Cararia."

"That's Cariari, Eddie."

"Whatever the hell it is. They wanted to come."

The first game for the team would be the game against Saprissa, one of the leading Division I pro teams. Their stadium was on the outskirts of San José and boasted the largest following of any of the Division I teams. Their board of directors was very progressive and initiated this tour of the United States national team. In the 1990 World Cup about one third of the starting team were from Saprissa's, including Roger Flores, the highest rated sweeper. Saprissa's dominance was much less today than before; however, their management and financial situation allowed them to pursue a vigorous international program of interchange.

The game went well for the United States as they dashed off to a 2–0 lead in the first half. Saprissa scored once in the second half, but the United States contingent won 2–1.

Kori was not pleased with their effort, however, and remonstrated them for lack of executing and not finishing scoring opportunities. "The difference," he counseled, "between a good team and a great team is finishing off your scoring opportunities."

For the first time, Scott felt he had let down the team. Twice he knew he was the cause of not scoring a goal, because he wasn't where he was supposed to be and did not anticipate the play action. Now he knew why he was taken out and substituted in the second half. He would be especially watchful for those opportunities in the future.

Their practice the next day focused in on finishing the plays and capitalizing on opportunities. Position of the players was crucial; anticipation and execution would create more opportunities for shots. Kori demonstrated these activities with such enthusiasm and fervor that the players enjoyed the session even though they knew they were being remonstrated for lack of performance in the game. Scott marveled that Kori could chew them out and that they would enjoy it. His already very favorable opinion of Kori went up another notch today.

The team had the rest of the day off, and because they had practiced very early in the morning there was plenty of time for sightseeing. Naturally Hernando was full of suggestions. He arranged for a mini-bus to take Scott, Nick, Robert, Rosibel, Marta, Pierina, and a girl named Vera to Lake Arenal, which lay in the shadow of the Arenal volcano. He explained, "It's beautiful, and the way out to there is just as spectacular. Bring your swimsuits; we can swim in the lake or go wind surfing or whatever you want."

When word spread of what they were doing, two more carloads of players followed them on the trip. Eddie, Ricky, Pu, and some girl Eddie picked up went in one car, while Marty, Cornell, and Chase went in a third.

The small caravan took off north from San José and climbed up the mountains. At the top Hernando took them to see Mount Poas, an active volcano with a beautiful turquoise-colored lake in the crater.

"Now this is why I joined the Navy," Eddie exclaimed. "To see the world. Don't got nothin' like this around my home town."

"It really is splendid. Almost takes your breath away," Nick volunteered.

"The only wonder of nature I've seen that I'd rank higher is the Grand Canyon," commented Chase.

"Hernando, this is great. I've always wanted to see a volcano."

"I know, Scott, you once told me that at the fraternity. I never forgot that."

"Thanks, buddy."

They didn't spend long at the volcano because there was much more to see and do that day and, surprisingly to the Americans, it was pretty cold up there. Some were shivering before they left.

"How high up are we? What's the altitude here, Hernando?' Nick asked.

"About seven thousand feet."

"No wonder it's so cold."

The group hurried back to their cars and headed down the other side of the mountain on winding narrow roads with no guardrails.

"Those canyons are beautiful, aren't they?"

"They sure are. They remind me of the terrain in the mountain scenes in the movie *Romancing the Stone*," Scott said.

"Look at that dropoff," Nick said as he looked down out the window of the mini-bus. "It must be five hundred feet straight down. The only thing to break your fall if we go off the edge is a couple of dozen trees along the way."

That brought a nervous laugh from the others.

Hernando, who was driving, waved it off as if it was of no importance as he chatted almost constantly and frequently looked over to Rosibel.

Unexpectedly they came around a corner to an absolutely beautiful waterfall, right next to the road.

Scott involuntarily took in his breath.

"Gorgeous, absolutely gorgeous," Robert exclaimed.

Scott smiled to himself as he imagined Eddie's "Awwrright" coming out for something other than a good-looking girl.

They all got out of their cars, as conveniently space had been provided for off -the road parking. They stood on the bridge over the river looking directly at the huge falls only twenty meters away.

"Did you guys see the second stage up above?" Chase asked.

"This is called El Angel. There are really three stages to these falls. You can't see the highest one till we get about half a kilometer up the opposite hill there," Hernando replied.

"Wonder how much water goes over that in an hour's time?"

Scott turned to Nick and said, "Watch this. Hey, Eddie. Why don't you climb up there and jump down in the pool?"

"Might. Just might."

Eddie led the girl he picked up—Scott couldn't figure out how Eddie did it all the time—by the hand along a path leading behind the falls.

"Hey, ya'll. Come here. You got to see it from here," Eddie shouted back.

That made everyone in the whole party trek the short way along the wet and not-so-secure pathway back to the falls.

Only Hernando stayed on the bridge with Rosibel. Hernando took some pictures of the group back by the falls.

Nick asked Hernando what the names of all those wildflowers were that appeared along the side of the road. "They look like periwinkles. Are they?"

"No, I don't think so, but they're probably in the same biological family."

Scott looked more closely at Pierina. She had on an orange jumper with a white t-shirt underneath. She looked so good that Scott knew he was tempted and that he would have to fight his natural male instincts. She is positively stunning, he said in awe. Immediately his conscience bothered him as his Christian beliefs once again dominated.

As if on cue Pierina turned to him and flashed a toothy-white smile. "Pretty, no?"

"Very pretty; very, very pretty," Scott twice agreed. If only you knew, he added in thought. Once again he weakened.

As they started to walk to the vehicle, Scott impulsively reached out and took her hand. She turned and smiled at him. Damn, damn, he silently cursed to himself.

On they went, back up the mountain. The falls, Scott noted to Nick, occurred at a low point in their way over the mountain.

Robert hollered out, "I can see the third tier from here," shortly after they left the falls. Hernando slowed down so everyone could look back and appreciate the vista.

As they traveled along, they could see off in the distance, on the other side of the canyon, a very tall waterfall, maybe two hundred meters high.

"Stop, Stop," Robert shouted. "I want a picture of this."

"OK—don't worry."

The others stopped as well.

Hernando basked in the verbal accolades as he remained silent, preferring nature to do the talking.

This time Scott followed Pierina as they evacuated the van. Certainly is romantic up here looking at such wonders of nature, he thought to himself, glancing first at Pierina and then at the distant falls.

Chase didn't have time to change his film from when they left the Angel Falls until they arrived here, so he was late in getting out of his car. "I'm going to have a slide show to beat all when I get back home."

"How many rolls of film did you bring?" Pu asked

"You mean today or on the whole trip?"

"Both."

"Four and nine altogether."

"Holy criminy."

"And the way things are going I'll have to buy some more. I've only got one more unused roll back at the hotel."

"Money doesn't seem to mean the same thing to Chase as it does to most of the rest of us," Robert noted to Scott.

"He comes from a very well-to-do family, as I understand it."

After traveling through another twenty minutes of spectacular scenery they descended into a valley.

"This is the Sarapiqui Valley," Hernando told them. "In the last few years there has been tremendous growth of orange groves and especially pineapple plantations. We'll try to buy a couple of fresh pineapples from a roadside stand somewhere. You'll like it. Nothing like the pineapple they grow here, really sweet."

They stopped for lunch at a little circular grass thatched restaurant called Rancho Leona. Hernando apparently knew the owner, Leona, for he greeted her and kissed her on the cheek. She turned out to be bilingual; her parents were half American, half Costa Rican, and she had lived for years in the States. In the restaurant were beautiful wood inlaid tables. Hanging around the exterior of the open-air structure were large stained-glass panels of tropical forest scenes. The work was well done and drew lots of favorable comments from the group.

Nick told Scott later that Leona's husband was a gringo from California and that he had made them. Furthermore, he used to make tables like these for Hollywood stars.

"How about that. You certainly don't expect to see something like this in a little town this size in Costa Rica, do you?"

"Nope. The town's name is La Virgen, which means 'The Virgin' in Spanish. Not that there are any of those here. Leona also runs a tour guide service and her husband runs kayaking trips on the river back behind the restaurant. He's got more than twenty-five kayaks. The river's name is Rio Sarapiqui, which is how the valley got named that."

"Busy people, aren't they?"

"Look at the kayaking pictures in the tops of these tables."

"That one picture of my husband was in *Life* magazine."

"Leona regularly gets fresh pineapple from one of the plantations nearby and has agreed to cut up a couple for this whole group—free gratis."

"Great, I'd like to taste them."

They couldn't believe how sweet and good the pineapples were.

"How come we can't get pineapple like this in the States, Leona?" Pu asked loudly.

"Well, these were picked yesterday and they were more ripe than what is picked for export. But I've tasted those that are picked for export and they are pretty good, too. I think the pineapple grown here in the valley is just a better fruit. I really believe that's the main reason. There are plantations from here to Puerto Viejo—about ten miles away."

"Damn, this is good," Eddie drawled as juice dripped off his beard. "Is there any more?"

"No, I had only two."

"Hernando said we'd try to buy some from a roadside stand along the way," Nick told Eddie.

"I vote for that. We'll buy all they have," someone else said.

"You can take pineapple back to the States, no problem, I understand," Leona added helpfully. "Don't take fully ripe ones though, they won't make it. Get ones that are at least half green in color."

"Thanks."

After saying their good-byes and thank-yous, the group resumed their travel. The caravan bought out two roadside stands along the way, each guy taking two or three apiece. They would have stopped at a third, too, if they had passed one.

It took another hour and one-half to reach Lake Arenal. In front of him Scott saw one of the most splendid and serene vistas he had ever witnessed. The lake was large, although you could see the very distant shoreline on the opposite side if you looked really hard, but all this lay beneath a magnificent volcano—Arenal, a very active one that still spewed forth ash and smoke several times a day.

Once again Hernando filled with pride at the effect the natural beauty of his country was having on his guests. "Their reaction makes all this worth the effort," he told Rosibel.

"You have worked hard to plan this and make it happen for them. I am very proud of you, Hernando." She reached up and gave him a quick kiss on the lips as she squeezed his arm.

"I'm not sure what's better; their reaction or your kisses. Now I'm doubly paid."

Rosibel threw back her head and laughed. She hoped they enjoyed Hernando's humor; he was fun to be with—everyone said so. Hernando was at his finest whenever he was showing off for others. He did it in a way that was attractive and offended no one.

They rented two sailboards and spent the rest of the afternoon swimming, wind surfing, and laying out on the beach.

Cornell could never get the hang of getting up on the board, but the rest of them more or less managed. Hernando was very good and made them all look bad. Pierina and Eddie's pickup were the only girls who tried. Pierina did pretty well, but the other girl was not at all good.

Scott could hardly take his eyes off Pierina. She had a magnificent figure in a bathing suit; she really looked good. Pangs of guilt struck deep within him as he thought of Diana, pregnant back home with his child. "My God, if ever I were to find someone to be unfaithful with, it's got to be Pierina. Here I am, far away from home. Diana would never find out. And this girl is so beautiful, she's almost wanton, without even trying to be." Scott could feel the struggle rise within himself.

Just after dusk the volcano shot fiery ashes high into the sky. The luminous eruption presented a spectacle all its own, unmatched even by events earlier in the day. Scott was standing next to Pierina gathering things together for the trip back to San José. He put his arm around her waist as they viewed the spectacle in the sky.

"Perfect, just perfect," Hernando whispered to Rosibel. "The timing couldn't have been any better. Just at dark, just before we leave. I love it."

"I love it, too, and I love you," Rosibel responded.

"Really! Really! You mean that?"

"Yes, I do."

Hernando grabbed his woman and kissed her hard on the lips. The kiss turned long and passionate as the two lovers cemented a bond.

Eddie saw Hernando kiss his girl and imitated their action with his own, seizing the moment of opportunity. Soon anyone with a girl was doing the same, including Scott, who had taken that first fateful step. There was something wonderfully romantic about that moment—something none of them would ever forget.

The trip home to San José was shorter than the way out, when they had taken a circuitous route to include the scenic spots. It also was a quieter trip, each person reflecting on the experience of the day.

Eddie normally liked to be the driver, but tonight he rode in the back seat with his date and made out most of the way back.

Scott was smitten, Hernando could see it. Pierina was everything one could want in a female companion. She was, of course, beautiful: the kind that stops traffic to watch her walk along the street.

Scott imagined what effect she would have, dressed in some elegant evening dress—black would look good with her blond hair—walking into their old fraternity house. He could imagine heads turning and guys staring at her. She had a sexual quality about her, too; something alluring, something that made her even more attractive. Scott decided the more desirable quality in a girl was sex appeal, even more than beauty. He couldn't tell enough about her personality or her intelligence except that she was a lot of fun to be with, and she showed she was definitely interested in him. If she had spoken more English he could tell more about her.

"How many brothers and sisters do you have?" he asked.

"More slow, please."

"How many…brothers and sisters…you have?"

"One brother only. Less. Fifteen years."

"Good. Good English. I understand. *Comprendo?*"

"*Si,*" she responded with a large satisfied smile.

Scott got the impression everything was OK with her. She seems too easy-going, as if she were "along for the ride," so-to-speak, he mused. Scott wasn't sure what he expected, but Pierina seemed a bit too placid. "Not that she lacks spark or enthusiasm, because she has those qualities.

It's just that everything is always OK: perhaps her character isn't deep enough. Maybe it's just the language barrier. Diana certainly has a better personality. Diana!

Scott knew at that moment that while he could and would enjoy this young lady's company and be attracted to her, he couldn't let himself fall for her, no matter how attractive she was.

The trip, they all decided later, turned out to be a huge success, thanks to the efforts of Scott's friend.

Around nine o'clock the next morning the phone rang to rouse the slumbering duo. Robert was first to reach the phone as he gave a sleepy answer. They each wanted to get up and eat a good breakfast, then to go and enjoy the pool. Hernando and the girls were again coming over at eleven to enjoy the pool too, and then they were going to do some close-range sightseeing. Hernando wanted to show them the ox-cart factory where colorful hand-painted miniature ox-carts were produced for the tourists in four different sizes.

At the factory they learned that years ago much of the nations' goods were moved by way of real carts drawn by oxen. Particularly farm produce coming to market was handled in this manner. The individual farmers took pride in the way their carts looked and painstakingly hand-painted them in colorful patterns. The walls of the factory office showed many pictures of such carts in action.

Afterward, Hernando drove them around San José and showed them the United States Embassy, a real fortress; the twin AID building about two miles away and said to be connected with an underground tunnel; and the Russian, Spanish, and German Embassy buildings. Scott was impressed with the apparent security of the United States Embassy, but was more impressed with the Russian Embassy compound from every other aspect.

The Russian Embassy was located in an upscale suburban community. The houses look like they would cost $300,000 and up around Atlanta, he thought. The group came away very impressed.

"You know, Hernando, often we hear of a two-class society in most Latin American countries. While there are some obviously wealthy people here, I perceive a broad spectrum of social levels existing here. It's not a two-class society," Scott pointed out.

"Right you are. Costa Rica has a broadly based middle class, same as the U.S.A. In fact, our poor people are probably much better off than yours. There are isolated pockets of shanties and low-class dwellings in every large city, but not really any slums to speak of. One thing you gringos do that perpetuated the poor people's condition is your welfare and food stamp program. A lot of people are born into it, live their whole life on welfare, and die never knowing anything else. Here we are different. Only if you are incapable, through illness, injury, or some debilitating condition, would you stay on the public dole for any length of time. Our belief is that prolonged welfare support of any individual or family is actually detrimental in the long run. It takes away one's incentive to improve one's way of life. That's why we have such a broad middle class here in this country."

"Quite a speech—one whose theory is consistent with my own thinking, incidentally," Nick retorted.

"I quite agree," Scott added. "I think we do millions of Americans a disservice with our welfare program. It simply is a product of our governmental system, where once something comes into government funding, it never goes away, even if it was supposed to be temporary. It just costs us more and more as the politicians expand and expand."

"Hey, neat, you guys would like it here. You know there's almost no violent crime here in Costa Rica. While there is frequent burglary, you would feel safe walking around town at night."

Nick looked at the girls with them and responded, "I know I could enjoy living here. I believe that while you don't necessarily enjoy all the material advantages we do in the States, the quality of life here appears to be just as good."

"I think you're right, Nick. Hernando, I'd have to say that everything you bragged about Costa Rica is true. I really didn't believe it all when you espoused its many virtues, but I do now. It's a wonder your country is not inundated with tourists. It's a tropical paradise here."

"We probably don't do as good a job merchandising the country as we should. I believe international tourism, however, will continue to grow and grow."

The tour group returned to the Cariari after eating lunch at Lucas' restaurant at the entrance to El Pueblo. The Corvina fish baked in butter sauce was every bit as good as Hernando said it would be.

They had a short practice in the middle of the afternoon, working on particular strategies Kori expected the national team of Costa Rica to employ. He talked of the young kids on the Costa Rica team, Paolo de Palmer and Alex de la Paz. "These two are as good as any I've seen anywhere. Paolo possesses instincts and talents usually found in someone much older. His major weakness is his concentration on the game, which I'm told he sometimes lacks. Scott, watch out for Alex. He's a devastating tackler and very aggressive. He did not play in the game with Saprissa; he was held out. You will meet the team tonight because the hotel here will host a get-acquainted dinner for both teams. Then afterward you will be invited to the Miss Costa Rica pageant held here."

"Awwrright," a group near the back chorused.

"Then tomorrow it's all business as we hopefully take this important step forward against a team that could be one of the better ones at the World Cup. Dinner is at six-thirty sharp in the restaurant."

Scott went back outside to the pool where Hernando and the girls still were. Rosibel had already left, having to get ready for tonight's pageant. Once again Scott was impressed with Pierina, who got up to greet him with a light kiss. Scott pulled off his shoes and shirt and dove into the inviting water, calling out to the others to follow suit.

They swam and roasted in the hot sun for another hour before Scott had to get ready for supper. The others promised to be back in plenty of time to watch the beauty pageant.

The combined dinner was fun. The mood was kept light and casual in order to forestall the building of tension between the groups. The organizers need not have worried. When Marty got done eating his lobster, the players couldn't have been any looser. He entertained them all.

To Scott's delight Fofi was one of the hosts. After the meal of baby beef and lobster, Fofi got up to say a few things to both groups. He told the U.S.A. team—in English—of some fond memories he had of the States, particularly his time at L.S.U. "It wasn't at L.S.U., though, that I got my academic education. I was too busy partying and having a good time. I have some especially fond memories of those years. But enough of me. Welcome to Costa Rica. We sincerely hope you have had a pleasant stay here. Judging from what I have seen and observed, I know you have. My good friend, Hernando Obando, has seen to that, I'm sure."

Fofi also addressed the Costa Rican team and several comments brought raucous rounds of laughter. Then he turned back to English.

"We hope tomorrow's game is but a prelude to the World Cup finals next year. The United States has come a long way in three short years. I do not think you are the same team that I saw in Italy. You are one to be reckoned with."

The English-speaking portion of the audience broke into applause and cheers upon hearing that remark.

"But so is Costa Rica one to be reckoned with."

The U.S. team applauded politely and less vigorously at that statement.

Then Fofi translated into Spanish. The Costa Ricans applauded politely at the comment about the U.S. team and then more vigorously when Fofi told them about the Costa Rican team. Several U.S. players joined in the applause for the Latin team.

After the formalities, Scott located Nick and they made a point to go introduce themselves to Alex and Paolo, who were standing together. Alex knew enough English that they could talk a little, and so an acquaintance of sorts was struck. Scott was young himself, but he could tell both of these players were even younger. He wondered how they would respond to pressure. Pretty good, he answered himself. I think Kori is right. These two are something extra special. Paolo's eyes have a bright sparkle, as though betraying mischievous thoughts.

"We go now," Alex told them. "Paolo doesn't want to miss the beauty contestants."

"OK. Good to meet ya'll."

"Ya'll?" Nick mimicked to Scott as they walked away.

"Habit, my boy. Habit."

The ballroom near the pool served as the location for the pageant. Hernando, standing by himself, signaled Scott and Nick to his area.

"They're getting ready to start. I'm nervous already. I wonder if Rosibel is, too."

"Take it easy, buddy. You're probably more nervous than she is. Often it's harder to watch than to participate."

"It's impossible to get comfortable."

"Where are Pierina and Marta? I don't see them," Nick asked.

"They'll be here, don't worry. I'm sure of it," Hernando said, as he smiled one of those big, toothy smiles of his.

Indeed, in just a few minutes Marta came up to them and warmly greeted them. She gave Nick such a kiss as to make Scott wonder.

"Where is Pierina?" Scott asked Marta.

"She'll be here soon," was the reply.

Scott saw Marta flash a glance and a smile at Hernando and figured everything must be all right.

The preliminaries began as all the girls were introduced. Scott was surprised at the enthusiastic response Rosibel got from the audience . He saw his teammates supporting her and got warm fuzzy feelings for the loyalty his teammates were showing to Hernando. Why not? he thought. Hernando has certainly gone out of his way to show everyone a good time, and she's as pretty as any of the others. Except maybe Pierina. Where is she?

There were fifteen contestants. When all fifteen were introduced, there ensued a very loud round of applause and shouts of good luck. Then Hernando leaned over to Scott and said, "Now they will introduce last year's Miss Costa Rica."

Scott almost choked when he saw Pierina, with a crown on her head, come out from behind the curtain. Her eyes immediately found his and her smile became a little broader.

Scott was incredulous. "Holy Cow, Hernando, why didn't anyone tell me, tell us?"

"We thought it was better this way. Could have caused problems among your team if everyone knew this at the beginning. But I knew you'd not want to miss her for that reason."

"You dog, Scott. Miss Costa Rica all this while and we didn't even know it," Nick gushed. "Whaddaya know!"

Hernando and Marta stood up as they began a standing ovation. Scott and Nick immediately joined them; soon the entire room was on its feet clapping for the reigning beauty queen. Scott had trouble focusing in on events the remainder of the evening. His mind was blown. If it hadn't been for Rosibel being in the contest and Hernando right there, he might have drawn a blank for the whole evening.

Evening gown and swimsuit competitions were held. In their group Rosibel was ahead of everyone else except an absolutely gorgeous brunette from San Isabel.

Sure enough, three finalists were chosen and Rosibel, the girl from San Isabel, and a blonde from Puntarenas were the lucky three.

Hernando was ecstatic! His girl was in the finals. He was jumping up and down and whooping and slapping friends on the back.

"She's gonna win it. I tell you, she's gonna win it. Whooppee!"

An interview session was scheduled to determine the winner. The emcee asked the girl from San Isabel her questions first. Hernando said she answered very well. Scott could see she had great poise. Rosibel was next. Hernando couldn't sit still, he was so nervous. Scott patiently waited until she was all done to ask what she was asked and what was her answer. Hernando recapped the dialogue for Scott and Nick as he clapped as loud as he could. He added that she too did well, in his estimation. The third girl appeared obviously ill at ease to Scott as he watched her being interviewed.

"She's having trouble," he leaned over and whispered to Nick.

"Yeah, she is."

Hernando was obviously excited and happy. "They are taking a commercial break now. I think she may have won. I dunno, it's hard to tell.

What do you think?"

"She ought to win it. It's definitely first or second, but I think she won."

"Rosibel certainly did well. She has a beautiful smile and a certain grace about her when she's up there. That other girl did well too, though. It's close, Hernando. I hope she won."

"Me, too. The winners don't have quite as demanding a schedule as yours do in the States from what I understand. You realize now how much less formal some things are here than in your country. Pierina obviously could go places unescorted, whereas winners in the United States are escorted everywhere for their year of reign. Otherwise I would not want Rosibel to win," he said with a chuckle.

The announcer had been handed an envelope. "*Damas y caballeros...*" he began.

The other girl from Puntarenas was named first, meaning she finished third, as expected.

When the announcer next named the other girl—with great fanfare and a drum roll—Scott thought Rosibel had won. As it turned out, though, in Costa Rica they announce the winner's name first instead of the first runner-up, as they do in the United States.

"She finished second, *amigo*," Hernando said out of the side of his mouth. "Second."

There was a lot of polite clapping for the new queen as Pierina came over to her and took the crown off her own head and put it on the winner's. Scott saw her cast a wistful glance and smile to Rosibel as if to convey her sorrow to the runner-up for not winning.

"*Raputa*. I thought she would win it."

"Don't feel bad, Hernando. She did very, very well. There couldn't have been much difference between her and the winner. And, the winner did very well herself. She was no slouch."

"Not bad looking, either, Hernando. Look, I agree with Scott. Rosibel did great. You should be very proud."

"I am, guys, I am. It's just that she was so close. It's hard to lose. I've never been a good loser."

"That's because you are a competitor. That's good. Good losers lose, remember that."

"I think congratulations are in order. Congratulations, Hernando."

"Yeah, congratulations."

"Thanks guys. Thanks a lot."

"Hey man, you really suckered me with Pierina. No wonder I thought she was so pretty. Miss Costa Rica. Wow!"

"Ha. Got you on that, didn't we?"

"You sure did. Say, how did you not know Nick would ask her to dance and not Marta?"

"I told Nick there was a special reason why Pierina was there for you, and I asked him to ask Marta to dance. Now you know why. What else could I do for my best college buddy than to set him up with Miss Costa Rica?"

"You're crazy, you know that?"

"She's really something, isn't she?"

"Yes, indeed. She is. You know on this whole trip it has seemed to me that she's been preoccupied with some thought or that there was more to her than what I was seeing. I just couldn't dig it out. I couldn't quite grasp what it was."

"She told me something like that. She wanted you to like her for who she is, not what she is. Incidentally, her family is very wealthy. Coffee. They own several large coffee plantations and two processing mills also. Big bucks. Their house is among the nicest in Costa Rica. It's beautiful."

"Yeah?"

"Holy cow, I'm impressed."

"Hernando, I can't say enough for what you've done for me and my teammates on our trip down here. You have done everything imaginable to make this trip a huge success. You have gone out of your way and at great expense to set up all this."

"Thanks, Scott. As you know from our college days, I love my country and I wanted to show it to you the very best way I could. I wasn't sure I'd ever get a chance to do this for anyone I'd known in the States. But I've always been ready, and I've always wanted to. I'm so glad you came here."

"Well, I'm glad, too. This has been an unforgettable experience for me. Having you here and being able to spend time with someone I know—and a good friend—has made it much more special. Add to that all the nice things you've done for us and it's made this trip the nicest one for me of all that we've been on."

Nick added, "I'll echo what Scott said, Hernando. You have really added to this trip. Plus you have shown us what a great country you have here. You'd make a great ambassador."

"Thanks. It's been fun for me, too."

At that moment Hernando's parents and Rosibel's parents walked up to them; all were dressed expensively, Scott noted.

"Mom, Dad, Señora Vargas, Señor Vargas, please meet my best friend from *Estados Unidos*, Scott Fontaine, and his friend Nick Jankowski from the national team."

"How do you do?"

"*Mucho gusto.*"

"You must be very proud of your daughter. She was terrific and very beautiful," Scott spoke in English hoping that they would understand since Hernando had introduced them using English. Not that it would make any difference, he thought.

"Oh, yes. Yes we are delighted. She did wonderfully. We are happy for her. Thank you."

"Not only is she talented and beautiful, Mrs. Vargas, she is such a nice person as well. We've been privileged these last few days to get to know your daughter and Hernando. They have made a great effort to see that we had a good time here in Costa Rica," Nick politely told them.

"We have certainly enjoyed your country; Rosibel and Hernando have made us feel most welcome here. They've been fabulous to us."

"Thank you for those nice things you have said. We are delighted to have you come and visit. You can be sure our home will always be open to you when you come here," Mr. Vargas graciously replied.

"Thank you, sir. We do feel that hospitality. Mr. and Mrs. Obando, your son was a very popular person who was well-liked, fun to be with, and a good student while he was at college. Everything he told us of Costa Rica is true and then some. We are really impressed."

"Here comes Rosibel and Pierina!"

Everyone congratulated Rosibel and it was a happy group that thronged around the runner-up.

Scott's eyes finally met Pierina's and he was certain they reflected how she had changed. Maybe it was because Scott knew so much more about her now. Maybe it was because her secret had been revealed. All Scott knew was that Pierina—and his feelings for her—had become different. Once again Scott was all mixed up. They each took a step toward one another and Scott reached out with both hands to her. She raised her hands to grasp his and stepped closer. Scott couldn't resist. He kissed her as he told her how beautiful she was. Somehow her close presence enveloped him totally. Under different circumstances he would have surrendered completely. Her force, her attraction, her ambiance was that powerful. Scott felt light-headed. He didn't know what to do. He could feel himself blush. At last he decided to hold her hand and try to relax.

Hernando announced that Scott and Nick and the girls were invited to the home of his parents for a celebration party.

Scott and Nick looked at their watches and then at each other before declining. "I regret to say our curfew is in half an hour and with the game tomorrow we really do need to be back in our rooms," Scott said.

"Scott's the captain and has to set the example for the whole team. The game tomorrow is important and so we must regretfully decline your gracious invitation. I know it would be fun, especially after tonight and with such enjoyable company," Nick added.

"You silver-tongued fox," Scott whispered.

"OK, too bad for you. We'll see you tomorrow, then? Shall we come here to the pool?"

"That's fine, although we can't swim or be out in the sun."

"All right. Tomorrow then."

Everyone said their good-byes and Scott and Nick went to their respective rooms. Robert was already there and getting ready for bed.

"Hey man. You do make the right contacts. You're something else."

"I didn't even know that she was Miss Costa Rica, honest. I was shocked."

Robert broke out into a big wide grin. "You're sure going to take some shit tomorrow from the guys. You know that."

"Yeah, you're right. I know I will."

That night Scott lay awake trying to deal with his feelings and what he knew was right and yet a strong urge was pulling at him in the opposite direction. He fell asleep picturing her walking out on that stage with a crown on her head in that white dress with the "Miss Costa Rica" banner across her front.

"If it rains this afternoon you will have to make some adjustments to what we have just gone over…" Kori was delivering the game plan chalk talk to the team before they hit the field.

Scott remarked to Robert, who was sitting next to him on the wooden bench in the locker room, that Kori seemed a little bit uptight today.

Robert agreed. "I think this game means more to him than he's letting on. He wants to show the people of Costa Rica what he's done with us."

"Yes, I believe you're right, Robert. You know Costa Rica wanted him back to coach their national team and was bidding for his services when the United States made him an offer he couldn't refuse."

When the coach finished, Scott asked for a moment alone with the team.

As soon as Scott started to address the players, some of them made comments about his relationship with Miss Costa Rica. Scott's fury was rising because he realized he couldn't control the mood.

Robert stood up and signaled for silence. "Listen, please, to what Scott has to say, it's important."

"Thanks, Robert."

"I thought it was obvious Coach Kori was uptight. To him, guys, this game today is the biggest game we will play prior to the start of the Cup games. This is where he used to coach, where he left to come and try to build a world contender with us. He wants this game more than anything else. He wants to show these people why he came to the United States. This game is also an indication of everything yet to come. We've had a good time, me most of all. But I swear I'm ready to play and ready to win. Kori deserves this. Let's win it for him."

Robert and Nick led the yells of enthusiasm, but privately Nick wondered whether Scott was really ready to play.

They found out in a hurry in the first few minutes as Scott took a lofted pass from Chase, controlled the ball, and made a neat deception to the left as he turned right to drill a shot into the upper corner of the net.

Scott noticed that after that play, Alex, the young defender for the team in red, played him man to man every time he got close. Alex had defended another forward when Scott beat the left fullback to score. Alex would not let that happen again.

Just before half, Paolo took a pass from his right wing and jockeyed around Eddie to gain a favorable shooting position. Because the field was now slippery from the light rain that had started to fall, Eddie couldn't recover in time to stop the shot. Paolo placed the ball with pinpoint accuracy, away from Cornell's reach and into the goal to tie the score.

Although Eddie cursed the wet turf for causing his slip, Nick and Scott conferred before the restart and decided Paolo would have to be defended differently. The move he made on Eddie was as fine a play as Scott had ever seen. Scott also tucked it away in his memory bank to practice on it himself later on. Scott could tell Eddie's appreciation of Paolo's skills were somewhat less enthusiastic than his own.

"I'll take out that son of a bitch next time he comes around me. If the field had been dry he never would have made that play," Eddie claimed to anyone who would listen. "Look at him."

Paolo, meanwhile, was playing to the crowd. He ran around with both fists up in the air and jumped into the arms of a teammate while still celebrating for the home fans.

The crowd suddenly was rejuvenated and came back to life. Paolo seemed to have a special rapport with his countrymen, almost as if no matter what the circumstances, as long as Paolo was in there, anything was possible. He would come through.

Scott was feeling magnanimous and told Paolo—just before the kick-off—what a nice play he made. Scott knew that was not normal, but he couldn't help but admire the man's adroitness with the ball. He also knew his compliment would catch him off guard— if he understood it.

Eddie's thoughts and words continued in a different direction. He was thinking of ways to take Paolo out of the game, to hurt him. Eddie always felt that way if someone beat him.

Alex knew Team USA would be smarting after the score. He also heard Scott's comment to Paolo and translated it for him. Alex interpreted the statement as a touch of class. Paolo mistook it for showing weakness.

No score occurred in the time remaining in the first half, so the teams went to the locker room with the score tied 1–1.

Kori was unexpectedly upbeat in the locker room. Scott had expected him to be upset that the host team had scored or that they had squandered two scoring opportunities. But no, he was ebullient about their prospects.

"You are in control. The ball belongs to us. They are the ones who are scrambling, who are nervous. That is good. That is very good. I think they will press a bit harder the second half. I also think they will try to give Paolo the ball and clear an area for him to work in against one or two men. Be wary, he is very good. He is a magician with the ball. Do not underestimate him. Eddie, you will need some help with Paolo. Nick, you're the man. Keep the ball from him, intercept the passes. I'm going to start Robert the second half. Robert, you will also have to guard Paolo, especially if he breaks away from Eddie and Nick. But the reason you are going in is to score offensively on a corner kick. I want the first corner kick of the second half to be lofted into the middle. Fong, you kick it. Robert, you lay back a little and come up at the last minute. Fong, you signal the final movement. Just like we practiced. It will work. It will also put pressure on them when they fall behind."

Kori became so enthusiastic, his attitude was contagious. The players fired up and added emotion to their arsenal.

Robert was ecstatic. Not only was he going to play, but he would be featured in a setup that could result in a goal. The coach had confidence in him—at both ends of the field! He would not let him down; he would show the other guys he deserved to be one of them. This would be the first really big game the coach had played him. He would succeed!

The game resumed with an even flow back and forth. It seemed the home field advantage was buoying up the Latin team with the crowd support matching the enthusiasm of the North Americans.

Halfway through the second forty-five minute half, the moment came. The United States had a corner kick from the right side. Fong went over to place the ball exactly where he wanted it in the corner. He looked around the field and saw Robert moving up. He lined up the kick and raised his hand, held it up, then brought it back down. Fong counted to two then kicked the ball in a soft arc toward the area in front of the goal. Robert ran in and jumped up to meet the ball. It proved to be elusive, however, as it sailed just an inch above his head and passed on harmlessly beyond, only to be kicked away from danger.

The United States team lost the wind that had filled its sails. They all saw how close the planning put them to the go-ahead goal. They all saw, too, that Robert failed to judge the ball quite right; failed to execute his assignment. It didn't matter that none of them could jump that high; he could. The jump was a fraction late and the ball passed before he reached the zenith of the jump. They said, "nice try;" they meant, "you blew it."

Robert was devastated. So much had been laid at his feet. The coach believed in him, the team believed in him, he had believed in himself. Everyone looks for that one chance that will set himself apart from the others. He had had that chance.

Coach Kori, on the sidelines, however, took a different view. His comment to the assistant reflected more about himself. "God, don't you just love to watch him jump? He's like a gazelle."

"He could've had that, coach."

"I know. He's still learning. He had to try that in a pressure situation and miss in order to be solid later on when we really need it. One day he'll do it."

Everyone within earshot of the coach knew then Robert was on the Cup team no matter what. Some of the others were not assured a position on the team, and they wished the coach would feel that way about them.

Alex took note of the play the United States tried. It was obvious his team had no one who could get up nearly as high as that black guy could. He'd have to watch for that in another corner kick situation so they could block him out.

The two teams learned a lot about each other and about themselves that day. They each pushed the other toward unknown limits; both understood how important this game could be. The media in Costa Rica had built up this contest such that not only the team knew this was important; so did the fans at the stadium and the public at large.

So it was that the tempo surged in the stadium as the pressure was increased on the visitors by the home team. It seemed the promise that remained hidden was starting to gel in the Costa Rican contingent. They were dominating the action, even outclassing the United States.

With ten minutes remaining in the game, Fong gave Scott a beautiful outlet pass. It enabled Scott to get behind the left fullback as he pushed up the right center of the field.

Alex noted what happened and moved at an oblique angle to cut off Scott. Scott looked up and over to his left wing to see Chase Anderson side by side with the right fullback, but Chase having the inside.

"C'mon, Scotty, see me now, see me now."

At the right moment Scott lofted a pass over the on-charging Alex. As the ball hit the ground the second time, Chase dribbled it forward. "A perfect pass. Way to go."

One more dribble and Chase blasted the ball past the Cujo, goalkeeper, low and one foot from the right post. The go-ahead goal had been scored.

Chase ran and jumped up into Scott's arms. "Great, great pass, partner, couldn't have been better," he yelled.

"Great shot. Boy, what a shot. You got us ahead."

All the U.S. players on the field came to congratulate Chase and Scott for their play. They were all jumping up and down in a demonstration of happiness.

So, too, was Kori. He was back-slapping and throwing his arms up and jumping all the while. "Way to go. Way to go," he shouted. When Chase looked over, Kori punched upward with his right fist. "Way to go." He was all smiles.

Despite a furious press by Costa Rica, they were unable to convert in the waning minutes. Twice Robert deflected passes coming into the middle to Paolo. It was evident the Costa Rican team was relying on Paolo in this desperate moment. The collapsed U.S. defense proved able to withstand the furious onslaught for the time remaining in the game.

After the emotional level of a close contest like this one, Scott was usually wiped out for several hours afterward. Physically and emotionally a game like this takes its toll. Kori Gaborakov was exactly the opposite. His emotions were flowing freely as he hopped around the locker room slapping backs and recreating moments in the game. He was so psyched up Scott was sure he had underestimated what this game really meant to the trainer, despite his speech to his teammates. He was everywhere, like a bumblebee laughing and talking and acting out plays on the field. Everyone was in a good mood, anyway, but Kori's infectious behavior made it all even better.

Scott had to admit it was a satisfying feeling. That's the best we have ever played, he said to himself. Great teamwork, great anticipation, and good execution. Kori was right. Costa Rica is good and this is a milestone. He's not only happy because we beat them, he's happy because of what we showed out there and what that means for us in the future—the Cup."

Despite all the warm fuzzies everyone was feeling, they did not spend a long time in the locker room. The team was to go back to the hotel to shower and change, and then they were all invited to a dinner party at the house of a friend of Coach and Mrs. Gaborakov. Supposedly it was a real mansion and the dinner party was large. Everyone was invited, including Hernando and the girls. Even the hostess who was with the team on the first bus trip away from the airport was coming. Given the atmosphere after the game, this ought to be one hell of a party.

As the transport bus pulled into the driveway, Scott thought the house was easily the nicest he had ever been in. The grounds surrounding the mansion were expansive and well taken care of. There was an eight-foot-high stone wall enclosing the compound all around, about three or four acres, Scott guessed. The entrance doors were oversized, maybe ten feet tall, and wide open. The central room was open and spacious. There must have been fifty people there already before the team and its entourage arrived. Even with the addition of the U.S. players the room was not crowded. The back of the room was open to the outside and a good-sized patio provided ample access to the outdoors through the means of four glass doors that all slid over to one side.

Hernando and about fifteen girls were outside on the patio talking with Fofi. Both Fofi and Hernando seemed to know how to entertain and charm the ladies. Actually their capacity for this sort of thing seemed insatiable. Both loved to be the center of attention and both loved the ladies. Truly, they were now in their element.

The approach of Scott and the other players changed everything. Hearty congratulations were rendered all around. Scott didn't realize how close Eddie and Pu and the others were, but immediately Eddie's drawl could be heard above the clamor and distant sounds of the band.

"Nice place to have a victory party. Hey, Hernando. Whadda ya'll think of American soccer now, huh? We've come a long way, baby."

"Hey, congratulations, Eddie. You and the team surprised us. You really played well. You have come a long way. Ours is a good team, but you might be better."

"Might, hell. No, no, you do have a good team," Eddie agreed as he changed his demeanor. "Actually one of the best we've played. We needed to. No, you do have a good team. That center forward of yours, Paolo, he's terrific. Got the best of me once. Made me mad. That won't happen again."

"Ha, *amigo*. Paolo has gotten the best of many a defender. You are not the only one to be burned by him. He is quick and crafty with the ball. I think he will be one of the stars of the '94 Cup. You have some excellent players on your team also. I am surprised my old school chum got to be so good. I had to teach him the finer points of the game while we were together at Georgia."

"Oh, you did, did you?"

"Scott, didn't know you were so close, or I wouldn't have thrown you a compliment. Nice win, though. Your team and even you played well."

"Thanks. As Eddie said, that was a very good game for us. Our team did play well. Kori is ecstatic."

"Kori. When the world sees you guys play in the Cup, he'll be able to write his own ticket, anywhere he wants."

"He can just about do that now. If we do well, you're right. You're absolutely right."

"Hey, hero, nice going," called a female voice.

It was Rosibel with Pierina alongside of her. Scott involuntarily sucked in his breath at the sight of the two of them.

"Thanks. You two look magnificent. I honestly can say I have never seen two more beautiful girls in my whole life than you two look right now."

Scott kissed the customary kiss on the cheek to Rosibel, but a more centrally located one on Pierina. Pierina gave him a big hug. Scott guessed it was her way of saying congratulations and all the other things she couldn't say in English.

In a couple of minutes when the first excitement cooled a little, Hernando sidled up to Scott and whispered, "Hey, *amigo*, I have the strong feeling that if you want to take Pierina to bed, she's all yours. In fact, she has been wondering why you have not already."

"I am going to have difficulty explaining to her that I won't be, either, without hurting her feelings."

"What?"

"I think she is one of the most terrific people I have ever met. Certainly one of the most beautiful. I am most flattered she feels that way about me. But I am married to Diana, and will not have an affair with anyone. I am fully committed to her and our marriage. If there ever was a tempting situation, though, this is it. Diana would never know and you can't do any better than Pierina. It absolutely is no reflection on Pierina. I just won't let myself. Believe me, I have struggled the last few days with just this situation, more than I have ever before. I need your help to make her understand. I don't want her to be hurt. She's a wonderful person."

"*Amigo, amigo, amigo,* I can't believe it. You have no Latin blood in you. Man, think of what you are saying. Look at her. Thousands would give their left arm to be in your position."

"I know, I know. I'm sorry, but I just can't do that to Diana. I couldn't look her in the eye. My relationship with her would be changed forever."

Hernando cocked his head a little sideways. "Man, you are really something. OK, I respect you for your decision and Rosibel will, too. Pierina probably won't understand. You are the only one anywhere who would refuse her."

"You might be right, she is a most enchanting girl, but I am happily married to my wife. It's really a choice I made a long time ago. Thanks anyhow for a most wonderful time down here. You couldn't have done more for us. I really appreciate it. I really do."

"No sweat, man. I've had a blast. You gotta know this has meant a lot to me, too."

"Yeah, I know." Scott stepped forward as the two frat brothers hugged each other.

The euphoria of the victory carried everyone beyond the sadness of knowing this was their last night here. So many friendships formed; one friendship renewed. The party mood sustained its lightness and happiness despite the clinging to one last opportunity and the knowledge this world would be left behind for another, more familiar one.

Pierina gave Scott a big hug and a kiss again. Then she pouted as she explained something Scott did not understand in Spanish.

Rosibel came to the rescue. "Pierina is very happy for you and your team. Her heart, however, still lies with our team and she did not really expect you to win. So she is sad for her team."

"I think her loyalty is correctly placed with Costa Rica. You have a terrific team. Let us hope we next meet in the finals of the World Cup. She should not feel bad about wanting Costa Rica to win. I do not expect her friendship for me would outweigh a lifetime of feelings."

Rosibel then translated to Pierina and a glow of warmth replaced that of sadness in the beautiful blonde's eyes.

"Tell her I respect her even more than before because she was able to speak openly about this."

"OK. You're a nice person, Scott."

"Thanks, you are, too."

Pierina coyly smiled at Scott when Rosibel passed the compliment along. Scott was pretty sure Rosibel had not yet told Pierina about the position he had taken, although Hernando had told Rosibel. He wondered what her reaction would be and how she would treat him after she knew. It was an ego trip for himself to know that a girl of that caliber would have been willing, even if he did not plan to take advantage of it. Would she be mad? Would she feel scorned? The questions remained.

At that moment Hernando came over and said, "C'mon. The owner of this house, the host, wants to meet all the U.S. players. You too, Pierina, come with Scott."

As the host met each player, he said something to every person, welcoming each to his house and to Costa Rica. Scott happened to be last and Pierina was next to him. Coach Kori, with his beautiful dark-eyed wife alongside, was doing the introductory honors, telling the host some bit of information about each player.

"Señor Trejos, this is Scott Fontaine, our team captain and an important part of our offense. He scored a goal and assisted in another today."

"Well, well. Almost single-handedly you destroyed our defense, Mr. Fontaine. However, you provided some exciting action for us all to watch. Very impressive indeed."

"Thank you, Señor Trejos. We had a good game. Your team is very good. May I say on behalf of my team how appreciative we are for your hospitality and the exceptional treatment we have received during our entire stay here in your country. Sir, allow me to introduce my friend Pierina Diaz to you. She has been helping to show us the best of all the local sights."

"It is no wonder you have enjoyed yourselves here. She is part of the beauty of our land. *Mucho gusto, Señorita*."

"Pierina is the former Miss Costa Rica."

"No wonder her face is familiar. But of course."

The host then launched into a brief conversation with the former beauty queen.

Then he turned back to Scott. "You cost me a sizable bet. I lost on the game today, young man. But don't worry, I intend to make that back and a lot more on your team in the World Cup tournament. I think your team and Kori will perhaps surprise more than a few doubters."

"Thank you, sir. I hope both our teams do."

"Ho! Well spoken, Mr. Scott Fontaine. Well spoken."

A band struck up the music again and Scott started dancing with Pierina. As he watched her dance, he grew somewhat lightheaded in awe of her physical beauty. She combines a beautiful face and nearly perfect body with a sensuousness in her movements, he mused. Some girls have a sexual quality about them that makes them more desirable. Pierina combines the best of everything. What a woman! he thought. She always seems to be having fun, too. One more point for her. She's not a bit stuck up, either.

After two fast dances the band played *Theme from a Summer Place*, one of Scott's favorites. Pierina automatically moved in tight for close, slow dancing. Scott's resolve weakened a hair, as they floated on the dance floor. *Moon River* followed without missing a beat except that the slow dance became slower and even more romantic. Scott couldn't help but kiss her as they looked into each other's eyes. Her lips were soft and yielding. He felt the passion welling up in his body as he became enchanted under the spell of her many charms.

Scott enjoyed the moment for what it was. But even though he was feeling wonderful, the guilt was rising.

"Let's take a walk," he told her, grabbing her hand and starting toward the open sliding doors.

The fresh air outside felt good against his skin. "*Muy fresca,*" Scott commented, using his expanding vocabulary.

"*Si.*"

They walked for a while in silence absorbing the quiet ambiance. The grounds behind the house were verdant and lush. The sounds of the band diminished in the background and the two became more conscious of themselves.

"Pierina, you have given me one of the best times of my life. You are wonderful. You are beautiful, and a good time." Scott held both her hands and looked deep into her eyes. "If circumstances were different I would fall in love with you. No, I am in love with you, but differently. Comprende?"

"*Si—mas o menos.*"

"But it just can't be," Scott cried out in anguish. "I'm married. I have a wife, a spouse."

"*Usted? Spousa?*"

"Yes, *si.* In *Estados Unidos.* Her name is Diana and I love her. Pierina, I have not been fair with you or fair to Diana. My emotions have been so mixed up. You are so beautiful, so charming, so enchanting. I have really fallen for you, and I shouldn't."

Pierina had separated herself from Scott to create some space for herself. She was not sure what to think. She knew Scott had told her he loved her—she had seen enough movies to know what those words meant—and she knew he had told her he had a wife in the United States. She could see the anguish in his face. But Pierina could not sort out her own feelings. Hernando had told her his friend was captain of the United States national team and that they had gone to school together. He did not tell her he was married. He explained his friend was good-looking and fun to be with. She had not expected to develop such strong feelings toward him. What did it mean for her? She looked over at him. He was from a different land, a different culture. But was he really so different?

She had not had a boyfriend who was as appealing to her as was this American. Now, just as her feelings for this man were changing into a deeper emotion, she realized he was not hers to have. Tears started to form in her eyes. She had not expected anything to come out of the gringo's visit and agreed, mostly because of Rosibel—at Hernando's encouragement—to be a companion for a few days to his friend. As she had watched the game today, and watched him play well, she felt herself changing her view of this new person in her life. She began to wonder if there might be something deeper developing between them. Both of them, she knew, were attracted to each other, not just by appearances, but also by personality. It was surprising how much they could communicate, even though words limited them. She knew they both felt comfortable in the long silences together, sometimes holding hands, sometimes looking at each other.

Now the feelings changed. Pierina could tell Scott was trying to communicate that he had a wife and would be committed to her. She felt an emptiness where new hope had arisen only earlier that day. She felt sorrow for herself, even though she knew she shouldn't.

It was with tear-filled eyes that Pierina at last turned to face the American. The look of deep sorrow on his countenance further forced the tears out. She held out her hands to him and he took them for a moment before wrapping his arms around her. They stayed that way for more than a minute before he pulled back enough to look at her. With great tenderness Scott kissed the tears on her cheeks.

"You are very, very special, Pierina. So beautiful, so wonderful. I love my wife and so I can't let myself love you. But if I could, I would. In fact, I do love you in a way I can't explain to anybody else. But you know."

"*De amo tambien. Usted es muy amable; muy bonito.*"

"*Gracias*, Pierina." Scott kissed Pierina lightly on the lips and had meant to stop it right there as a fitting conclusion to this conversation. But both of them grabbed for something more as the kiss escalated.

Then it was over. Scott hugged her briefly and took her hand as he started back toward the house.

As they entered the house Scott was embarrassed to find out they had been looking for him to accept an honor presented to the United States team. To his dismay his teammates razzed him loudly with cat-calls and embarrassing questions about where he had been. Worse, both he and Pierina blushed in response.

Although the coach had lifted all curfews, Scott took Pierina home before midnight and was back to his hotel by twelve-fifteen. The plane left at nine A.M. the next morning and they were to be at the hotel lobby, packed and ready to go by eight.

Hernando and Rosibel had promised to come to see him off at the airport, but Scott had recommended they not bring Pierina—that they had already said good-bye. "It would just make it harder on her and me," he explained.

Everyone was in the lobby on time, except Eddie and Ricky. Just as someone volunteered to go to their room and get them, they drove up to the entrance with great big smiles on their faces.

"Hold the bus, we're coming," Ricky yelled. They both got out of the Cressida and gave their girls one last big kiss.

"Awwrright," chorused Pu and Robert and Scott and Nick, mimicking Eddie.

The two prodigal sons raced toward their room with Eddie flipping the bird to them as he ran by. The players just laughed.

Armida was, once again, on the tour bus returning them to the airport. Scott did not listen to what she was saying as he was pensively remote in his own thoughts.

At the airport Scott once again invited Hernando and Rosibel to come to the United States when the World Cup is played. "Thanks, buddy. This couldn't have been better. I'll never forget this trip—ever. Rosibel, please tell Pierina I think she's the greatest, the sweetest person one would ever want to meet. No question, I fell in love with her. I wish her all the best for the future. Please tell her."

"I will, but I think she already knows how you feel. You might want to know, you are the first man she has ever fallen for."

"She'll find someone, I know she will."

Scott hugged Rosibel and gave her a kiss on the cheek. As he hugged

Hernando the emotions made him cry. "These are happy tears because you put so much of yourself into showing us a good time. Hernando, it just couldn't have been better. Good-bye, buddy."

"Good-bye, *amigo*. Good luck to you and the team next summer. You'll have a lot of friends rooting for you."

"*Hasta luego. Vaya con Dios.*"

CHAPTER 12

From all over the world journalists descended on Las Vegas to attend the drawing for the 1994 World Cup. The major newspapers from every participating country were there in the form of both photographers and writers. Sports magazines from many countries were present, sometimes digging into whatever side issues they could find, looking for material out of which might come an interesting extra story for their employer. TV cameramen and reporters were everywhere.

Each group had been prepared for the events surrounding the draw by special briefings FIFA conducted the day before. By providing a sequence of events and the timetable in which each was to happen, FIFA supplied the media the ability to organize itself more effectively and prepare ahead of time for each aspect of the draw. Where every group would be playing was important, as well as which teams got grouped together. The lead teams had been announced or rather leaked out already, but not how each of the other teams had gotten classified: as a second level, third level, or bottom level of the draw. Each group would end up with one team from among the best and one from each other group as the teams got rated. The media often played up this aspect of the draw, as they did in '90 when England got placed at the top to ensure secure playing locations on the islands of Sicily and Sardinia. That upset the Holland contingent, which thought it, not England, deserved the top slot.

In addition to all the media, there were significant numbers of FIFA officials and some of their families members. Attending the festivities were many dignitaries and VIPs from all walks of life. The United States Soccer Federation had invited several famous athletes to partake in the ceremonies. Magic Johnson, Gayle Sayers, Joe Montana, Jim Courier, Pelé, Andre Agassi, Barry Bonds, and Greg Lemond were attending, all invited by the United States Soccer Federation to increase the publicity and awareness of the everyday sports fan for the World Cup. In addition, top executives and their spouses from the companies that sponsored soccer, particularly the '94 World Cup effort, were here at the USSF's invitation. To add glamour, some Hollywood stars were present also. Several well-known musical groups were here to be part of some festivities. From Argentina, a performer known world wide as The Puma was here, along with Julio Iglesias, to add an international flavor.

FIFA had organized three separate social events for the favored VIPs as a part of the proceedings. Most of the media people were included in the large party given the night after the drawing. This gave them a chance to work up side material for their stories, as well as to have an enjoyable evening. The affair was first class. This was to be an example of how the whole tournament would be run. FIFA well understood the value of good public relations.

The closed party for invited special guests the night before the drawing included the FIFA officials and their spouses, the president of each country's soccer federation and his spouse, four invited guests from each country, as well as all the entertainers and special athletes. Included, too, were various political dignitaries from the States.

The luncheon just before the draw included everybody and offered time for conjecture and heightened interest for the main event.

The drawing had become a very big event in its own. TV now covered it live and so much social activity attended the draw that in itself it had become a significant event. It was held early in December and, by virtue of the timing, kicked off the Christmas party season in Las Vegas. The results of this draw would have great bearing on the tournament itself. Often it was the luck of the draw that helped one team make it into the second phase. Sometimes that allowed a team that was not playing especially well to recover and go on to do very well.

The USSF had seen to it that the public would have news about the World Cup placed in front of them almost daily from this point forward. It was crucial to build grassroots support for the tournament that would result in larger attendance of United States fans at all the games. More than half the attendance—even for the important games—would have to come from the States. Limited fan support would come from the home countries. Brazil, Germany, Argentina, and Italy would have large follow-ings, but couldn't begin to fill the largest stadiums. Cameroon, Egypt, and Costa Rica wouldn't even fill one section in a stadium. Throughout the world there was doubt, considerable doubt, the United States could effec-tively host the World Cup and fill the stands. Logistically, America could handle a tournament of this size. That was a given due to the various suc-cessful Olympics held in this country. The 1988 Olympics was particularly well received around the world. The trick was to translate fan support into attendance. Toward that end the USSF was working hard to publicize through the media, state and local soccer organizations, and corporate involvement.

Each venue selected to host a game had to guarantee one-half of the stadium capacity pre-sold locally for every contest held there. Much of the effort was placed in the state and local soccer organizations' hands. By active promotion, the youth soccer programs had accounted for nearly the one-half requirement in every case. Where they didn't, the very active corporate sponsorships made up the difference. In fact, some of the games had commitments exceeding sixty percent of the capacities of the stadium, once reserved areas for the press and those reserved for USSF dignitaries had been discounted. Every state soccer association had submitted commitments for the games. Some groups would have to travel more than ten hours by bus to reach the closest game, yet each organization was enthusiastically endorsing and supporting the big tour-nament. What better audience could the tournament play to? This was just what was needed to inspire the young players to achieve higher lev-els. Most people in America could go relatively short distances to watch quality football, baseball, or basketball, but not soccer. This might be a once-in-a-lifetime opportunity for most of them.

The USSF and in turn the FIFA officials were extremely pleased at the favorable developments. FIFA officials had been lambasted by a number of organizations for choosing the United States as the host country. "There is no soccer there. Where will all the fan support come from? Give it to a soccer nation," were the kind of comments heard by FIFA ever since they disclosed the United States was being considered as the site. Now United States reaction and execution was making them look good. Most of the world was unaware of what was going on and wouldn't believe it anyway. Only when the games were televised and the viewers could see the full stadiums would the USSF's efforts speak for themselves and be a positive commentary on America's interest in soccer.

Some aspects of this interest were being provided to the press. The information communicated to the media revealed most of the games had already pre-sold most of the entire U.S. allotment of sixty to seventy-five percent. That would astound most detractors.

So it was that activities leading up to the main draw had been carefully planned and orchestrated for many months and many long days. The sub-group of the USSF that was responsible for the drawing was worn out and ready for it to be over. The tired bodies and faces of those responsible were evident. Mr. Priestaps noted this and made a decision to expand the planning group for future events so as not to burn out those involved.

The moment had finally come! The first team drawn was Germany. They would head group A. Then in succession were Brazil, United Sates, Argentina, Belgium, and Italy. These teams were seeded first in each group. The draw landed the United States in the "C" group with England, Spain, and France. The "E" group contained Belgium, Greece, Uruguay, and Costa Rica.

While Italy and Germany were considered the favorites, neither of these other two groups was considered easy. France, stung by their fail-ure to make it into the Italian World Cup, had really made a concerted effort to improve. Their recent record amply demonstrated that. In fact, the French were incensed that they were placed in the last level instead of the third. Spain, as always, would be tough. The United States was listed as a gross underdog despite the improved showing demonstrated in the past two years in international play. Belgium, Greece, and Uruguay made for a really tough lineup for Costa Rica. The Costa Rica Soccer Federation had lobbied hard to get it placed as a third-tier team, but to no avail. They pointed out their strong showing in Italy as their chief reason. However, FIFA stood resolute. Once the draw was made there would be no changes. So Costa Rica, France, and the others had to accept things the way they were.

Italy was not happy, either. They weren't as worried about who was in their group so much as they had drawn the stronger half by all appear-ances. Again they would likely have to face Argentina in the semi-finals. But Belgium had also been particularly strong in the last year and was rated the third best team in the tournament this year. Some scribes even ranked them ahead of Italy. As bad as that was, Italy could see that they would probably have to face either Cameroon or England in the first game of the second phase—the eighth finals. All in all Italy just probably had the roughest schedule to get through to win the tournament. They knew there was no use in complaining. They were just letting the press know what they faced. The Italian officials pointed out how dangerous the team from Cameroon had been in the last World Cup and that they proved to be the hardest team to defend against. This time they could be even stronger, as noted by FIFA, who had granted them second-level status this time.

The results of the draw were proclaimed throughout the civilized world, providing fodder for many discussions the next day and for several weeks. The carefully planned campaign to promote soccer, especially the World Cup, within the United States was drawing praise from all corners of the globe. Combining this information with the improved results of the U.S. national team made for a much better feeling everywhere that, yes, after all, the World Cup was in capable hands. While no one thought the American team would be a serious contender, the United States was winning support for its efforts throughout the world.

As Andrew was getting on board the Lacsa plane with Godfrey, he double-checked the his list of items he was carrying with him. He feared always he would leave a bag or some other carry-on item behind at an airport or on the airplane. He liked to count the number of items he had so that if he couldn't remember what he was supposed to pick up each time, he would know how many and not miss any.

They were taking newly printed Chamber of Commerce brochures about Ashton as well as certain representative items that Ashton employers had provided, such as three jackets made by the Henry-Wright Co., the apparel maker, and fifty souvenir pins with thermometers in them from Bradley Gent and Sons thermometer plant. They also carried a photo album of various scenes and facilities in town, maps, and a newly printed hotel-restaurant guide.

The purpose of their trip was twofold. First was to meet with the Costa Rica Soccer Federation officials and to present their town as a viable option to locate their headquarters, and to show them how interested they were in having them. Second, was to gather information about Costa Rica to bring back with them so that they could better plan events to make the Costa Rica team feel more welcome and to educate the Americans more about Costa Rica.

The teams selected to play in the group scheduled for Giants Stadium in East Rutherford were Belgium, Greece, Uruguay, and Costa Rica. As soon as the draw was made and the teams were known, Ashton's investigations were begun into the teams, the cost, and the countries. Belgium was ruled out—way too expensive—so efforts were concentrated on the other three.

What had weighed most favorably for Costa Rica was the kind of country it was: peaceful, with no army, an agrarian society, winner of the Nobel Peace Prize, and a country that had taken a leadership role to change Central America through dialogue, not war. It was also the second oldest democracy in the Western Hemisphere, electing a president every four years. In researching information about Costa Rica it was surprising to find out better than ninety percent of the registered voters vote in their presidential elections. In the United States, by comparison, often fifty percent is a good turnout in many places. They also have more school teachers than policemen, and have an extremely high literacy rate. Costa Rica's primary exports were coffee, bananas, beef, sugar, pineapple, and orange juice concentrate.

It was a beautiful country. As the Ashton city council was reviewing slides of each country, the natural beauty of Costa Rica was very evident. The rugged mountain terrain, the beautiful waterfalls, the volcanoes, and the wonderful coastline all made for pictorial splendor.

The town council had narrowed their choices to Greece and Costa Rica, figuring they would provide the best return on the dollar invested. After some time passed, almost everyone found himself leaning toward Costa Rica, and so the final decision had been an easy one.

Flying, Godfrey discovered, was not so unpleasant after all. He had flown before, of course, but not for sometime now. As the plane entered Costa Rican boundaries he intently viewed the landscape below. He could see both the rugged mountain scenery and the Pacific Ocean with the long beaches, then San José, their destination.

The meetings with the soccer federation officials went very well. Godfrey and Andrew were able to generate some interest for Costa Rica to consider Ashton as their headquarters. Of importance to the Ashton city council members were answers obtained to questions about expected accommodations required for housing and practices, the daily schedule, travel needs of the team and its contingency, types of meals, and other details. They learned the team would more than likely spend a few nights elsewhere; that generated more revenue for the team, as those places paid fees to them, too.

Both Andrew and Godfrey hit it off with Ricardo Servilla, the Costa Rica federation president. Ricardo was a friendly, thoughtful, well-spoken man, fluent in English and fun to be with. He had lived in New York for a number of years. Ricardo had told them what a positive experience they had in Mondovi, Italy, at the Italian World Cup. "The people couldn't have been nicer or made us feel more welcome. Everywhere they went it was the same." Mondovi even organized a carnival, culminating in a disco that featured the players.

"The town really supported the team. On one occasion they arrived very late in the night, maybe one-thirty in the morning actually, and there were over one hundred people waiting for us. Our team had just upset Scotland. The people were yelling and cheering. It really perked us up; made the team feel like heroes."

Ricardo invited them to his house for dinner that first night and also arranged for transportation and a bilingual guide to take them around to see San José and some of Costa Rica. Godfrey and Andrew felt almost like they were the ones being wined and dined—that the tables were reversed, the roles interchanged. They were made to feel very welcome.

Two things really impressed them about Costa Rica. One was the friendliness of the people. The second was the level of knowledge about soccer and the World Cup possessed by the average person. They expected Ricardo and the other officials to know a lot, but everyone they met could tell them who won the last five World Cups, what teams they beat, who were the great players, and where the World Cups had been held. They were taken aback by how much soccer meant to these people. Godfrey and Andrew had decided the lack of any other real competing sport in this country made soccer, and people's awareness of it, just that much more dominant.

While in Costa Rica they were treated as special guests to a soccer match between Saprissa and Heredia, two of the best teams in the first-division pro league there. The game was held in Saprissa's stadium. Purple and white were everywhere. The stadium was impressive in size for a country whose whole population was only three million. Saprissa won the game 2–0. Eight players from Saprissa's team, Ricardo explained, played on Costa Rica's Italian World Cup national team. This year the number might only be five as some of the other teams had developed good young players.

Ricardo had told them of the success their younger, under twenty-three team has had over the last six years and that for the first time this youth corps, plus the experience gained in Italy, would mean their team could very well be competitive with even the best teams. He felt they were a stronger team now than they were for the last World Cup, but they would have to be stronger to really compete.

In watching the game Godfrey and Andrew realized soccer was played on a higher level here than what was played in the United States. As they discussed the United States soccer efforts they realized both had joined the camp of those who thought the United States would never be competitive until they had a first-rate professional league. The league would develop the skills necessary to compete, but more importantly encourage consistent application of the mental aspects of the game that other World Cup teams treat matter of factly. Andrew recalled reading that the United States team committed a great number of basic errors that other teams and players just didn't do because they faced difficult competition regularly and it became second nature to them. He remembered one example in particular, when an American defenseman was beaten in the United States—Austria game. The Austrians made an easy goal because no one else was there to help the goalie. What should have happened is the defenseman who was beaten should have fouled the Austrian! Although this set up a direct kick outside the penalty box, the defense was given the advantage of a situation that could be defended by a human wall helping the goalie. It's a normal, regular event with all other teams. Instead the United States let it happen twice; it would have been unforgivable anywhere else.

In the game they just watched, the defense for both teams fouled a player who had beaten them, thus preventing a one-on-one situation against their goalie. Twice there had been blatant fouls, where a player had reached out and dragged an opponent down. The referee had given them yellow warning cards, but in neither case was any goal scored.

Andrew knew from his experience with kids recreational soccer that it took two yellow cards against any one player before he is thrown out—or in the case of a vicious foul, a red card could result in an immediate ouster from the game—making the team one player short. Even if the team plays one short it's better than giving up an almost sure goal. At the World Cup level any player getting a one-on-one situation ought to score.

Señor Servilla, it turned out, was also the president of Saprissa. The Americans were invited into the dressing room afterward to meet the players and coach. The players were nice to them and willing to talk. About half knew English, and Ricardo translated with the others. When Ricardo introduced Andrew and Godfrey as representatives from a town in the United States that wanted to host Costa Rica, they were very enthusiastically received by the players. Ricardo explained that they all know from the ones who went to Italy how well they were treated by the Mondovi and Finale Leguri townspeople, so the players came to regard anyone hosting their team as valued friends.

Andrew looked at Godfrey as they both realized what a special situation, a special opportunity they had here. Andrew wondered whether they could effectively communicate the feelings and observations they were experiencing on this trip. Both resolved to themselves that Ashton would not disappoint Costa Rica if chosen.

Andrew started planning some things that could be done in advance to raise Ashton's level of awareness. He hoped the local newspaper would be cooperative. He could provide some stories of how the townspeople in Italy had supported the team—meeting them late at night, the carnival, the good treatment of fans of Costa Rica—perhaps challenging the town of Ashton to do as well. The wheels in Andrew's mind were spinning one hundred miles per hour as he considered the things that could be done. He had to involve the newspaper. Schedules, elementary Spanish lessons, personal interviews, human interest stories, 1990 World Cup events, information about World Cup, rules of soccer—all of these were items of which the newspaper could help inform Ashton townspeople. If developed properly, it could serve many purposes. The newspaper could build clientele, inform townspeople about Costa Rica, soccer, and the World Cup, publish schedules and events, build enthusiasm and support for what Andrew hoped would develop out of being the host and a good neighbor.

When Andrew and Godfrey left Costa Rica they were more determined than ever to win the privilege of hosting the Costa Rican team and their federation officials. The two talked about working with some other communities to develop an overall package to present to Ricardo Servilla that included some nights away from their community. Also some discussions with Ricardo indicated a possibility of one or two separate single-event occasions—a dinner, a dance, or a practice in another place, all designed to generate additional income for the Costa Rican team. Andrew told Ricardo he was resolved to present a package deal to them that could be all-inclusive or leave one or two open options for the team to separately negotiate. Ricardo acknowledged that the open options might be desirable and might allow interesting opportunities for them to pursue.

Ricardo thanked them for making such a special effort to come to Costa Rica to find out about them and to show such interest. While not obligating themselves, the Costa Rican soccer officials informed Andrew that Ashton would certainly be considered and that they were very appreciative and impressed with all the effort and preparation already given to providing a bid as the host for the team's headquarters. It was obvious they were sincere and willing to provide suitable arrangements. Ricardo then expressed interest in meeting and negotiating with them at the time of the FIFA Congress in the United States.

Upon their return to Ashton, Andrew and Godfrey took the opportunity to present to the town council, as well as to various civic clubs, garden clubs, and other organizations, what they had seen and learned of Costa Rica and what would be expected of Ashton as a host city. The slides they took served as a wonderful visual aid for these presentations. Both men were delighted at the level of interest by all these groups. While obviously interested in Costa Rica, each group centered on what the Costa Rican Soccer Federation had to say about coming to Ashton. Each group was told, "This was a preliminary presentation. While no decision could be made yet, we felt well-received and consider that Ashton has an excellent chance to win the position as headquarters for the team and its officials."

The newspaper cooperated fully, doing an extensive article on their trip and what happened to them while they were there. Andrew used the newspaper to keep the citizenry informed as the situation developed.

So it was that most of the town was informed, through a front-page article, that the Costa Rican soccer delegation was coming to the United States to scout locations. This signaled the single most significant change in the town. People started painting, fixing up their houses and lawns, and planting flowers; the city workforce was also sprucing up. The day that article came out was the day the economic boom began for the town.

The arrival of the delegation from Costa Rica was kept low-key, although everywhere they went to view practice facilities, hotels, and restaurants people waved, introduced themselves, and were just plain friendly. Godfrey thought the visit couldn't have gone better.

Ricardo had made several requests for changes or additional capabilities, none of which seemed a big problem. The relationship already established in Costa Rica continued to be friendly and cordial. All the city council, the newspaper people, the chief of police, the high school superintendent, and the recreation soccer league officials and their spouses were invited to dine with the federation officials, giving an opportunity for all the right people to meet Ricardo and his entourage. Included too were the state senator from Ashton and county and state government officials involved in providing financial support.

All went well and Ricardo promised some correspondence from them within the next two weeks. Sure enough, nine days later a fax was received in Godfrey's office confirming Ashton as the chosen site for Costa Rica's headquarters. Godfrey immediately sent a fax back to Ricardo confirming receipt of the message and telling them how pleased he and all the others were that they had been selected. He added reassurance that to the best of his ability he would make sure it was a pleasant experience for all.

———⚽———

Brad Wilkerson was amazed at the pace at which things seemed to be happening. For the World Cup tournament he had been put in charge of the public relations sector. He enjoyed the challenge of this responsibility and was determined to carry it out to the very best of his ability. Things were on schedule for printing game schedules and maps that would be made available by the hundreds of thousands throughout the country, but particularly in and around the nine cities chosen as venues. The schedules and the maps served two functions: one was to provide needed information, and the other was to hype the tournament within the United States. He was very impressed to hear the positive results achieved by the ticketing group, which had excellent success promoting soccer with the various state and local soccer organizations. Somehow, they had enthusiastically supported the tournament so that already seventy percent of the tickets were committed.

Brad's frustration came from the lack of defined strategies in place to deal with the media. He and his assistant had obtained details of the procedures at the Italian World Cup and were determined to improve upon them. Part of selling the United States as a World Cup host was making sure the media had everything it required in the way of facilities, phones, equipment, and food. He had decided to provide word processors, fax machines, and office space at each stadium. A double-wide, forty-five-foot trailer was to be set up at each location. Then for the semifinals and the final, he would move one of the trailers no longer being used to those sites to provide double the space. Also, two trailers would be available for each site that the U.S. team would play.

Brad felt good about the deal he had worked out with the manufacturer. Brad found his relationship with the sponsor group was a tighter one than he expected. The sponsor group had been instrumental in locating a manufacturer who would donate the office space. As a matter of fact, many of the things he needed were obtained through the sponsor group. The maps and schedules were provided by a soft drink company, which requested exclusive advertising on those. In return, no other official maps or schedules would be used. Use of the 1994 World Cup logo was forbidden on any non-authorized maps and schedules. That was a good deal for both the advertiser as well as the USSF.

It was hard to get his hand around the media issue, though. Certain details, such as providing interpreters, were already being arranged. At least two interpreters would be needed for each game, unless one or both of the teams spoke English or the same language, even if it was not English. In the stadium itself, there was a minimum of two hundred and fifty media spots for which space had to be provided. Each spot required a forty inch section at a table with word processing as well as audio recording capability. Brad was relieved to find out that audio capability simply meant electricity and a few back-up recorders in case one failed. Then he had to provide a minimum of twelve sound booths for announcing teams to provide individual language transmissions back to their home countries. Every game would be covered by at least five cameras. Important games might have twice as many.

Brad still did not have a clue as what the press passes would look like. Those, like the game tickets, would be printed up at the last possible moment to keep counterfeiting to a minimum. He had requested, but not yet received, an official list of media representatives from each country. In addition to those representatives from the twenty-four countries involved, he knew there would be quite a few from other countries just here to cover the tournament. Trouble was, he couldn't even begin to predict how many would cover the tournament; having it here in the United States probably meant more than the usual number would come. Brad had the numbers from the last three World Cups. In each case the number of media covering the tournament had grown. As a planning tool he added thirty percent to the number who had gone to Italy; however, he fretted that he might be way off.

Arvon Bresnev, the celebrated coach for the new Commonwealth of Independent States team, smiled to himself. Yes, it would work, but they could only try it once. They had better pick the right spot for using this valuable present Nicholai had suggested. He must remember to include this innovative contribution in his next report on his assistant. Indeed, he had shown he was capable of creative, useful strategy, and that his coaching abilities were growing and maturing. Nicholai was the third coach on the national team. He had proven his value several times before in creating specific plays that, when practiced, showed some measure of success. Surprise was a very important element in top-level competition, and their team would not be found wanting in this regard.

The play they had practiced on was a sort of reverse defensive trick. Nicholai had walked through it with a certain gleeful spring in his step. In a man-to-man defense it was possible to draw a penalty kick by having one of his players unintentionally run into by a defender who wouldn't even know the other player was there. In a quick circling maneuver the offensive player could work himself to the blind side of the defender. With more work the timing could be developed to have two offensive forwards criss-cross with a third player, passing the ball at the right moment. The key man would purposely place himself in the path of the charging defender, who couldn't help but crash into the forward who would be just receiving the pass. Timing. Timing was everything. The "fouled" player would also have to be a great actor, tripping and falling to the ground at the perfect moment. Especially if they got exactly the right footwork down so that it looked like a real foul, the action would fool even the best of referees.

Arvon could see that it would not be everyone who could pull this off. He would have to experiment with Sartov, Jeckai, and Boris to see who would develop the most realistic situation. These three had shown the most potential in practice. Jeckai Prozinkop might just be the best, although it was likely he would be a substitute. Because he was not a main player, that meant Arvon would have to substitute him into the game, if he were not already in there.

Arvon mused about Jeckai's background. He lived and breathed soccer. His father had played on the Soviet World Cup team twenty-five years earlier. Jeckai, if he could, would let nothing interfere with his becoming a member of this team. Arvon knew that this one all-consuming drive would make him practice this trick until he became the best, if that's what it took to be sure he would be on the squad. Jeckai even wanted to wear the same number as his father—five—as a way to remember him. His father had died under very mysterious circumstances one night. The boy had nearly come apart when that happened. It had always been a hope of the lad that his father would one day see him play in a World Cup. That was too bad.

Coach Bresnev generally was pleased with how the squad was developing. Zantorovich, the keeper, had progressed nicely, as had several of the others. The most pleasant surprise had been the outstanding play of young Charko Popov, who had become far and away the high scorer on the team. The man had an uncanny ability to find the back of the net. The coach said to himself, Charko might just be the best athlete I have ever coached. Never have I had a player before who could jump like him. Charko Popov's father had been an Olympic high jumper, winning the national championship for Russia at least twice, he recalled. But it wasn't just his jumping ability alone that made him such a dangerous threat;

Charko could deflect a high pass with absolute precision every time he headed the ball. He had remarkable concentration. Combined with his three-meter-plus jumping ability and his concentration, his head control made young Popov a unique weapon—perhaps unparalleled in the soccer world. No one could jump like him! No wonder his father was a high jump champion! Truly he was "a chip off the old block," demonstrating so many of the abilities his father had had.

"Scott, Scott, Wake up. I think the time is here. I've felt contractions for the past couple of hours. Now they're getting stronger."

"Why didn't you wake me up?"

"I knew I still had plenty of time. The contractions were not so hard and were pretty far apart."

"How far apart are they now?"

"The last one was one minute and fifteen seconds."

"My gosh, that's pretty quick. We'd better get ready and go to the hospital."

"Will you call the doctor? I have his phone number written down next to the phone."

"Sure, you bet."

Scott kind of got a kick out of speeding and running red lights on his way to the hospital. He figured this was only one of a very few legitimate reasons to go through red lights. No reasonable cop would give him a ticket on a mission such as this. In fact, he almost hoped one would stop him just so he could explain why he was hurrying.

Diana started moaning a little from the pain of a particularly strong contraction. What was fun and games to Scott all of a sudden became more purposeful.

Scott went to the emergency room entrance, not wanting to waste any time. He helped Diana out of the car and into a wheelchair that a watchful nurse was already wheeling out to the car by the time he got around to the passenger side.

Scott filled out the admission papers as Diana was wheeled up to the maternity suite. He was trying to hurry extra fast after he heard Diana say she felt the urge to push. Arrangements had been made earlier for him to attend the birth in the delivery room. He knew he had to hurry, though, because he had to put on a green scrub suit, complete with booties that covered his shoes.

He rushed upstairs, taking the steps two at a time. When he burst through the door into the maternity suite a smiling nurse was waiting for him with his gear. He slipped the booties on and, at the nurse's encouragement to hurry, he put the cap on. He ran to the delivery room as he was tying the gown around him. No sooner did he enter the room than he heard the doctor telling Diana "Don't push, not yet. Oh, good. Scott's here."

Scott went to Diana's side and grabbed her hand. "Hi, I'm here."

"Good. I was afraid you weren't going to make it. The baby is about ready to come out. We just made it here in time."

"Everything's going to be…"

"Ooah, ooah. Doctor I've got to push."

"OK, push. That's fine. Everything is going fine. Push. I see its head. Here it comes! You've got a brand new son; a fine-looking baby."

Scott quit his praying and looked up. He couldn't help himself. He counted the fingers and toes even though he knew that was trite. And, yes, it was a boy.

Diana wearily looked up at him and smiled. "We've got a boy."

"Yes, a beautiful baby boy. He looks just like you. He must, he doesn't look like me."

The doctor put the newborn on top of Diana's stomach and helped her hold him. Immediately the touch of the baby made Diana's maternal instincts peak. After a few minutes the doctor asked Scott if he wanted to hold his son.

"My son. He said 'my son'," Scott proclaimed. "This is my son."

Diana watched the blissful expression on her husband's face as he held his son for the first time. She knew everything would be all right as she watched him.

Back in the recovery room hours later, Scott and Diana called both sets of parents.

"We are going to name him Andrew Joel Fontaine. Yes, tell Andy we named the baby after him. He'll like that."

"When can we come there to see everyone?"

"Diana wants you to come right away. She's anxious to have you here."

Scott frequently got down on his knees to thank his Lord for the miracles He had wrought. He prayed for the health of his wife and his new son. He also prayed for strength for Diana in these next several months in which he would be so tied up with soccer. Scott found that his prayer life grew much stronger now that he had a child.

The happy event was therapeutic for Scott. Somehow the hectic schedule of preparing for the tournament was becoming onerous. The coach had granted him a full week off to be with his family. After getting to spend time at home with his new son and wife, he was especially grateful to the coach for the lengthy stay.

In Ashton, five Girl Scouts were talking with one another about normal young teenage things when Andrea stopped them cold.

"The soccer team from Costa Rica will be coming next week; why don't we go see them come in and see if we can get to talk to them and watch their practice and everything?"

"Soccer team? What do you mean?" Amber responded.

"You know, the Costa Rica soccer team is supposed to come and live here and practice here while the World Cup is being played. Don't you know Ashton was picked as the site for their headquarters? They'll be staying at the Carlton Hotel and practicing at the high school and at the soccer complex. The World Cup is a big deal," she said, exasperated at the lack of response. "Teams from all over the world are arriving in the United States to play for the world championship of soccer. It's a big deal that Ashton got chosen by one of the teams. Doesn't anyone know what's going on around here?"

"I heard something about it," Megan said. "My Mom and Dad were talking about all the changes that were happening here in Ashton and that it was due to the soccer team coming."

The other two girls, Molly and Paige, just kept quiet because they didn't know anything about what Andrea and the others were saying. But they knew they would follow Andrea's lead because she was always thinking of and doing neat things.

"Let's go and at least see what they look like. We can decide from there what else we want to do."

"OK, I'm for that," Megan declared.

With Andrea and Megan in, the others also now were all for it.

"When are they coming?" Amber asked.

"Wednesday, one-thirty in the afternoon, the paper said."

"I've got a great idea. Let's make a welcome sign for the team—a banner that we can all hold up. I think they'll like that. Imagine getting off the bus and seeing some people who took the time to make a sign. We'll make it a nice sign."

"I know! I know! They speak Spanish. We'll do it in Spanish so they can understand it," Molly piped up.

"Let's do it in red, white, and blue like the colors of their flag," Andrea said.

"Oh, is that what all those striped flags are for?" Paige asked. "I wondered why all of a sudden these streamers and flags were appearing all over town."

"Those lighted signs, too, Dummy. Anybody notice all those signs that say 'Welcome Costa Rica' and '*Bienvenidos*' and the real giveaway—'Ashton welcomes National Soccer Team of Costa Rica.' This is a big deal for us and them, too," Andrea scolded.

The afternoon passed quickly for the girls. By the time they had finished getting the materials—paper and paint—they had looked up the Spanish wording they wanted and set about getting the banner done. When they were finished they all stepped back and together inspected the result. The ten-foot sheet of butcher's paper, compliments of Amber's daddy, had been transformed into a very colorful, if not professional, welcome banner. They were all very satisfied with how it looked. Linda's art ability showed clearly in the end product. Molly had done the most painting after Linda outlined the letters, but all had worked hard and felt ownership in it.

"We'll let it dry here if that's OK, Megan. Your Mom won't mind, will she? Then next Wednesday we meet here after lunch at twelve-thirty and pick up the banner and go to town. Let's keep the banner rolled up, though, until we see the bus. That way we'll surprise everyone with it."

So they all agreed to keep quiet and not tell anyone about the banner. They all left with an excited, expectant feeling.

"Hey, Carlo, hurry up we're all waiting for you," Antonio shouted.

"He's on the phone," answered Vinnie. "I don't think it will be long."

"OK. First, let me tell you the boss has approved everything we decided on at the last meeting. Specifically, the ladies and bookmaking of any type; he does not want to try fixing any games. He doesn't believe there are enough controls to make that work. The boss is against extortion or kidnapping, also. First, let's go over the plans to do the bookmaking."

Nick stood up. "We can tie in very nicely with the official book in Vegas or here in Atlantic City. I'm impressed with the immensity of this market. The research we've done says that vast amounts of money are bet on these games in many different countries, centering in England, Italy, Germany, and France in Europe; Argentina and Brazil, primarily, in

South America; and in the Far East, Japan and Korea. We're talking big bucks here. The estimated amount gambled in the last World Cup was a startling $14 billion."

"$14 billion!"

"Fourteen big ones!"

"Yes, incredible as that seems, that's the estimate, or so I've been told. Remember there are thirty-three games played, eighteen in the preliminary round and fifteen in the final rounds. What makes it really interesting is that sometimes the best teams lose or tie in the preliminary rounds and it is not a big deal. In other words, if they already have a final round spot sewed up, they may rest their best players and end up losing or tying a game they would otherwise blow away. That sometimes makes the betting get crazy. Every game is bet and odds given. Every game also gets an over-under, like we suspected. Big betting occurs before the tournament even starts, with odds given on every team. What's really great is that the odds vary from country to country, and we can be sure to make money if we tie into the gambling interests in some of these other countries. Let me give you an example: United States vs. England. Naturally the odds given the United States here would be less than the odds given the United States over there in England and, in fact, all over Europe. Don't you see? We could take money in here at 2–1 and lay it off at 5–1 over there. People will bet with their heart when their national team is playing. It's a wonderful opportunity. It's a guaranteed way to make money, big money."

"Good report, Nick. You are in charge of the gaming. You pick whoever you want to help you—other than the people in this room and their number one's. Everyone is to cooperate. Understand? It sounds like this is a real opportunity. I want people placed in the major centers of the world. I want people in Vegas and London. Let's do it right. Carlo, what about your end?"

The dark-haired man with large, bushy eyebrows responded, "OK. First of all, there are nine cities that the games will be played in. Each team will have a town that sort of becomes their home base. At each of these places we will have a strong presence. We will get the word out that we have girls available and maybe even do a little bit of light discouragement for the independents. In most places we can deal with any organized effort, either driving them out or working together with them. I'll put Roscoe in charge of those efforts, if that's OK with everyone. I've learned the United States Soccer Federation will even help us by estimating how many visitors from each country they expect to come to the States. All my sources say to expect a huge influx of tourists. Joe has already done a great job of arranging extras to be mobilized from location to location. Joe, you take it from here."

"Thanks. As Carlo said, this is already starting to get lined up. Boss, I may need some private planes to fly the girls from place to place."

"That can be arranged. I'll speak to the chief about that."

"Thanks. I'm also going to work on getting some girls from Europe and South America. I figure we can be a leg up on anything else if we have some girls that speak the same language as some of our visitors."

"Good, I like that. That's something else the bossman might help with. He's got a few connections across the pond."

"We can get a lot of girls from places in South and Central America, like Columbia and Brazil, for peanuts. We can fly a few jumbos full of girls up here for a month and hardly pay them anything."

"Just make sure the *girls* aren't jumbos."

The boss's joke brought laughter from everyone except Carlo. He didn't think it was so funny.

"All right, it sounds like everything is being planned. I want twice-a-week reports from each of you on how things are going."

"What about the extortion or kidnapping?"

"I don't want to do something dumb. I for one don't relish being behind bars. This other stuff we've talked about is harmless and won't get the feds down on our butts."

"Boss," Vinnie pleaded, "there's a way to tie in a kidnapping with the advantage gained in making book. I think we ought to consider something like that, at least to make a plan. If it doesn't look like the right opportunity presents itself, then we can scrap it. I think there will be enough sightseeing by the players in their days off that security will not be an insurmountable problem. I just don't think we ought to quickly dismiss this idea."

"I'm leery of taking on something like that. Too many things to go wrong. Too much chance to bring the wrong kind of people down on our heads. I'll continue to keep an open mind. Remember, though, my decision is final."

The big day was finally here! After months and months of planning, meetings, and hard work, this was the day the team from Costa Rica would arrive in Ashton. Andrew reflected back on the events that led to the decision to host a team. Not surprisingly, there were many detractors.

It was too much money. There would be no peace and quiet. We won't realize anything from it. A waste of time and money. This is what some people said. However, somewhat unexpectedly, the majority of people in offices and the city government were very supportive. Even more amazing was that the average person on the street was excited about it. Once the decision was made to go for it, the whole town had really rallied behind the effort. The steering committee had continuously received calls of offered help from civic groups, church organizations, and hundreds of citizens. Godfrey and two other town officials had told Andrew they had never seen the town so united in one cause like this. Whether or not they actually hosted a team, to have the town rally together around a cause and unite as one was worth it.

So much had been accomplished with the specter of national and worldwide TV imminent, the businesses fixed up their storefronts, sidewalks got repaired, houses painted, bent light poles replaced, streets repaved, and hotels remodeled. City flower beds never looked better, and there were more flowers planted at homes around town than ever before.

Already their investment had been repaid. There was virtually no unemployment; so much had been done in the last six months that employment had gone up from ninety-two percent employed to ninety-nine percent. Better yet, city tax receipts had climbed steadily so that the town, which ranked monthly between one hundred ten and one hundred twenty of the largest in the state, had improved to where they were now sixty-sixth largest. The businessmen in the town were responsible for much of the grassroots support.

Andrew and Godfrey had surprisingly little trouble in raising the finances for this cause. The city pledged an initial amount of one fourth of the total, the county had matched one half of that, and the state government came in for fifty percent. The remaining amount was raised by a special two percent sales tax levied for six months, to run through the end of the World Cup. Impressively the whole amount was raised in three and one-half months instead of the planned six months. So now the city found itself the recipient of additional unanticipated revenues; in fact, they had already doubled the amount expected, and the tournament had not yet even started.

One favorable development had been the forming of a new group that would work with the city's Chamber of Commerce to help host tourism events and aid new people in town. The group, called LaBelles, consisted of high school girls who volunteered to help stage events the town had organized to help promote tourism. The World Cup and all that surrounded it would present the perfect opportunity to utilize this resource. However, since the group was still fairly new, it would be a baptism by fire for the pretty, youthful ladies. They were chosen for their personalities, scholastic achievement, and beauty. The chamber was pleased at the response. Immediately, it became a status symbol to have been chosen for this group.

Godfrey looked at his watch. It was three-fifteen. The bus bringing the players, coaches, and managers would be here in ten to fifteen minutes. He dug a worn piece of paper out of his pocket. On it were phases written in Spanish. Godfrey, like so many others in town, had recently taken some Spanish classes so that at least he could say "Hello," "Welcome," and a few more things. He knew that, in general, the American people were unwilling to learn other languages, creating an image problem throughout the world. Godfrey wanted at least for the Costa Ricans to know he cared enough to learn some very basic Spanish. He had been able to attend three of the evening Spanish classes that were being offered, although many of the townspeople took advantage of all ten classes. The newspaper had done such a super job informing folks about Costa Rica—where it was, the size and population, about its volcanoes, the agriculture exports—that a sizable portion of the town's population knew more about Costa Rica than any other foreign nation. The Costa Rican delegation would be pleased to hear there were already several groups of people planning sightseeing trips to Costa Rica, including next year's senior class. The local travel agency had even made available two slide shows for the library, which a lot of people had taken advantage of.

The first sight Godfrey caught of two state highway motorcycle patrolmen leading the white FIFA bus into town made a lump come to his throat. Each motorcycle had a little American flag on the left handlebar and a Costa Rican flag on the right handlebar. He looked around. The town and county had purchased over three miles of special streamers in the same colors as the flag of Costa Rica—blue on top, then white, then red, then white again, and blue on the bottom—five horizontal stripes in all, each equal in size. These streamers had been tied to every light pole and every telephone pole in the town as well as avenues leading into town. They had also erected a large sign that said *Bienvenidos Seleccion National de Costa Rica,*" which meant, "Welcome Costa Rican National Team." Then a second sign: "Ashton, New Jersey salutes you," and *"Buena suerte En La Copo del Mundo '94,"* which is "Good Luck in World Cup '94," in a third sign all done with the colors of Costa Rica.

The caravan of FIFA vehicles included the team bus in the lead followed by four vans and two cars, all of which were white, with the '94 World Cup emblem and FIFA on both sides of each vehicle. Bringing up the rear was a state highway patrolmen in a highway patrol car with its blue lights flashing.

Just as the bus pulled to a stop the high school band began playing *America The Beautiful.* Andrew was on board to show the driver the way and had previously planned the route and the precise stopping point. As the team disembarked the crowd of two hundred people clapped and shouted "Hello," "*Hola,*" and "*Bienvenidos.*"

Standing alongside Godfrey was the one family in town from Costa Rica. Godfrey had invited them to help receive the team and officials into Ashton and to make them feel welcome. Mr. and Mrs. Quiros were delighted and feeling very proud to be asked. They had provided so much valuable information and had volunteered much of their time getting ready for this event that it was fitting for them to share in the spotlight.

The team members were all wearing red blazers with white shirts and predominately blue ties. Godfrey had a very favorable first impression of the team. They were good-looking, clean-cut young men. As the entourage got off the bus they were forced to walk between two lines of the LaBelles. Godfrey shook each player's hand and introduced himself as mayor, while the Quiros family followed behind him taking more time with each player. Godfrey went on to greet each member of the Costa Rican encourage as the other vehicles unloaded. After everyone was greeted, Godfrey went to the microphone and gave a two-minute welcome speech, praising the team from Costa Rica, its officials, FIFA, the country of Costa Rica, and the town as well for all it had done to get ready. Godfrey purposely kept his speech short so that the new arrivals would not have to stand around a long time. Mr. Quiros translated as Godfrey spoke so that his words were communicated to the new guests. As soon as they had finished, Andrew escorted Ricardo Servilla to the microphone. Ricardo was introduced as the president of the Costa Rican Soccer Association and the one who made the decision to locate here in Ashton.

The crowd enthusiastically cheered for twenty seconds before it was quiet enough to allow Ricardo to speak. The players looked around with wonder at the enthusiasm shown by the people. Several leaned to their fellow countryman and commented on the crowd.

Ricardo thanked everyone for providing such gracious hospitality and for extending such a warm welcome. He was sure, he said, that they would enjoy their stay here and hoped that the team would do well and reflect good things upon this special town, their temporary home.

The official hostesses—six in all—went to the players and pinned the Ashton Chamber of Commerce emblem on each one. Two of the players kissed the girl on the cheek who pinned them. Both hostesses blushed, and the crowd was amused at their embarrassment.

Andrea, Molly, Amber, and the other Girl Scouts—their group had grown to eight—squealed with delight when three of the Costa Rican players came over to personally greet them and say "*Gracias*" for making the signs they held. One of them, Andrea noted, was "fine" and had a sexy smile. When he gave Amber a quick kiss they all thought they'd faint.

The team was staying at the Carlton Hotel, one of two hotels in town. The two hotels were augmented by five motels, creating a total of three-hundred-sixty-two rooms available for this event. Both hotels and three of the motels were renovated to some extent and looked very nice. One motel was just recently built, so no renovation had been required. The officials and their families were staying at the Hotel Ashton. It was a little larger and a little nicer, but it was nearer to the busy downtown area. The Carlton Hotel was in a less noisy area and would provide a more relaxing atmosphere. All the rooms at the hotels had been booked by Costa Rican fans following the team, except for the ones kept in reserve by the management. The motels were not all booked up; there was a problem that made the Costa Ricans hesitant about staying there. It was learned that in Costa Rica the name *motel* means it is used for a purpose other than family-sanctioned events. It is traditionally used for taking one's girlfriend or mistress for a few hours. Efforts had been to counteract that aspect but had not totally been successful. One of the motels put a banner across its name changing it from "Motel" to "Hotel" very quickly after learning of the situation.

The local press was there in full force for Ashton's red-letter day. Flashbulbs were popping all over as locals and newspaper photographers were making the most of the moment at hand. It was a truly momentous occasion for this small town. Old and young were here in attendance; rich and poor; athlete and non-athlete.

The World Cup opening ceremonies had been touted by many as something not to be missed. Chicago had been chosen for its heavy population base, and to give the Midwest venue a certain exclusivity. The United States Soccer Federation had long ago approached the Wilt

Tinsley Company to inquire of their interest in providing a memorable opening to their showcase event. Happily, the situation suited them and their need for international exposure, and the people of Tinsley threw themselves into the task of planning.

The result was magnificent. The Tinsley characters played a make-believe game of soccer in the center of the field, creating a delightful routine featuring the antics of the characters Sequoia Sam, Robby Rat, the seven gnomes, Beanstalk Jack, and others. The sell-out crowd loved it. Specially trained actors, who were also soccer players, filled some of the roles because highly skilled tricks were required of them. Of course, the main character costumes were worn by those people who normally wear the outfits and who had to undergo extensive training to be able to perform today. Tinsley would not compromise the several key characters for fear of not having a consistent image for the few that formed the flagship of their stable of characters.

The pageantry and colorful figures moving around on the field made for a spectacular display. The twenty-four nations participating in the World Cup were recognized in a colorful way. In the midst of a most stupendous laser-light show, the flags and the names of each of the countries were, one by one, ignited by a laser streak. The colorful fireworks display took fully thirty-six seconds from when the first one was lit until the last one was lit. They burned on for another forty-five seconds before the first couple started going out.

In the darkness of the early night the vestiges of fireworks burned on. Then a very clever thing was arranged. Instead of a time-consuming teardown of the fireworks stands, cables were attached from the fireworks stands to a center ring and then a helicopter hoisted the displays up and away. The removal took less than two minutes and, as the displays disappeared into the air, an explosion of bright, colorful fireworks emanated from the base structure as it was hauled upward. Higher and higher it went, showering light, color, and noise on all those present. Just before it disappeared the letters U-S-A appeared, lit by a timed fuse.

The unexpected finish drew a strong reaction from the assembly below, as they responded enthusiastically to the awesome display unveiled before them. Then the laser-light show resumed as children and adults alike looked on in wide-eyed wonder.

Shortly after the laser show ended, a banner was brought out that read "Fair Play, Please." This was paraded around the track on the perimeter of the field. After they made a complete circuit, they stopped in front of the tunnel to the locker rooms. The two teams appeared and waved to the stands as they were led to the middle of the field. There the introduction of the players and head coaches were made and a ceremonial coin was tossed. The tournament was ready to begin!

CHAPTER 13

The locker room was a happy place. Not only had the Americans shown they belonged, they had beaten the aggressive French team 2–1. Favorable turns of events resulted in several good scoring opportunities. Scott had immediately established himself as a star, scoring both goals. One was on a breakaway produced by his dazzling speed, and the other was a head shot into the corner of the goal on a ball Chase Anderson had unselfishly passed after drawing the keeper to his side. Scott had outjumped the defender to put the ball away.

Kori's eyes shown brightly as he chatted easily with reporters after the game. "Yes, yes, I am pleased with the play of my charges—with almost all aspects of their play," he answered one reporter. "Our defense worked well together, our transitional game was strong, and obviously we can score."

"Do you think the French team underestimated you?"

"Yes, I do, but that's no surprise. We are better right now than we have ever been."

"What about this Scott Fontaine? Did you know he would be this good?"

"Scott had a great game. He's been playing solid ball all along, but one should expect the captain to be a leader. He certainly was today."

"Does this mean your next game with Spain will be that much more difficult? You're not a secret anymore."

"I would guess they had a scout or two in the stands."

Favorable comments appeared in newspapers throughout the world, not just because the United States upset France, but also because of how they had played: with precise passing, a hard-nosed defense, and a good transition game from defense to offense. In no area did they look deficient or outclassed—not even in ball-handling skills. France had been highly regarded itself, but the United States had come a long way since the 1990 World Cup.

When he was interviewed, Scott gave all the credit to Kori, the other players, their talents, their dedication to excellence, and their unselfish play; he claimed only to have been in the right place at the right time when a good pass was made.

Diana was delighted and took great pride in the accomplishment and composure of her man as she watched the taped interview on the TV later that night. She also felt a little invaded as she realized she must now share her husband with the public. Still feeling fat and unappealing after the recent childbirth, she was keenly noting the obvious adulation of the young ladies who clamored for his autograph and attention wherever he went.

For the first time in his life Scott was appearing in closeups on TV as he was interviewed. His light brown hair had a wind-blown look; his slightly curly locks presented an unkempt, disheveled appearance. That just made him all the more appealing to young female members of the television audience. Scott didn't realize at the time how much impact his image would have on the American public. He became very popular in photo sessions and it wasn't long before posters of him began to appear on the souvenir stands.

Although not a starter, Robert had been substituted into the game and had performed well. The coach had wanted to give him some playing time without placing on him all the pressure of a starting role. No unusual opportunities to make any great plays came his way in the twenty minutes he was in the contest; however, he was being evaluated by three keen eyes: two were Kori's and one was the eye of the techno camera.

Mild interest was shown among the public as they listened to the sports news to learn of the upset by this young American contingent in a sport in which they had no business being competitive with any European nation. As Americans opened their newspapers the next day they saw a small note on the front page referring to the World Cup victory, with several good stories appearing in the sports section. Prodded by the USSF, which had lavished extraordinary attention on the members of the U.S. media in order to garner increased exposure, the 250 million American people had

splashed in front of them a myriad of stories about the World Cup, yesterday's victory, and the significance of the win over France, a highly
regarded European team.

Alex De La Paz could feel that same awful sensation starting to complain in his stomach. He knew what it was and what caused it. It was from
a growing realization that he would not be on the main team. Alex had
felt so good when he was informed he had won a position on the national
team of Costa Rica. It truly was an honor to be selected, and the
perquisites and fame that subsequently came to the '90 Cup team could
again be his, if they did well at this World Cup. The '90 Cup team had
reaped bonanzas beyond what they could have hoped for: several got pro
contracts for teams in Europe, many got contracts to endorse products, all
had their salaries as professionals increased, the government allowed special tax considerations, and countless freebies came their way.

What Alex really wanted, though, was to be a part of the winning
effort, the main team. To be a substitute, perhaps not even to play, was to
be on the outside looking in. It was not the same as being a starter. You
were included, yet not totally. You were a part of the team, yet not a key
part. You had to watch the others play and could not help them from the
bench.

The growing realization that he would not be a starter did not make
Alex bitter, just disappointed. He had done his best. He was in the best
shape of his life; he felt like he could run forever. In addition to the team's
workouts, Alex had run ten kilometers three times a week and once a
week did twenty kilometers. These runs were at a fast pace. Alex could
run ten kilometers in just under thirty minutes, but normally made the
run in thirty-one. Because he was a fullback he knew the importance of
having speed and endurance at the end of a game. Often the last ten minutes were crucial to the final outcome. That time period could many times
be controlled by those least tired. Sometimes a one-step edge was all that
was needed to break free for a shot. As a defender he wasn't going to let
that happen to him. Just as important was the ability to shrug off physical
contact. Players grabbed, held, obstructed, and pushed opposing players
to gain an advantage—anything and everything the other team could do
to hinder an opponent and help get a shot off. Toward the end of a game
it was increasingly hard to break that contact. Those in shape could do so
more easily.

Alex had not been told yet that he had not made the starting team. It was more of a feeling he had. He would not let himself get down about it, however. He knew that nearly every game in the World Cup had at least one or two substitutes play. After the first couple of games, frequently one or more players became ineligible because of red or yellow cards they had received. In the final against West Germany, Argentina had five players ruled ineligible because they had accumulated two yellow cards. Often a substitute made a very valuable contribution. He thought back to the Italian World Cup and realized Hernan Medford had made an impact for Costa Rica and impressed several pro teams enough that he was offered a contract. Also, Salvatore Schillaci had come in as a substitute and not only earned himself a starting role by his play, but had become the idol of all of Italy and the whole World Cup with his stellar play and many scores. Medford set up the tying goal and scored the winning goal. No one could stop him. The papers called him Costa Rica's secret lethal weapon. Nobody had heard of him before. Yet, in the last fifteen minutes in the game against Sweden, five times he either broke past the last defender or was fouled as he was about to go past. The Swedish team changed defenders on him three times, trying to find someone who could control him. One of the Swedish players stated on TV that they had no one who could stop him. He had made all the difference in the game and enabled Costa Rica to come from behind and beat Sweden.

Costa Rica had become the darling of the press, the surprise team of the tournament, and had garnered more than its fair share of TV and press coverage. The third game victory against Sweden was pivotal. It established Costa Rica in the Italian tournament. The first game upset against Scotland was regarded as something of a fluke. Little and lightly regarded Costa Rica had come into its first World Cup as one of the three longest shots to win it all. They were supposed to get whipped soundly. They didn't. Instead they beat a not-so-good Scottish team and then beat a fairly good Swedish team by coming from behind to score two goals in the last fifteen minutes, the only team to come from behind and win in the first phase. All of this was made possible primarily because of the impact of one player—a substitute. So enamored was the sports press that they had named three of Costa Rica's players to the best twenty-two players in the tournament through the first phase: Flores as sweeper, Conejo as goalkeeper, and—most amazingly—Medford as striker, even though he had played less than twenty minutes in one of the matches.

"Incredible," Alex thought, "that one player, a substitute, could have that much impact." But it was what kept his spirits up and kept him feeling that he had to make the most of any opportunity that came his way. Alex felt sure that he would at least be one of the five players chosen as eligible to be a substitute for each game. He was sure that sooner or later he would get the opportunity for which he had worked so hard.

The subs came out first and walked over to the protected benches. Alex had been told by the coach that he should prepare himself, that he might get in the game today. The other four potential substitutes were Cujo—a goalkeeper, two midfielders, and a forward. Alex was the only fullback. He had stretched his limbs and loosened up, but had not yet warmed up. The subs did not warm up before the game. They generally did at half-time. Unless an injury brought a player out, it was unusual to change a player in the first half.

Alex looked up at the stands. One neat thing about the World Cup was all the flags waving in the stands. Greece, Costa Rica's opponent today, had sky blue and white in their flag. Costa Rica's, of course, was red, white, and blue. From what he'd heard, fewer than 500 fans from Costa Rica had gone to the Italian World Cup. Comparatively, today's crowd was a refreshing sight. He could see North Americans also had some flags and were supporting his team. Other nations' flags were waved vigorously, adding to the colorful panorama. He saw some from the United States, some from Argentina, Brazil, and Germany, and even the new Russian flag. There were also some he couldn't recognize.

The stadium held 73,000 and only a few of the seats were empty. Maybe those would fill up soon. This was their first game and Alex did not know what to expect. Ronald Gonzales, their star midfielder, had told him some of what it had been like in Italy. None of Costa Rica's games had been filled to capacity, and some were played in a stadium that held only 45,000.

Alex guessed that fans from the United States would pull for them because Costa Rica is in the Americas and because there are such close relations between the two countries. Then, too, they were both in the Concacaf region.

This was the first game, the real thing. The feeling was different from all previous matches—much different, Alex decided. They had practiced in the stadium twice before—once during the day and once at night under lights. The atmosphere today was charged by the noise of over 70,000 spectators. Goose bumps formed on his arms, and the hair on the back of his neck prickled. The realization set in: he was playing for his country, not just for his own team. This was for everything back home.

Alex reached the bench and took a seat next to Jaime Turin, a midfielder from Puntarenas. Jaime was having a hard time adjusting to the bench. He had never been on the bench before. Jaime had withdrawn into himself and was not engaging into the usual banter that took place along the sidelines.

"Jaime, this is really something, isn't it?" Alex was trying to get Jaime back to a nearly normal state. Jaime would be of no help to the team unless he came out of his mood. "Jaime, can you hear me?"

"Yeah. What is it?"

"You look like you are in some kind of deep trance. Come back to earth."

"Aw, I was just wishing I could be starting. The whole feeling, this whole experience would be different. Right now I can't really feel a part of it. Maybe if I get a chance to play it will be different."

"Same here. It must even be worse for those not even on the substitute list. If we feel the way we do, it's got to be even worse for them."

Alex looked up when he heard the noise of the crowd announcing the appearance of the starting teams. The four officials—two linesmen, the referee, and the extra official who oversaw substitutions—preceded the ball boys, who were carrying the "fair play" sign out of the tunnel. Next came the captains of each team, followed by the remaining players, coaches and the trainer. The players and officials lined up on the far sideline, waiting for the national anthems to be played. As the Costa Rica national anthem began, the players on the bench stood up and put their right hands over their hearts. How pretty the music is, Alex thought. Again goose bumps rose on his flesh as he thought about representing his country on global TV.

Alex had a lot of national pride. He was a loyal person, too. He would not criticize his coach the way Jaime sometimes did. That didn't mean he agreed with everything, but he wouldn't talk negatively about the coach or the team to any outsider.

The national anthems ended and the trainers were on their way over to the benches. The main players readied themselves, kicking to each other, stretching, and making short runs to warm up their muscles.

The whistle blew to call in the extra balls and get the teams ready. One minute before starting time now. Alex was nervous just watching. He knew half the team had played World Cup in Italy. They would be called upon to provide a stabilizing influence on the new players. All had extensive international experience, however, and should be prepared. At least he hoped so.

The game started. The first few minutes were a feeling-out process.

Both teams controlled the ball without taking large chances. Each team probed almost to the other penalty box, only to lose the ball. So far it was looking even. One of the things we have to look for, recalled Alex, is the center forward for Greece. He's big and tall. Like Skuhravy for Czechoslovakia in the Italian Cup, he's a threat every time they cross the ball over the middle, he thought.

No team had a decided advantage throughout the first half. Both teams squandered opportunities by not being daring enough or misplacing passes. Costa Rica typically had played a defensive ball game. This was the same strategy they had used successfully in Italy . In all their games there the team had played a very defensive first half.

At half-time, Alex and Jaime warmed up together. The starters were in the locker room with the coach, getting a pretty lively talk, he imagined. The coach would tell them what was not being done right. Defense was what he concentrated on, and Alex was sure he would go over the things that made him uncomfortable or led to dangerous situations that had to be corrected. He also, however, was good at uncovering vulnerable areas in the other team's defense. The coach would explain ways to exploit that.

All five substitutes then got in a circle and passed the ball in the air to one another, using all parts of their bodies except the hands. Then they practiced a keep-away drill in which the four outside would keep the ball from one in the center. This was a good way to get ready for the game action: quick moves, reacting to pressure, getting the heartbeat up.

Soon the teams came back out again. Alex went over to Roger Flores, the captain, to get an indication of how things went. Roger was optimistic. He answered Alex's query, "I think we've got them. They haven't figured us out, but we have them. Watch us create some scoring opportunities. They are no better than we are. In fact, *we* are better."

Alex felt better as he trotted over to the bench. He told Jaime what Roger had told him.

"Yeah? Sounds good," was Jaime's reply.

The second half began with Greece pushing hard. They were trying things they hadn't in the first half. Their midfielders were making forward runs without the ball, looking for the pass. The first three times the pass had been intercepted. The fourth time their center halfback took the pass and got a shot off, but their world-class goalie, Conejo, made a good stop. Alex looked over at the coach to see how he was reacting but was surprised to see him impassively sitting there.

I couldn't be so calm, Alex thought. If that's what it takes to be a good coach, I'll never be one. I can't stay still; I can't keep quiet, he mused. In fact, Alex had been shouting encouragement to his teammates as he sprang up and down from the bench.

Then all of a sudden Greece got caught too far downfield, and Costa Rica got a three-on-three fast break going. Juan Cayasso took a shot that just missed wide to the left. It was Costa Rica's best chance at scoring in the game so far. The chance had been made by a series of three quick passes: Cayasso to Gonzalez to Rojas to Gonzales, then a good cross to Cayasso, who took the shot in the air.

Alex could see that this play had set the Greek team back on its heels a little. It also excited the crowd. Much louder now, the crowd was cheering its approval for a more open, more lively game. The U.S. audience likes offense, he had heard. Some forcing tactics by Ronald Gonzales got the ball within the penalty area; with a deft maneuver he juked past a defender and made a good pass to Cayasso, who took another shot. The keeper, on a diving save, deflected wide past the goal. Corner kick.

Here comes the kick—a little long, but a good one, Alex told himself. Goal! Paolo De Palmer knocked a beautiful one past the goalie on a spectacular bicycle kick as the pass from the corner had been perfect. Goal! What a tremendous shot that was! Alex found himself jumping up and down in front of the bench. The players were all jumping on Paolo. The change in tension was measurable. Costa Rica 1, Greece 0; eighteen minutes into the second half. Costa Rica could now breathe a little easier.

Indeed, as the action began again, Greece began pressing furiously. They weren't yet panicking but it was clear they were now in a position they had not expected. The Europeans had been favored and their attitude of confidence had been badly shaken by Costa Rica's goal. While one loss was not fatal, losing to the lowest ranked team hurt one's chances in future matches. Costa Rica, in turn, more or less adopted their first-half strategy of playing a strong defense.

The first indication of this strategy Alex saw or heard was Jaime jumping up and going over to the coach. Evidently the coach had called his name, because he went to warmup on the sidelines. In another minute Alex heard the coach call his name. He too was to warmup. The blood started coursing through his veins in a vastly different way. He could feel his heart pulsing. Not just beating, but *pounding*—reacting to the new demand conveyed by his brain. This is it, he thought. This is my chance. I'm going to make the most of it. I wonder who's coming out?

In two more minutes the coach submitted a substitution request to the alternate FIFA official responsible for substitutions. Jaime got called over and told to take his warm-up off and go in the next time play was stopped.

Jaime replaced the left midfielder, bringing fresh legs onto the playing surface. The coach now converted the team into one goalkeeper plus four fullbacks and three defensive-minded midfielders. That left only two forwards.

Greece continued to press. Alex could see their frustration mounting. Their players lacked the individual acumen to dribble through the fence put up against them. Their team play was not so effective when everyone came back on defense. Too many legs.

Twenty minutes to go. We've got to hold on, Alex thought. Look at all the pressure they are putting on us.

Just then he heard Roger shout to three of the players to make a push up the right side at next opportunity—even a fast break, if possible. Then he told the right fullback, Alberto, to watch for a good chance.

A loping pass to the middle gave Greece a corner kick when Roger headed the ball over the end line. Alex could see Roger was starting to tire a little. So was the left fullback, Constantin. Too much was being asked of them.

The corner kick for Greece came in an arc that brought the ball curving toward the goal as it got to the center. Alex reflexively jumped a little as the ball came dangerously close. It went over Constantin's head to where a Greek forward was crashing in to head the ball in the goal. Jaime got there first and headed the ball away and to the right. Ronald Gonzales took off like a shot when he realized the ball had gotten beyond all but two defensemen for Greece. He just beat the defenseman to the ball by reaching out with his right foot and toeing the ball further out to where Hernan Medford was running. Medford took off, galloping up the right sideline. Cayasso dashed up the middle slightly behind and with an opponent's shadow alongside. Ronald jumped over and pursued the twin thrust. The lone defenseman was shouting to the others as he moved toward Medford to slow him down or take the ball away.

Medford was going against the captain of the Greek team, one who had superlative defensive techniques. Hernan's got to use the others, Alex thought. C'mon guys convert, convert. Alex heard Ronald holler, "Three to two," meaning Costa Rica had the advantage.

The crowd noise escalated quickly. Everyone could see the dangerous situation for Greece and the opportunity for Costa Rica.

When Medford reached the point even with the penalty box he executed a nice step-over fake, faked a stop, then one quick dribble further forward against the off-balance defender to loft a crossing pass toward Paolo, who was streaking toward the goal.

The goalie took two steps out before he realized he wouldn't get to the ball. The ball was crossed slightly behind De Palmer, making a head shot impossible.

Paolo stopped, jumped, and instead of trying a head shot, hit a pass with his head down to Gonzales, who was trailing to the right. Ronald took the pass in the air with his left foot and smashed it into the right side of the goal.

"Goal! Goal!" Alex screamed as he jumped up and down, still halfway loosening up.

The roar of the crowd was deafening. So well executed was that play that the crowd was cheering not just the score, but also the skill with which it had been executed. Three players had made three good moves in a combination that was just marvelous. The crowd roar continued for a full twenty-five seconds before any abatement, then even longer at a lower level.

So absorbed was Alex in the events that had just transpired that he didn't see or hear his coach signaling him to get ready to go in. Another sub had to come and grab him to tell him he was going in.

The FIFA official was holding up the number 12—Constantin's number. The coach told Alex to take Constantin's place. "Watch number eighteen for Greece, he's the most dangerous. He's their playmaker. You guard him man to man."

Alex now knew the coach's strategy. He was using a fresh sub, one whose defensive strength lay in quick reactions. Alex was good at man-to-man coverage, and even though he preferred zone defense he knew that in this game his role was defensive man-to-man coverage. As Constantin came off Alex gave him a high-five slap and told him he had played great.

Alex's adrenaline surged as he came into the game. He knew he was fresh and the others were not. He was determined to carry the burden assigned to him. The coach had called on him with confidence, and Alex resolved to play to that level.

Roger asked what his position was as Alex ran into the game. Alex had almost forgotten—every sub is required to report to Roger any and all instructions from the coach. It is the one legitimate time a coach can provide instruction or direction to the team, other than at half-time.

"I've got Constantin's spot. I'm to cover number eighteen man-to-man. 'Keep up the good work and try to utilize Alberto a little more on their striker; keep an eye out for the counter-attack; especially to the right side,' that's what the coach said. I think you guys are doing great. I feel terrific." Alex added the last part and expected Roger to smile. He didn't. He just nodded his head and went to tell the others what instructions were sent in. Alex realized he could not feel, could not comprehend on the sideline the level of intensity felt by the players on the field. In an instant that realization struck him and he adjusted himself away from selfish thoughts and on to those felt by his teammates.

The frustration continued for Greece and they were unable to penetrate the defensive alignment thrown at them by Costa Rica. When the game ended Alex was able to jump around and hug the other guys because he had been part of it. He looked over at the substitutes and the ones who were on the squad but not listed as a sub today, and he saw happiness—at least outwardly. But for all the jumping around and happy faces and the shaking of hands he knew it was not the same for them as it was for those on the field of honor. That could be me except for the whim of the coach, he thought wonderingly.

Alex reflected back on his performance in the game and was satisfied for the events as they transpired. He had made no major errors and had hustled the whole while he was in the match. His coverage of number eighteen had been excellent. The man never touched the ball except twice, and then he did nothing with it. He even felt good that he bruised his thigh slightly when number eighteen had kneed him. It was his "red badge of courage" of sorts. Alex, having tasted the action, knew it might be even harder the next time to watch from the sidelines if he didn't get in.

The coach was sufficiently pleased with Alex's performance that he decided to start him in the next game against Uruguay. He played so well against the South Americans that he distinguished himself as a top defender, and a mainstay of the tough Costa Rica defense.

Mrs. De La Paz couldn't believe her ears. Here before her, all smiling, was a delegation of town folks who were holding out in front of them three airplane tickets to the United States for her to see.

"Mario, Pepito, come here, quick," she called.

"Good afternoon, Mr. and Mrs. De La Paz. We are very happy and privileged to inform you that it is our pleasure to give you the opportunity to go to the United States and to see the World Cup games. We appreciate your family and would like to do this for you. Alex is on the team and contributing to our favorable fortunes. We want you to be there to see him play, and to see them win. Please, you go for us; we can't all go. We want to do this for you, for Alex, and for us."

"We have a sign for you to take," another said. "Take this and display it at the stadium for us to see on TV. It says 'Salute to our National Team—from Puerto Viejo.'"

"Alex can get you match tickets; they give each player some tickets for each game. You'll have to figure out where to stay, though."

Mr. De La Paz could only stand there, tears streaming down his face. All these people in front of him, many had been life-long friends, and now they wanted him to represent them, as though he were doing them a favor. He looked over at Pepito standing at the edge of the porch. Joy sparkled in his eyes and his countenance was radiant. He was trying to be calm, although Mr. De La Paz knew better. He then looked at his wife, who was dabbing her eyes with her tattered handkerchief. She nodded her head slightly. His mind made up, he responded, "Thank you. We accept your kind offer, one we know entailed great sacrifice." He struggled to get out a second "Thank you." After a moment, he said, "This gesture you have made is one of great sacrifice and of great friendship. There is noth-ing…no way I can ever repay you."

"We don't want to be repaid, Mr. and Mrs. De La Paz. This is some-thing we want to do for you; a present from us. Allow us this pleasure, for you and your family have given to us in so many ways. Furthermore, Alex represents us on that team. Part of all of us is out there facing the Englands, the Brazils, and the Germanys of this world. No, Mr. and Mrs. De La Paz, this is something we want to do for you."

"Your generosity is overwhelming," Mr. De La Paz responded. "We appreciate your thoughtfulness as well as the money you have given in sacrifice to do this for us."

"Sir, it is strange that the greater the sacrifice we feel for this, the more pleasure we have derived from this same thing. You go, you be there in our place. Know that while you are there we will be here watching and lis-tening."

"God bless you all. Bless you for giving us this opportunity."

The next night the town of Ashton had a banquet in the team's honor. They made a really big to-do about it. Included among the guests was Paul Ott, an entertainer from Mississippi. He sang several songs on a patriotic theme, including one particularly emotional one saluting our men at arms in past wars, called *The Right Arm of America*. As he explained, "The United States has a lot to be proud of. Democracy is a manifestation of freedom. Costa Rica is a good neighbor to the south, one who has been the standard-bearer for Central America; a country who has shown the world that democracy can work, even when surrounded by communism and evil dictators. It was for *everyone's* freedom, not just the people of the United States, that we fought our battles. Not just freedom but the right to be free."

It went like this:

MANY TIMES I HAVE STOOD IN DEFENSE OF THIS
   GREAT LAND
WHENEVER AGGRESSORS RISE, YOU'LL FIND ME
   CLOSE AT HAND
I'VE BEEN CALLED AROUND THE WORLD THAT
   ALL MEN MIGHT BE FREE
I MARCH BEHIND OLD GLORY, I FIGHT FOR LIBER-
   TY

AND I WAS THERE WITH WASHINGTON IN VALLEY
   FORGE'S BLOODY SNOW
RAGGED, BUT DETERMINED MEN, WE OVERCAME
   THE FOE
I WAS CALLED THE VOLUNTEER, THIS TIME IN
   NEW ORLEANS
WE DENIED THE CROWN, WE HAD NO NEED FOR
   EARTHLY KINGS

WHEN TRAVIS CALLED, I ANSWERED, THE ALAMO
   WAS LOST
BUT I RETURNED WITH HOUSTON AND WE
   SHOWED THEM WHO WAS BOSS
WHEN BROTHERS FROM THE NORTH AND SOUTH
   BEGAN THEIR BITTER FRAY
I COULD NOT CHOOSE A SIDE, SO I WAS BLUE AND
   I WAS GRAY

THEN AGAIN WHEN THE CHALLENGE CAME, A
   CHALLENGE DEEPLY FELT
AND I WENT DOWN TO SAN JUAN HILL WITH
   TEDDY ROOSEVELT

THEN IN NINETEEN HUNDRED AND SEVENTEEN I
    WENT OVER THERE
TO FACE THE KAISER'S ARMIES, AND I WHIPPED
    'EM FAIR AND SQUARE

I WENT AGAIN IN FORTY TWO BEFORE ALL
    EUROPE FELL
TO HITLER'S RAGE AND TYRANNY IN A WAR THEY
    CALLED HELL
AND I WAS THERE IN THE PHILIPPINES BY THE
    SIDE OF GENERAL MAC
WHEN THE RISING SUN FLEW O'ER OUR LAND, I
    FOUGHT AND WON IT BACK

I HAVE BEEN ON PORK CHOP HILL AND IN THE
    JUNGLES OF VIETNAM
WHEREVER I AM NEEDED, THAT IS WHERE I AM
THEN IN JUST FORTY THREE DAYS, I CALMED THE
    DESERT STORM
I FOLLOWED THE BATTLE PLAN OF GENERAL
    SCHWARZKOPF TO THE KUWAITIS' OPEN
    ARMS

I AM THE ARMY, AIR FORCE, NAVY AND MARINES,
    AMERICA'S FINEST DAUGHTERS AND SONS
I'M SOMETIMES CALLED THE NATIONAL GUARD,
    I'M HOW THE PEACE WAS WON
GREEN BERETS, THE 24TH, TOP GUN, THE SEALS,
    PARATROOPERS AND THE FLYING TIGERS
    TOO
MANY ARE THE UNIFORMS I'VE WORN, AND
    THESE ARE JUST A FEW

ON THE BATTLEFIELD AND AT HOME, I'M YOUR
    SECURITY
TOOLS OF PEACE FROM FREEDOM'S FORGE, I'M
    WHAT KEEPS YOU FREE
NOW, THERE ARE THOSE WHO SAY I'M EVIL, THEY
    CONDEMN ME AND THEY DAMN
BUT THEY ARE FREE TO SAY THE THINGS THEY

SAY BECAUSE OF WHO I AM

ACROSS THIS HALLOWED LAND OF FREEDOM
WHERE OLD GLORY FLIES SO FREE
I AM THE BRAVE MEN AND WOMEN OF AMERICA'S
ARMED FORCES...IN PURSUIT OF LIBERTY

What he was saying and what he sang about struck a chord deep within the audience. The fires of patriotism burned more brightly after the war in the Persian Gulf. There was a relationship between countries of the Americas, especially democracies, that made them brothers against oppression and the villains of the world.

Señor Servilla got up to speak. "It is with the deepest feelings of appreciation that the people of Costa Rica thank the United States of America for the many things you have done on our behalf. As you know, we have no military in our country and no ability to participate in wartime activities. We have chosen a different path to lead our war against oppression—through peaceful efforts.

"This was recently evidenced in the awarding of the Nobel Peace Prize to our former president, Oscar Arias. That your country's leaders took the initiative and made a very tough and maybe not such a popular decision to address the problem in the Middle East has made this world a better place in which to live. That is typical of your country. It is a decision that has been made for the betterment of mankind a number of times by your leaders. Costa Rica depends on you, as do a great number of other countries that are unable to defend themselves. The special relationship we feel for the United States is unparalleled. So, too, however, did we take a leadership role in establishing peace in Central America. We chose dialogue, our only weapon. Fortunately the outcome was successful. I think we are good for each other.

"Just like this town and how we have been treated by so many fine people. This is one more example of the good relationship that we hope to foster through our participation in this World Cup. We are but a tiny, almost insignificant country in terms of population and land mass, but we hope to make our presence felt beyond our physical characteristics. I know I speak not only for the players and the coaches, but also for all the people of Costa Rica. Thank you so much for all that you've done for us, and may this be a truly happy union of two peoples."

Antonio grew concerned over the attitude he saw developing in Vinnie, one of his more ambitious underlings. He knew, or rather he sensed, that Vinnie was planning an independent action. Probably a kidnapping and ransom, unless he missed his guess. He and Number One had already decided that some activity like that was just too risky. Vinnie had indeed come to him and presented his idea. It was not something that was in keeping with their long-term plan. There had been too much heat on the various families of the underworld; to provide cause for further investigation or tightening of enforcement was to invite trouble, big trouble. Vinnie's plan could possibly yield some significant fiscal gain, but it was just not worth the risk. Vinnie had taken the rejection hard. In a way he was a throwback to the old gangster days of Prohibition. He liked action. He liked to use muscle and guns and terror to show how much power he wielded. Vinnie was always on the outer edge. That's why he was useful as an enforcer for the organization. Antonio decided Vinnie was no longer going to be a part of any strategy sessions. From now on he would report to Carlo.

Vinnie took the news hard on both accounts. One, that his plan had been rejected and that he had been warned not to proceed any further; and two, that he had been demoted and was no longer a part of the council. Now he had to go through Carlo for everything. His pay and responsibilities were not affected, yet in the eyes of everyone he knew he had been taken down a notch. It wasn't worded quite that way when it was announced. It had been said that Carlo was being promoted. The real effect, however, had been to demote him. Vinnie knew it, and so did everyone else.

Something inside of Vinnie began a long, slow burn.

Alex made arrangements for someone to pick up his parents at the airport. He was delighted to get the phone call from the soccer federation officials that his family was coming. Apparently someone at the headquarters took the phone call from the Costa Rican Soccer Federation, giving the flight details. Alex had no idea how his parents could afford the trip up here. Maybe they had some money tucked away somewhere he didn't know about. He wondered what they might have sold to raise the cash. No, he decided they had some money somewhere. Certainly he would ask about that when they came here.

Actually Godfrey heard about how the De La Paz family came to be traveling to the United States before Alex did. People with the soccer federation let it be known to the host organization. Godfrey made a few phone calls on his own prior to the arrival of the family at Newark.

Much to the surprise of Alex and his family, a reporter and a photographer as well as several people he recognized from the Ashton World Cup committee were there at the airport to greet them, and really make a fuss over them. Pepito was treated like a king.

Upon their arrival at the Ashton headquarters for the Costa Rican team, the family saw that a small crowd of twenty-five or thirty people were there to warmly welcome them. Two of the hostesses and eight of the LaBelles greeted them. All of the De La Paz family were still puzzled until it was explained to them that people had heard how the family had been sponsored by their village and how so many people had given a little bit in order for them to come. "To us here in the United States, we just think that is a great human interest story," Godfrey told them. Our whole town would like to know about you and your village and the details of how you happened to come here. It would please us to be a part of the good neighbor policy initiated there by your hometown friends. Please allow us the privilege of continuing your sponsorship here in Ashton."

When this was translated to the De La Paz family, they were overcome with emotion. That these people would be so nice to them, people they had never even met, seemed too good to be true.

Godfrey continued, "Your country's team has done a lot for Ashton also. This is but a small token of how we feel about everyone from your country who we've been associated with. In no small sense Costa Rica has become *our* team, too. Your son has contributed to the success of the team, and so we are indebted to him for that."

When that was translated, Alex felt ten feet tall. He could feel the hero-worshipping eyes of his younger brother looking at him. When he looked into the faces of his parents, he could see the happiness in their misty eyes.

Later, when the family was able to talk among themselves, Alex asked a question that had been very much on his mind. "How is Maria Elena? I miss her."

"Oh son, I'm sorry. I brought a letter from her to you. Here it is in my purse. She said to tell you how proud she is of you. She indicated many people have spoken to her about your spectacular play here."

"Everybody says that, Big B. You're a hero back home."

"Thanks, Little B. It's so good to have you here with me."

The next day the *Ashton Herald-Tribune* carried the story of the family's arrival and how the people in the village scraped together the funds to send them to represent their town at the World Cup. The story even carried the details of the delegation coming to their house. "It's just a little three-room house. It's not so large as these houses we see here in Ashton," Mr. De La Paz explained. "We are a poor people compared to you here in the United States. Yet we have plenty to eat and a robust zest for life. It is a good life there in Costa Rica."

The reporter was intrigued by what Mr. De La Paz did for a living on the pineapple plantation. However, it was almost by accident he delved into the close relationship between the two brothers. The more questions he asked, the more interested he became in their family history. So it was that the paper carried almost a full-page story of the coming of this family and a feature on both Alex and Pepito as well as Mr. De La Paz himself. After the paper came out, many people wanted to meet this special family who had traveled all this way. Some even sent gifts to their hotel room. There were flowers and gift packages from several of the stores in town.

The reporter summed it all up nicely when he stated, "We too are a small town and can relate closely with what happened down in Costa Rica to a family that is very popular and for a local boy who brings fame and honor to his family, neighbors, and town."

Some major surprises surfaced during the first phase of the tournament. Of course, the good results for the United States were much better than almost everyone expected. To finish second with the strength of its bracket was no small accomplishment.

All of the favorites in each group qualified; all but the U.S. finished first in their own groups. Costa Rica flashed hot and cold, tying two games and winning one. They allowed a tie in their contest against Uruguay after dominating most of the way. Against Belgium, the group favorite, they showed brilliantly, looking every bit as good as the European team. That the game ended in a tie was deemed fitting by those sports scribes who attended the action. Words of praise emanated from the many articles that followed. Paolo De Palmer on offense and Alex De La Paz on defense, particularly, were singled out for their stellar performances that day.

Unified Germany dominated. No one in Germany's group even got close, either in the action on the field or in the final tally. They dominated at both ends of the field, holding one team to one shot and another to only four attempts on goal. On offense they rolled up impressive results, scoring six, five, and three goals, respectively. In short, they were awesome.

Italy also had a good first round, winning all three games and being the only team other than Germany to do that. They showed particularly well on defense, having shut out every opponent—the only team to do so. People were already talking about the possibility of an Italian-Germany final. As the top two seeds of the tournament, they were placed in opposite brackets in the championship rounds.

The Commonwealth of Independent States also had a good first round. They had proved solid in all phases of the game and had revealed a very dangerous offense, led by Charko Popov, who demonstrated uncanny abilities inside the box to outjump the opposition and direct effective head shots into the goal. So productive was he that he was tied for first in individual scoring during the first phase.

The rest of the teams performed more or less as expected. Cameroon once again had demonstrated a very potent offense. They were capable of scoring on anyone, using a surgical, penetrating attack that no one had been able to stop. Their trouble was an inability to recover and defend. Cameroon's games were judged to be some of the most entertaining. The American audience certainly appreciated them as their games were all high scoring; not one had fewer than five goals. After the first game they played to nothing less than a sell-out stadium and huge TV audiences.

Overall scoring was up significantly from the low averages in the Italian and the Mexican World Cups. As if to accommodate the fickle U.S. audiences, the games averaged one and one-tenth goals more than in the 1990 Italian Cup.

The televising of the games was superior to any the United States had done on previous occasions. Commercials were overprinted on the bottom of the screen or shown as a split screen, while the soccer action continued to be televised live. Of course, time out for injury and immediately after a score allowed the network to show commercials regularly without infringing on the action. Things had improved so much that not a single goal in a televised game was missed.

In the United States the announcing team of Kyle Rote Jr. and Jimmy Greenawalt had done a respectable job. They did all of the U.S. games as well as two others. Those broadcasts were received throughout North America, including Mexico. Highlights, announced by the pair, had made many of the news shows around the globe. In contrast with earlier occasions, getting no negative feedback was considered to be a positive sign by Kyle, Jimmy, and the network.

———⚽———

With a few days off between the last game of the first phase and the round of sixteen, Coach Gaborakov wanted to make good use of the time available to work on some weaknesses. As a matter of fact, he scheduled two practices the day after the third game in the first phase. He wanted to work very hard the first day, a normal amount the second day, and then to have a fun practice the third and last day off between games.

Kori was very pleased at the way the tournament draw had worked out. Getting Russia, or the CIS as it was known, was not a bad draw. Having Germany in the other half was also very favorable. The path to the finals he figured would be the CIS first, Argentina second, Italy in the semifinals, then Germany. He felt his fledgling stars could more than stay with the CIS and Argentina. Beating Italy was another matter, however. The Italians were definitely superior, but soccer was a funny game; not always does the best team win. First, though, they had to beat the CIS team. He knew his U.S. team would be the underdog in every match, but that was the way he preferred it. The practices consisted of preparing for the CIS and in correcting the weaknesses he personally saw and those which the techno program identified.

One thing Kori was happy about was that the United States outplayed every team in the last fifteen minutes of each game, indicating their conditioning was superior to that of the others. That would be particularly important if any of these games end up tied and have to go into overtime, he reflected. Thank God for their attitude and willingness to sacrifice all else to prepare for these games. All the hard work they had endured brought them closer as a unit. They shared the pain and misery, Kori thought as he shook his head in wonder. The technical advances that aided them were vital to their superior conditioning. The Strength Shoe, the parachutes, the techno analysis, the body analyses to determine specific diets—all these aided the young Americans. Who would have thought these things would have yielded so much benefit?

All the periodicals were espousing the speed and athletic ability of the U.S. squad. Kori was sure there was not a team in better condition than his, and none faster. I love the ingenuity and resourcefulness of the Americans. If I can just keep the injuries away…, he mused.

He went on with his thinking and planning. One thing the players needed to improve upon was recognizing when and how to take a fall when tripped or fouled. If there was one thing I wish our players were better at, that's it. They don't go down when struck. Other teams and players do it as a matter of course to draw the whistle. Especially they needed to do that when they were in the penalty box. Americans probably did less acting than any other nation. It's part of the game, though. You need sometimes to draw the fouls. I'll have to give some more demonstrations and have them practice those.

CHAPTER 14

The big board at Cleopatra's Palace in Las Vegas, despite the unexpected success of the United States team, was not very kind in analyzing the United States' chances against the Commonwealth of Independent States. The odds were set at 3–2 and even though the CIS was no longer a world power, the United States team's chances were lightly regarded. Their public goal achieved, reality would soon set in, or so the thinking by the odds makers went. The CIS team showed consistent evidence of the level of commitment and resources poured into its Russian national program years before. And while the betting was extremely heavy in Las Vegas on the United States to win, Cleopatra's was laying off money as fast as it could. The betting elsewhere in the world was even heavier against the Americans despite odds of as much as 4–1 in favor of the Russians. Early efforts to plan for this facilitated the bookmakers' abilities to handle the volume of transactions. Direct conversation was not necessary for each separate bet. Elevating levels of "credit" to lay off were being arranged with phone calls. The contacts were located in England, Germany, Argentina, Monaco, Panama, Italy, and Korea. So much money was being wagered that records were being broken that had been set during recent Super Bowls.

Privately, the United States was pleased with drawing the CIS in the first round of the second phase. The CIS was considered one of the weaker teams to have advanced. In fact, only the United States and Hungary were more lightly regarded. Italy, Germany, and Brazil were the heavy favorites. Not always do the best teams win their group in phase one, because sometimes the teams don't always play to win. For a variety of reasons they don't always show their best. Coaches, at times, play substitutes to evaluate personnel or to hide strategies. They may rest their star players, or not want to show their strengths before critical matches. The idea is to reach the second phase wherein the tournament becomes single elimination. The first phase can be an evaluation period. To their credit, some teams, like Germany, had used the early matches to ring up impressive victories, hoping to build momentum and to intimidate opponents.

Even after *perestroika* and more friendly relations with the USSR, and then the tumultuous overturn of the Soviet Union and the formation of the Commonwealth of Independent States, a great rivalry continued to exist between the United States and Russia. All through the years since World War II the two nations had opposed one another politically, militarily, and athletically.

The soccer world was also viewing this as the real test for the American contingent. Things got serious once phase two started. There was a pervading feeling that somehow the teams in the United States' group were either overconfident against them or just didn't play well in front of the large partisan crowds. This obviously would hold less of an impact once the teams had it all on the line. Skill would prevail over emotion.

The crowd was in a festive mood, having "tailgated" for up to four hours before the game. The stadium in East Rutherford was a complete sellout. The normal capacity of 77,000 was reduced to about 73,000 to provide for the security requirements of FIFA. The demand for tickets was so great they could easily have sold an additional fifteen to twenty thousand. Outside the stadium were hundreds of people looking for tickets. They had arrived early in the morning. Some of them were able to get a few tickets from those who had extra, but by far most fans were disappointed.

Jimmy Greenawald and Kyle Rote Jr. were finalizing preparations for the game. Both had interviewed each team during the past four days. Kyle noted how calm the American players were about the notion of making the second phase. He was amazed when he realized how poised the players were, and how their mindset was focused beyond the first-round games. "It's sort of like driving through a powerful punch in boxing," he said. "One doesn't box successfully unless when he throws a punch at someone, he aims six inches beyond the other guy's face," he told Jimmy. "Our guys expect to win tonight. Kori has done a magnificent job on the mental aspect of the game."

"The usual pageantry is preceding the start of the game. Here come the teams marching together onto the field, led by their respective captains, Charko Popov and Scott Fontaine. These are the only two teams left in the tournament that have the center-forward or striker position holding the captaincy. With most teams it is a midfielder or a fullback," Jimmy told the television audience.

Jimmy was nervous tonight. He couldn't quite come to grips with the fact there were over a half a billion people watching this game around the globe. Of course, in many countries, natives would be providing the dialogue and doing their own play-by-play announcing. Still, it was staggering to think how many would be listening to Kyle and himself. He surely was glad to have someone as experienced and capable as Kyle doing their play-by-play.

As the national anthem was played it became even more obvious that the overwhelming percentage of U.S. fans in the crowd and the volume of voices singing—or cheering—would be a positive factor for the less experienced American contingent. The fans seemed to really be into it. U.S. flags were waving everywhere at the conclusion of the song. As each game had progressed, many fans had adopted more and more the World Cup custom of carrying and waving the flag of his country. Today there were thousands of Old Glories, big and small alike.

Eventually the game started. Kyle walked the viewers through the starting players and told his audience what to expect from the game strategies as told to him by the coaches in the past day or two. He also told them who were the players to watch on each team.

"A most intriguing aspect of tonight's game is the matchup of number 10, Charko Popov, the striker for the CIS and number 17, Robert Hastings, the United States sweeper. These two men have extraordinary jumping ability—perhaps the two best in the whole tournament. Both players have recorded jumps of considerably more than one meter—that's roughly thirty-nine inches—in a standing vertical leap. Charko's strength is heading the ball into the goal. So far in the tournament he has gotten five goals, all but one from head shots. This will indubitably present opportunities throughout this game for them to go 'head to head,' so to speak."

"Kyle, I don't know why it is, but I'm getting chills up my spine and the hair is raised on the back of my neck. I'm so excited right now...just filled with anticipation."

"You're right. This is a spectacular opportunity for the United States. All the elements are here for a tremendous game. Of the sixteen teams left in the tourney, this matchup ought to provide as good a game as any."

The CIS dominated the early minutes of the game, frequently pushing well upfield, deep into United States territory. The midfielders for the home team were clearly being outplayed by the bigger CIS team. The noise level of the stadium had dropped considerably as the home team struggled.

Midway through the first half, at the twenty-eight-minute mark, Charko headed in a sharp shot on a beautiful crossing pass.

"…and on a well-executed maneuver the Russians draw critical first blood. That was just the way you diagram it on the chalkboard, Jimmy."

"That's right; pretty play. I think the right forward for the CIS is a bit too quick and a bit too clever for the fullback, Jackson, to stop his crossing pass to the center. We might well see that play again."

"Good observation. We could see Kori play Charko a much closer man to man, using Robert to guard him. If you can't stop the pass, then you've got to stop the shot."

The game restarted and once again the team from the old Soviet Union controlled the play. It soon became evident that with a lead, the Russians were going to be more physical. The Norwegian referee had not called a very close game thus far, opening the door for these strong-arm tactics.

The opening game for the United States in 1990 with Czechoslovakia had not been forgotten. The inexperienced Americans lost 5–0 to a physically dominating Czech team, who simply intimidated the new kids on the block. It looked like the CIS was now shifting to that type of game, hoping to rattle the U.S. players. Twice in the game the linesmen raised their flags to indicate a foul on the CIS players, only to be waved off by the center referee.

Kyle began inserting words in his commentary like "hard tackle" and "strong body charge," but it was an effort not to make his language stronger. He knew he must remain neutral as much as possible.

Jimmy was somewhat less restrained. "Kyle, things have gotten a bit rough out there. Our boys are getting clocked with nary a peep from the referee. I'm struggling to control myself. I'm sure it's beginning to wear on them as well."

As Viktor Vladimirov dribbled toward the middle, he cut quickly back away from the end line. As he went to make a pass, Eddie Jackson ran into him from behind—hard, trying to stop the cross.

At that moment the whistle blew, stopping play. The referee called Eddie to him and gave him a yellow card. Eddie stomped around in anger for the unfair treatment the official was granting the CIS team.

"That sucks, Mr. Referee. Call it on them once in a while, too. They're doing the same damn thing to us."

"CIS gets a penalty kick from that call. The United States bought itself a bad situation with that one, all right. Getting behind 2–0 could spell disaster," Jimmy intoned.

"That was a good call by the referee," Kyle commented. "Eddie ran up his back, which is a foul, and it was in the penalty box. That's the area within which a foul results in a free kick on goal, with only the keeper allowed in the zone to stop the short, twelve-yard kick. Eddie's got to control his temper. He let it get the best of him there. Now it's a penalty kick. This also shows the inexperience of our players. It could also prove to be the undoing of the team. The question here is, can the United States come back from this adversity?"

The contingent from the Commonwealth converted the penalty kick to go ahead 2–0. Scott went over to talk to Eddie and calm him down.

"That bastard's been grabbin' and shovin' me all day. The first time I get him back, they call me on it and give me a card."

"I know how you feel, Eddie, but if we're gonna have any real chance to win, we can't give them any more freebies. Now get tough and shut 'em down. We're going to win this. No giving up. Let's go."

Then he turned to the team. "Let's go, guys," Scott shouted. "Turn it around right now. Let's come back. Fire up!"

A very perceptible change took place among the American delegation. They started taking it to the Russians, finally penetrating deep into their territory. Up to the point of the second goal by the opposition, the United States had gotten off only two weak shots. In the next two minutes the Americans got off one "fair to middlin'" shot, as Eddie called it, and one notable shot by Scott off a good pass from Chase. That shot would have gone in except the opposing keeper tipped the ball up over the goal as he stretched out, diving to his left.

At that moment the whole game scenario changed. Marty started jumping up and down and up and down, waving his arms upward to draw the lifeless crowd into the game while he shouted to his teammates. "This is it! This is it! This is it!" Then two or three other players started encouraging the crowd. The people seized the moment. The crowd as one stood on its feet and a deafening roar dwarfed all else. The stadium was rockin' and rollin'.

The Americans played like a team possessed. Three times a shot just missed the goal. On the last one, again the keeper tipped the ball over the crossbar. Corner kick for the United States!

Scott called out, "Primary R, Primary R," to all his players. As Fong took the corner kick and lofted a beauty into the middle, twelve yards out from the goal, Robert came running all the way from his sweeper position at midfield, unmarked—he actually started before Chase kicked the ball— and jumped up high to head the ball down into the corner of the goal. Score!

"Goal! Goal! Goal! Hot dog, we've got us a game now. This team is on fire," Kyle cheered.

"What a great play that was, just terrific," Jimmy gushed.

"Yes, a great call, Jimmy. The Russians weren't ready for that at all, and it was well disguised by the movement of the other players. They didn't open the middle until just before he kicked the ball. Most of the U.S. players were moving away from the middle, and the defenders had to follow them. That left a good opening for our great leaper, Robert Hastings, to do his thing. Well executed all around; a very pretty play."

"Kyle, it was obvious that was a planned play. Who called that, do you think?'

"Well, it's hard to be sure. I'd say either Scott Fontaine, or Coach Kori through someone else. It was a situation play that they would try under certain circumstances."

"Looks like they picked the right one."

"Yes, and now it is a different ball game. We are playing better, much better, and the crowd is a big asset."

"I hope you people at home can hear this crowd. This is as loud a stadium as I've ever heard."

Kyle initiated the play-by-play as the game resumed. "The CIS team has picked up the pace a bit. Dimitre gets the ball over to Charko, back to Yuri. He gets around Marty, but is picked up by Pu Thatcher. Nice team defense."

The game went back and forth the remaining four minutes of the half, with neither team gaining much advantage. Chase got off a long shot that was easily handled by the opposing goalkeeper.

As soon as the referee blew the half-time whistle, the crowd gave the home team a tremendous ovation. The players on the field responded by waving to the fans in recognition for the part they played.

"Kyle, I'd say that was an unusual half. What do you think?"

"It sure was. The Americans were timid during the majority of that first half. We didn't play as well as we should. But after that goal, the second for the CIS, we saw a different team. In those ten or fifteen minutes that followed, Jimmy, I believe we could have stayed with any team in the World Cup tournament. *Any* team."

"We did look good. We played aggressive, hard-nosed soccer with good ball control and well-designed runs at the goal. And that goal Robert made off the corner kick was superbly executed. He must have been a foot above the defense when he struck the ball. Magnificent."

Kori felt much better about the team at half-time than he had during the first sixteen minutes of play. He could see the fire in their eyes, hear the enthusiasm in their voices, so he changed his talk to one designed to keep them on their high. He was excited and let his players know it. "Now you're playing. Now you're doing it right. Now we've got it going the way we want. Keep it up. Keep it up."

In the other locker room Arvon Bresnev was furious. "We had them down. Step on them. Put them away. You have let them get back into this game. We must reassert our dominance. We *had* them."

The CIS players, while they knew he was right, somewhat resented the coach screaming at them. They had played an excellent first half. Some of them didn't know what had happened. All of a sudden that crazy guy for the United States started jumping around and before they knew it, the whole stadium was shaking.

The coach eased off and spoke more rationally. "All right, all we have to do is play our game. You fullbacks, I want everybody covered, don't let anybody get open in front of the goal. Watch your passes and communicate to each other. Now let's go get them."

Kori was relating to his players some defensive tendencies the CIS team showed that the techno team had picked up on the high-speed analyzer. He instructed them how to best exploit them. Time was up. The FIFA man called them back out.

"Before you go guys, remember this," Kori instructed. "The first five minutes of the second half are crucial. They are everything. Even if we don't score, win the first five minutes. Hands together now."

At Scott's request the team had begun having a short prayer not just before the game, but also at half-time. At the end of the prayer, they all counted, One-two-three. Let's go!"

Scott added three words silently, "For you, Joel!"

The second half opened with both teams psyched up. Once again it became a very physical game. The CIS players were playing rough. Their two main targets were Scott and Robert. Twice time was stopped by the referee to allow first one, then the other to hobble up and regain some physical normalcy.

The ball moved up and down the field, with the squad from the States generally getting the better of it. They produced two good chances but could not convert. Then disaster struck. As Scott went up for a high ball to head it at midfield, Viktor Vladimirov, who had been playing particularly rough anyway, went low and took Scott's legs out from under him. The sound of Scott's body crashing to the ground made Chase, who was closest, sick. The two linesmen immediately raised their flag as a flagrant foul had been committed. The referee saw it, too. The sound of the whistle pierced the air. Viktor was being called to the referee. Out of his shirt pocket the referee pulled his cards.

"Which will it be, Kyle? Red or yellow?" Jimmy asked.

"It deserves a red card, but the way he has been calling I expect a yellow caution. No, look! He gave him the red card. Viktor Vladimirov has been ejected from the game. Good call. Good luck for us, too. CIS has to play a man short now."

Scott sprawled on the ground. He couldn't get his breath. Worse, his ribs felt like they were on fire. He tried to sit up but couldn't even raise his head.

"Referee, Referee, he's hurt. He needs attention," Chase called.

As soon as the referee recorded the number of the player ejected and the game time, he looked over at Scott and Chase. Turning toward the bench area, he then waived onto the field the team doctor and assistant.

"What hurts?" the doctor asked as soon as he came upon Scott.

All Scott could do is point to his side. He still couldn't talk. As the doctor felt his side, Scott winced in pain.

The doctor said to his assistant, "Broken rib, I believe. We need to get him off the field. Take your time. Can you breathe yet?"

"Just short, tiny breaths, Doc. It really hurts to take a deep breath."

"Can you stand up?"

"Yes, I think so," he managed to grunt.

"Let's get you up and on the sideline and see what we can do."

"Okay, whew."

"Bad news, Kyle. We can't afford to lose Scott. He's the heart of our offense and the leader of the team," Jimmy moaned.

"You're absolutely right. Unless I miss my guess, though, Kori will probably wait to substitute to see if he can come back with some help from the doctor and some time to recover."

The game resumed with only ten players to each side. Kori did not substitute immediately, preferring to see if Scott could continue later. He was well aware that to substitute for Scott would make him ineligible for the rest of this game, according to the rules of World Cup soccer. Each team played evenly, with no one creating any scoring opportunities. On the sidelines Scott had his shirt off and the doctor was wrapping him around the waist with an elastic bandage. When he finished he added adhesive tape, also. The finished bandage was about ten inches in width around his body. Back on came the shirt, and Scott took a light jog of seven or eight steps holding his side. Each time he took a practice run he got faster and better. After a five-minute hiatus Scott was ready.

The crowd cheered loudly when the referee waved Scott back onto the field. You could see the players lift their heads a notch too. Although still hurting, their captain was ready for action.

Now a man heavy, the United States dominated the action. With few exceptions the ball stayed on their offensive end of the field. Still the United States couldn't score. With the defense retrenched tightly into preventive tactics, scoring opportunities were limited.

Then on a simple give and go, Scott passed to Jebedoah, the most skilled ball handler on the team. One fake outside, then Scott cut for the goal. Jebedoah deftly returned a great pass through two defenders to lead Scott as he charged past the line of defensive men. With one control touch Scott put the ball in front and saw daylight between himself and the goalkeeper. One more step, then *POW!* A shot blasted past the goalie into the net.

The stadium erupted. The players all danced around and round. The noise was deafening. Tie game, two all.

"Wonderful execution. Just your basic wall pass—the give and go. The most basic play in soccer. Nicely done," Kyle exclaimed when the deafening roar from the crowd subsided. "Now it's here for us to win."

"You asked if we could come back from adversity, Kyle. I think that question has been countered with a determined reply."

"And how. An impressive turnabout."

Despite sterling individual performances by the U.S. offense, the old Soviet team held off any further scoring. Eddie Jackson verbally worked over each Russian every chance he got.

The game ended in regular time, tied at two apiece. Neither team could capitalize on any new thrusts into enemy territory.

"All games from this stage forward must have a winner, no ties," Jimmy informed his audience. "Now it's going to come down to two ten-minute periods of overtime. If it's still tied after that, it goes to a five-man shootout."

"You can bet each coach is utilizing this short rest period to transmit updated strategy and to exhort his team on to victory," Kyle reported.

"Yes, they are reviewing defensive strategies and also talking about what will work offensively for them. I imagine Kori is also making sure Fontaine can hang in there."

Play resumed after the CIS substituted number five for number eleven, a seemingly insignificant change.

"Number five, who is that?" Kori asked one of his assistants. "What do we know about him?"

"Not much. I believe this is the first game for him."

"Call upstairs and see if they can find out."

"OK."

The assistant coach called and talked to the techno team, then he told Kori they had nothing on this new guy, Jeckai Prozinkop.

"Nothing?" Kori echoed.

"I'm afraid not."

Just two minutes into overtime the CIS were again pushing forward offensively.

"With eighteen minutes left in the extended game, Kyle, I expected the CIS to sit back and play for the tie, being a man short."

"I don't understand their strategy. The CIS coach made a substitution on our last score and put in a little-used player named Jeckai Prozinkop. They've become offensively minded again. Maybe this Prozinkop guy is some offensive weapon we aren't aware of. Maybe with eighteen minutes and being undermanned, the CIS coach, Arvon Bresnev, believes he can't hold off the United States team, which appears to be in better condition. I don't know," Kyle replied.

Russia was pressing forward and had once again become very physical. Yuri and Charko were putting on a dazzling display of ball handling and passing. They controlled the ball for a long time.

The first half of overtime ended with no change in score. The teams switched ends of the field. Once again play resumed as the partisan crowd watched from the edges of their seats.

During one break in the action Scott went over to Pu and told him something. Pu nodded his head as the action started again.

The CIS once again began dominating the action as they pushed forward well into United States territory. They were bringing everyone into the action except their sweeper, who stayed close to midfield. Nicholai brought the ball to the middle of the field. He spied Yuri making a cut toward the goal.

The pass to Yuri was behind him such that he couldn't snag it despite contorting his body. As it rolled past him into open area, Pu raced toward the ball. He smacked it hard across and upfield toward Scott. The sweeper came forward to intercept the ball. He didn't reckon on Scott coming back as fast or as far as he did. Scott beat him to the ball and deflected the ball over the sweeper's head just as they crashed together.

Chase Anderson realized the opportunity and anticipated well. He took off downfield after the ball. Chase made it look easy as he worked the ball around the advancing goalkeeper and put the go-ahead score into the goal.

Bedlam reigned throughout the stadium and across the nation! In clubs, bars, and living rooms, at big-screen theaters and arenas everywhere, celebrations erupted. In the space of one hour, eleven players in blue uniforms had won the heart of America. A huge underdog and down 2–0, the team had come back with courage and determination to capture the emotions of the nation, which by now was totally absorbed by the tournament.

Scott staggered to his feet in time to see Chase score the goal, but almost overcome with pain, he couldn't join in the celebrating. He couldn't move much.

Three to two and the lead.

Five minutes to go and the CIS came back more intense than ever. Pu, Eddie, Ricky, and Robert had their hands full as the CIS team made run after run toward the goal.

Three minutes to go and the United States team kicked the ball out to Scott, who lost it because injured, he couldn't make his normal moves. Right back again came the CIS. First a crossing pass one way, then the other. Robert had to keep position on Charko to keep between him and the goal and to be able to step in front and keep the young Russian from getting his head on the ball. Twice the ball was headed out of danger by a leaping Robert.

Two minutes left. Terry O'Shay intercepted a pass and just blasted the ball down to the other end of the field. The CIS goalkeeper came way out of his box to stop the ball and get it to a teammate headed back up the field.

Eddie was having a particularly hard time with the new substitute, number five. The idiot ran disoriented patterns and kept bumping into him. What he was doing seemed to make no sense at all.

The goalkeeper for the CIS was now all the way up past midfield. A shot went wide of the goal but was deflected off Ricky. Corner kick, Russia.

One minute to hold out for victory.

The kick came across the middle. Robert and Charko, the great header for the CIS, both went up for it, but it sailed above their heads. On the far side the CIS gained control once more.

"Jimmy, the pressure out there is extremely intense—on each side. The CIS team has to score and we have to keep them from scoring. If they get a goal and we go into a shootout, I'd have to say the odds favor them. They have some outstanding shooters. We're only average, and Scott's hurt."

"I'd feel a lot more comfortable if we could get the ball on their end of the field. No danger to us if it's out there."

"Right. Ball goes back to Strolin at midfield, then over to Yuri on the right. Forty seconds left. He controls the ball to the left, dribbles past Jackson, passes hard to the middle to Nicholai; he back passes to Prozinkop three yards behind him, who returns it to Nicholai. Prozinkop cuts through! Pass forward to Prozinkop. Here comes Pu Thatcher flying across to intercept. Prozinkop steps forward to kick, and then he makes a sudden, crazy move to the side! Uh! Thatcher slams into him. A whistle. Oh, no, a whistle."

"That's going to be a penalty kick. The infraction was in the penalty box."

Kori came flying off the bench. "That's no penalty. He caused that himself. No penalty, Ref.," Kori cried.

Kori didn't realize it but he was shouting in Yugoslavian, not English. It wouldn't have mattered. The referee wasn't listening anyway.

Although Jeckai could hardly catch his breath, he knew at once all the practices and his coach's faith in him had paid off handsomely. He had done his job!

Kyle whispered, "Prozinkop is lying on the ground. The referee has stopped the clock. I saw him stop the watch."

"That gives them time to set up the kick. The U.S. players are protesting vehemently."

"Yes. It's the prerogative of the referee. In a situation like this he obviously feels the CIS should have a chance to play out this kick and any rebound, also." I'd guess that stadium clock is correct. It shows twenty-two seconds."

"Kyle, this would be awful to have the game tied now. Everything these boys have worked for is now on the line."

"I don't like the odds. More than seventy-five percent of penalty kicks are made. Our risks are high here."

"It's all up to two players: Yuri Brenislev and Cornell Davies. I have a sinking feeling in my stomach."

"It's going to be a great play if we stop them. The referee is issuing his instructions to the teams."

For Cornell, time slowed almost to a stop. Every movement became slow motion.

Through a foggy daze the U.S. goalkeeper watched the referee issue instructions to the players to keep out of the penalty box until the ball is kicked. He said it twice, once in English and once in Russian. The voice sounded like a record played on too slow a speed. Cornell's eyes saw the referee talk to the one who would kick the ball, but his mind was elsewhere. The goalie had gone into a mind-clearing, focusing process. All else was blanked out. He knew what he had to do. He knew what his chances were.

When he came out of his trance, the referee was standing close to him. Cornell heard the words but did not listen. He knew what was being said, anyway.

Then he heard Scott call out, "Think, Cornell. Think techno."

That reminded him of the research done by the technical staff for this game, as they had done for every other game. Analysis was conducted on each and every player on the opposing team who was likely to take a penalty shot, predicting who was most likely to be chosen. For every candidate, they kept a complete history of where they kicked the ball during this World Cup. Most important: left or right. Kori had also taught the goalkeeper how to dive and lift his feet at the same time in the event they tried "El Centro," a blast up the middle, especially in situations where the guardian was an excellent diver.

All that information was fed into the high-speed computer program to suggest the percent chance of which way the top five on each team would direct the ball. It even broke the data down into early in the game, late, or in a shootout. As importantly, the techno team analyzed the films to attempt to differentiate even minute changes in the player's approach to the ball in order to provide the keeper with insight up to the last split second.

Cornell remembered each detail of what had been prepared for him. Number fifteen, Yuri Brenislev, would make the play. He had studied it over and over these past several days. Scott had even reviewed it with him to help. Cornell smiled at the way Scott called his attention to the research without tipping off to those English-speaking opponents that we had more than a guess of which way to go.

Kori said to the back-up goalkeeper on the bench, "Which way do you think he will go?"

"Percentages say right, seventy-two percent. That's the way I'd dive, to my left, his right."

"Good. You too, must always be prepared. That might be you out there next time, with your country depending on you."

Time for Cornell to assume his position. The world moved in slow motion. He blocked out every sound, save the pounding of his own heart. His feet on the line, spread comfortably apart, the legs bent for maximum thrust sideways, his body vertical to show no tendency either way, Cornell was ready.

Scott lined up just outside the penalty box, to the right of the kicker. He, too, knew the percentages. If the ball hit the crossbar or was blocked, he'd be there first, if possible. Robert was on the other side ready to charge in to give their two fastest players maximum goal exposure.

Deep in the back of his mind, Cornell heard the whistle. The Russian started his move. Left foot, right foot—it seemed an eternity—two more steps, plant. Now! Like a Patriot missile protecting the homeland, Cornell exploded to his left. Launched in flight, hands out stretched, fingers taut, Cornell Davies dove. He dove for his team, his coach, his family, his friends, his country, and himself toward that missile of destruction hurtling bullet-like toward its target.

Scott could see Cornell had a chance to stop it or knock it out. He had made a spectacular leap. One could also tell he would not control the ball and so the captain headed wide to where the play would likely end up.

Robert darted for the center. His job was to cover the kicker when the ball went to the other side. Time was of the essence.

Focused on that moving missile, Cornell judged exactly the point of intercept. But could he reach it? He thought his fingertips would strike the ball. He hardened his extremities like steel. The ball struck the top of his outstretched gloves. He pushed that last fraction of an inch to best change the direction of flight. Cornell heard two quick sounds. First the ball struck his gloves, then it rapidly caromed off the sidepost, back into play.

The keeper's body no sooner touched down than it bounced back up. The job was not yet done. He could see the ball heading straight back to Yuri again. Cornell had almost regained a crouched position as he took note of the Russian once more planting his foot to shoot.

Scott couldn't react to the change in direction, and his momentum carried him out of the play. Robert was boring in on Yuri Brenislev like a locomotive. I can't get there before he kicks it, he told himself.

Nineteen seconds showed on the stadium clock that no one saw.

"You mother," Robert shouted as he dove feet first in front of the kicker.

Yuri's instinctive direction was to the other side of the goal from where the keeper was. To that intent he nailed the tying shot.

Robert's outstretched foot deflected the ball away from its intended area, more toward the middle of the goal.

With just one step, Cornell again launched himself back the other way and out a little from the line.

The deflected shot smashed into Cornell's face and bounced high into the air immediately in front of the goal on the right.

Cornell came down hard, losing his senses for the moment. Everyone seemed to be in slow motion. As he landed, he rolled slightly onto his back. Through groggy eyes he saw high above him a round object floating. Nothing made sense. Where was he, what was going on?

"The goalie saved it, deflected the sure score, but the chance is back to them again as the ball comes back out—high," Kyle shouted.

Charko spotted the rising ball and thanked fate for this opportunity. His position was excellent, about ten yards away, with no one between him and glory. Adrenaline pumped through his every fiber. All that work, the time spent endlessly practicing as a child for this one moment, to leap high into the air and head glory into the goal.

Scott was horrified to see the ball rise high up in the air directly in front of the goal. It seemed to float tantalizingly in midair. I'm too far away, can't get there, he cursed himself as he fought through the bodies in front of him.

Worse, he saw Charko coming. No one could jump like Charko.

Except Robert.

"Robert," Scott screamed. "Robert."

Cat-like, Robert whirled to look up at the ball. As he took his first step he saw Charko.

The goalie lay on the ground, powerless to move. His eyes saw the ball. Then he saw Charko. Still his brain could not command his body to respond.

Charko charged in like a bull.

Fourteen seconds to play.

Cornell struggled to move. Two tons of weight impeded his muscles. His eyes left Charko as he focused on the ball above him.

Like an enraged lion charging, Robert closed in.

The ball started dropping down through air charged with electricity.

Awestruck, the crowd watched breathlessly as the two opponents neared the white and black ball.

Two steps. One, and Charko propelled himself high into the air.

At the same instant Robert catapulted himself into space.

"Popov, their best jumper, a great header, has a clear shot at the ball. No, wait, here comes Hastings. What an athlete! It's going to be just the two of them," Kyle shouted into the microphone. "The ball is fourteen, fifteen feet in the air. It's man against man."

Not to be denied, Robert jumped for all he was worth.

With a scant three inches difference, the man from New Jersey struck the ball with his forehead as the Russian's head crashed into his ear.

"He did it! He did it! Hastings cleared the ball. Amazing! Amazing," Jimmy hollered.

The ball bounded over to Marty, who wheeled and fired it out of bounds, out of danger.

Pandemonium reigned! The exultant assemblage shook the stands in a throaty roar. Blissfully, the crowd celebrated.

Every soccer player, every fan watching the game live or by broadcast, was caught up in the moment of victory.

The crescendo of noise dissolved into "Seven…Six…Five…Four… Three…Two…

One." The crowd kept time with the clock.

"Unbelievable, Kyle. I swear Robert Hastings jumped more than four feet off the ground."

"He had to. Popov was at least that high."

Just as Cornell regained his feet, two bodies smacked into him from above. One black, one white. One blue shirt, one red shirt. One winner, one loser.

Even the CIS players were impressed; you could see it in their eyes.

"USA, USA, USA," the crowd chanted as the game ended.

Up in the section reserved for dignitaries, Alan Priestaps was tearfully hugging his wife and then all those around him. All the effort, all the time, all the people, all the money poured into this program over the past four years had paid off—big time.

All across the nation, in cities and in towns, people poured out of their homes into the streets in wild celebration. Cavalcades of vehicles, horns blaring, flags waving, paraded through the streets of hundreds of cities. Houses and bars emptied of their occupants. The impromptu jubilation attracted all walks of life. Street parties sprang to life as diversity melded into a common feeling of oneness.

The United States bench poured onto the field, led by the coach. Excited beyond bounds, Kori was a kid again. Bouncing and running and jumping, he made his way toward the pile of players on the ground. He, too, jumped on top.

By the time they unpiled, Cornell thought he'd never walk again. Somehow, though, he found himself on his feet, with everybody hugging him.

"Way to go!"

"Great save!"

"That's using your head," Marty kidded.

The goalkeeper-turned-hero recovered enough to join the mob around Robert and squeezed through to give him a bear hug.

"Nice play, big guy, you saved the game."

"So did you. Twice."

"Kyle, I can't remember seeing a finish any more exciting than that," Jimmy yelled above the roar.

"It was a great play, a humdinger of a finish. The United States team played very well after a sluggish start. Some great individual efforts, especially on defense. The United States of America has now qualified for the quarterfinals."

Kyle then recapped the scoring and the general flow of the game, including for the audience some of the more dramatic plays of the game.

"If we can play as well as we did in today's game, I am hopeful of our chances against the winner of tomorrow's game between Argentina and Hungary," Jimmy said to Kyle and a worldwide TV audience. "At times we evinced a standard of play capable of competing with the best. Consistency was the only ingredient lacking. Today the Americans showed poise, hustle, imagination, and coordinated team play. The next game, however, the competition should be a little tougher."

Far up in the stands, above the dignitary section, scouts from Argentina and Hungary as well as other delegations were still writing in their notebooks and talking into recorders.

CHAPTER 15

Antonio, anxious to find out if Vinnie was staying in line, telephoned his investigator. "What'd you find out, Juan?"

"It's like you said, Mr. Montini. He's gone out on his own as far as this plan to kidnap someone. He's contacted Sabatini and Virgilli to enlist their efforts and interest."

"Sabatini! You sure?"

"Yessir. He met with him at Corky's Grill day before yesterday for about an hour."

"I don't like Sabatini at all. He is involved in too many risky things, and would like to ease us out of some areas we're now in. Could Vinnie have any other reason to be dealing with Sabatini?"

"I do know from another patron in the restaurant that they talked about the World Cup. I even found a discarded napkin with a list of four countries on it."

"Good work; there will be a little something extra in your pay next week."

"Gee, thanks, Boss, it really wasn't too difficult, though. Vinnie ain't too bright, in my opinion."

"What were the countries on that list?"

"Argentina, Germany, Holland, and..."

"Yes?"

"And the United States."

"The United States! That idiot. OK, Juan, you've done well, thanks."

After Antonio replaced the phone in the cradle, he sat in his high-backed, luxurious chair, thinking for a few minutes. Then, having made a decision, he dialed Number One in New York.

A tremendous shout went up in the sports betting room in Cleopatra's Palace. The big-screen TV showed the United States scoring on the Argentina team. The announcers, Kyle Rote and Jimmy Greenawalt, were screaming into the mike just to hear each other. The tumultuous roar in the stadium was deafening. Ninety-eight percent of the crowd was rooting for the USA.

"What a shot! What a shot! What a shot!" Jimmy yelled.

"Absolutely," Kyle answered, "a most impressive shot, but every bit as good was the transition play and the pass made to set up the shot. Great team play. The United States goes up a goal: 1–0."

The large crowd was watching the game with much vested interest. Many had placed wagers on the game; for some it had been their first time betting on a soccer game. Most had a double reason to place wagers. First was the opportunity for a handsome economic gain, and second was that they found themselves cheering a little harder for their own soccer team than they might have otherwise. Many new fans were converted to the sport of soccer this way.

All during the tournament the odds on the United States national team had been long—very long indeed. Their chances of beating Argentina were posted at 1–6, although everywhere else in the world the odds were considerably worse.

So active was the betting that Cleopatra's had come up with numerous ways for the individual bettor to wage his money. Not only could one bet on the winner of the game, the betting possibilities included odds on spotting goals, such as United States plus one and one-half, plus two and one-half, plus three and one-half, and plus four and one-half goals. These odds ranged from 5–2 against the United States to 20–1 in favor of the United States, all of which were profitably laid off internationally by the Cleopatra's Palace bookmakers. One could also bet an over-under wager on total goals scored. The line for total goals scored was four today. Then, as always, the bettor could take any team remaining and the odds to bet on who would win the overall championship.

The room full of people were whooping and hollering. As far-fetched as it once seemed, the American team had a chance to advance to the semifinals against either Italy or Belgium. It was as though the spectators were at the game themselves. That's how loud it was. Most of the people in the large room stood to gain appreciably if the United States could hold on. Some had only bet two dollars, more out of patriotism than any other reason; some, though, had studied the United States team's progress these last four years and knew it was a good risk, so had bet a lot of money. The largest bet today had been one hundred thousand dollars to win on the United States.

Cleopatra's was loving every minute of it. They had a group of people constantly on the phone, laying off the bets as they came in. With the differential in odds between those offered in Europe and these in Las Vegas, the casinos were raking in big profits. No wonder Cleopatra's and all of Las Vegas treated the World Cup with such aggrandized appreciation. It was turning out to be a month-long Super Bowl. No sporting event in history had ever come close to generating the betting dollars that this World Cup had—especially with the United States doing so unexpectedly well.

With every game the United States won, the betting on the next one increased fifty percent. The numbers—and profits—were becoming mind boggling. Cleopatra's was doing the best it could to cope with the swelling interest. Plans were being made to lease a facility and set up a telephone bank of fifty people making phone calls to lay off the bets. The management at Cleopatra's knew they had to be prepared to handle an extraordinary volume. Already people were telling them other casinos were turning away bettors, that they couldn't handle the volume. Cleopatra's had a reputation to uphold. They did not want to be in a position they couldn't handle.

The loud cheering from the betting room made several things happen. First, the manager ordered all TV monitors everywhere in the hotel to be turned to the game so people could watch anywhere. He shrewdly figured people in a good mood would wager more than they would otherwise. The level of intensity rose several notches in the sports room, and with that rise was an accompanying rise in noise and cheering, which attracted even more people. Before long, the room was jammed with people shoulder to shoulder. Then the manager had the scoring of the goal and the fact that the United States was leading Argentina announced on the PA system, both inside and outside the building. He did that for two reasons. Obviously, it would hype the soccer team's success; also, he knew a large number of Cleopatra's employees were soccer fans. Soccer in Las Vegas had grown substantially in the last several years. Most everyone with young children had someone playing soccer.

The excitement was contagious. Twenty-two minutes now remained in the game. The announcers were describing the play-by-play, all the while inserting comments about what a stunning upset this would be.

Argentina, meanwhile, had awakened to the fact they had been playing a lackluster game and had turned up the juices. The offensive pressure was extraordinary. If they didn't score, they were out. The U.S. defense was beginning to frazzle under the strain; cracks were developing, creating opportunities for Argentina. With five minutes and change to go, the Argentinian left wing, Canniggia, made a run toward the goal.

Kyle Rote shouted into the mike, "The United States is weakening, we're in trouble. Watch out, watch out, Claudio Canniggia is open, here comes the pass —just barely too high. Jimmy, they missed an almost sure goal there. Canniggia jumped to head the ball in and was just inches less than what he needed to achieve an almost certain goal. In fact, I think it skinned his head. That was a dangerous play. We were fortunate."

"Yes, Kyle. That would've been a goal if it were better executed. Our defense looks in disarray out there. This is a very dangerous time."

"Argentina has control again. They are working it around the perimeter with sharp, quick passes. The United States is doing a respectable job marking the players. The ball is outside, in front of the goal again. No question the United States would be losing now if Argentina had played like this from the outset. You have to ask yourself, why weren't they?"

"Good point, Kyle, the difference is amazing."

"Nice pass. Uh, oh. There's a shot. Nice save by the goalkeeper, Cornell. Nice save. He stretched out flat to reach and deflect that ball up and over the goal. Beautiful save. Corner kick for Argentina. They're hurrying to get the ball back in play. Here comes the kick. Good kick. Look at Cornell. Did you see that? He knocked down two Argentina players, bowled them over, to get to that ball and knock it out. The strategy there for Argentina is to place someone, two people in this case, to impede the ability of the keeper to get to the ball, giving their offensive headers a chance to put the ball in. Instead Cornell manhandled whoever got in his way to reach that one. Very impressive."

"That play is reflective of Cornell's maturity and international experience he has gained these last four years as a pro over in the European leagues. The Argentineans tried to play hardball, but Cornell was harder."

"Good insight, you're right. Here comes Argentina again. Sharp, quick passes again make them hard to defend. The South American style of play is being evidenced here by Argentina. This United States team is being tested. The ball is over on the right again. There goes Canniggia again.

Watch him. Here comes the pass, he's open! Unbelievable! I don't believe my eyes. Our sweeper Robert Hastings just jumped four feet off the ground to head that cross out of the way. Four feet. Every time I see him do it I can't believe it. What a play!"

"That man is reputed to be the best leaper, not only on the United States team but, as far as we know, in all the World Cup. From a standing position he has more than forty-four-inch vertical jump capability, an extraordinary ability. And I agree with you. He definitely jumped four feet off the ground on that one."

"That'll make every highlight show in the world tonight. I hope they show that in slow motion. I can't believe I saw that. He would have hit his head on a basketball rim ten feet off the ground."

"With the adrenaline flowing, I'll bet Robert has exceeded his normal leaping capability."

Kyle went back to the action. "The United States just intercepted the ball. Pass to Fontaine, pass back to Anderson, he takes it down the field. Finally some relief from the pressure. We need to use up some time on the clock. There can't be more than a minute left; according to my watch, we are into injury time and there hasn't been much of that. We lost it! Stolen by Canniggia. Look at that. Both teams are sprinting up the field as fast as they can—every player. It's all on the line now. Marty slows Canniggia down, forces him wide to the left. Eddie catches up. They are double teaming the dangerous left winger for Argentina."

"Cornell, our goalie, is shouting instructions to his defense. He's making sure every man is marked. C'mon, guys, hold them, hold them just a little bit longer!"

"I see the referee is looking at his watch. That's good. Canniggia passes back out to his midfielder, who passes across, pass back to the left. They're moving the ball. The midfielder, Souilla, lofts a cross in front of the goal. Cornell knocks it out. The right fullback of Argentina gets the ball. He immediately kicks it back across in front of the goal. They're desperate. The United States heads it away. Another cross to the goal. Cornell snares the ball. Hold it, just hold it. Yes, he waves everyone down the field. Still he holds it. Argentina is appealing to the ref. Cornell kicks a long one. The South Americans trap the ball on their side of the field. Time's up, ref, call the game. Here they come again. The ball goes to the right, back to center, back again. It's over! It's over! We did it! We did it! We won! We beat Argentina! Can you believe it? The players are jumping up and down. The coach and bench players are all on the field."

"The Argentina players are stunned, Kyle. They can't believe it.

There's no way this is supposed to happen!"

"The noise is unreal. 85,000 fans standing and cheering. They're making so much noise it's hard to hear. What a feeling Jimmy! I can't help but get goose bumps. What a game; what a victory; a 1–0 shutout."

"This has got to bolster significantly the game of soccer here in the United States. Perhaps we finally will see the development of a legitimate competitive first-division professional league here."

"You're right, this will have a major impact," Kyle responded. "A very positive impact on the development of soccer at every level of the game. I think the United States is poised and the timing perfect for an explosion in the popularity of the sport. This is just what the doctor ordered."

"What a glorious feeling for all Americans."

Logistically, Cleopatra's had a problem now. Because the odds were so high they had to make special arrangements to get an extraordinary amount of cash in order to pay off their winning customers. Knowing this possibility, they had posted signs reading, "All bets over $10,000 will not be paid immediately in the event the United States wins. Arrangements will be made for payment within a two-day period. However, credit for other wagers will be granted immediately."

The reason for this, of course, was that Cleopatra's would need some time to collect its money from everywhere in the world it had laid off the bets, and to handle the unwieldy logistics involved in safely transferring that much cash.

The income in recent years from races and sports betting had become a more significant element in the overall makeup of Cleopatra's profit. A really big event like a major fight could net as much as three or four million dollars for the company. Normally the way the bets or odds were structured, it didn't matter who won or lost; they generally tried to make the betting even on both sides, relying on the ten-percent "juice" to produce reliable profits.

In the case of this World Cup, though, every time the United States won, not only did Cleopatra's make money by laying off the bets, but the effect was multiplying because of the high odds being paid to the bettors choosing the United States team. So, the betting expanded explosively. More and more people were betting, and more and more money was being placed on each bet. Armored trucks were hired to bring the vast sums of cash to the casino, whereas normally the armored truck's role was to take cash to the banks. The banks with whom Cleopatra's did business were being taxed to provide enough hard cash to the casino, so great was the demand. All the while Cleopatra's bank accounts were building rapidly from the largess of profits emanating from abroad. The success of soccer bets in the sports room had a vastly stimulating effect on the action at the tables as well. Some bettors lost all their soccer winnings when they switched to traditional casino gambling.

A very special feeling enveloped the team during dinner. Well-wishers from the town, FIFA officials, USSF officials, and the players' family members were all trying to crowd their way into the restaurant.

The team, their spouses, and the few children who were present ate together in the same room as the coaches and USSF officials. The FIFA officials, town officials, team hostesses, and the owner of the restaurant ate in an adjacent room. Many members of the press were served a similar meal in the outer room.

To win in the quarter finals! The feeling was euphoric! Impossible, the experts had thought. Argentina had too much experience for the young, upstart American team. The United States had done well, *very* well to reach the quarter finals, but beating the CIS team was not the same as beating Argentina. So much tradition, so much poise. Truly, it was thought, Argentina had an easy trip to the semifinals. Was it overconfidence? Had they been too cocky? The blue-and-white-striped gladiators had thought it might come easily. They had played flat.

The sports world was turned on end. The upstart U.S. team had disposed of a vastly superior team from South America with soccer skills second to none. It was thought only the German team and the Italian team could upend Argentina. Now that was past. How much longer could the United States sustain this level of play?

As the team finished their meal, there was nothing really to mark so momentous an occasion. The players did very little reminiscing about the game—much less than one would anticipate. Scott remarked to Marty about how subdued everyone was. Perhaps it was the relief of having the pressure off. In the round of sixteen against the CIS there had not been so much pressure, because very few people expected them to beat the CIS or even to do well. Their early success was such that most people regarded it either as a fluke or that they had "shot their wad." Getting to phase two fulfilled most goals of American soccer fans and officials and had surpassed predictions of experts and media throughout the world. Practical, rational analysis, prior to the game with the CIS, would have indicated the end of the road for the North American team. After all, one loss at this point, and that's it. With the great victory over the CIS team, however, dreams were renewed, seemingly unrealistic expectations were revived. So many were saying, "What if?" And yet the team and the coaches believed in themselves.

So it was that many of the players were simply reflecting on the good things and giving quiet thanks to a higher power for the blessings that had already come their way. Seven of the players had been contacted by one or more representatives from professional leagues. Scott and Robert had garnered the most attention. After today's game Robert's stock had climbed considerably. The United States Soccer Federation had contracts on almost all the players. Those contracts had terms that gave the federation the right to sell their contract rights to another professional team. The USSF had set a minimum fee of $125,000 for anyone to be released from their contract prior to the commencement of the World Cup tournament. That figure had been raised to $200,000 after the victory over the CIS, and certainly would be higher for some of the individuals. In fact, originally the optimist within the USSF said one or two United States contracts could be sold for $250,000 to $500,000 if someone played particularly well. Now, almost certainly, the contracts for Scott and Robert would go for much more.

The sports writers who followed the World Cup and who ranked the players' performance on the field had Scott ranked number one at his striker, or center forward, position, and Robert ranked tied for third as sweeper. Robert's rating was sure to go up after tonight's performance. Reports were getting back to the team that the sports writers were really making a big deal out of Robert's four-foot-plus jump to head that ball defensively near the end of the game. That made two games in a row Robert had saved a game-tying goal by his ability to leap into the air to whatever height was required to outjump his opponent. The save against the CIS involved simply outjumping the Russian forward. Tonight's save involved an element of timing also, as the ball was traveling fairly fast, almost horizontal to the ground. When Robert headed it, the ball was fully ten feet off the ground. The mere mortals participating as players possessing human limitations stood helplessly watching the ball soar over their heads. Not Robert. He did admit afterward that he wasn't sure if he could reach the ball when he went up for it.

The announcers had been right when they predicted that play would make highlight shows around the world. ESPN had played it back to back three times in a row, each time making a bigger deal of it. They played it in every highlight show from then on. In Germany, Italy, England, France, the Czech Republic—all over Europe—reporters were giving Robert his due, calling his feat the play of the tournament so far. Even in Argentina, the words *incredible* and *magnifique* described slow-motion film clips of "The Play." Even while the South Americans mourned the exit of their team from the tournament, they begrudgingly gave credit to Robert—and the U.S. team—for playing competitively. In fact, a new opinion of the United States was beginning to be heard in many quarters throughout the globe; it alluded to an improved level of play, even that the United States was deserving of that prise and that after all these years, maybe the United States was ready to join the fraternity of serious soccer-playing nations.

At the end of the dinner the coaches asked all of the guests except wives and family to give them five minutes alone with the team. After the other diners had exited, Coach Kori told his team how proud he was of their effort today, how well they had played as a team. "You know, I have gotten reports from one of the Federation officials that even now, in at least a dozen known places—and probably a lot more—there are wild celebrations going on by your fellow citizens all over the country. We've had phone calls from Dallas, New York, Washington, New Orleans, Las Vegas, Pittsburgh, and others telling of the huge street celebrations, all for what you men have accomplished. This is a first for the United States of America. The people out there are rallying behind you like they've never done before. Never has any national team had the impact on America that you are having. Gentlemen, because of your dedication to the game, soccer in America has arrived.

"You have got to feel good about what you have accomplished. But there is more to do." The coach paused. Lester was quick to whip out a white handkerchief and, making a big show of the act, hand it over to Kori. The team all laughed, at the humor and Kori smiled at the joke. "You are carrying the banner of your country. People all over America are now behind you; in big cities and small towns. Ladies, I want these next several days—through the final—to be as stress-free for these players as possible. No arguments, no negatives. Help your man to concentrate on the task ahead. If anyone has a situation that will detract from the focus on our next game, I ask you to report it to me and I will get you whatever kind of help you need. There is no limit to what we can do for you on this occasion: baby sitters, a loan, use of a car, I don't care what you need. Just please let me know.

"Now I want to propose a toast. To our continued success toward the capture of the greatest prize in sports."

"Hear! Hear!"

"Yeah!"

"Awwrright!"

It was with a very special feeling that the team left the restaurant. They were still quiet and contained. Most of the players were reflecting on the game or on the amazing announcements the coach had made.

"Somebody better get the hell out there and find him! He's got to be somewhere. I'm not going to Mr. Montini and tell him we've lost Vinnie; that no one has seen him for two days; that he's not been doing what he's supposed to be doing."

"But, Carlo, we've searched everywhere and we've had his house watched. We've even tapped his phone. Nothing."

"He'll show up. Keep an eye out for him in Corky's Grill and at that broad's house over on Fourteenth Street. He's liable to show up there if not at home. We'll give it one more day before I bring Number One in on this." Carlo slammed the phone down in exasperation.

Unknown to his own people, Carlo had been told by Antonio just three days ago to watch Vinnie. He had told Carlo what Juan had reported to him, but not who had reported it to him. Carlo had been surprised at the news. No one goes against a decision or goes out on his own. Carlo had not seen that in the five years he had been in Antonio's organization.

Carlo pulled a World Cup schedule out of his desk. Tomorrow Costa Rica was playing Brazil, and Germany was playing Cameroon. Tonight Italy was meeting Belgium, and the United States had just finished upsetting Argentina. That astounding upset would be yielding big bucks to their organization as the betting volume certainly would continue to grow. There would be handsome bonuses in this for everyone—unless that idiot Vinnie screwed it up. Three more quarter final games, and then the two semifinals. Carlo guessed that if Vinnie had gotten together with Sabatini and planned some kind of kidnapping, the best timing for them would be before the semifinals. Only two teams on Vinnie's original list were left in the tournament. Carlo guessed that the way Vinnie worked, he would not switch off of that original plan. So, only Germany and the United States were to be considered. Let's see, Germany plays either Costa Rica or Brazil, probably Brazil, he mused. Then the United

States plays Belgium or Italy. Italy!

"Damn," Carlo exploded, hitting the top of his desk before exiting his office.

Scott woke up feeling good. He had slept surprisingly well. The good feeling, though, really came from the oneness that the players all felt for each other. Yesterday's victory had drawn them even closer together. His unit during the Italian trip had developed a lot of *esprit de corps* , but this was a different feeling. There was a goal out there to be reached. One that had significance. The coach's words had a profound effect on Scott and, he guessed, on many of the other players as well. The eyes of the nation were now on them. Even on their bus trip from the Celebrity Restaurant back to their hotel, the amount of people lining the route had increased fivefold over the earlier crowd. People cheered them everywhere they went. This morning Scott had been awakened by noise from outside. When he looked out the window he couldn't believe his eyes. Outside there must have been a hundred and fifty people milling around the hotel. Apparently some player must have gone to the window, because the crowd was looking up and pointing. When Scott looked out the window, several people below saw him and pointed, and he again heard a few shouts from below. Scott stepped back away from the window and shook his head. His watch said it was 7:45. Mighty early for that many people to be here, he thought. Almost too early—most of the guys will still be sleeping. Hope they don't wake everyone up.

At practice the coach had the offense work on kicking crossing passes to the middle in front of the goal, with the player there taking the ball in the air with a hard kick on goal. It was an exercise that they worked on at least once every other practice, because exact timing was needed to be able to make a shot on goal with the ball traveling forty miles per hour or more. They also practiced heading the ball in on crossing passes. Both ends of the practice field were used simultaneously for shots on goal. That way each player enjoyed more practice opportunity. They practiced in a stadium of sorts, with police cordoning off the perimeter of the stadium.

The coach had insisted on a closed practice so his players could concentrate. The external distractions were growing to be more of a nuisance, even though the team's obvious popularity was a very positive motivating factor. The coach had to prepare them to play a team whose style of play could be totally different from those teams they had already played.

While not practicing, the coaches were watching videos of Italy. The Italians epitomized the European game—fast transition, fast play, attacking offense, never a "slow down" game. The defensive pressure put on an opponent by Italy could wilt the niftiest of offenses. In their first four games they had taken a total of fifty-four shots and made fourteen goals, tied for third highest among the playoff teams, behind only Germany and Cameroon.

The United States techno staff was already hard at work, even before Argentina's game, analyzing both Italy and Belgium. They used a high-powered computer to predict tendencies by the teams and by individuals on each of those teams. The computer could pictorially portray the most likely scoring plays that would be used by each team, as well as show defensive reactions to certain situations. By reviewing this type of analysis, the coaches were able to set up situations to practice against offensively in order to exploit the tendencies and weaknesses of the opposition. The defense could also better anticipate the movements of the opponent on offense. The techno staff would prepare this printout of the analysis so that the coaches could review them, in addition to viewing the actual footage of the games. The techno crew was getting good at this. The World Cup was really the first "trial by fire" after months of staged laboratory analysis and operations. The members of the sports technical unit were really excited about the possibilities. They felt that with each game their analysis technique was improving, giving the United States a better chance than they would otherwise have. The Americans would be ready for their next game with effective, prepared strategy.

When practice ended the team returned to the hotel and ate a light lunch. By the time they finished, the afternoon game between Germany and Cameroon was on the TV. Germany showed itself to be a real juggernaut, running roughshod over a strong Cameroon unit. The game ended with Germany on top, 5–1.

Tonight the game between Brazil and Costa Rica would decide which team would fill that one open slot in the semifinals, joining Italy, the United States, and Germany in that distinguished company. Brazil was a heavy favorite. Costa Rica had accounted well for itself in the first phase and had played steadily, finishing tied for second. Then in the first game of the playoffs, they had surprised England 2-1, pulling off the upset of the tournament—at least until the United States had beaten Argentina.

Brazil seemed to have Costa Rica's number. Five times in the last five years these two teams had played; five times Brazil had won. Costa Rica had surprised everyone in the last World Cup by reaching the second phase. In this year's Cup they were rated higher and expected by some to reach the first round of phase two. There it should have ended. England was regarded as one of the strongest teams in the cup. Some expected them to reach the semifinals, where they would meet Germany.

Even with the victory over England, Costa Rica was an underdog to favored Brazil for two reasons. Brazil had a better offensive game and statistics, and Brazil had not lost to Costa Rica in recent times. Tradition in soccer circles often was the difference in winning or losing the big matches. That was evidenced in the last World Cup, wherein tradition-rich Argentina managed to reach the finals, despite being outplayed in five of its seven games.

Costa Rica, on the other hand, had to overcome decades of tradition when going against Brazil. Brazil has one of the most storied histories throughout all of the World Cup championships. The 1990 Cup in Italy, however, was Costa Rica's first.

The only believers in Costa Rica's chances to win were faithful Costa Ricans, those teams they had beaten on their way to the quarter finals who knew how good they really were, and the residents of Ashton, the team's new hometown. The players were shown frequent reminders of their country's motto; "The little country that thought it could."

The situation in Ashton and even in the whole state of New Jersey was really a wonder. A tremendous pep rally was held in the team's honor the second night of the phase-two matches. As it turned out, the rally became a double celebration because the United States team's stupendous victory over the CIS had occurred just the night before. Periodically during the rally, chants of "U-S-A, U-S-A, U-S-A" broke out. The short speeches given by the captain of the team, the coach, and the president of the Costa Rica Soccer Federation were all very gracious and supportive of the United States team and its success. The combined result was a welding of the emotions and feelings by the fans and team members toward both teams. In a way they felt like kindred spirits, brothers in the cause. Knowing that they could only meet in the finals helped to foster the close feeling. It was extremely unlikely either team, let alone both, would make it to the finals. So it was with little concern that they were supporting a rival; because of the circumstances, both teams' fans were free to support

Costa Rica and the United States. The supporters felt no conflict, but an alliance instead. Each team was a heavy underdog, each team was from the Americas, each country was a democracy, each country opened its doors and shared—through its residency policies—a number of inhabitants with one another. Then, too, so many had read about how the Costa Rican team had been adopted by the town of Ashton. Americans as well as Costa Ricans now had two teams to root for.

Lucinda was nervously looking for things to do. She had already done the dishes, mopped, and waxed the kitchen floor. She thought to herself, If it wasn't for these times I need work to calm my nerves, much of my housework would not get done. As she looked outside at some passing vehicle she noticed the dusty condition of her windows. OK, she thought, the only time I'd ever do windows would be at some time like this. That's what I'll do—the windows. She had just started gathering newspaper to wipe the windows when the phone rang.

"Hello, Lucinda?"

"*Si?*"

"Flora here."

"Hi, how are you doing?"

"Fine, how about you? Are you getting nervous as usual before a game?"

"Oh, yes, I'm over here doing housework—things that keep me on the move—physical things that keep my body occupied so my mind can't think."

"Well, how about going out to a disco with me tonight, and have a few drinks, dance some, and have a good time? C'mon, it would be good for you. Maybe you'd be able to take your mind off of everything else."

"Oh, I don't know if I could go. I would be thinking of Paolo a lot and, and…"

"You'll have fun, and besides, I want your company. I'll pick you up at eight-thirty. We'll go to El Pueblo."

"OK, I'll go. Thanks, Flora."

Lucinda hung up the phone softly, thinking how nice it was of Flora to think about her, especially to understand her need even more than she herself did. Flora was right, the disco would be a welcome change of pace. Now I'll have to hurry with the windows to get ready and fix supper in time, she thought. A lighter mood fell on her as she was cheered by the prospective evening ahead. It must be six months or more since she had been dancing—almost as long as she had been living with Paolo. His involvement and training regimen for soccer had not permitted many occasions like that.

Paolo—wonder how he's feeling about now, if he is awake yet. They have a late-evening game against Brazil. Paolo said Brazil was playing very well and that would be their toughest game yet. They were to play under the lights at the Coliseum in Los Angeles, and have been practicing at some high school stadium at night to get ready for this. The light, Paolo said, affected Conejo, the keeper, more than anyone else.

They knew they could get scheduled for some night games, so Paolo has practiced under all kinds of lighting conditions for eight weeks, just to get used to the ball. He liked to toss it around with Conejo at night without lights on. He said it improved his night vision and his reflexes. A tear fell from Lucinda's eye right then, as she misted up, thinking of her boyfriend and that he had already been away over three weeks.

Alex and Paolo met together in their hotel room before they were to leave for the stadium; Pepito was there, too. This had become a ritual for them that they did not want to change. Paolo, especially, was superstitious and insisted Alex meet with him just like the other two times prior to victories

Paolo told Pepito that three teams had already made substantial offers for his contract but that his team refused to consider selling it. Alex noted once again that Paolo was whining and complaining. As his star status became brighter and brighter, Paolo was given over to wanting his own way even more than before. The trouble with Paolo was that he knew he was good and expected everyone to curry his favor.

By the time the team reached the stadium, the FIFA escort had trouble getting through the crowded streets. As Costa Rica advanced one more level with each new win, more and more Americans flocked to their games to see the "Cinderella Team" of the tournament. Costa Rica had become darlings of the press. The writeups in the papers about how the small town of Ashton, New Jersey had adopted this team and claimed them as their own, and how this small town had stuck its financial neck out to host any team, had caught the fancy of many a person across the land. Emphatically their popularity was enhanced by the fact that they were an underdog that had already toppled some better teams. Costa Rica was getting some very good press; the natural beauty and attractions of the country were espoused in more than one sideline story. When mighty England fell to these Central Americans, the sportswriters had had a field day.

From the outset of the action it was evident that Paolo was a marked man. At no time did he get near the ball anywhere in scoring range without defenders all over him. Ronald Gonzales, Hernan Medford, and Juan Cayasso knew that they would have to take the pressure off Paolo by attacking areas the Brazilians left vulnerable because of the overshifting onto Paolo. Ronald also found himself with a shadow whenever he pushed dangerously forward. The Brazilians had scouted them well and were trying to shut down Costa Rica's two potent weapons.

That strategy was precisely what got them in trouble when, in the seventeenth minute, Hernan Medford broke loose to receive a pass beyond the line of defense. He took two short dribbles and, with a pinpoint shot, put Costa Rica ahead. Brazil protested that he was offside, that he had gone beyond the last defender before the ball was kicked, but to no avail.

All the Brazilian flags that had been waving suddenly found rest. Up went the Costa Rican flags of red, white, and blue. Those impartial North Americans that had come to watch a World Cup match immediately developed a newfound allegiance to Costa Rica. The Ticos felt heartened by all the fan support. It was almost like playing at home.

With a lead, Alex knew he would play a better game. It enabled him to take more risks than he would otherwise. He was determined to shut down the team from Brazil if at all possible. That they were perhaps the best passing team in the tournament did nothing to deter Alex's zeal for the shutout. He thought it was possible; therefore, he would attempt to achieve it. The whole defense felt the same way—enough so that Costa Rica was the third-best team against scoring in the whole field of twenty-four when figured on an average goals per game. Their team had been particularly tough to score against once they got the lead. Much of the solid defensive effort had been laid at Alex's feet. For a player to have started out as a substitute and then come on and been rated one of the better fullbacks in the whole tournament gained Alex a lot of attention.

Brazil failed to capitalize on a chance to tie the game shortly before the half when their left forward chested a long pass down to the ground and split Roger Flores and Alberto Martinez. Just as the forward took his shot, Alex threw himself close enough to distract his attention such that the shot went high, but not high enough. Conejo, the goalkeeper, couldn't quite reach the ball as it hit off the crossbar and bounded back out. Fortunately, Roger was there to clear the ball out as he kicked it out of bounds.

At half-time, the coach went over the strategy he wanted followed in the second half. Nothing was new, because by now a familiar pattern had developed. The plan depended on the two side fullbacks to close down certain areas in the penalty box while the rest of the defense played man on man. The forwards for Costa Rica were often playing a vital part in the defensive scheme. This hacked Paolo off, and was often the point around which arguments started. The more success Costa Rica had, however, the more Paolo came to realize the coach was right. Furthermore, the more the success of the team, the more valuable he knew his contract was worth. Thus, as the tournament progressed, Paolo griped and complained less and less about having to play a defensive role.

The second half started out well for Costa Rica. In fact, the possession time was well in favor of the northern team. Brazil started to show signs of frustration. Here was a team that they were supposed to blow away, one that had never beaten them in the previous fourteen meetings since the 1930s. After fifteen minutes of the second half the Brazilian coach made his two substitutions to try to instill new life in the squad. A change in strategy became evident as the South American team began to adjust offensively. It was obviously something that had been planned if the second half the action did not turn favorably toward the Brazilians.

The whole team knew it was a good call. The striker for the green and gold had definitely been tripped when he got by the stopper, Alberto. Penalty kick for Brazil. The kick was easily converted as Conejo dove the wrong way. Score, 1–1.

Alex was trying to figure out what it was that had changed. He knew they were in a different formation and that the way they were attacking the goal had suddenly varied from their typical pattern. Roger Flores figured it out. Alex was thankful that their captain had so much experience and could discern the changes taking place so that their own team could adjust.

Brazil returned the favor four minutes later as Rogilio Arias was fouled inside the box. Paolo took the kick and sent it straight up the middle. The keeper dove to his left and the ball passed over his feet. The score was 2–1 as the crowd cheered the underdogs.

The Costa Rican team remained dangerous on offense. One of the moves made by the Brazilian coach was to replace a fullback with an extra forward. This weakened their defensive alignment and reduced the coverage on Paolo. On one foray into the penalty box, Gonzales was able to pass it into Paolo in the middle. There was single coverage on him and he had his back to the goal, so Paolo flipped the ball up in the air and, laying back, shot the ball over his shoulder in his now familiar bicycle kick. The resultant goal for Costa Rica shook the stands!

Alex ran all the way up to where Paolo was just getting up. Paolo jumped into his arms with both fists raised high. The papers later extolled the talent of the Latin magician, calling Paolo "among the very best."

Brazil came back with a vengeance, attacking from all sides. Alex couldn't believe how fast they could move the ball. Finally the sleeping giant had awakened. Three times the green and yellow team from Brazil had good shots but couldn't convert. The activity was almost entirely down at Costa Rica's end of the field. The South American champions were finally playing like they should.

Alex was no longer so sure he could shut down this marvelous machine. Whereas before he had confidence in himself and the other defenders, now he wasn't so sure. As it turned out, his premonition was accurate. With 6:25 left in the game, Brazil put in a head shot on a magnificent crossing pass to make it 3–2.

Roger gathered the team together while Brazil was celebrating and told them, "Everything we have worked for is now on the line. This is it. We've got to move the ball further up the field. We can't let them camp down at our end. If we can hold out six more minutes we go back to New Jersey and to the semifinals. Let's do it!"

Never had Alex or any of the other teammates played a more frenzied period of soccer. The action turned rough as Brazil got more and more desperate with the passage of time. Conejo was having to make save after save. While the defense was giving up shots, it never allowed a really good chance for a goal to be scored. When the referee finally blew his whistle to end the game, the Tico players were all expended. Alex didn't know what he could have done if the game went into overtime. The stress and tension was exhausting. Looking around, he could see the others felt the same way.

"Ladies and gentlemen. The management of Coco Loco has a very important announcement to make: a final result in the World Cup. Your attention please. In Dallas, Texas, in Estados Unidos, the game has ended. Final score is…Brazil two–Costa RRRRica three. Incredible! Victory for Costa RRRRRRRRRRica!"

Everyone in the nightclub went crazy. The dancers and waiters and bartenders were jumping up and down and hugging one another. The music was turned up louder and all the people were deliriously happy.

"Unbelievable, Lucinda," Flora was shouting to be heard. "Lucinda, I can't believe it! Aren't you ecstatic?"

Lucinda was shaking from the emotions racing through her mind and body. Paolo, she thought. My Paolo, you must have done it. Out loud she answered, "How could we have done it? Paolo told me nobody could beat Brazil, or Germany, or Belgium, or Italy, except each other, that they were so much better than the rest of the teams."

"Amazing, isn't it? I'll bet Paolo and all the others are as happy as they could be."

Lucinda thought about Paolo and Alex and some of the others that she had gotten to know. Then she thought about Maria Elena, whom she knew must have watched the game. That girl is an angel, everyone loves her, she thought. She is so unselfish and loving toward others. Of all the wives of the players, she is the one who treats me the best. I hope Alex played a good game, and I hope she is very happy.

"Tonight we celebrate. It is too great a feeling to let this pass."

"Doesn't this put us into the semifinal round? Semifinals!"

"Yes, two more games to go."

"Can you imagine?"

The word spread quickly. Out into the courtyards and walkways of El Pueblo came the people. Jubilant and ecstatic, the celebrators were jumping and shouting, living for the moment. High fives and hugs were readily exchanged. Cars on the street were honking to the beat of "Cos-ta Ri-ca, Cos-ta Ri-ca."

Details of the victory spread. Ordinary players became heroes, heroes became gods. The smallest nation in the tournament felled one of the largest and the best.

Every radio station in the country was now relating the details of the game, with intermittent breaks to announce the final score. Wondrous praise, indeed, was told that night. Many were saying it was the finest sports moment in Costa Rican history.

Downtown San Jose was jammed with traffic. Drivers who had stopped at the center of activity didn't want to move their cars, so those behind were stuck. The Central Park was mobbed with revelers. The mood was festive, indeed.

La Sabana Park was attracting its share of visitors as well. Before long three thousand celebrators filled the east end of the park. Someone brought fireworks and cherry bombs, which were set off to the delight of the throng.

A large group decided to parade up Paseo Colon, the main avenue, to join up with the others they knew would be celebrating in Central Park. As this group set off, nearly everyone joined in. Soon the sizable throng of crusaders took the formation of an enormous dragon, writhing and weaving its way down the three-mile path to meet its "mate" downtown at Central Park.

All through the night the fiesta remained alive and active. Only when dawn came did the party-goers head home.

CHAPTER 16

Sheila left the church with a good feeling. Her choir director had been totally cooperative, even enthusiastic, about her idea. She had figured he would be. He was going to contact another choir director, his friend at the Baptist Church. Sheila, meanwhile, would roust out the president of the local soccer league and try to get the word out—fast—to a lot of interested people. There wasn't much time to get everything ready. The United States team was flying in this afternoon at 1:15. Sheila had found out the team's schedule for practice and for dinner, and even for a team meeting at the hotel. She knew the precise timing for everything, thanks to her friend Shane, who was dating one of the hostesses for the World Cup.

Sheila had been a soccer player for several years in the girls' youth league around Chicago. When she heard the city had won the bid to get one of the semifinal games, she was ecstatic. Long a soccer fan, she felt somewhat alone in her following of professional soccer and especially the World Cup. Recently, however, nearly everyone in the bank where she worked asked her something about the rules or how teams got eliminated in the tournament or comments on games they'd watched. Everyone, it seemed, was tuned into the games on TV.

Sheila had wanted to do something to help psyche up the team in their game with Italy. It was too good to be true. Not only was a semifinal game being played in Chicago, but the United States team was part of it. Sheila had thought about making a nice banner to take to the game, but had decided her contribution should be something that was bigger and involved more people. She thought maybe she could get a lot of people to line the route the team bus would take, but thought maybe that was too big an undertaking. An inspiration made her remember a moment in college shortly after she had gotten pinned, in which her pin-mate's fraternity and her sorority organized a welcome home reception for their basketball team, who had stunned nationally ranked Indiana. How special she had felt! What an impression they had made on the team when everyone there had sung the school fight song! It was a moment she would never forget. Sheila and that boy had broken up later, but that didn't dim her memories of that occasion.

It was not a big jump in thought to conceive of how the United States team would feel with hundreds of people serenading them at their hotel tonight. If only nothing was changed on the team's schedule, the nine o'clock timing ought to be good. It was exciting to think she, Sheila, was planning something that could have a very positive effect on the U.S. team. In a small way she thought of herself as helping her country. It gave her a warm sensation inside as she envisioned tonight's activities.

Sheila met with the team logistics coordinator to alert him to the plans. She requested that the team not be told exactly what was to happen. She wanted them to be surprised. She asked the coordinator to let the team know only that they should be available for something special the community had planned.

Another idea occurred to Sheila. Making two phone calls, she had lined up a trumpet player and a drummer. Those two were to get a couple more if they could. A small band would provide the music to accompany the singers. Seven or eight instruments would help a lot, she thought. Sheila told the two musicians about a few of the songs she had in mind. Now, somehow, she had to find copies of the songs she wanted. Fortunately, the library had every one of them. When she made the necessary copies of each song using both sides of the sheets of paper, she felt she was ready.

The president of the soccer league, whom Sheila called, was also caught up with the idea of serenading the team. He and Sheila had decided to get as many people to the hotel as possible and to have them bring flags and candles, if possible. The president called two other league presidents and a coach in yet a third league. Carefully he explained what was going on and what he wanted them to do. All agreed and got busy making phone calls. Coaches from the many leagues around the city received phone calls and were asked in turn to phone the kids on their teams.

Sheila also called all the local TV stations to tell them about tonight's plans. She thought if things went according to plan the TV stations might just get a very newsworthy story to show on the eleven o'clock news. She went to the hotel where the team was staying to scout out the best location to hold the serenade, and to see where the team should be and where the crowd could be.

Today was the day of rest between the rounds. That made it easy to not have to work out a schedule around whatever game was being played. She knew the players would want to watch any games televised. Tonight, however, posed no conflict, so the idea was made valid and workable.

"Mr. Montini, this is Carlo. We've got Vinnie, but he won't talk. We can't get any information out of him."

"Where'd you find him?"

"At that broad's house on Fourteenth Street. Got him trying to sneak in the back way about an hour ago."

"Persuade him a little, maybe he'll talk. The fact that he won't talk means he is trying to go through with that plan of his."

"We're going to have to persuade him a lot. We've already used mild persuasion, and that didn't work."

"Try threatening him with his family or his broad."

"Alright. Let you know."

Fifteen minutes later Carlo was back on the phone with Antonio. "You were right, he cracked. He cracked just like his fingers on his hand. A little pressure, a little more, then (pop), they broke. He says it's a plan to get Scott Fontaine, captain of the United States team. Can't understand where his loyalty is. First a fellow American; then, even worse, the guy's got an Italian name. That Vinnie's not too bright. We got a problem, though. I have the distinct feeling that the plan will be executed with or without Vinnie."

The last bit of information really made Antonio mad. "Get as much information out of Vinnie as you can. See if you can get any other names, any timing, and where they planned to do it. After you get as much as you can, get rid of him. He's a liability."

The only new information Vinnie yielded was not much help. He admitted to being involved with Sabatini, and he gave a name that no one knew. Antonio angrily paced around the room, trying to decide what to do. Then he dialed the phone. "This is Antonio Montini. Get me Sabatini—it's urgent. Freddy, this is Antonio. You need not look for

Vinnie anymore, you won't find him. I'm calling to try to persuade you to give up this foolhardy idea of kidnapping someone, particularly a premier player, on one of the soccer teams. It just won't work."

"Whatever do you mean? Vinnie came to me and offered this plan to kidnap someone, but I, like you, thought that was just pure stupidity. I told him to take a hike. He came back to me with a revised plan, but I told him that we still weren't interested. You haven't got a problem with me."

"I'd like to believe you. Trouble is I'm just not sure. I will say this: if something like this happens, you will personally answer for it."

"Don't worry about it. We keep our noses clean."

Antonio called Carlo to verify the exact words Vinnie spoke when he talked of his involvement with Sabatini. Carlo seemed sure there was an ongoing plan in the works, although he couldn't be sure Sabatini was still involved. As soon as Antonio hung up the phone, he called New York.

Within two hours the phone at the new USSF headquarters in Chicago rang. An anonymous caller told Brad, who was the only ranking person available, that he had knowledge of a plan to kidnap the captain of the United States soccer team before the semifinal game with Italy. When Brad tried to get more information out of the caller, the line went dead. Goose bumps rose all over Brad's body, and a sinking feeling struck deep inside him. Antonio called Carlo one more time and suggested some measures to take to help ensure that no problems would surface. Carlo accepted without question the direction of his boss. When he hung up, his forehead furrowed and his large, bushy eyebrows drew together in thought.

The triumphant Costa Ricans were welcomed back with great fanfare. Two bands played at the airport as the players disembarked and came into the concourse. The rather large crowd made it quite congested but exciting for all concerned. In addition to the players were the rest of the Soccer Federation officials, several from FIFA and several from USSF, and, of course, there were the many privileged folks, such as the De La Paz family, who traveled with the team.

Fifty-eight vehicles formed a cavalcade that came down the interstate to Ashton. Many of the cars had signs and flowing streamers. They were led by two motorcycle cops and the white FIFA bus. It was difficult for the casual observer not to know what was going on.

When they reached Ashton there was an even larger welcoming crowd waiting for their arrival. Heroes in their own right, the players felt even more important with all the hoopla showered upon them. They talked about it that night when they had a team meeting. Not one person said anything but how well they had been treated here in their home away from home.

Anticipation was high. Costa Rica was again at Giants Stadium, where the luck of the draw brought them back to the venue near their hometown headquarters. The town of Ashton was riding high. All the networks had been here more than once making documentaries about the city as host for the surprise Cinderella team of the tournament. Here they were, a team given almost no chance, only two victories away from claiming it all. Publicity for both Ashton and Costa Rica was extremely favorable. Already Lacsa, American Airlines, and many travel agents had seen future bookings for this tiny democracy rise well above normal.

Andrew and Godfrey were sitting in the mayor's office reminiscing about all that had happened. "You know, none of this would have taken place if I hadn't happened upon that Mr. Cothern from the USSF. Fate must have placed him in my path."

"Lots of folks would have let this all pass by. You seized the moment of opportunity and pounced on it."

"I'd rather be lucky than good. It was a bit of good fortune."

"I believe luck is the meeting of opportunity and preparation. You make your own luck."

"I like that; never heard that before."

"Do you realize our tax receipts are already estimated to be well over triple what we projected to the city council?"

"No, but I knew we were doing very well. Every single hotel and motel has been turning away business since the Costa Ricans arrived."

"Even the neighboring towns have done well. All the way from beyond Rutherford to Madison, business activity has been high."

"I'll give you credit for one really smart move, and that was to exact a fee from the other towns that wanted to share in the specific events in which the team participated. That alone has accounted for $75,000."

"Well, it probably wouldn't have been nearly that much if this team had not done so well."

"Or lasted as long."

"Right."

"Maybe the best thing has been the way so many of the citizens became involved, even those you wouldn't ordinarily think would get caught up in this sort of thing. I saw Mrs. Diamond chasing autographs today. She's eighty if she's a year."

"Really. Hey, I've seen the same thing. Little girls, too, from six years old and up. That group of junior high girls—those Girl Scouts—have been very closely involved ever since that first day. Remember the ones that made those huge welcome signs…and in Spanish?"

"Yeah. But maybe the greatest event that stimulated Americans everywhere, and probably contributed the most to putting us over the top, was the arrival of the De La Paz family. No other single thing captured the imagination and interest of the nation more than that."

"Preparation and opportunity."

Dinner for the players and coaches was finished at eight P.M. Coach Gaborakov then moved them to a conference room where he had a team meeting to talk over game strategy for tomorrow's game with Italy.

"They will come out hard and fast. The first five minutes are the key to the game. If we can come through the first five minutes tied or ahead, we can win the game. I feel sure they will try to blow us out. It's a tactic they have used successfully before. But I'll tell you this: If they put their all into scoring at the beginning and they don't score, then that's certainly a psychological boost for us and, more importantly, it is obviously a psychological downer for them. Not only that, but I believe you men are in better shape than they are. I don't believe there's a team left in this tournament who is in as good shape as you are. Remember back to all that work you did to get to where you are now. Have confidence in your strength and your conditioning."

He showed them what offensive formations and plays the computer analysis said would work, as well as defensive tactics to employ under certain conditions. He reviewed tendencies the analysis showed Italy would use. Salvatore Schillaci was their money player on offense, but not as dangerous as Roberto Baggio, in the opinion of the coach. Schillaci had lost a step or two from the '90 World Cup, in which he had emerged as the star of the Italian team. He was just as aggressive, just a slight bit less effective.

"Eddie, watch out for your strong side swap. The midfielder is likely to swing around to the outside, kind of sneaking over there, when he thinks you're not aware. Talk to each other. You can't over-communicate. Cover up when someone is drawn away from his area.

"Guys, I want to tell you, you have done more, accomplished more, than many out there thought possible. You have ushered in a new era to World Cup Soccer. The United States has arrived! And by God, we're going to state that in capital letters by beating Italy. You have stirred the emotions, tugged at the heart strings of the nation. Millions upon millions will be watching you tomorrow night. The attention of the nation will be riveted on you. Lester, where are those newspapers you brought?"

"Right here. Look at this. *America Today* headlines: 'Americans topple Argentina in World Cup.' *Dallas Afternoon News*: 'U.S. Upsets World Champs!' *New York Journal*: 'Incredible! U.S. soccer team advances to semifinals.' Then a subhead: 'U.S. proves itself to be a new world power in soccer'. It's the same all over the country. We're getting good press because you are *making* good press."

The coach followed that up by holding up a fistful of mail that had just come in. "These are from people all over the country. Some of them are for you individually. They are faxes and telegrams from your fans. Let me read one." The coach read a fax to the team. It said pretty much what they expected: how proud the nation was of them, and how much they had already accomplished, and so on. What surprised them was who had sent it. The fax was on White House stationery and signed by the president. Other celebrities had sent them faxes too: several governors, Burt Reynolds, Magic Johnson, Pelé, and Donald Trump. The coach read several more, then passed the batch to Lester to pass out to the team.

After a few minutes to allow the team to read some of them, the coach said, "Boys, you can't let all this adulation and attention stop you from concentrating on the task ahead of us. Your job is not yet done. The game tomorrow is at night. We will have a light practice tomorrow at twelve-thirty. After that we'll eat a big meal at three. Get lots of sleep tonight."

The meeting ended, the players filed out of the meeting room and went out into the lobby. There all the hostesses were waiting for them with smiles. "We've got a surprise for you," several players were told. The hostesses asked the players to wait until everyone had caught up and assembled together.

"Follow us, please," the hotel manager said to the group.

They walked outside to the outdoor eating area. There on the edge of the terrace were two TV cameras with their lights on, obviously filming them. The manager led them over toward the waist-high concrete wall surrounding the patio, where a young lady in a white dress was waiting for them with the mayor and ten others. As they got closer, the team members and their wives and children noticed another camera, then another.

These additional TV cameras were not facing them, though. They were facing the girl.

The manager stopped when he got beside the girl and turned to them and waited until the rest of the group had joined them. Then he said simply, "This young lady's name is Sheila Van Camp and she wants to tell you something."

She stepped up to the several microphones to address them. "The city of Chicago is proud of what you have achieved and the spirit with which you represent so well the United States of America. On behalf of the people of Chicago and those all across the land, we would like to say good luck in tomorrow's game and to offer you this salute."

Sheila then was handed a candle by one of the others and a third person lit it. As the flame grew strong, she walked the few feet over to the wall and as she looked out over it and down to the grassy area below she raised her candle high. The several people with her, the mayor and others, also produced candles and lit them.

From below a small band started playing *America The Beautiful*. A swelling volume of harmonious voices joined in singing the song.

All the players and coaches and wives moved over to the wall to look below them. To their amazement there stood at least two thousand people, many of them with candles. The small bright flames pierced the darkness and lighted in kaleidoscope fashion the many faces joined in the musical tribute.

The group on the terrace above, led by Sheila—all with candles in hand—also joined in song. Each one had a small sheet of paper with the song obviously copied for them, so that they could follow.

The players were speechless and taken aback by the tenderness of the moment. Here they were in the good ol' USA, experiencing the best life's got to offer. Embodying the newly awakened spirit of the country, and expressing the sentiment felt by the millions in towns all over the United States, were these two thousand plus people paying tribute to their team. The gesture, the effort made by these people, packed such an emotional charge that more than half of the players either cried outright or at least had tears come to their eyes.

Scott couldn't help himself. Seeing all these wonderful people out there serenading them immediately flooded his eyes with tears. Scott wished he wasn't so sentimental but that was a natural character trait of his, something he could not change. Those people, those marvelous people, he thought. They're doing this for us. This is incredibly moving.

Down below, as Scott looked at the people, the flames burned brightly.

More and more people were coming to join in. Scott could see the faces of many children among the crowd. They look like soccer players, he thought. In fact several uniformed teams were grouped together. Scott looked over at the girl in the white dress. She had light brown hair about shoulder length, lightly curled, a slim figure nicely shaped, and the dress she wore was a white formal strapless gown that looked absolutely stunning. She had a happy, contented look on her face. He wondered if she was in charge of putting this together. Why else was she up here with them? Could she have won a contest? He was determined to ask.

The words from the song, *America The Beautiful*, were profoundly meaningful tonight. Scott looked around to see if any of the others were affected the way he was by this demonstration. Almost every wife there was crying; some had handkerchiefs and some used Kleenex to dab their eyes. Some of the players were smiling and waving appreciatively to the crowd. Others were just pensively staring out into the many faces of the crowd. Marty, for some reason, was gazing up at the stars, no doubt contemplating the meaning of it all or conjecturing on some other great philosophical theory. Several players, Scott noticed, were rubbing away tears from their eyes. One surprise was Eddie. Scott had figured him for an unemotional type of guy; a lot of hard bark on him, but not so, apparently. His armor was obviously pierced tonight!

Robert was very openly weeping. Scott knew how much this meant to him. He had given up a potentially lucrative career in basketball or football in order to pursue soccer. Maybe, just maybe, the financial rewards would come to him anyway. Scott had heard talk that several division-one teams in Europe had already approached the USSF about him. Scott guessed it could become quite a bidding war. Numerous articles had appeared in newspapers about how good an athlete he was and included stories of his days playing football, basketball, and track when he was in high school. The stories especially played up the fact that Robert did not play soccer until comparatively late. Most everyone else he would be playing against, or with for that matter, had played all their lives. Robert, more than any other player on the team, had captured the interest of the sportswriters and the soccer world. He grew up in a black section of New Jersey, not far from New York City. His family was very poor, his father was a disabled veteran of Vietnam, who for some reason wasn't receiving full disability pay from the military and couldn't work another job. This too had been explored by the media. Robert was the single unifying factor in the united support of black and white America for the team. Helping that was that there were no racial controversies surrounding the selection of the team or in the team's day-to-day activities. Scott, like all the others on the team, felt a close togetherness with every other player. The fact that there were three blacks on the team seemed a non-issue. Scott focused back in on Robert and felt very, very happy for him.

Immediately following the end of the song the small band began the song *God Bless America*. The players, Scott noted, were all singing as well. More tears flowed down the faces of these guys representing their country.

As soon as that song finished, the band started playing the theme song from *Rocky*. The enthusiasm and electricity that swept through the crowd was very evident. Every player was waving to the crowd and jumping around—a natural reaction and posture for Marty. Like Rocky Balboa, the USA team was waging an uphill fight against a superior opponent. Overcoming the odds as an underdog was the essence of their popularity.

Toward the end of *Rocky*, before it was quite over, a chant of "U-S-A, U-S-A, U-S-A" was begun. The volume escalated as the United States players joined in. The place was rocking.

After two or three minutes of the "U-S-A" chant, the mayor of Chicago stepped up to the microphone to quiet the crowd. After four attempts, the crowd quieted down enough for him to be heard. When he spoke next he addressed the team and the crowd fell silent.

"You men have made us all proud. Everywhere in the United States of America, people are following your games and rooting for you. These good people of Chicago are just like those everywhere in our country. We love you, we honor you, and we salute you. Good luck tomorrow against Italy. Win it for yourselves...and for your country. God bless you and your families."

The crowd started shouting and cheering, and some renewed chanting "U-S-A, U-S-A." But then the band started playing *The Star Spangled Banner*, and everyone joined in lustily singing the national anthem. A flag was produced from the group on the terrace and all faced it. Every player to a man, Scott noticed, had put his right hand over his heart and, with tear-filled eyes, was singing along with the crowd.

At the end, the players, wives, and all in the team contingent waved to the crowd below in grateful thanks. Those on the terrace, who were not on the team moved among them shaking hands and wishing them good luck. The players quietly and genuinely expressed their thanks.

Scott and Chase purposely positioned themselves to be the last ones to congratulate the girl in the white dress. Scott wanted to do more, to say more than just thanks. As she approached, he could see she was attractive. Kind of dark-complected, or very tan; he thought she probably had some

Latin blood. Her dark complexion made the stark contrast of the white dress stand out all the more.

"Hi, I'm Scott Fontaine, and this is Chase Anderson. Your name is Sheila?"

"Yes. Hi. Oh, you're the star, aren't you?" she said to Scott.

"No, everyone's the same. Our team doesn't really have a star. Did you organize this? Or were you chosen to do this for some other reason?"

"It was my idea. I kind of organized it. We did all of this in one day, just started this morning. I thought of it last night in bed."

"What you did was special, very special. You have given the team a real lift."

"I know I got more out of it than anyone. I have never felt better about anything I've done in my whole life. I feel so alive."

"This turned out great. For me it is something I'll remember the rest of my life."

"You're very nice. I'll be there tomorrow watching you. I know you'll win!"

"They're good. It'll be a difficult game for us. But knowing there are people like you for whom we're playing, we'll try a little harder."

Impulsively, Scott leaned forward and kissed her cheek.

Chase followed suit. "I...I'd like to see you again. Will you come to the team dinner after the game tomorrow night—as my guest?"

"Will I? Yes! Yes, yes. I'd love to. Oh, thank you. Thank you very much." Sheila threw her arms around Chase and hugged him. "I'll be there, win or lose. Thanks."

"OK, good. I've got to run. 'Bye."

"'Bye, Scott Fontaine, 'bye Chase Anderson." Sheila smiled and waved prettily as they walked away. Looking back at her, Chase smiled and waved again.

All night long Chase thought about Sheila and the serenade until he dropped off to sleep. It was good to have something take his mind off the game.

"I want it airtight—metal detectors, airport security stations, bomb detectors, and the like at every entrance. It should be so impregnable a small pocketknife wouldn't get through. Everyone will be frisked, all purses searched, all carry-ins confiscated except binoculars, radios, cameras, flags, tape recorders, and umbrellas, if it's raining. And make sure these items are in fact what they seem to be. Post signs at all entrances and make radio and TV announcements—and make those sound routine, matter of fact, gentlemen—emphasizing that excess baggage will *not* be allowed in. You obviously will need police of both genders at the gates.

"Next, I want air coverage, with at least two helicopters available and a fighter plane at the nearest base or airport. We must have the helicopters visible and showing a presence of security enforcement. Have the fighter plane make a couple of passes at the time the teams are traveling from the hotels to the stadium.

"Now, when they come out of the hotel, the players must be protected. No slipups; got that? I want a plan for the protection on my desk in the morning."

David Starr was in control. He was pleased with the reactions and the effort everyone was putting in; however, nothing less than that could be tolerated. So much was on the line.

CHAPTER 17

Scott felt like a real celebrity. It was a combination of the security required for the players as well as the adulation showered upon him by the kids and the many girls that screamed at the sight of him. When caught in a crowd, Scott couldn't resist the fans who insisted on getting his autograph. Scott tried hard not to deny anyone, but sometimes time didn't allow him to satisfy them all, even though the ever-present security force screened the autograph hunters. The same situation existed for all the players, even the ones who had not yet gotten in a game. The individual players had all been photographed and written up in all kinds of periodicals. In essence, the team had become the darlings of the media.

That night Scott and Diana got to stay together—surprising before a big game. It was only the second time since the tournament began that they could relax with each other. Her parents were keeping the baby. Scott really missed her companionship. She was a real morale booster. Scott liked to hear her perspective of the games and of all that was happening in the outside world. Scott had largely lost touch with what was going on elsewhere, so focused was he on the games.

"I know you really wish that Joel could be here enjoying all of this."

"He *is* here. He's watching from somewhere up above. I firmly believe that. Still, it's not the same."

"Honey, I know that you would thrive on the support and friendship he would have given you. I'm sure there remains a void in your heart for a best friend that you grew up with and spent all your time with. You have lots of friends, but you can't replace the one best friend in your life."

"*You're* my best friend now. You mean so much to me."

"That's a nice thing to say. Ditto here."

Later that night when Diana was already asleep Scott reminisced about days gone by with Joel. His mind focused on a big game they had played against East Atlanta when they were fifteen. Game time had been two o'clock, and it had been probably one of the hottest days of the fall. Scott and Joel had joined a premier team from Bethel, made up of players from their side of the city. The Decatur, or East Atlanta, team was the one, however, that had the big reputation. The year before they had won Southeast regionals, and finished second at the nationals.

Scott had run up to the front door of Joel's house, knocked, then went in as usual. "Joel, Joel, hey, Joel. C'mon down, let's go outside and kick the ball some."

"Hi, Scott."

"Hey, Ms. Cindy, how ya'll doin?'"

"Fine, Scott. You look like you're in a good mood."

"Sure, it's Saturday, it's fall, and we have a game today."

"Have a chocolate chip cookie, I just brought them out of the oven."

"Man, they're my favorite."

"Get some milk too if you want."

"Hey, thanks. This sure looks like it's going to be a good day."

"Joel will be down in a minute or two, he's cleaning his room. It's a mess. Isn't your game today against some kind of star team?"

"Yes, ma'am, its a premier team from East Atlanta, they're supposed to be a real strong team. It is one of those teams where they charge $200 just to try out for the squad. They get over a hundred and fifty guys trying to make this team. They get to travel all over the country and even go to other countries to play in tournaments. They're really good. Several of the players are from the Decatur area. Decatur always has strong soccer. We've played Decatur teams frequently in various tournaments. Alone, they're good, but adding in all those others makes this team really strong."

"My money's on you guys. I don't see how anyone can beat Bethel as long as you and Joel are there."

"Aw, Ms. Cindy, we have a good team, but there are better ones some-where."

Just then Joel had come bounding down the steps two at a time.

"Hey, Joel, I came over to see if you wanted to kick a few around."

"Sure thing. I just had to finish my room first, but that's all done now."

"Let's go." Scott and Joel had burst out the kitchen door, with Joel dribbling the ball as he went. As he ran out he had tried to pick the ball up from behind his heel and flip it over his head and in front; the ball hadn't quite gotten there. "Look at that, would ya? I'm gettin' better; won't be long before I'll have that down pat."

"I know you're better. So am I. Watch me." Scott had then tried it and did just about as well; the ball had hit him on top of the shoulder. As they separated to a distance of about twelve yards and started kicking the ball back and forth, both boys showed a little nervousness about the upcoming game, normal in Scott but unusual in Joel. A win today would be a big boost for their team.

As they rode to the field together, Mrs. Adams remarked that she was glad Joel and Scott decided soccer would be their sport instead of football or basketball or baseball, because she liked to watch the games better. Scott and Joel had looked at each other and smiled. They had been glad they chose soccer, too.

During warmups Scott had observed that the other goalkeeper had trouble moving quickly to his left. He had decided then that his shots would be in that direction.

The game had started strong for both teams. Play ebbed and flowed back and forth, with neither team able to get a good shot. Scott had one weak shot that didn't reach the goalie because a defender had intercepted it. At one point in the game the players struggled for control of the ball near the sideline where Mrs. Adams and Joel's sister Amanda were watching. Joel had gained control and passed off to a teammate who took the ball up the field. Joel lingered a moment near the sideline to catch his breath. In a wink Amanda was tottering out on the field with a plastic squeeze bottle, holding it up to him. Joel saw her and laughed. He ran to her and picked her up, gave her a quick kiss, and carried her over to the sideline and lovingly admonished her to stay off the field.

One of the parents on the sideline said, "Isn't that just the cutest thing you ever saw?"

"That was darling."

Joel had played a great game, very aggressive. Scott had loved to watch Joel play, because he was so physical and could outmuscle, outrun, and outplay almost every opponent. And they always seemed so surprised that he could do it time after time. Joel was the soul of their defense. By the end of the first half, the other coach was warning his team to beware of "The Animal." Joel frequently seemed to be sacrificing his body, but seldom received any bruises or scrapes, even when he slide-tackled. Joel was doing his usual great job back there on defense, so much so the other coach was getting mad at his players for not being able to beat him. The half ended without a score.

Scott and Joel's coach was happy. You could tell he hadn't been so sure his team could stay with the East Atlanta team. The coach was telling them they had to spread out more and quit dribbling so much. "Pass more," he said, "and dribble less." He also told them the other team's right fullback tended to come too far into the middle when the ball moved clear over to the right side, and that a good long crossing pass to Scott might just leave him unguarded enough to get an open shot. He asked how tired everyone was, so he could make a decision to substitute. Joel and Scott hardly ever came out of the games, though.

Shortly after the second half started, Scott scored a goal on a crossing pass from the right wing. As the coach had noticed, Scott was open. Scott took the pass, made two dribbles toward the goal, and made a high hard shot into the upper right corner of the goal. Score: 1–0.

The other team had a strategy conference before they kicked off. Their plan became apparent when both Scott and Joel were unfairly assaulted at every opportunity. The Decatur team had put their biggest player at center forward, right where Joel had to play defense. The big guy bowled Joel over twice. On the second try the ref gave him a yellow warning card and told him one more time and he'd be out of the game. Joel came up limping slightly, but stayed in the game. About halfway through the second half the big guy broke through with the ball and just smashed home a goal, hurting the goalie's hands as he tried to stop the ball. Score: 1–1. Scott went back and talked to Joel before the kickoff, then shouted at the goalie not to worry. "No one could have stopped that shot," he called.

The game played even for a while. There was a noticeable pickup in the other team, though. They seemed to get more confidence and play with greater enthusiasm than before. Scott recognized this situation; he'd seen it many times before. It was a critical, dangerous time for his team. They also had to play harder to take the momentum away from the other team. Scott's team was successful in keeping the ball on the other team's half of the field for a while. That helped to blunt the momentum.

Then the game seemed to get played on their defensive end—not a good sign. Scott hoped Joel would get the right opportunity to try the maneuver the speedster had suggested to his buddy in their short conversation after the tying goal was scored. The idea depended upon two things: first, the other team probably didn't know how hard Joel could really kick the ball, and, second, the right situation had to present itself. Their team used color signals shouted verbally as communication on plays to move the ball from defensive to midfield to offensive positions. "Red" had worked best today. That was a play with a lot of short passes, working the ball up the field gradually from Joel to midfield, then to Scott, with some passes in between. Scott noticed, however, that the other team had already picked up on that call and was tending to closely follow both Scott and the midfielder backward toward Joel to try and stop them. Scott suggested a different play to Joel when he called, "Red two."

Just then he saw it—the exact situation he hoped for. The ball was rolling out past the penalty area, about midway up on their half of the field.

Scott heard Joel holler, "Red two." He took a couple of steps back toward Joel, then quickly spun and started sprinting down the field. He heard Joel kick the ball with a hard smack just before crossing midfield and being offside. Scott looked to his right and noted the last defender was just turning around. Good ol' Joel, Scott thought. After six steps the ball whizzed over Scott's head. He was sprinting toward the other team's goal as fast as he could. Scott caught up with the ball with no one between himself and the goal except the keeper. Scott felt the thrill of the breakaway and sensed this was the one big chance he'd never get again in this game. He dribbled the ball four times until he was close to the goal, then he shot it hard and low to the right.

Goal! Goal! He bounced up and down and ran back to hug Joel. "What a pass! You must have really blasted it to get the ball out in front, especially with as big a lead as I had," Scott said to his friend.

Everyone on their sideline was jumping and cheering. Scott looked over at Joel and said, "Don't that feel great?"

"Sure does," agreed Joel.

Scott hadn't noticed before how many people had gathered along the sidelines to watch. Several other games on nearby fields had finished, and many people had wandered over to watch this highly touted team from East Atlanta. They stayed when they learned Bethel was holding its own against them. Scott was gratified to hear the crowd cheer when he scored. He looked again; there must be two hundred people along their sideline. What a great feeling to know his score didn't go unnoticed, but was witnessed by so many people who either knew him or had heard of him. Maybe even he and Joel would get their names in the paper! Scott would make sure Joel got the credit he deserved.

The spirit was gone from the other team as play resumed and the game ended 2–1. What a game!

Afterward, on the way home, Scott and Joel had told Joel's mom how they had planned the winning play. She had told them that showed the cleverness and resourcefulness that it sometimes takes to win. She had said they ought to remember this lesson because it would apply to other situations later on in life. Joel had asked what she meant by that. His mom had then explained that often in life when a plan is not working or you appear to be prevented from progressing toward your objective, it is necessary to devise an alternative plan and reach your goal by another route. You become a tougher person if you have experienced obstacles and been forced to work around them. "In a way, that's what has happened today," she had said. "You two found a way to beat that real good team by using your heads to make a plan that worked. You fooled them, then capitalized on your speed, Scott, and your power, Joel, to gain an advantage. When you scored, they became disheartened. It was great to watch the crumbling effect on the other team and the dramatic switch in momentum. Your team was sky-high after you got ahead. By the way Scott, have you ever been timed in the hundred-yard dash?"

"No, ma'am, but I've been timed in the forty-yard dash. My best time is 4.56 seconds, but I can regularly beat 4.6 seconds."

"That sounds fast. Is it?"

"Well, really fast times for professional football players are under 4.35 seconds. I sure hope as I get older I can bring my time down—maybe even below 4.30 seconds."

Joel had said, "Quickness is just as important as speed and you, Scott, start like a jackrabbit. I never saw anyone as quick as you are. When Scott plays touch football, he can run the length of the field without anyone touching him. He fakes left, then right, then goes left where the defender just left to cover the right."

"What?"

"In other words Mom, he fakes you out of your socks."

"Joel, you sometimes do the same thing to them in football, you just won't toot your own horn," Scott had said.

Joel answered, "Not like you, though. No one I've ever seen is as good as you."

Just then they had pulled into the driveway and conversation ended.

The next day Scott and Joel had been pleased and surprised to see their names in the paper in an article that called their game a battle between the two best young soccer teams in the state. Joel and Scott had been really excited because they were unaware they had gained such a reputation.

Joel had been beside himself. "Look at this, it says here 'Joel Adams made a sparkling lead pass to Scott Fontaine, streaking toward the opponents' goal. Displaying superior speed, Scott blasted his second score of the day past Arnold Master, the Decatur goalkeeper. These teams and players bear watching in the future.'"

Scott remembered all of this as if it had happened yesterday. Feeling very sad, he dropped off to sleep.

Outside the stadium the next day the German and Costa Rican colors were very much in evidence as people carried their flags proudly. Additionally, the clothes often reflected their allegiance. Hats were popular as well as a myriad of T-shirts depicting the hopes of the fans. Every once in a while some odd-ball would really have something crazy on, reflecting his loyalty. The air was crackling with the electricity of anticipation.

Attendance from the town of Ashton was very high. Tickets had been obtained from a variety of sources. Many people had developed good connections, and information was published early and often as to what the public should do to gain admission.

One enterprising individual had made T-shirts in the colors of Costa Rica proclaiming, "Ashton, home of the Costa Rican National team." These seemed to be plentiful all around the stadium.

The Costa Rican team knew what their chances were against the unified German team. No one had really tested the European juggernaut. In every game, they had dominated the other team. Only two teams had even scored on the Germans.

Paolo realized that the burden for the offense would fall on his shoulders. He had had a very good tournament so far. Some premonition told him, however, that this opponent was going to be more than their team could handle. All the films they had watched showed a superbly organized unit that functioned extremely well together.

Despite a valiant effort, the Costa Rican team was dominated by a much stronger German team. The final 3–0 score was a fair indicator of the difference in the two teams' strengths. The European game plan had been well thought out to thwart the strengths of the Tico players. Paolo was double-and triple-teamed throughout the contest; Alex was purposely drawn away from the intended point of attack; and Ronald Gonzales was neutralized by using the German star, Thomas Doll, mostly as a decoy.

As soon as the game ended the crowd stood in ovation while both teams waved to the faithful. The Tico players ran inside the perimeter of the field, accepting the acknowledgment of the fans for an exceptional performance throughout the four weeks.

The international press gave Costa Rica and Germany their just due. Few faulted Costa Rica for a bad game; rather, most praised Germany for having one of the best teams of all time.

The Costa Ricans were treated like royalty, even after the loss. Somehow they had risen above the contest and its results. The people of Ashton welcomed them back one more time, inviting them home as if they had just conquered the world. One last banquet was held in their honor, with many people vowing to come down to Costa Rica, at the same time being told they would be as welcome there as this team had been welcomed here.

"Aw, Quentin, you're speaking from your heart, not your mind. The United States doesn't have a chance and you know it. The odds in Great Britain show Italy a 5–1 favorite. That's unheard of in a semifinal game. Even Las Vegas shows 3–1 odds. Italy will dominate the game like they did against every other opponent, and probably worse. Don't bet with your heart, too. Remember, Italy has been here before, we haven't. Don't underestimate the notion that the United States has already exceeded everyone's expectations and will be satisfied even if we lose today. The Italians, however, would face the ridicule of the world. It would be a national tragedy, literally, if they lose."

"It's eleven against eleven on the field, Harry. While what you say is perfectly true, so too was it true in the quarter finals. Look back just a couple of days ago and the feelings were the same. Argentina was on a roll, beating a superior team from Belgium. Yet the United States not only beat Argentina, they outplayed them. Everyone attributes it to a horrendous day for team Argentina, but I'm not so sure. I think the United States is a legitimate contender. We have superior speed, perhaps better athletes, and the ball-handling skills have nearly caught up with the rest of the world. The one thing they still lack, in my opinion, is game experience. Our ability to recognize situations, to play creatively, is still a couple of notches behind the best teams. Don't worry, I'm not going to bet the farm, but I do confess I've made a small wager."

"How small?"

"Five hundred dollars."

"Five hundred dollars!" Harry exclaimed. "You've got to be crazy!"

"Its worth the risk. I'm going to enjoy it afterward, being able to say I believed in them and had the guts to bet it. Yeah, I'll probably lose, but the thought of winning conjures up such a sweet picture it's already been money well spent."

"To each his own. Am I picking you up this afternoon, or are you picking us up for the game?"

I'll come get you at about 12:45. Even with traffic, that ought to get us there in plenty of time."

The two golfing buddies finished putting their clubs away in their cars after changing shoes. This morning they played only nine holes instead of their normal round of eighteen. Quentin Aaron was still almost a scratch player, even though it had been years since he had played it seriously. Harry Weems and he were good friends who had enjoyed golfing together regularly. Harry was not as capable a player as Quentin, but he, too, could sometimes play par golf. They cut their golfing short today to allow time to get home, eat, and spend a little time with their families. The men had sons who played soccer together on the same team. As a matter-of-fact that's how they had met five years ago, when their boys had played soccer together for the first time. Their sons were now in junior high school and were delighted when their dads agreed to their request to get tickets for the semi final game so the four of them could go together. Earlier, the two boys had gone to two of the first games together and one quarter final game with their whole team. They had come home talking excitedly about the games, the players, and the action, both on the field and with the spectators.

"The flags, Dad, the flags. You should have seen all the flags waving. It was terrific," Brian said to his father after the first game.

Harry listened to his youngster, admiring the youthful exuberance with which he greeted each new experience. Brian seemed to be the type of person who absorbed life like a sponge soaks up water. He will never lack for friends or for something to do, Harry thought. He admired that quality in his son. Neither he nor his wife possessed that zest for living to the degree his son did. I wonder where he gets that, he mused.

Harry and Quentin had planned to leave two hours earlier than necessary to take their sons to the hotel where the American team was staying. The hope was that they could see, and even meet, some of the players. Sons Brian and Quentin could not only name every player on the team, including the substitutes, they also knew all of their hometowns and colleges and where, if anywhere, they played professionally, and who had scored goals and how many during this tournament. Newspapers, magazines, and TV shows had made much of the various players on the team. Brian and Quentin were sure they would recognize any they saw. Prominently displayed in front of the public were the speeds and jumping ability of Scott Fontaine and Robert Hastings. Every young soccer player in the country knew those statistics. The two lads were particularly anxious to see Scott and Robert in person.

Harry drove home without hurrying. Nowadays it seemed he was always in a hurry to get somewhere, so it was especially nice just to relax and take his time. His house was near the country club and, with only light traffic to negotiate, Harry was home in five minutes.

"Hi, Dad," was Brian's greeting as he came in the door. "Did you play well?"

"Yeah, I did OK today—even par."

"Gosh, that's good, Dad. Did you beat Mr. Aaron?"

"Yes. For a change I did. He usually beats me you know."

"Maybe that's a good omen, Dad. You coulda brought the United States team good luck."

"I don't think my golf and the soccer game today are at all related. Brian, don't get your hopes up too much. The United States is liable to get blown out of the water 4– or 5–0."

"Not a chance, Dad. Look how we handled Argentina. We're going to do the same with Italy, just you watch."

Harry smiled at his son's youthful innocence. He's at a great age to combine hopes and dreams, with no need to be practical, he smiled to himself. That'll change before long, probably when he wakes up thinking about girls.

"Italy is far stronger than Argentina or any other team for that matter, except possibly Germany—and the United States has probably been playing above its head. But that's why they play the games, Son, isn't it?"

"Yeah, I guess that's right. You watch, Dad, you're gonna be surprised. Fontaine will blow by them and score two goals. The team's gonna play well. I'm not afraid of Italy."

The four of them were surprised at the large number of people around the hotel. They were disappointed to find out that, without authorization such as a press pass, no one was allowed inside the hotel. It was impressive, however, to feel the electricity and excitement in the air. The white FIFA bus was close to the main exit and was clearly visible to all. Everyone was excitedly talking about the chances of the amazing Americans. There was much talk and fellowship among people who had been strangers before, but who, in just a few moments, became bonded through their common interest and enthusiasm for the team and the game just ahead. The talk focused on the upcoming game and everyone's thoughts on the U.S. chances to win, and on the great plays that occurred in earlier United States contests or other closely fought matches.

It wasn't long before two police cars and a van full of armed policemen drove up to the hotel entrance and positioned one car in front of the FIFA bus and one behind. The van pulled alongside the bus before it came to a stop. In addition to the normal sidearms, the cops had full riot gear: helmets with visors, billy clubs, and shotguns.

Harry turned to Quentin, "I didn't realize the extent to which they would go to prevent an incident from occurring. It's almost scary."

"This guy over here is telling me that they received some sort of a threat earlier and feel extraordinary precautions are necessary," Quentin replied.

"Is that so? My God, I hope nothing happens."

Two of the tallest and largest policemen went inside the hotel, accompanied by the captain of the police squad. The crowd closed in around the building's main exit doors. The police unwrapped a ribbon barrier supported by portable stands. They forced the crowd further away from the main doors and to a distance of more than twenty-five feet from the nearest vehicle. In a few minutes, shouts by those most able to see revealed that the players could be viewed inside the lobby. The noise level rose appreciably.

"The hair on the back of my neck is standing on end," whispered Brian.

"Mine too. This is great," replied his buddy.

The two men and their sons had found a little knoll that offered them an unobstructed view of the front doors. The boys could see over the heads of all those in front of them. As they looked around they could see that the size of the crowd had swelled to almost a thousand people.

Out of the corner of his eye Quentin noticed a commotion to his left. A swarthy, dark-haired man with large, bushy eyebrows was helping another man, who had apparently fainted, get to an open area to lie down.

A shout preempted the opening of the doors. The first one out was a photographer who turned around and backed up toward the bus. A young man in a suit, who carried a clipboard, was next. One of the managers for the team, dressed in USA sweats, led the players out of the hotel.

"Look, there's Eddie Jackson. I recognize his beard."

"He's bigger than I thought he was."

"He's six-three and one-ninety."

"There's Chase Anderson and Pu Thatcher."

"And look, there's Hastings. Boy, he just looks like he can jump to the moon, doesn't he?

After four more players exited, the largest cop stepped out, waited until all before him were aboard the bus, and led the other two cops out, bracketing Scott Fontaine. They hurried onto the bus, closely followed by Kori Gaborakov.

"There he is, Dad. There he is. That's Scott Fontaine!"

"Well, it's obvious who they were protecting the most, isn't it?" Mr. Weems remarked to his friend.

"Looks like that report we heard was accurate, and the target must have been Fontaine."

A chant of "U-S-A, U-S-A" started up and was acknowledged by the players on the bus. As the bus pulled off, it was noted that the largest cop occupied the window seat next to Scott Fontaine.

The players were leaping in the air, running around, arms held high in victory. The bench cleared immediately at the final whistle. Players hugged each other. The crowd stood in ovation for their lightly regarded but gutsy team. Giant Killers. That's what they were called. The United States had upended first Argentina and now mighty Italy. The nation of Italy, who publicly jeered Argentina and had bragged about how they would destroy the impetuous Americanos, now lay in mourning. Shamed by their team who had lost to an admittedly weaker team, no more were they the elite of the soccer world. No matter that the best pro leagues in the world were there, no matter that the best players in the world were there, they lost to the United States. The United States! No one could have imagined it! Italy, where the nation stops and shuts down tight when their team plays. The Italian newspapers scoffed at the chances of the United States team upsetting the Italian nationals. Now there would be heavy accusations. Blame will be liberally administered. Perhaps, too, some credit would go to the Americans for building up their program, for even reaching this point.

Very few fans left the stadium. The scoreboard was flashing "Victory, Victory, Victory," then "1–0, 1–0." Then, "Incredible, Victory, 1–0," "Incredible, Victory, 1–0." Then, "Do you believe in miracles!" The Italian team, some of whom had exchanged jerseys, were now circling the field. Although defeated today, they would go out recognized by the crowd as champions. The American crowd applauded them enthusiastically.

As the Italians exited the field the thunderous chant of "U-S-A, U-S-A" began. The team waved to the crowd. Some players grabbed towels and waved them around and around above their heads. Everyone was celebrating and enjoying the moment. The United States team made a circle well within the confines of the field boundaries. It seemed the team was saluting the crowd for their great support almost as much as the crowd was saluting the team for their exciting play and incredible victory.

"I know not everyone in the audience can appreciate the magnitude of this victory today," Kyle Rote, Jr. was saying. "To gain the finals of the World Cup is a special achievement, especially to have beaten a world power like Italy to do it. Jimmy, this was an outstanding game. The whole defensive unit played superbly, we controlled the transition game, and we made the few opportunities we had on offense count. Hastings, Jackson, Thatcher, Cornell Davies—they all played an extraordinary game."

"They sure did, Kyle. That shot by Matt Fong turned out to be the winner, too. He took a marvelous pass from Fontaine and nailed it from two feet off the ground, without the ball ever touching down. The keeper for Italy never had a chance."

"That pass showed good intuition and awareness. Fontaine anticipated Fong clearing just enough to drop that pass into him. There was no room for error."

"I'm still shaking from the excitement. The crowd certainly was a significant factor as the stadium was solidly behind our team."

"Just to recap, the United States has qualified for the finals against Germany on the merits of a 1–0 victory over Italy. Matt Fong scored with twenty-eight minutes left in the game on a beautiful pass from Scott Fontaine. The action started with a nice transition authored by Nick Jankowski, who took advantage of an overly aggressive Italian unit. Very few of the fans have left the stadium, even though the game ended more than ten minutes ago."

As most players agreed afterward, neither their win over Argentina nor the one tonight over Italy would have happened if the tournament had been played anywhere else except the USA.

Once in the locker room, Chase's thoughts turned to dinner and his "date" with Sheila. He hadn't thought about her since he first woke up. Like most professionals Chase had the ability to "put on his game face"— in other words, to concentrate and focus in on the game at hand, to eliminate all other thoughts and distractions. He planned, reviewed, and visualized how the game would be played. His mind reviewed instructions from the coaches, strategies to be employed. These had been committed to memory on such a level of consciousness that he would recognize immediately any special situations. Each player had been given a booklet full of diagrams and information that had to be studied and reviewed. This was the result of the techno staff's findings, as enhanced by the computer. All were familiar with the information by game time. Chase was not sure whether he was more excited by the victory or by the anticipation of seeing Sheila. He knew there were really two different levels at which he was excited and one didn't compare to the other, yet the girl was very much in his mind.

Scott talked to lots of reporters. They were interested in his pass, what the sensation felt like, his not-yet-healed ribs, and the supposed threat to kidnap him. Fong also was surrounded by reporters. He was the man in the spotlight, having scored the only goal of the game.

Scott was the recognized leader of the United States team. Much was made of his captaincy and leadership he provided the squad. Scott deflected much of that praise, saying, "Jebedoah, Pu, Eddie, Cornell, Robert, Ricky, and others deserved much of the credit, they are the heroes, they shut down Italy—cold. Their experience on a high level of play was the leveling factor."

After a while the reporters cleared out and everyone showered and dressed. Scott was tired of answering questions about his injury and about himself. The change was welcome.

The team boarded the FIFA bus to go back to the hotel where they would eat. The bus came right to the locker room, and outsiders were kept away. So, when the bus pulled away, the team was amazed to see a gauntlet of fans lining the way from the stadium. They all clapped and cheered. The trip from the stadium was about three miles or so, but the whole way along the route people acknowledged the team. When they drew close to the hotel the large crowd was again evident. Many people waved American flags in tribute. In the middle of the route the people had been at most one deep along the side of the road; near the hotel, however, they were eight to ten deep on both sides. Once again the chant "U-S-A, U-S-A" was loud and imposing. As the team disembarked, the crowd cheered loudly. From one point in the crowd a group started to chant, "We want more, we want more…" That chant never really took over the whole audience, but it was enough to have been clearly heard. Most of the team members smiled and either waived or clenched a fist high in the air.

Inside the hotel were a number of dignitaries: FIFA officials, USSF officials, town officials, the governor, and several other state VIPs, as well as family members. Red, white, and blue streamers were everywhere. Scott overheard Chase say, "It looks more like a political convention. The only thing lacking is the band."

The dining room was big. It looked like it was set up for two hundred people. At the front of the room were blue and red covered tables set aside for the team and family members, while at the back the majority of the tables were covered with white cloths. Each table had a little center-piece with a miniature red, white, and blue checked soccer ball mounted between two small American flags.

Chase said to Marty when they came into the room how neat it felt to be winners and representing your country. "I mean, we are America's team. It feels good, gooooood."

"Yep. It just doesn't get any better than this."

"Look at that sign up there." Chase pointed to a large banner on the wall. It said, "VICTORY—WE LOVE YOU—CONGRATULA-TIONS." "Somebody was planning ahead and had a lot of confidence in us—or else is a very fast painter!"

"Yep. Ain't that sumptin'. Makes you feel all tingly inside."

"The newspapers that I've read so far are really making a big deal out of how much the level of patriotism in the country has gone up since the start of the Cup. It's a happening. Not only are people being tuned into soccer more now, but they're also tuning into America. To know we are affecting the country that way really gives me goose bumps. I mean to say, what's happening across our nation is a big deal."

"Yep. Kinda scary to realize we're doing it, isn't it? Ever wonder about what the kids you grew up with are thinking? I wonder sometimes whether they are proud they've known me and tell people, or whether they are cynical or jealous and maybe run us down. What do you think?"

"Oh, I think most of them claim us. There may be a few that don't, but the majority will."

After Chase located the dining room, he came back out into the lobby area to look around for Sheila but was unable to find her. Where could she be? I wonder if she got lost in the traffic or tied up somewhere? Maybe she's not coming. Trying to look casual, Chase stood around a bit in the lobby looking for her. She was nowhere to be found. Maybe she's sick and didn't even go to the game. Boy, that'd be a shame.

Several people came up to Chase to speak to him and wish him con-gratulations. Pretty soon a small crowd had gathered around him. Several thrust something for Chase to sign into his hands. Signing autographs at first had been a novelty and made him feel like a bigshot. In the past several days, however, it had become less a positive thing and more of a burden. It was a burden he willingly suffered, though. Chase knew as a kid how he felt when he got near a sports hero. He wasn't about to refuse any kid's request for an autograph. He considered it a privilege as well as an obligation to do so.

All of a sudden she was there. It took him by surprise. She had a patient, knowing smile on her face, standing almost right in front of him—just a little to the side—with a pen and program in her hand waiting childlike for her turn to get his autograph.

"Hi," Chase said as he smiled at her.

"Hi. Nice game. You were great."

"Thanks. Glad you got here."

"I wouldn't have missed this for the world."

The small crowd soon disbursed as everyone made their way to the dining room. Chase looked more closely at Sheila. She looks as good tonight as she did last night in the dark, he thought. That was somewhat of a relief to him because too often he had been impressed with the way a girl looked the first time he met her, only to be disappointed when he saw her the second time. Sheila, true to her patriotic spirit, wore a blue pants suit with a red ruffled blouse set off by a white sash tied around her waist. She looked stunning once again.

"You look tremendous. Wow! Ready to eat?" he asked.

"Sure," Sheila answered as she took his arm.

When Chase and Sheila walked into the room some of the players took notice and nudged each other. Pretty soon they were all looking up, watching the two walk in.

"By the way, what's your last name? I didn't get it last night."

"It's Van Camp."

"Well, Sheila Van Camp, thanks for coming here."

"It's my pleasure. This is really a treat for me."

Chase looked at the players' tables and saw an eight-person table with Scott, Diana, Marty, Pu, Robert, Robert's sister, and two open seats.

"Let's sit over there," he said.

As they got to the table the four players stood. Scott looked at Marty, who had one eyebrow arched in a silent question, and smiled.

"This is Sheila Van Camp. Sheila, this is Marty Wilcox, Chase Anderson, Robert Hastings, and Cynthia Hastings—Robert's sister—and you met Scott last night. This is his lovely wife, Diana."

A light came on in his eyes as Marty said, "Chase, you smoothie! Isn't this the girl from last night at the serenade?"

"Yep. We talked for a little afterward. I thought it would be nice for her to come here tonight after all she did to organize that tribute to us last night. Wasn't that a great thing? It really psyched us up—me, anyway."

"That was fantastic, really super—the serenade last night," Pu said. "What a spectacle that was. I was turned on by that."

"I loved it," Robert intervened.

"You know what that was? It was romantic, very romantic," Cynthia added with a perceptive look.

Marty jumped in. "Yeah, I agree with Cynthia. It was romantic, but it was also patriotic. I felt all gooshy inside."

Sheila tilted her head back and laughed.

Scott watched her reaction and liked the way she handled herself.

Chase retorted. "Gooshy, what's that?"

"You know, a combination of wanting to cry and feeling very good about what was happening," Marty added.

Everyone at the table enjoyed that comment, because it accurately described how they all felt.

"Well, I found it inspiring," Chase said.

"Yeah, we can see that," Scott answered.

Sheila blushed a bit, and so did Chase, as the others all laughed at the innuendo.

The team nutritionist had specified the meal the players were to be served after the games. Every time it was steak, baked potato, broccoli, fried beans, and a green salad. Then the meal changed as another game approached. For instance, on a day when the game was in the afternoon, no one was allowed milk or milk products, pancakes, or waffles. On those days the player drank juice and ate eggs and bacon or sausage for breakfast. The meals were nutritious, tasty, and attractive, yet carefully programmed to be an asset, not a liability. The night before a game was pasta night, when the players loaded up on carbohydrates.

As the meal progressed Sheila, when prompted, told in some detail how she had thought of the serenade and what she did to organize it. They all commented on the favorable TV coverage that had made the nightly news at eleven o'clock. The serenade had wrapped up around nine-thirty. The news crews, she said, flew back to the stations in helicopters. She was told the story was shown nationwide that night and frequently throughout the whole day.

"We couldn't have had a better sendoff to go into our game with Italy. I think we won as much because of emotion and fan support as skill; maybe even more."

"The crowd was a big help. That's something to hear the roar of the crowd and to have it be so noisy. Do you guys remember some of the games we played a year ago? Ten to fifteen thousand people don't begin to give you the same feeling as seventy-five thousand do."

"Got that right, man," Robert added. "It really gives me a boost to hear the crowd. Glad we're playing at home. It'd be a lot different someplace else."

After supper was finished, the coach got up and told the team and the crowd in the room how pleased he was with their effort. "We played with intensity and discipline," he said. "I've got a favorite saying that the first five minutes of the game and the second half are the key. Well, we came out firing on all four cylinders. Those first ten minutes of this game were among the finest played by two teams that I've ever seen. We beat a great team when they were playing well. We showed the world today that United States soccer has arrived!"

The room exploded in applause. A few people in the back of the room stood up. Quickly more followed until all were standing and clapping. Diana, Sheila, and Cynthia stood just after the first ones in the back got up. They were proud of the team and it showed with an extra sparkle in their eyes. Each of the girls looked down and smiled at someone very special to them. The guys at the table looked up at them and returned the smiles.

When the ovation finished, Chase leaned over and whispered something to Robert, who told Cynthia. Chase got out of his chair and, staying low, went over to another table and told them something, then returned to his seat. As soon as the coach had finished speaking and the applause for him died down, Chase picked up his spoon and clinked it against his water glass. Marty and Robert did the same thing until they had the room's attention.

Chase stood up and announced, "I think it's appropriate to hear a few words from our captain and the high scorer of the tournament."

Scott started to decline, holding his hands up in protest. Right away some team members started chanting "captain, captain, captain." Scott realized he'd have to get up and say something. As he made his way to the microphone his mind raced as he tried to think of what to say.

"It just doesn't get any better than this."

The team led the applause.

"Today was truly a team effort; everyone played well. We stood toe to toe with one of the best teams in the world and didn't back down. We couldn't have done it, though, without the strong fan support we've had. Ya'll have been tremendous. Particularly helpful to our morale and determination was hearing the support and noise in that stadium. What ya'll did last night at the hotel was particularly moving. Every player, to a man, was bolstered by the singing." Scott looked at Sheila and smiled. "Chase exercised player's privilege to invite the young lady who organized that event here tonight. Sheila, will you please stand? This is Sheila Van Camp. Sheila was perhaps the one most responsible for our win today. Thank you, Sheila, from all of us."

Sheila stood, but blushed heavily at all the attention. Scott had to pause several seconds to allow the clapping to die down after he asked her to stand. Several players clapped as much at how pretty she was tonight as much as for her contribution to last night's serenade.

Chase made sure that he got her phone number and address before the evening ended. Scott did him one better, though, by going to the president of the USSF and requesting a ticket for the final game as well as plane passage with the soccer federation officials in light of her extraordinary contribution to the success of the team. He was surprised a little when Mr. Priestaps granted his request. Scott told Chase and Sheila the good news, and he was rewarded by a hug from Sheila and a strong handshake from Chase.

"Thanks. Thanks a lot."

"Oh, I know someone in Los Angeles. I'll just stay with my friends," she gushed. "That will work out fine. Thanks."

Kori made sure the team got out of there at a decent hour so they wouldn't get overly tired. They had two days of rest before the finals, but it wouldn't do for them to get exhausted tonight.

CHAPTER 18

S cott, there's someone here who wants to talk with you. I think it's a team agent. You want Sam with you?"

"Yeah, if that's what you think he is."

As the success of the team produced victories it also created a significant demand for a legal representative to serve as the bargaining agent for the USSF, because any contracts signed by a player had to consider the release of the player by the United States Soccer Federation. The values of those contracts had increased sixfold in most cases, with some, like Scott's and Robert's, increasing twenty times or more.

Scott had already been approached by seven teams: two from the Italian league, two from Germany, one from Brazil, one from Spain, and one from England. All had made a pitch for his playing services and all had offered attractive money. Scott wisely had not committed himself earlier, and as the tournament continued his stock rose in value—dramatically.

He met Sam outside the conference room and was mildly surprised to see two business-attired gentlemen already seated inside the room.

"Mr. Fontaine? I'm Carlo Venturi and this is Mr. Jean-Franco Boscotti. We are from the Italian leagues, but represent no particular team."

"How do you do? This is Mr. Sam Case. He will represent the USSF."

"You boys keep a pretty tight security. We were frisked three times and had to show credentials twice. They kept us in here for the past half hour while they checked out our story and our references."

"We've had to be careful," Sam answered.

"Mr. Fontaine, Mr. Case, we will come right to the point. We represent the entire Italian professional system. We want you in our first-division soccer league and are prepared to deal in those terms. We have been given a good bit of latitude to negotiate, as most of our teams have demonstrated an interest in having you. Instead of having individual teams keep approaching you, we've decided a better tactic would be to approach you as a league, then later decide on the team. If I'm not wrong I believe two of our teams already have made contact. Is that correct?"

"Yes, that's true."

"And I believe that was prior to your team defeating Italy. Is that not correct?"

"Yes, sir."

"After you beat us we consulted as a group to develop this strategy. You have been remarkably resilient to some very good offers. I suspect others, too, have approached you. No, that's not fair, I know that to be true. You have been wise to wait. Your fortunes continue to rise with each surprise of the tournament. What we want to accomplish today, Mr. Fontaine, is to establish a base guarantee on an offer that, depending on actual team offers, can only be bettered by what finally comes out in the bidding process. Mr. Case, has the USSF set a selling price for Mr. Fontaine's contract?"

"Yes, sir, we have."

"Can you reveal that at this time?"

"Yes, I can. The sales price is $5.6 million."

Scott involuntarily jerked, violating his self-imposed control during a negotiating session.

"The Federation met late into the night after the celebrating ended, for the purpose of reviewing the values of those players whose contacts had not yet been sold. You're after our number-one man," Case continued.

Mr. Venturi looked over at Mr. Boscotti, who nodded slightly.

"OK, we will agree to pay that, although it is beyond what we were authorized. However, I told you we have been given some latitudes. For you, Mr. Fontaine, we can offer you $4 million a year as a minimum; it could possibly be higher, but maybe that's all. There is a three-year guarantee plus use of a vehicle. Housing will be provided, commensurate with your standard of living, of course. We will also provide language instruction for you and your wife, as much as you can handle. You see, we want you in our league."

Scott could tell Sam was delighted. He knew they had set a huge figure on himself, observing the considerable interest so many had in him. They weren't sure they would get it, but it was their asking price. The offer from these men was substantially more than any other he had received, although he had to figure that those offers would be upped after his play in the semifinals.

"You have made a generous offer that should be earnestly considered. Let me tell you where I'm at. I like Italy. I really enjoyed my travels within your country. I won't make a decision until I talk with my wife, and I won't sign until after the finals. However, if you will provide a signed contract for me to review, I will not sign with anyone else without giving you every opportunity to match a better offer, if one comes in. And, I won't nickel-and-dime you. If we decide Italy is where we want to play, only a substantially higher offer would be brought back to the table. I guess I'm saying you've made a very fair, even generous, offer. I'm favorably inclined and will treat you right, yet without closing all the doors to other offers. Sam, does the USSF agree to hold that price, no matter what comes about in the next few days?"

"Yes, we will sign a contingency contract with them, setting the price."

"May we plan to meet with you after the game finishes?"

"Yes, of course. That would be fine."

Scott called Diana to tell her the good news.

"Oh, Scott, that would be wonderful to live in Italy for a few years. I can't understand them throwing good money away like that, but heck, that's terrific. We're rich!"

"Yep. Now I can afford to support you in the style to which you've been accustomed. I'm sure I'm going to sign with them; we may not have anything to say about choice of city, though."

"That's OK. I'll go where you go."

"I love you. I love you more every day."

"I love you, too. Am I going to see you tonight?"

"Yes. You have to come to the hotel, though. The team has to stay together."

Scott was glad that his parents and sisters, Diana, Andy, and their parents would be able to come to the game in Los Angeles. Surprisingly, his mother told him Susie was coming also. She had called to congratulate them on Scott's outstanding performance after the game with Italy and mentioned she was currently living in Oxnard, California. Mrs. Fontaine had asked her if she wanted to go, and that she was sure she could get an extra ticket. Susie said yes. Mrs. Fontaine was glad, knowing the long trek back to a normal life with which Susie was still struggling. Scott was happy to hear the news.

In the locker room beneath the stadium, the United States team was finishing changing into uniforms and getting pre-game treatments and tapings from the medical staff. Scott's side still needed to be taped from the injury incurred against the CIS team, when his legs were taken out from under him as he jumped. He winced as the doctor gingerly pressed against his side.

"You're gonna continue to be bothered by that, I'm afraid. At least two ribs are cracked. The X-ray was not definite on the third, but it also may be cracked. How much does it hurt to breathe when you're out there running?"

"It hurts to get a deep breath. Shallow breathing isn't so bad. It's nothing I can't put up with for one more game, Doc. Thanks for fixing me up. The taping makes a difference in the level of pain I feel."

"Cracked ribs are a painful injury, especially in soccer and basketball, where there is so much running."

"Yeah. A good tennis match, too."

"I can't give you what we used to use to help the pain. When they drug-test you it would show up as a bad element."

"That's OK, Doc. I can endure it for ninety minutes. Plus I have this modified flak jacket the techno team designed. This rubber material is hard enough to absorb and dissipate a blow, yet not so hard as to be disqualified by the officials. It's made of a dense foam."

"I would still try to avoid any hard knocks. You'll feel an elbow regardless of that flak jacket."

Scott grinned. "The papers have made a big deal of my ribs, so the Germans certainly are going to test it. My job is not to let them know it hurts. If they see that it's having an effect, it will just be worse."

"We're waiting on you, boss man."

It was Robert who had come to the door of the training room. The rest of the team was already gathered in the main locker area.

Scott gingerly slipped into his flak jacket and tightened the Velcro straps. Then he put his shirt on over the jacket and tucked it into his shorts. He was ready.

The atmosphere was unlike that of any other game. The team knew there was nothing beyond today. None of them would ever play a more important game. They had already accomplished far more than had been expected, yet reaching the finals was not enough. Kori was adamant that the German team could be beaten. The techno team had worked around the clock since the semifinal with Italy, preparing strategies, evaluating weaknesses, and building defense mechanisms that would work against the juggernaut they were to face.

Kori stood up. "Gentlemen, I am very proud to be associated with this team, with the United States, and with you as individuals. We have accomplished much. Our work is not yet over. All my life I have dreamed of winning this game. We have a chance to do it today. Our goal was not to reach the second phase, not to reach the semifinals, or the finals. Our goal has been to *win the championship*. You must concentrate on all that we have worked on. All your training, all your experience, all your talents must be focused today. We have the golden opportunity to turn the soccer world upside down. Everyone of you will reap enormous financial benefits when we win. Endorsements will come so fast you won't have time to spend the money you'll make. Most important of all, this one's for your-selves, your families, and for your country, the United States of America."

On cue, the theme from *Rocky* played over the locker room sound sys-tem. As if programmed, the players reacted with electrifying energy. All those *Rocky* movies the coach made them watch, all the time the music was played at practice, had instilled in them an involuntary reaction that pumped adrenaline through their bodies.

As the cheering crescendoed and the players were on their feet, psy-ched up, Scott got them huddled close together, hands clasped together in the center. He led them for the last time in prayer asking God for His blessing, a game free of injury, and that they do their best.

Scott got to the exit first and, one by one, shook everyone's hand. Some reached up and messed his hair or patted him on the shoulder as they went by. As they passed beneath the doorway, most reached up and touched the sign above that said, "For The Glory." The team waited for him to catch up before they went out into the sunlight.

As usual, the substitutes, assistant coaches, and medical people went out first. The crowd noise rose perceptively.

First, the team from Germany was introduced. From the German sup-porters, flags waved and the fans stood and loudly cheered; their support was surprisingly strong.

Then one by one the Americans heard their names announced.

Strategically, and because he was the captain, Scott was the last player. Scott waved to the crowd as the roar for him was deafening. As he trotted out to the center of the field he was amazed at all the United States flags being waved.

"They've certainly caught on to the flag bit, haven't they?" he said to Chase when all the hand-slapping finished.

"Yep, don't ya just love it?"

"Yep. This is the big time."

The crowd again went crazy for Kori Gaborakov, the miracle worker, as the papers had been calling him.

Scott's eyes misted over when the national anthem was played. He found himself at times singing louder than usual and at times unable to sing at all. He fingered the captain's arm band and the one underneath.

"This is for you, Joel."

Final Game U.S.—Germany

The Place: The Rose Bowl. Capacity: 102,000

At Cleopatra's Palace: Odds were placed at 3–1, Germany. The betting was especially heavy, big money being placed both ways.

"Well, Jimmy, this is the big one," Kyle Rote, Jr. bubbled at the Rose Bowl before the last game between Germany and the United States. Who would have guessed we would be in this position?"

"There aren't ten people in the world who predicted this event. Can you imagine? First the women win the very first world championship over in China, and now here we are playing for the men's championship."

"The American women were favored, though. It's almost the exact opposite here. Some had us ranked dead last of the twenty-four teams."

"This promises to be an exciting game. The question is, can Kori work his magic one more time?"

"We'll soon find out. Here we go."

Germany won the toss and elected to kick off. They looked confident and imposing.

Things didn't seem to be going right. Even at the outset the American team seemed disjointed against the European powerhouse. Bad passes resulted in loss of possession, and individuals were unable to control opponents one on one.

"Kyle, I don't like at all how this is going. We are not playing our usual game."

"I think the team is tight. They need to loosen up a bit and play better if we're going to stay in this game."

"The Germans are confident and are playing dominating soccer."

"Not only are they passing well, Jimmy, the other players are moving aggressively without the ball, creating effective offensive opportunities."

Scott was frustrated. He had only touched the ball twice. The team had been unable to move the ball upfield without it being taken away. Because the team couldn't control the possession, Scott moved Chase Anderson and Matt Fong deeper on defense to try to create a more secure guard. This was something Kori had directed be done if this situation arose. The two outside midfielders, Marty and Jebedoah, backed up to help the defense form a blockade loosely encircling the goal area.

Nick Jankowski was the one bright spot on the whole team. It would be his stellar play around which the team regrouped. He seemed to always be in the right spot, intercepting passes and thwarting the dangerous German machine.

Scott was impressed with the other team. Not only could they handle the ball well, but their passing was more creative and they moved extremely well, anticipating openings and passes from their teammates. Scott felt a difference between this caliber of play and the rest of those they faced. Yet he realized it was exactly what they had viewed on film time and time again.

Nothing is substantially different except we are feeling it instead of seeing it, Scott realized.

At that moment Klinsmann made a beautiful loping pass to Franz Bauer, who got clear and near enough to the goal that he headed it in. Result: 1–0, unified Germany.

Scott took the opportunity to gather everyone together while play was stopped.

"Guys, let me tell you what I just now have recognized. We have each been intimidated without knowing it—me, too. The reason is we are feeling their power and their skill out here; we're not just watching it on the screen. What we have to do is realize we too have some ability and to play our own game. Rely on Coach Kori and the information from the techno group. It's gotten us this far. Play these guys hard and tough, but play them *our* way. Let's go. Let's change right now."

"Well, the advantage goes to the favorites," Kyle informed the viewers.

"Sometimes teams can be outplayed tremendously and hold the game scoreless. Argentina did that in the final four years ago through three-quarters of the game. This is going to make it that much tougher."

"And this comes against, arguably, the best team ever assembled," Jimmy added. "We have to recognize that no team in this tournament has come within one goal of tying this German group. In every game, they have had at least a two-goal margin."

"That's extraordinary in a tournament like this."

At Cleopatra's Palace, odds were changed to 9–1, Germans.

Play resumed, with improved results. The Americans moved the ball with more confidence and were able to push upfield, deep into enemy territory.

"I see a change. The United States has begun settling down. This looks better."

"Right, Jimmy, sometimes the first score breaks the ice and gets everyone into the game. This looks more normal."

Scott felt a huge cloud lifting from over the team. It was as if they could see more clearly. They had cast off the fog of uncertainty and the darkness of intimidation. Now we can play our game, he thought.

And play they did. The contest became an even match, with opportunities created at both ends. Neither team could score.

"The crowd has gotten into this and they are seeing a really good match now," Kyle said excitedly.

"Yes, we are playing well. You can tell we have earned the respect of the other team's players."

Scott was starting to take a good bit more physical punishment now that he was more involved in the action. Four or five times someone had hit him in the side. Twice his arm had been down to absorb the blow, but the other times had been painful. His breathing became a little more labored.

The Germans mounted an attack, pressing inward. The action was furious in front of Cornell. Twice the ball was cleared just before a shot could be taken. Then the right forward worked free and shot hard and high to the right. Cornell dove and tipped it out and over the crossbar.

Corner kick, Germany.

"Thus far we've been effective on defending corner kicks. Robert Hastings has proven truly to be an asset in that anything within reach has been controlled by him."

"Here comes the kick, it's out a little from the mouth of the goal. Oh no! Goal! Goal scored by the Germans on a nice header into the open area. Jimmy, Robert was no factor on that one."

"No, he wasn't. The Germans boxed him out or prevented him from getting involved somehow. Look, he's limping!"

"Damn it, Ref," Robert was complaining loudly down on the field. "He stood on my foot to prevent me from jumping!" Robert shouted angrily as he pointed to number sixteen of the opponents. "He fouled me! Call something."

"What happened, Robert? I saw you shouting at the ref," Scott called.

"Number sixteen purposely tromped on my foot to keep me from jumping as the guy on my other side boxed me in toward him. They knew the ball would go over my head. They planned that play. The ref wouldn't call it."

"He's not going to call that kind of play. You have to use your hands more to keep them away. Be more physical. We have to start taking more chances. That includes provoking cards against us."

Scott passed the word about what happened to Robert and that they had to play with more assertiveness, even at the risk of getting carded by pushing to the physical limit.

At Cleopatra's Palace, odds were now 60–1, Germany

"Oh boy. 2–0. Kyle, not good at all."

"No. A deficit of two is going to be awfully tough. While Germany is known for their high-powered offense, no one yet has scored more than one goal on them in the entire tournament. I don't like our situation at all. Twelve minutes to go in the first half. It would mean everything to us if we could get one score back before half-time. Kori is a genius at making adjustments at half-time. He's the Joe Paterno equivalent in soccer."

It was quickly apparent that the game had gotten more physical. Mid-air collisions became more violent; frequently, a player was slow to get up from such an encounter. The United States was more than holding its own as they made several penetrations into the goal area. Scott always found himself surrounded by defenders, whether he had the ball or not. As a result he had only taken two off-balance shots thus far in the game.

Once again the United States forced play deep into opposition territory as Marty made a nifty exchange with Chase and took the ball up the right side.

"Wilcox makes a great move on a give-and-go as he leads the defender by half a step. He jukes around to clear a pass and crosses the ball to the middle," Kyle relayed to the listeners.

Scott could see the ball coming. He knew if he could get to it first he stood a good chance of getting a clean head shot. Just as he leaped for the ball, someone from the other team put his head into Scott's side. The air exploded out of his lungs as the ball went harmlessly overhead. Scott's vision went black before he hit the ground.

"The ball goes over everyone's head. Wait, Fontaine is down! He's on the ground. The ball is coming fast up the field. The Germans have a five-on-four play here. Fontaine's still down. Two quick passes and a shot—caught by Cornell Davies! He boots the ball clear up into the side stands, stopping play for the United States."

"Fontaine hasn't moved. The United States medical staff has gone onto the field."

"They're moving fast. They were already up the sideline waiting their chance."

"Listen to the crowd. They don't like having their star player down."

"Neither does the team. There's two shoving matches going on right now. Here comes the referee to break them up. No cards shown."

"Kyle, Cornell also sent a message to the referee by blasting that ball up into the stands."

"Yeah, he sent it a long way."

"They're administering aid to Fontaine. It looks to me like it's his side."

"I'm sure he's been worked over all game. There's six minutes to go in the half. It's probable that if Scott can't continue now, Kori will wait until half-time to see if they can get him back into action."

"I think they've signaled for a stretcher. Yes, here comes one now."

"I can hardly breathe, Doc. I can't catch my breath," Scott whispered.

"We're going to take you into the locker room and see what we can do for you. Only a couple of minutes till half."

The players gathered around Scott as he was lifted onto the stretcher.

He gave them a weak thumbs-up sign as he was carried off the field.

"Kori signaled ten men. They will go on without Scott," Kyle announced.

When the field was clear, play resumed with a German throw-in from the sideline. In a gesture of fair play, the German team retreated to midfield while their player threw the ball back to Cornell.

Kyle explained to the viewers why that was done. "The reason Cornell kicked the ball out of bounds was to stop play so the medical attendants could come onto the field for Scott. The Germans simply returned possession to the Americans."

As the United States brought the ball up the field, the Germans waited. Several probes were made but were blunted by the Europeans. The team made advances toward the goal by carefully working the ball back and forth. They were in a dilemma, not wanting to give up possession when they were undermanned, but needing desperately to score. Chase used another player to pick his man off and got free just inside the penalty box. Jebedoah Wright got a pass to him and, as players converged, he shot.

The German goalkeeper made a nice diving save, preventing the score. At once the Germans attacked.

The United States regrouped defensively and went into a preventative posture, while the Germans worked the ball around the perimeter. Twice passes into the middle were broken up, only to have the visitors retain control.

Eddie watched for his chance. The midfielder who had knocked Scott out of the game was over on his side. Eddie would find a way to make him regret taking the captain out. Then it came. Someone passed the ball toward his mark, even as Eddie made his move. He had to reach him before the ball crossed the line into the penalty box.

That's just right, he thought.

Just before the ball got there waist high, Eddie went in, cleats up. As he deflected the ball away, he followed through into the groin of his target. The intended result occurred as revenge was carried out.

The side linesman raised his flag and caught the eye of the referee, who was partially shielded from the play.

Eddie expected a foul to be called, so he was not surprised at the whistle. He knew he had jumped into the man.

The referee, having stopped play, ran over to the linesman. The German lay on the ground.

"That's the bastard that got Scott," Eddie told Nick.

"That might get you a card," Nick replied.

"I know, but I've got one to give."

"The referee has made a decision," Kyle indicated. "It's going to be a yellow card for Jackson. I think Eddie knew that was coming. It could have been a red card in view of the fact that Eddie's action was clearly retribution."

"Maybe the fact we are already playing one short and Scott was laid low on a questionable play had a factor in his deciding just a yellow card," Jimmy added.

Just then the referee pointed toward the penalty spot, indicating a penalty kick—a free kick—with only the goalkeeper to defend.

The United States players went crazy.

"That was outside of the box. Not inside!"

"That shouldn't be a penalty kick!"

"You're full of crap, Ref! Open your eyes!"

The players crowded in on the referee, arguing in vain.

"Oh, that was a bum call. I saw it clearly on this side of the penalty area. Kyle, the player fell into it afterward."

"The linesman is the one who made the decision because he saw the play. His position was back, closer to the end line. He couldn't tell, yet that's exactly what they've called. I'm afraid there's nothing that can be done to change his decision. Penalty kick it will be."

"And look, the referee's giving another yellow card to someone for arguing. It's Jankowski. Nick Jankowski."

When the referee from Brazil got everything settled down, Jergen Klinsmann lined up to kick the ball.

Cornell positioned himself on the line and thought through the percentages for Klinsmann.

Sixty-two percent he goes left, and thirty-eight he goes right, he remembered. I'll have to watch how he plants his left foot, and make a guess. Hope he goes with the percentages.

Cornell watched Jergen come to the ball.

Left, he judged.

As he dove left the ball went right, into the net.

"Uh-oh. Three nothing. I dunno, Kyle. What are your thoughts?"

"Pretty tough from here. Realistically, we've got to keep this from being a blowout. I don't see much chance to come back from where we are now. We are playing a good game. The action has been about even ever since they scored that first goal."

⚽

At Cleopatra's Palace, odds shot up—300 to 1, Germany. Then the odds were raised to 650 to 1 to counteract the big money being placed on the European team.

The United States kicked off again and, using conservative ball control, ran out the clock.

The players were mad and frustrated at playing a good game, yet being behind 3–0—not to mention having to play without their captain. Scott was not in the locker room when the team got there. He had been taken to an area within the stadium where there was an X-ray machine.

Kori addressed the group.

"Gentlemen, we now have an uphill battle ahead of us. Do you remember we set as our goal winning this game? It can be done and I'm going to tell you how. I've been on the phone with our techno group, and they have identified a major weakness in their defense that has never been exploited by any other team. We have run simulations, I'm told, and two out of three times it works."

The coach went on to explain the strategy and then to make observations about the defense alignments he wanted them to use.

When he finished, Pu asked, "What about Scott?"

"I don't know anything yet. The doctor has him in X-ray. We won't know until they get back."

"What if he can't play?" Chase spoke up.

"Then we will substitute. Until then we wait. I owe the man that much. *You* owe the man that much. I won't take his chance away from him."

Diana had watched in horror as they carted Scott off the field on a stretcher.

"I'm going to him," she announced to her family, Scott's family, and the couple of friends who were with them.

"I'll go with you, Diana," Andy said.

So the two of them left the stands to go down under. When they got to the locker room entrance, the guard said the doctor had taken him to X-ray.

"Where's that?"

"Go this way about sixty or seventy yards. On your left you'll see the main first-aid station. That's where he is."

The two took off running. Before they got to the first-aid station the crowd noise told them something had happened, something not good.

"Must be a bad call. Listen to the jeers," Andy told his sister.

"Great, just what we need."

When they arrived, the guards at the door wouldn't let them in.

"Sorry, no one goes in. Orders."

Shortly the door opened and one of the trainers came out.

"How's Scott? How's Scott?"

"They're developing the X-ray now. He's hurting a good bit and can't breathe deeply. He got whacked pretty good in his bad side. Excuse me."

"Wait, wait. Help us get in to see Scott. It might do some good."

"OK. Guard, this is Scott's wife. Let them in, please."

"Scott, Scott, are you all right? I couldn't bear to see you on the ground and then being carried off."

"It sure hurts. Especially when I breathe."

"Then don't breathe," Andy added helpfully as he grinned.

The doctor came out of the dark room with one large X-ray picture in each hand. He noticed Diana and Andy next to Scott. Diana was holding her husband's hand.

"Well, Scott, you've got one more cracked rib now. You're getting quite a collection."

"Can I play again?"

"There's no danger of you causing great internal injuries just by playing. But if someone were to hit you hard there, they could push the rib bone enough to puncture your lung."

"Oh, Scott," Diana pleaded.

"How bad's a punctured lung?"

"Not too good. If that happened you sure couldn't play and you'd be out of commission for close to a year."

"But I could recover?"

"Yes."

"Then let's try it."

"OK. I'll spray freeze solution on it and on the flak jacket. I'll soak it good. The trainer went to get some stiff plastic splints we'll tape onto the flak jacket to try to prevent more damage. I'll put cotton over those so they're legal."

"Go get them, Big Boy. We need some scores," Andy said as he tousled Scott's hair.

"I love you, Scott," Diana added.

"I love you, too, Honey. Need a kiss, though."

"Silly." She kissed him twice. "Good luck."

"You guys can beat them. I know you can," Andy said.

Scott put his shirt on just as the trainer came back through the door.

"Got them." The trainer held up the four ivory-colored plastic strips. "By the way, it's three—nothing. They got it on a penalty kick. Eddie got the guy back. Their guy is out of the game. They substituted for him."

"Eddie?" Scott questioned.

"Got a yellow card is all. Nick, too, when the referee ruled it was a penalty kick. Everyone thought it happened outside the box."

"Hurry up, half-time's about over."

"Jimmy, our information sources say Scott's playing the second half is still very much in question. As soon as they take the field, we'll know."

"Yes, either Scott's there or someone else will be. My guess is it'll be Gates."

"Well, there they go. I don't see Fontaine's number. Wait: six, seven, eight, nine, ten. There's only ten. That must mean he's going to play but he's not ready yet or else they don't know."

"See if we can find out, Jimmy."

The game started ten against eleven. The play continued to be physical yet controlled, as if the score had been settled; an eye for an eye. The ball moved up and down the field, with possession changing several times.

"Kyle, we've got our response. Scott's broken another rib, but the doctor has given the OK for him to come back. He's getting ready."

"The team is playing surprisingly well down a man. We've got the ball deep in their territory. Anderson passes back to Marty Wilcox, over to Wright. Oh, good run! Anderson cuts past Wright, who leads him nicely. Anderson makes a nice move to avoid the sweeper. He scores! He scores! Listen to the crowd."

"Short-handed we scored! Wow! That's really something. Nifty play by the United States."

"That's the old post play. Pass to the pivot man and cut for the goal. Same as the common tactic in basketball."

The last bits of tape were being applied to Scott's armor when the roar went up. Scott jerked involuntarily when the stands vibrated from the noise level.

"We must have scored. Am I out?"

"I'm told Kori was holding it open."

"We scored down a man? Hurry."

"Scott, do it for Joel," Diana encouraged.

"For Joel and for you," he answered.

As soon as the stays were covered and taped, Scott threw on his shirt and ran out of the first-aid room. Diana and Andy followed him.

Play had already restarted when Scott burst out of the tunnel. When the crowd saw him, a crescendo built to thunderous proportions. Flags that had been put down were once again waved. Fans stomped in rhythm on the floors of the stadium stands.

At Cleopatra's Palace, odds fell to 95–1.

Scott could see the striker position was not filled. He looked up at the stadium clock to see 6:28 showing. Scott was aware of the crowd reaction as he trotted over to the bench. Coach Kori caught him up on half-time developments and projected strategies.

"How do you feel?"

"It hurts, but I'll make it."

"OK. Go on."

Scott reported to the FIFA official at midfield. He raised the marker indicating a substitute. When the ball went out, last touched by a German, Scott was waved into the game. The crowd was back into it.

The play stayed even, with both sides taking shots, but nothing dangerous. The morale of the Americans was boosted higher with the sight of their captain in the fray.

As Scott got the chance, he told Marty, Nick, Pu, and Eddie to try to pass him the ball as he came back to it to help move it up the field. The strategy worked. The United States had an easier time getting the ball into the front half of the field.

Of course, thought Scott, It helps to have eleven men on the field.

Scott and the team didn't make the maneuver every time, but when it was used Scott always called out, "Red two" or "Red three." Scott discovered his running was less encumbered than he thought. At no time, however, had he sprinted all out. In fact, he was careful to make it look worse than it was.

"Take advantage of what's given you," his coach had taught them.

Both Pu and Nick had the leg to make it work from deep in their end of the field. Of course, Marty or Jebedoah could easily work it from further up the field. Scott was careful and calculating to show pain.

"Once again the United States is playing its game. The Germans are by no means dominating possession. It does look, however, that Scott Fontaine is not at full speed. It's obvious he's hurting," Kyle announced to the audience.

One more time to set it up, thought Scott. When Pu got the ball Scott came back and Pu made a perfect pass to him. Scott dished it off to Chase, who moved it up the field. Scott turned and trailed the play. Chase gave it back to Scott and sprinted for the goal. Scott timed it right and lofted a pass to Chase, who, on one bounce, blasted a shot toward goal. The goalkeeper made a nice save; it was close.

On the way back down Scott explained his strategy to Pu and Nick and Marty. Nick said he would tell Eddie and Jebedoah.

The Germans almost scored again when a long shot soared above the corner of the goal. Several minutes passed and the Germans continued to press offensively.

Then it came. The ball kicked out toward Pu. Scott started back and hollered, "Red two." When Pu was three steps from the ball Scott whirled and started upfield. Immediately he knew it was a good move. He could see the look of surprise on the faces of the two defenders in front of him. One he passed, the other turned in time to stay even.

Scott couldn't hear Pu kick the ball—too much crowd noise. But when the roar came from the crowd, he knew.

Pu laid the ball well out in front.

"He must have kicked it two thirds the length of the field," Kyle said in wonder.

Scott now had one step on the German. He could feel the enemy grab at his shirt. Scott yanked the shirt out of his grasp and took off. The level of sound was deafening. Incredible! It engulfed everything.

The goalkeeper made a bad decision. He waited too late to come out. Scott got to the ball first, dribbled to the left, and around the charging keeper, who dove for his feet. Scott jumped, clearing the keeper's flailing arms, and dribbled the ball into the goal.

Pandemonium set in! The fans were on fire.

"What a play, what a play!" screamed Kyle.

Kori and the United States bench were jumping up and down. The score stood at three to two.

———⚽———

At Cleopatra's Palace the odds were lowered to 2–1, Germany. There were fourteen minutes to go in the game.

The happiness of making the goal didn't block out his body protest. Scott ran a few steps in triumph before he doubled over in great pain. He couldn't catch enough air. His teammates realized this before they aggravated the injury by celebrating.

"Oh boy. We've got us a humdinger now. The crowd is really into it. Look at those flags. Listen!" Kyle cheered.

The Germans came back, pressing for a shot. The defense held. Cornell gathered in the weak shot and threw it out to Eddie, who passed it upfield to an open Jebedoah. Once again the United States was on the attack. Scott and Chase exchanged places. The midfielders moved in.

Nine fifty-four to go in the game.

Scott passed to Chase at the post and cut for the goal. Chase deflected the ball back to Scott, charging hard. Two men were on him quickly, so Scott took a long shot. It looked good—upper left corner. But the ball curved and hit off the left post, and the Germans kicked it clear.

A short-lived shout from the crowd said it all. Close, but not good enough.

Once again the Americans came storming back. The visitors collapsed their defense, trying to close down the passing lanes. Short, quick passing opened enough of a crack to permit effective attacking.

"Fong shoots. Oh! It's deflected over the end line. Corner kick— United States."

"Look, Kyle, the United States is bringing up the whole defense— everyone, even the goalkeeper. The whole crowd is standing."

"Yes, with two and three-quarters minutes to play, you don't worry about defense. You've got to score."

"You can bet that ball boy is hurrying. He knows what's at stake."

"Time continues to run even when the ball goes out of bounds."

"Matt Fong will take it. He's the shortest."

"And he has nice placement," Kyle added. "Everyone is in place, here it goes. A tie sends this into overtime. The kick is in the air, what a kick! A dozen go up for the ball. There's Robert! The keeper has it! Nice shot, but no goal. Uh oh, the keeper kicked a long one. One German is clear, he's out in front! It's Bauer. The ball is coming down beyond midfield. Everyone is tearing back up the field. Look at Fontaine go! He's gotta catch him. The ball bounces, the German heads it further forward. He's gonna shoot it! Fontaine slides. He's kicked it away! Pu Thatcher is there to get it. Now the whole field is reversing. The American goalie stays up on offense."

"No question. The pressure is all-out now. They're going for broke," Jimmy announced.

"Anderson sets up at post. Quick, rapid passes. Fong cuts in, but no one can get the ball to him. He's back out. They take the ball to the side. Wright's got it. Marty passes to Fontaine, back to Wright. Marty shoots. Blocked by the Germans! Fontaine's got it again. He crosses the ball. It's over everyone's head. Nick Jankowski has it. He shoots! The ball hits the crossbar and bounces out and to the other side. Marty's going to get to it. He stepped over it. Fontaine kicks. The goalie dives out and punches the ball. Robert collects it, turns it over to Nick. Into Anderson. He turns and fires. Blocked! Jackson kicks. Blocked again! The Americans regroup and close in."

"In the air, in the air. Use Robert!" Kori screamed. "Less than thirty seconds. Thirty seconds!"

"Something has to give here, Kyle. Only seconds left."

"Anderson lays it off to Wilcox, back to Anderson. Fontaine cuts, good pass. He nails it. The keeper deflects it outside on a dive. Corner kick. All the ball boys are at this end of the field. Fong is running over to the corner. The crowd is standing. Three to two; we gotta score!"

"It's a great kick," Jimmy interuppted. "Hastings goes up for the head. What a shot! Oh! Headed back out by one of the three Germans positioned on the goal line next to the keeper. It caroms out toward O'Shay. He shoots! Oh! The ball hit the crossbar and kicked out to the other side. Toward Fontaine. He's open!"

Scott saw it coming. He also saw Robert was well positioned on the far side. The keeper was to the near side. Best chance—to Robert.

Voice communication was impossible. The stadium crowd, as one, was screaming.

Two steps, one. The pass was perfect.

"The referee is signaling time's up! No! It doesn't count! Robert Hastings heads the ball into the net just after time expired. It doesn't count! The game is over!" An emotional Kyle grasped for control.

"The game's over! The referee has signaled. Two seconds too late!"

"No one can hear his whistle," Jimmy shouted.

It can't be over, it can't be! A little more time. Please, somehow. A mistake. Give us a little more time, Scott lamented.

The fact that the game had ended and there was nothing that would change hadn't registered yet. Before reality sets in, there is hope, a wish that it were different without realizing it's not possible. This was Scott's mindset just after the final whistle blew. It took fifteen or twenty seconds before acceptance and resignation set in. Only at that time would he acknowledge defeat and accept what was. Only then could he shake the hands of the opponents and accept compliments offered by them. Even so, he was halfway through shaking hands before he could say anything. Then he told each one he shook hands with, "Great game, good game."

Franz Bauer came up to him and said simply, "Change?" as he took off his shirt.

Scott said, "Yeah, I'd like that."

"You ver gut, man. Gut game," Franz added.

"Thanks, you too. Tremendous."

Scott stood for a minute in the middle of the field to think about the opportunities missed, about the mistakes he had made, and about decisions he wished he could have made differently. He also felt sorry for his teammates; they had come so far, worked so hard, sacrificed so much.

So have I, he reminded himself as his thoughts turned inward. He was oblivious to his surroundings, not seeing, not hearing, not feeling. So it was with a jolt that he felt someone grab his arm. It was Robert.

"C'mon, man, we need you."

The United States team was grouping together and facing the crowd where there was the highest concentration of United States flags and clapping their hands above their heads, waving to the crowd, claiming their tribute for so much accomplished and so valiant an effort. The crowd responded vociferously. Loudly, gustily, and happily, the crowd cheered and clapped for their team. This was *their* team. The players, the team, represented a portion of each person in the stands. The spirit and energy of the hundred thousand or more fans were out there, too, in the bodies of those players. And they couldn't have been more proud of them at this moment. As one they all stood on their feet in tribute to both teams and the great game they had witnessed.

Preparations were being made to conduct the award ceremonies. Shortly the teams were called to the hastily erected stage. Robert sought out Scott and Marty so that the three of them stood together.

Marty said to the other two, "Nice try, you two played one heck of a game. I've never seen you play better, both of you."

"Thanks, man," Robert answered.

"Thanks, Marty, not quite good enough, though."

"Look. We played a great game. *Easily* our best game yet. Look how far we've come. Nobody, but nobody, expected us to get this far. Heck, we weren't expected to get to the second phase! Think what we've done for soccer in the United States. More has been accomplished in these past four weeks than in the past century of soccer here in the United States."

"Next time we take it all. OK?"

"OK," Scott smiled as he looked at both of them. "To '98!" he shouted. The three of them all clasped right hands above their heads in a commitment for the future.

The president of FIFA and the president of the '94 World Cup Tournament then presented second-place medals to each of the United States players, coaches, and managers, while right behind them came Miss World Cup '98 handing out a bouquet of white carnations with baby's breath to each of the players, coaches, and managers. Scott withdrew inwardly then as tears came to his eyes. He thought of his lost pal, Joel, and knew Joel was watching and smiling. Scott looked up toward the heavens, held up the bouquet, and said, "Joel, this one's for you. I love you."

The other players saw Scott hold up his bouquet and followed suit. The crowd renewed a thunderous roar as again they paid tribute. Scott looked around through teary eyes and smiled. Then the team held up the other hand to the player next to him so that the whole team was linked together. Even the Germans were smiling and applauding. Then the FIFA officials and the girls repeated the presentations to the Germans as the announcer spoke over the loudspeaker. "…Champions of the world, champions of World Cup '94, the team from Germany."

The crowd again gave a thunderous applause as the Germans, too, held up their bouquets in salute. The United States team acknowledged them with clapping as best they could with one hand full.

Scott said to himself, They deserve it. They are the best in the world. There are so many things yet to learn. How did we ever come so close? It's a *MIRACLE*!

He then looked around him and found an aura of peace within himself; so many memories of practices, of games played, and of moments shared. He looked at Marty, next to him and smiled. Then he laughed, "You're special, Lobster; don't ever change."

"What?"

"Don't ever change. Just stay the way you are. The world needs people like you."

"Thanks, I guess."

Both teams jumped off the platform and started to circle the field in a victory lap. The crowd once more responded heartily. They had certainly gotten their money's worth tonight. At that moment a loud and wonderfully explosive display of pyrotechnics began just outside the stadium. The crowd cheered the event. Some Germans came to some of the Americans and held up hands together as they trotted around the field. Then some Americans did the same with other German players. When the players got to the end of the field again, a couple of the players slipped through a part in the three-foot barricade surrounding the field and broke into a faster trot toward the stands as they continued circling the field. The throaty roar of the crowd grew voluminous at that end of the field. First one player, then another and another threw his bouquet into the stands. Before long all had thrown their flowers into the stands as the fans roared their approval. It was the players' way of giving something back to those who had supported them, in attending and cheering and being good sports. It was one of those special moments in sport when the players and fans harmonize in mutual admiration.

Scott still held his bouquet. His eyes looked ahead to the players' section, where the families and friends of the players sit. He continued his victory trot with the others toward this section, firmly holding his bouquet. As they drew in front of this section he reached up under his captain's arm band, pulled off his small black elastic armband, and wrapped it around the bouquet of flowers. Tears were streaming down his face. He stopped in front of Susie and his family. As he threw it up into the stands he shouted, "Susie—for you." He waved to his family as Susie caught the bouquet and he shouted, "Love ya," to them all.

Susie was crying uncontrollably after she caught the bouquet with the black armband around it. Only those close by understood the significance. Most who had seen it misunderstood.

God bless you, Scott, she said silently; words would not come.

"Look at our son, look at him," Scott's mother said. "He's our son," she said to the crowd.

"We're proud of them all," Mr. Fontaine said.

At that moment all the stadium field lights went out and a grandiose laser light show began. The World Cup committee timed it just right not to take away from the glory due the players. The Tinsley company began their thing. The fans roared their approval. Spectacular was inadequate to describe the show, seen by millions all over the world. This was World Cup—United States style. When the light show finished, once again the players shook hands as they departed for their separate locker rooms.

Robert said, "Scott, what was that you did? That wasn't your wife."

"Friend of a friend," he answered. "My best friend's friend."

Something about the way he said it and the significance of the black armband, kept a secret from so many all this while, made Robert grasp the significance all of a sudden.

"Sorry, man. I feel for you. Want to talk about it sometime, I'm here. OK?"

"OK, thanks."

AFTERMATH

Scott and Diana were again back in Florida at her parents' house. It was a time of relaxing and unwinding after the tumultuous period of celebration, parades, appearances, and other demands on his time. They were sitting by the pool watching Andy playfully dunk Karen and Dawn, reminiscing about the events that had so wondrously transformed their lives. Both sets of parents were in the house getting better acquainted, having found friendship with each other.

"Scott, I almost forgot to tell you. Susie told me she has met someone very special. He's going to graduate school at USC and plans to be an environmental biologist."

"That's wonderful news. Susie needs to have a loving relationship. She'll never get away from the past unless she can put Joel far enough in the back of her mind. She really is a very nice person."

"I thought so, too, even though I only saw her at the game in L.A."

"I'm so glad she could make it to the game. On top of everything it was to all the spectators, it had to be an especially emotional experience for her. I think, perhaps, it may have had a sort of cleansing effect on her. It may have been just what she needed."

"It was nice of the Milan team to give you an extra week here at home before we go there."

"I insisted on it. Otherwise I wouldn't have been ready for that level of competition day in and day out; not for a whole season, anyway."

"We'll have to start packing our bags soon. There will be so much to take with us, with the baby and everything. I'm really looking forward to going. I'm glad things worked out that you will be playing in Italy. I'm anxious to see all those wonderful cities I studied in art history class: Florence, Venice, and Rome. I'm excited about the chance to spend weekends exploring the ancient artifacts from civilizations long ago. And you know we'll be near Switzerland and Austria. Oh! I've always wanted to see Salzburg. Can we do that sometime?"

"We can do all that and more. Whatever you want, we will do." Scott reached over to take her hand. "I love you so much."

"I love you, too. You mean everything to me."

"Wouldn't it be something," Diana continued, "if we had a baby over there in Italy?"

"Yeah. He could have his choice of which country he wanted to play World Cup soccer for."

"And maybe, just maybe, 'he' will be a girl."

"Maybe. That would be OK with me. I like girls. Andrew needs a sister, anyway."

"That's good. I'm glad."

"You know what I wished could have happened that didn't?"

"No, what?"

"I really wish Hernando could have come to the tournament. He did so much for us when we went to Costa Rica. It's too bad that things didn't work out so he could come. Did you read the letter he sent?"

"The one about his car accident and his broken leg?"

"Yes, it arrived the day before yesterday at my parents address, just in time for Mom—before she left—to bring it here. He's a great guy. They don't make friends any better than he has been."

"I want to go to Costa Rica some time. Will you take me there?"

"I'm ready any time you are."

"I love, you."

"I love you, too."